BIRMINGHAM ROSE

Annie Murray graduated from Oxford in 1983. She has worked as a journalist and a nurse, has had short stories published in several magazines, and won the *SHE*/Granada Television Short Story Competition in 1991. She now lives in Birmingham with her husband and four small children. *Birmingham Rose* is her first novel.

BIRMINGHAM ROSE

ANNIE MURRAY

PAN BOOKS

This edition first published 1995 by Pan Books

This edition published 2001 by Pan Books
an imprint of Pan Macmillan Ltd
Pan Macmillan, 20 New Wharf Road, London N1 9RR
Basingstoke and Oxford
Associated companies throughout the world
www.panmacmillan.com

ISBN 0 330 33658 4

11 13 15 17 19 18 16 14 12 10

A CIP catalogue record for this book is available from
the British Library.

Typeset by CentraCet Limited, Cambridge
Printed and bound in Great Britain by
Mackays of Chatham plc, Chatham, Kent

ACKNOWLEDGEMENTS

With special thanks to: Carl Chinn, Tom Golding, Barbara Martin, Pat Oakes, Betty O'Brien, A. M. O'Meara, George and Jackie Summers and Eric Taylor.

For John

PART ONE

BIRMINGHAM

1931–1940

CHAPTER 1

JUNE 1931

'Look at this Ronald!'

Catherine leaned closer to the window. Water was streaming off the glass outside. It was the height of the storm, the heaviest Birmingham had seen for twenty years.

'How dreadful – we must do something for her!'

There was silence from the other side of the room. The only noise came from the rain, a constant solid sound as if there were not individual drops but a torrent poured from some great vat in the sky.

Catherine, still holding the spoon she had been using for the tea, tapped it against the window. Ronald, who had been sighing over the latest unemployment figures in *The Times*, finally flung down his newspaper in irritation.

'*Look*,' she insisted. 'That poor little girl.'

Across the street a tiny figure huddled low against the garden wall of a house. Petals of mock orange and yellow roses lay in a sodden covering over the ground. She was squatting sideways, pressed hard against the bricks as if blown there helplessly like a moth by the strength of the wind and beating rain. The arm closest to the wall was stretched out straight as if to stop her from toppling over; her left arm clutched something white close to her body.

'Poor little mite,' Catherine said. 'She can only be about six. Well, she can't stay out there in this. I'm going to fetch her.' Without stopping for a coat or hat she ran through the darkened hall and unlocked the front door.

'Do you think you should?' Her husband followed her. 'You could catch a chill. And the wind's quite dreadful.'

'Don't be ridiculous Ronald. What is the matter with you?'

The door she was opening was flung out of her hand as she spoke and she had to push all her weight on it to clip it shut. She ran down the short path, steadying herself against the wind. In seconds her white blouse was soaked and clinging, her pink flesh showing through.

From the sitting-room window Ronald Harper-Watt watched with a mixture of pride and exasperation as his impetuous wife ran down the path. Oh Catherine, he thought. Here I am always sitting thinking about doing things and you just get on and do them.

Out in the road the only sounds were the uneven roar of the wind, the swish of the rain and water gurgling along the cobbled gutters. Catherine saw a chimney pot hurled down from one of the nearby houses.

Heavens, she thought, there'll be roofs off next.

She expected to find the girl tearful and distressed. Not wanting to spend time comforting her and getting even more drenched, she lifted her up by the waist and twisted her round into her arms.

'Come on – I'll look after you little one,' she said. 'Let's go and get into the dry, shall we?'

While she was mainly concentrating on getting back into the house, and taking in as she went the fact that the guttering at one end of the vicarage was wobbling precariously, Catherine was conscious that two dark and quite tearless eyes were watching her face intently. She bent forward, holding the skinny child close to her, and reached the shelter of the front hall gasping. Her light brown hair with blond lights in it had been teased out of its pins by the exhilarating wind and rain and was uncoiling down her back.

Her straight green skirt and the girl's thin cotton dress and bloomers dripped on to the patterned tiles in the hall. Catherine stood smiling at the little girl who had, it seemed, been blown to their door. The child stood staring back with a penetrating, solemn gaze.

'Ronald?' Catherine called out.

To her amazement he was already half-way down the stairs with large white towels. 'The guttering's coming down,' she told him.

Catherine took the girl's free hand as she was still holding tightly on to the white thing with the other. 'Come on, let's get those clothes off you and get you dry. One of my girls is a bit older than you so I'll find you something you can wear. Now, what's that you've got under your arm?'

The child held out the object which turned out to be an enamel dish. Her brown eyes were taking in everything hungrily from under her sodden black fringe. Her hair seemed to be cropped in a rough pudding-basin shape round her head.

'What's your name, my dear?' Catherine asked her as they climbed the stairs.

'Rose – ma'am,' she added. She was looking at the deep red staircarpet in wonder.

'And where do you live, Rose?'

'Number five, court eleven, Catherine Street,' she gabbled out.

'Catherine? Well, you won't have any problem remembering my name – it's the same as your street.' She called over the banisters to her husband: 'Catherine Street. That's a way from here isn't it?'

'The only Catherine Street I can think of is about two or three miles away. It's in the Birch Street area. Not this parish, certainly. Probably St Joseph's.' One of the slum parishes, he thought. I wonder why she's strayed away from home – a runaway perhaps? Again he felt a sense of hopelessness overcome him. Recently it seemed that Catherine had a far greater instinct for dealing with people than he did, he who had once felt this was his gift.

As they crossed the landing upstairs the sound of children's voices could be heard chanting loudly in one of the bedrooms: 'Rain, rain, go away, come again another day!'

'Now Rose, what are you doing this far from home?' Catherine asked as she knelt rubbing the little body with her towel. The child's skin, spotted with bug bites, seemed to cover only jutting bones. Rose reminded her of a tiny kitten or a newborn foal, all bony knees and staring eyes.

'Been to me sister's,' Rose said. 'She's expecting, so Mom gave me the custard and raspberry leaves to take over. It's our Marj's first babby you see.'

'I see,' Catherine said doubtfully. 'So your sister – Marj – does she live here in Moseley?'

'Oh no! She lives up Sparkbrook with her husband Fred. Mom says the babby's coming in November. And she says if she takes the raspberry tea it'll stop her coming on so bad with the pains.'

Catherine smiled at this grown-up knowledge, thinking of the patched, infantile dress lying on the floor beside them.

'So you're going to be a little aunt then?'

'Yes. And Marj wants me to sleep over her place sometimes after the babby's born. I'm not sure I want to though, 'cos it'll be blarting half the night and our Marj is bad tempered enough as it is.'

Struck by the amount of talking this little person suddenly seemed capable of, Catherine asked her how old she was.

'Nine. Ten next January,' she replied promptly.

'You're nine?' Catherine managed to prevent herself from speaking the rest of her astonishment – how small you are, you poor child, how undernourished – and just said, 'Gracious, you're the same age as my Diana.'

She pulled one of her daughter's old dresses over Rose's dark head, wondering whether the child had lice, though she couldn't see any obvious signs of them. The frock hung limply on her, well down below her knees.

'Will that do you?'

Rose nodded solemnly.

'Now, you just stay there a minute and you can meet my children.'

Rose was left standing in the high-ceilinged room.

Without moving her feet she looked up and round, twisting her body to see the soft, comfortable-looking bed with its eiderdown well plumped up, the black and white wooden rocking horse in one corner, the shelf full of books on the top of which stood small china ornaments, hedgehogs, squirrels and cats. What caught Rose's eye particularly in all this splendour was a large black elephant, the top of its head and ears decorated with tiny pieces of mirror glass and beads. She was still staring at it when she heard Catherine say, 'Rose? This is Diana, and these two are William and Judith.'

A girl with light brown curls bouncing round her cheeks ran into the room and then stopped and stared at her. Outside the door, held back by their mother, Rose had a brief glimpse of an older boy who had the same broad face and grey eyes as his father, and a little girl with dark brown hair down her back who was trying hard to see into the room.

For a moment Diana stood staring at Rose, and Rose gazed back at her, looking at the pretty cotton print dress and white cardigan the girl had on. Then Diana said, 'You're not really nine are you? You're too small.'

'I am,' Rose said. 'And me brother Sam's ten, and me sister Grace is eight, and me brother—'

'Goodness, how many brothers and sisters have you got?' Diana wanted to know.

'Er . . .' Rose thought for a moment. 'There's Albert and Marj – but they're off married so they don't live at me mom's any more. And then there's Sam, and me and Grace and George. And me mom's expecting. So's me sister Marj.'

'Gosh,' Diana said. 'Well I suppose you can't help being small. Come on, I'll show you my room.'

'Where d'you get that elephant?' Rose asked, going over to it. She thought it was one of the loveliest things she'd ever seen.

'Daddy brought it back from India,' Diana said. 'Here . . .' She pulled out some books from the shelves. 'Come and sit on the bed and I'll show you these.' Rose obediently sat down, one hand stroking the soft bed-covers. 'Now, let's have a look at these. I'm going to be a teacher when I grow up. What are you going to be?'

'I dunno.' Rose had never once thought about it. 'Where's India?'

'It's . . .' Diana ran to the bookshelf again and came back holding a tiny globe on a stand, which swivelled around when she touched it. 'There. And England's here. Daddy's a vicar, in case you didn't know. He worked with a missionary in Madras, before he met Mummy. India's part of the British Empire.'

Rose wasn't sure what a missionary was. 'Do they have elephants like that then?'

'They have real elephants and tigers and snakes. Daddy brought back lots of things. Here, if you want an elephant, I've got a little one.' She jumped off the bed, opened a couple of drawers, rummaged around and came back with a smaller elephant, about two inches high.

'I'm afraid some of the bits of glass have got lost. But you can have it – there.'

Rose looked at her, her eyes stretched wide in amazement. 'Won't your dad belt you for giving it away? You could pawn that.'

Diana laughed. 'We don't go to the pawn shop. That's only for poor people. Are you very poor?'

This was another thing Rose had not thought about before. Most people in Catherine Street seemed to live like her mom and dad. She knew there were houses where rich people lived because her mom used to go charring for them. Otherwise the only people everyone talked about were the king and queen. Grace was forever on about them.

'I dunno,' she said again. 'Are you very rich?'

'Not very, I don't think. But Mummy's daddy has a lot of money. Daddy gets a bit cross about it sometimes but I don't know why because it means we can have a lot more things. Anyway, they won't mind about the elephant. You keep it.'

Catherine called them down for tea a few minutes later

and as they went Rose said, 'What's your other name? Isn't your mom called Mrs Something?'

'It's Harper-Watt. But just call her Catherine – she'll laugh otherwise. She's like that.'

Rose sat in the big front sitting room with the family, drinking tea and eating sponge cake with strawberry jam inside and gazing round her. On either side of the fireplace, where there was a vase of dried flowers standing in the grate because it was summer, were rows and rows of books. They were arranged on shelves reaching almost to the ceiling and they had grey, red and brown spines with faded gold lettering. There were never any books in Rose's house. Everyone thought reading anything except the *Gazette* or the *Sports Argus* was a bit barmy unless you had to do it. But Rose liked reading at school and her favourite teacher, Miss Whiteley, said she was coming on a treat.

Catherine poured tea out of the silver teapot and Rose saw that all the cups matched. At home there were never enough to go round and none of them had the same pattern. Little Judith stared at her so much that she kept missing her mouth with the cake and dropping lots of crumbs. Catherine told her to watch what she was doing. William pretended to ignore her, but kept staring at her when he thought she was looking somewhere else. Rose wanted to make a face at him but she thought she'd better not.

'So, Rose,' the great big vicar said to her gently. 'Did you get lost on the way home from your sister's? Moseley isn't really on the way to Catherine Street, is it?'

'No, I wasn't lost. I just wanted a walk round. Sometimes,' she announced, 'I like to have a bit of peace.'

The two adults smiled at each other, both hearing the echo of Rose's mother who presumably often needed to make the same claim.

'Well, I'm not sure if you've had that exactly,' said Mr Vicar, as Rose called him to herself. 'But we shall have to get you home soon, or your poor mother will be worried stiff. I'll walk that way with you myself. The rain is easing off now.' Partly he wanted to make up for his lack of initiative earlier.

By the time they had finished tea, the sun had come out and the heaviest clouds seemed pushed away by its warm arms. The air grew hot and heavy with moisture.

'You can keep the dress,' Catherine said and, seeing Rose's eyes full of happiness at the thought, continued, 'and please come and see us again if you're out for a bit of peace, won't you?'

'*Can* she?' Diana asked, jumping up and down. 'I like Rose. Go on, say you will, Rose.'

Diana demanded to be allowed to walk home with Rose too. The gutters were still running with water and there were puddles all over the pavement. As they walked, trying to keep their feet from getting too soaked, they saw broken tiles, glass and pieces of branch and twigs with leaves on. At one point a large tree had been torn up and was lying across the pavement.

'I do hope people haven't been injured,' Ronald said. 'Thank heavens it didn't happen yesterday when the shops were open.'

As he spoke, he noticed that Diana had taken Rose's hand. He smiled, moved by the sight. All her mother's warmth, he thought. And once more he felt his own inadequacy.

His despondency deepened as they walked towards the middle of the city, the seething, smoking core which circled the Bull Ring, the market at its heart. The houses here were smaller and meaner, crammed back to back in street after grimy street, with factories and mills and small workshops. Those living in their two or three bug-ridden rooms lacked space and light, and their children lived – and often died – in squalid shadowy courts covered with refuse and filth, knowing little of any other street, any other life or possibility of improvement. At least this was his impression that day of this part of the city of which he in fact, to his shame, knew little.

And what about Rose, this curious little person who had suddenly been flung to their door? He watched her as she walked in front of him with his daughter, the two of them chattering as if they had known each other for months. She was hungry for something, knew there was more than her own life was showing her. Surely, he thought, I can learn from this child. He found this more cheering than all his sterile prayers of recent weeks.

Catherine Street was a row of three-storey houses, crushed together, their bricks darkened by the sooty air. The street stood on a rise above the great belly of the city. Walking down it you could see the reddish grey roofs, closely packed, and the church spires and factory chimneys poking up above them. For miles around you could make out the long, pointed spire of St Martin's Church in the Bull Ring.

'I'll go now, ta,' Rose said suddenly, and she started to run off down the slanting road.

'But I was going to explain to your mother!' Ronald's voice boomed along the street so people turned to look.

Diana ran after her. 'Are we going to be friends or not?' she demanded.

'If you want,' Rose said. 'I mean yes – please. You'd best not come to our house though. Better go now.'

Diana went back to her father and they watched Rose's small form skipping down the street, the long dress flapping round her legs.

Ronald noticed that the sky was beginning to darken again. He steered Diana round to walk home, taking a last glance back at Rose.

'Extraordinary child,' he said.

CHAPTER 2

Carrying her old dress and enamel dish, Rose ran down Catherine Street. She thought she might go off pop, her head was so full of all the things she had seen that afternoon: the dress and the elephant in her pocket and Diana. But going off pop was just what she wasn't going to do.

I'm not telling no one about what's happened, she said to herself. Not Geraldine, not even our Grace. I'm going to keep it all to myself. She watched the cotton dress with its tiny pink roses flying up and down in front of her as her feet took her fast along the familiar blue bricks of the pavement.

I bet when Diana got this it was *new*, Rose thought. She began to skip so that the roses lifted even higher.

Then she saw her father. As she reached the entrance to their court she thought he must have seen her – the smile, the running and skipping and the new dress. She stopped abruptly and began to walk, holding the enamel dish against her stomach as if it was a teddy bear, her old dress rolled up and hidden inside it. She hoped he wouldn't ask any questions.

Ever since she was a tiny child Rose had had secrets. They were often very small ones, and quite unnoticeable to anyone else: a rounded pebble hidden under a leaf by the wall of the brewhouse or a word of praise at school from Miss Whiteley. It might be what she had seen on one of her walks – often not far, but alone – to neighbouring streets. She felt as if she, Rose Lucas, was the first person in the world ever to see them.

At the sight of her father, though, she felt as if everything she had been thinking must be clear from her face, every detail of it. But as he dragged his large frame towards her, his laborious gait managed on one leg and one rough wooden crutch, his eyes watching the path in front of him, she realized he had not even looked up. When he did notice her he said gruffly, 'All right Gracie?'

'I'm *Rose*,' she said angrily, and instead of walking in with him she left him to struggle home by himself and ran ahead into the yard. Couldn't he even get her name right?

The sky was half covered by piled grey clouds. A peculiar harsh light was shining down catching one side of the court, the wet bricks and the small windows on which soot and grime accumulated again as fast as they were washed down. The other side, the wall where the tap for the yard was fixed, lay in deep shadow.

Her brother George, who was three, was standing dressed only in a grubby vest, chewing on a hard finger of bread crust mingled with snot from his nose and stamping his bare feet in the puddles. His bottom was naked and his little peter wiggled about with each stamp. Freddie and Daisy Pye from number six were standing with him on their bandy legs. All the family except Mr Pye had rickets.

When George saw Rose he beamed all over his grubby face and ran towards her with his arms out, saying, 'Rose. Pick me up! Nurse me, Rose!'

Rose got a bit fed up with George's endless hunger to be picked up. No one had the time, that was the trouble.

'Look at the state of you!' she said. 'I can't pick you up now. You'll have to wait.' The little boy went back to his puddles, wiping his nose with the back of his hand. Rose disappeared into the house. She shot across the downstairs room where her mother stood slicing bread and went dashing up the stairs.

'Rose!' Her mother stood at the foot of the stairs, bread knife in hand. 'Where've you been?'

Rose paused for a second to make up her mind whether her mother was really angry. She decided things didn't sound too serious and carried on climbing the bare boards of the stairs, remembering the banisters at the vicarage, the pedestal at the bottom shaped into a huge shiny acorn.

'Got caught out in the rain, didn't I?' she called back. 'Down in a mo.'

'You haven't been at Marj's all this time – I know you,' her mother shouted. 'And where the hell did you get that dress?'

Rose climbed up to the room at the top of the house where she and Grace shared one single bed and Sam and George shared the other. She wanted to hide the elephant before anyone else saw it. She'd have to think up an explanation for the dress, but they needn't find out about all that had happened that afternoon. Not yet anyway.

She had tried hiding things up there before, but it wasn't much good. There was only the black iron rim of the bedstead under the mattress and you could hardly fit anything in there. And if she put it under the blanket Grace was bound to find it.

The Lucases' furniture had dwindled over the years. This was all part of the change, the decline from 'before' when Sid and Dora lived in a house with two proper rooms downstairs, where they had their first two children. Before, when Sid had been a promising apprentice engineer, until he had come home in 1917 without one leg and the lower part of his left arm, and also missing some less tangible part of himself, perished in the scarred pastures of Flanders. All, in fact, before Rose was born. Albert, the oldest child, could just remember his father before the war. As a six-year-old he had taken weeks to accept that the maimed and haunted figure who appeared one day in a greatcoat at their door was the same man.

Rose moved the chest of drawers a fraction from the

wall and hid the elephant behind it. That would do for now. She's find somewhere better later.

Downstairs, her mother had disappeared and her father was easing himself awkwardly on to one of the family's two easy chairs. He propped the crutch against the wall beside him. Grace was sitting bent over a steaming bowl of water, her head covered by a strip of sacking. She was wheezing heavily. Rose realized she was trying to stave off one of her asthma attacks. We're in for a bad night then, Rose thought, not feeling very amiable about it. She felt irritable being back here with pee in a bucket in the bedroom after the new things she'd seen in the afternoon.

'Get me some tea,' Sid demanded, pushing the muddy shoe off his one foot and putting it against the fender to dry. Rose went to the hob and found there was freshly brewed tea in the pot. A tin of condensed milk was waiting with the bread on the table. She sugared the tea and passed it over without speaking. Sid gave a grunt of thanks.

'Where's Mom gone?' she asked.

'The lav – sick,' Grace gasped tetchily from under the sacking, as if she'd already answered the question once. She pointed in the direction of the four toilets at the end of the yard, shared by the six houses. 'Rose,' she whispered. 'I need a drink.'

'What did your last slave die of?' Rose snapped and then, realizing how unkind she was being, poured out more tea and placed it on the floor by her sister.

Grace peered up through her wispy fringe. 'Ta.'

'You bad again?'

'S'getting better now.' She looked up with a pink, damp face and tried to smile. She took in a deep breath so that her shoulders pulled back and her lungs whispered the air in.

Rose looked at her and then moved her gaze to their father, raising her eyebrows at Grace as she tried to gauge what mood he was in. Sid was sitting silently with his copy of the *Gazette*. There often seemed to be some intense emotion caged up in him which couldn't find a way out. When it did, they were terrified of him. Their mother took the worst of it: the lashings with his tongue and the force of his fist. Sometimes he left the house abruptly, saying nothing, and went off pulling himself round the streets for an hour or two, trying to repress the violence inside him which he so loathed. Sometimes he came back easier in himself. Other times the mood had deepened so the children hardly dared open their mouths.

It was hard to read his mood now, but Grace pulled down the corners of her mouth and rolled her eyes as if to say, 'Better watch our step.'

Through the window Rose saw her mother's thin figure walking across the yard, in her faded brown and white dress. Her arms were folded and pressed into her middle and she was holding herself rather bent forward as she did when she felt ill. Rain was falling again, and hurriedly she went to the tap across from the house and swallowed a few mouthfuls of water before coming inside.

Rose waited for her mother to start on her but Dora sat down at the table as if drained of any strength. She was working four nights a week and in the second month of another pregnancy. She felt constantly faint and sick.

'Get me a cup of tea, Rose,' she said weakly. 'I want you carding tonight. Sam's at the Pyes and Grace ain't up to it, but you can get on with some of it or we'll never get them back.'

Rose groaned inside at the thought of another evening of work. To make ends meet they took in work from local factories. Rose had spent many evenings of her childhood sewing pearl buttons on to cards in the precise stitches expected by the factory until her eyes stung and watered under the gaslight. This time it was safety pins – fixing them on to cards for the shops. They'd get tuppence ha'penny a gross, and that, as Dora was forever pointing out, was worth a bag of sugar.

'Why can't Sam come back from the Pyes and do some too?' Rose asked. 'He always gets out of it.'

She saw her father's dark eyes swivel away from his paper. 'Don't give your mother lip like that,' he said. 'That's no work for a lad anyhow.'

Dora, sipping the tea with dry lips, waved her other hand at Rose to shut her up. 'Any road, they're feeding him, so that's one less of us. Aaah – that's better.' The colour was coming back into her cheeks. She sat nibbling half-heartedly at a piece of bread. She was already a slim woman, and every pregnancy, each baby carried and suckled shrank her thinner and made her look more gaunt and bony. In the overcast light of the evening her cheekbones were emphasized by the shadows beneath them and the skin under her eyes showed blue half-moons of exhaustion.

'Was Marj all right then?' she asked. 'Did you make sure she's taking the raspberry leaf? Which reminds me . . .' Dora got up and went to the kettle to prepare her own dose of the brew. Rose thought it smelt horrible, all sour. But Dora had an almost religious faith in herbs and drank it through every pregnancy.

She didn't tell Dora that Marj had said in her most petulant voice, 'She needn't think I'm drinking this muck,' and had thrown the leaves out straight away.

'She's showing a lot,' Rose said. 'She says she's already sick of carrying that belly around.'

'Huh,' Dora said. 'She's only just bloomin' started. Wait till she's at it with a crowd of other babbies running round her. Then she'll find out what it's all about.'

As soon as they'd eaten their bread with a scraping of jam and Sid had shuffled off across the yard to the Catherine Arms, Dora rounded on Rose. 'Right,' she said, emptying the pile of tiny silver safety pins on to the worn American cloth. 'Where've you been all afternoon? Where d'you get that dress from? And where's my bowl?'

'It's upstairs.' In her hurry she'd left it on the bed with her dress. 'I'll get it.' She stood up to go to the stairs.

'Oh no you don't.' Dora grabbed her arm. 'Sit down. Come on, let's hear it. You go off with a bowl of custard and come swanning back in a new dress. What's been going on?'

Rose sat down again. 'I had a soaking,' she explained. 'Right to the skin. And the wind was so strong I nearly went flat on my face. You saw what it were like! This lady saw me from her house and took me in to dry out. She put the dress on me and she said I could keep it.'

'What lady? Where've you been wandering off to this time?' Dora tapped her finger hard on the table. 'Where was this house? Up Sparkbrook?'

'It might've been Sparkbrook,' Rose said, reluctant to give away even the vaguest details. 'Or it might've been a bit further out.'

'And you don't know where of course?'

'I was ever so wet,' Rose said, staring hard at the pins on the table.

Dora couldn't help smiling at her daughter, knowing she wasn't going to get the full story. 'You're the bleedin' end sometimes Rose, you really are,' she said. 'Come on – get cracking on these or we'll be here all night.'

They sat pushing the thin wire of the pins through their cards. Dora was still feeling sick, even having eaten the small amount of food. She looked across at Rose's dark hair, the same wavy black as her father's, bent over the pile of pins next to Grace, whose hair was a lighter brown, more like Dora's own.

Her pregnancy with Rose had been the third after the war. First there had been the twins – remembering now sent a sharp twisting pain through her. They were born too early. The little mites, only the size of kittens, had barely snuffled their way into life before dying within hours of each other: two boys, Sid and Percy. Next there'd been Sam, a huge, healthy baby who she'd thought would split her right apart as his head forced out of her.

And then Rose. All her babies had been born at home except Rose. Always was a wanderer, Dora thought.

She had been working in that big house in Sparkhill.

Albert and Marjorie were ten and eight then and at school so she had to leave Sam with a neighbour.

That morning as she set out to walk to work the sky was low and grey over the rooftops and the ground coated with frost. It looked as if it was going to snow and Dora pulled her coat round her belly as well as she could. She'd felt very down in the mouth that morning, which made her think the baby wouldn't come for a few days yet. Usually, right at the end she felt a mysterious surge of energy and well-being, even when she was quite run down in herself.

Maybe I just can't feel lively any more, she thought. Too many things have happened to us. P'raps I'm just too old.

At twenty-eight sometimes she felt aged and slow, as if everything had been torn and sucked out of her. Today the lower part of her body felt taut and heavy as she walked.

She went down the Ladypool Road, where the smell of fresh bread mingled with the usual road smell of horse manure. People were just coming out on to the streets to walk to work or give shop windows a polish. A delivery boy from the baker's shop whisked past on his bicycle, pushing down hard with his legs on the pedals.

Even now, five years after Sid had come home, she could feel tears suddenly in her eyes at the sight of a young man doing so carelessly all the things her husband was no longer capable of. It reminded her with a deep ache of the whole young man, full of dreams of what he was going to achieve, whom she had kissed goodbye and cried for early in 1915.

Sid had not come back to the home he left before the war. Instead he had returned to find his wife living in one of the courts of back-to-back houses which sprawled in a ring round the centre of Birmingham. He came back to a woman who had struggled to keep herself and her children on whatever the shortages of the war would allow, who had worked in factories churning out munitions to fuel the war and who had, with hardly a break, been working in factories ever since. He had watched her age, get thinner, lose her teeth. She snapped more and swore more and her laughter – once loud, generous laughter – came harder now and more rarely.

That change of address on Dora's letters had not prepared Sid Lucas for the losses he had to face on every side when he came home – of not only his limbs, but his livelihood, his dignity and of the way he and Dora had been together before. Before.

Sometimes, when she was at her lowest, when Sid had been silent for days or sweated and sobbed in her arms at night, she wondered if it wouldn't have been better if the mud and water of Passchendaele hadn't buried him completely instead of leaving her with half a person.

Work that morning turned out to be even heavier than usual. Dora did all the routine dusting and polishing with Mrs Stubbs, the elderly woman who worked mornings there.

Then Mrs Stubbs said, 'Right, I'd best go and do that silver she's on about in the pantry. You can go out and shake the rugs.'

Dora looked at Mrs Stubbs' plain, rather stupid face and wondered whether she was being spiteful. She decided she was just thoughtless, but the advanced state of Dora's pregnancy should have been obvious to anyone.

'Couldn't we do them together?' she suggested.

'I'll come and give you a hand if it gets too much for you,' Mrs Stubbs said serenely and limped off to polish the silver.

Dora dragged the two large rugs through the hall to the bricked area out behind the house which faced on to a large garden. It was beautiful in the summer. The brewhouse was tucked in at right angles to one end of the building and she and Mrs Stubbs heated the water for the wash there each Monday. The bread oven was in there too, so it was often a warm place to be. Dora was glad that the small building jutting out protected her from the main stab of the cold wind.

She picked up one end of the first rug, unrolled it and

started to shake so it rippled heavily along the blue bricks of the terrace, giving off great wafts of dust. Dora's arms immediately felt exhausted, as if the carpet was made of lead. She rested between the vigorous shakes, her heart thumping harder and harder. She grew hot and faint.

The pains began suddenly and very strongly. After the first couple of harsh, breathtaking contractions she stood bending forward, her hands pressing on her knees, taking in gasps of air.

My God, she thought. How'm I ever going to get back? I've got to get home!

It felt so urgent, so far advanced, that she knew already that she'd never make it back – not on foot.

She waited for a lull and then stepped over to the brewhouse. It was a bit warmer inside and rather dark. There was nothing to sit on except the scrubbed quarry tiles. Dora squatted down with her back to the stone sink. It was very quiet apart from the faint scratch of winter jasmine and rose thorns against the window. Dora knew she should get help, that she needed a midwife, but between the contractions she had no strength and couldn't raise the energy to move again.

'Please God,' she prayed. 'Don't let anything be wrong with this babby – not with me all on my own. Just help me – please, please!'

She loosened her clothes and took off her bloomers. They were wet like her legs and the back of her dress, where the warm force of her waters breaking had soaked her. A couple of times she had to pull herself up to vomit into the greyish yellow basin. Her face was shiny with sweat.

'God,' she cried, the words coming out hoarsely. 'Oh God, God!'

She knew the baby was not long from being born. As she sobbed and panted through the next contraction she heard Mrs Stubbs' voice outside, 'Dora? Dora? Where are you? I thought you was getting started out here at least.'

In a moment her head poked round the brewhouse

door and she saw Dora kneeling, her eyes stretched wide with pain.

'Gorblimey – Dora!' she shrieked. 'You can't have a babby in here. This is where we bake the bread!'

And then, seeing Dora's wet face, her hair hanging in lank brown strings and her clothes all undone, she came closer and said, 'You poor little sod. There ain't time to get a midwife now. It's all right, I'll help you. I've had a few myself in my time.'

She went to the door saying, 'It's all right, I'm not going to leave you. Back in a tick.' A moment later she reappeared with a ball of string, the big kitchen scissors and a towel. She knelt down and pulled one of Dora's arms over her shoulder. 'Go on – you're all right, you're all right,' she kept saying as the young woman writhed and screamed beside her. And then: 'Sssh – keep it down a bit for God's sake.'

Soon the little girl's head bulbed out from her body as Dora cried out for the last time. The pink slithery body followed, and Mrs Stubbs tied the cord and they wrapped her in the old strip of clean towel. Finally, Mrs Stubbs went off to fetch help.

'I'm going to call her Rose,' Dora said when the midwife arrived. 'I mean, if I'd been any further outside I'd've been in the blooming garden, wouldn't I!'

As they sat carding the pins in the unsteady light, Dora suddenly said, 'You're a funny kid you know. Go on – get off to bed. That's enough for tonight.'

Grace was already asleep when Rose lay down beside her in bed that night, listening to the soft rain against the windows. Something scuttled across the floor in the corner of the room.

She thought about Diana and her house and of how one day she wanted to have carpets and comfortable beds and shelves and shelves of books.

During the night she half woke, hearing sounds from the bedroom below, the painful, incoherent cries that her father made sometimes in his sleep. The shouts grew louder, until she heard him cry out, 'No. NO – over here!' and some more words she couldn't hear. Then her mother's voice over his, comforting him until his sounds stopped with hers and they could all sleep.

CHAPTER 3

Her first thought when she woke the next morning was Diana. How soon could she go back there? After all, they had asked her – twice. Rose was just resolving to go as soon as possible when she realized she must have woken extra early in her excitement.

Usually on school days Mom called up the stairs, 'Come on – get yourselves down here. No messing about. You'll be eating your breakfast on the way, else!' But even George was still half asleep. Rose could hear voices outside and she pushed the blanket back and went to the window, pushing it open a crack.

The sun was shining, lighting up one corner of the yard, and the ground was still very wet. Smells of sodden dirt and rotting vegetable peelings wafted through the window, though they didn't overcome the stink of the pee bucket. Rose had a quick peep behind the chest of drawers to check that yes, the elephant was still there and she hadn't dreamed it.

It was wash day. When Rose and the others got downstairs, Dora was hurriedly bundling up all her washing, though she looked pale and was bent over with nausea. She pointed at the table with her free arm. 'There's tea and you'll have to take your slice with you.'

Rose, Sam and Grace hurriedly drank down some stewed tea and left the house. George was standing rather forlornly by the washhouse with his slice, watching Gladys Pye rocking on to each of her bowed legs in turn as she pulled out the heavy mangle. Rose, feeling suddenly sorry for George, went and gave him a cuddle. The little boy's face shone with delight.

They called for Geraldine Donaghue and her brother Jo and the five of them set out, walking to the church school along the sunny street still littered with the debris of the storm.

'Our dad says the roof's gone off Woodgates,' Jo said.

Rose wasn't listening. She was picturing herself one day walking to the school as a teacher who'd stand up grandly in front of the class. She'd wear clothes just like Miss Whiteley's, a straight grey skirt and a white blouse with a frill down the front, and a little fob watch like hers pinned on to it. She'd be very calm, she'd know ever such a lot and all the children would love her.

'What are you going to be when you grow up?' she asked Geraldine, trying to sound like Diana.

Geraldine peered at her, bemused. 'You all right?' she asked. 'What's the big idea?'

'What are you going to be when you grow up?' Sam mimicked her. 'Getting big ideas, Rose? It'll be the factory or the big house for us. What else is there?' Sam scuffed his already well-worn shoes along the pavement. 'We're not exactly going to be King and Queen of England are we?'

'I want to be a teacher,' Rose said.

Sam snorted with laughter and Geraldine looked horrified.

'You don't want to be like Miss Smart, do you?' she asked. Miss Smart was a sour woman, given to almost savage outbursts of temper. It was whispered that she'd been jilted on the eve of her wedding a few years before.

'No,' Rose said. 'But Miss Whiteley's nice, isn't she? And she knows about ever such a lot of things.'

Geraldine looked puzzled. 'What d'you want to do that for? I'd never do that. I'd like to be a singer or one of them dancers they have on at the Hip.' She preened and posed in her skimpy dress along the pavement as if it was the stage of the Hippodrome.

'Geraldine!' her brother said. 'Everyone's looking.'

'You're both daft,' Sam said. 'Dream away. I'm going to be Rudolph Valentino. But it's only dreams. People like us don't ever do anything different, do we?'

This dampened Rose's enthusiasm straight away.

'Who d'you know who's ever been anything special then?' Sam continued.

'Mom says Dad was doing all right before he went to the war,' Rose said.

'It was still the factory though. And nothing's the same now, is it? That's what Albert says.' Sam always looked to his older brother, whom they scarcely ever saw, as the source of all information and authority. 'Anyhow, you have to stay on at school to be anything special, and there's fat chance of that.'

Rose felt very down in the dumps after that. Was Diana going to stay on at school? No one she knew in the court had carried on after they were fourteen. She'd never questioned it before, how you couldn't do anything much with your life unless you had money.

Rose knew that some time during the morning her mom would bundle up Sid's Sunday suit and shoes and they'd be down to the pawnbroker's at the end of the street until Friday when she got her money from the factory. Sid joked grimly sometimes that they ought to get 2d extra for the shoes because he only ever wore the one. Rose wondered if her mother was going to pawn her new dress.

That day she stared adoringly at Miss Whiteley as she stood in front of them next to the blackboard, the portrait of the king behind her head. She imagined Diana standing there with her curls tied back, telling them all about rivers and jungles and the kings and queens in history books. And then she tried to put herself in the same position, as she had on her walk to school before all the things Sam had said. All she could think of now were the thick darns on the elbows of her cardigan and her faded old clothes and the way she spoke, which was different from Diana.

I could never be like Diana, she thought.

As she turned from chalking up some names on the

blackboard, Sarah Whiteley noticed Rose at her wooden desk wiping her eyes with the back of her hand and sniffing.

'Are you feeling unwell, Rose?' she asked kindly.

'No, Miss Whiteley,' the girl said quietly, and she blushed such an embarrassed pink that the teacher decided not to pursue it just then.

When school finished Miss Whiteley said to her, 'Rose, would you come here a minute?'

Geraldine whispered to her, 'You're for it now. I'll wait for you outside.'

'No, you go home,' Rose replied. 'And take Grace with you or Mom'll be on at me.'

She stood solemnly by her teacher's desk when all the others had made their way noisily out of the room. She could hear them laughing and yelling as they trailed off down the street.

'Are you all right, my dear?' Miss Whiteley asked, sitting behind her big table at the end of the classroom. 'It's all right, don't look so worried, you're not here to be punished. I saw you crying earlier. Is everything all right at home?'

'Yes, Miss Whiteley,' Rose said.

The teacher looked at the serious brown eyes which were gazing apprehensively at her and she smiled suddenly. She had a soft spot for Rose.

'Are you happy at school?' She was sensitive enough to realize that something was going on inside Rose, and she also knew that whatever her disadvantages in life, this was a child with potential.

Rose just said yes again. She liked Miss Whiteley and trusted her, but standing alone in front of her she felt small and shy. She kept her eyes on the scuffed wooden boards of the classroom floor and her even more scuffed boots.

Sarah Whiteley decided to try once more. She came out from behind the desk and brought her chair up to sit next to the child.

Rose looked into Miss Whiteley's lovely plain face with

her round pink cheeks, quite unlike Miss Smart's angular, rather pretty face, which was so often full of spite and irritation. Miss Whiteley seemed to give off comfort, like someone handing out buns.

'What if I wanted to be a teacher?' Rose blurted out. ''Cos Sam says people like us don't do things like that and it's daft of me to think of it. Only my friend Diana's going to be a teacher.' And without expecting to she found she was telling Miss Whiteley all about the storm and Diana and how different her family were from Rose's own.

Sarah Whiteley was startled. This was not what she had expected at all. She'd thought perhaps things were especially difficult for Rose's family, as they so often were in the homes of the children she taught. She had met Dora Lucas a number of times and had taken a liking to her. She'd found her brisk, with the kind of hardness of someone who has no energy left to spare for niceties. But she isn't rough, Sarah thought. Just worn down. And again, Sarah had perceived intelligence. She hadn't met Rose's father, but she knew he had been injured in the war and could not get work.

With these thoughts in mind she struggled for words to answer Rose's eager questions. She wanted to be positive and realistic at the same time and the combination was not easy.

'Whether you could be a teacher is not an easy question to answer. I think you're a clever girl and you do well in your lessons. But I expect you'll have to leave school to go to work soon, won't you?'

Rose nodded miserably.

'But perhaps what you can aim to do is get the best work you can. If you do well at school we might be able to find you something in an office, and you never know what opportunities might come your way. And there are such things as evening classes where you can further your education if you have the means when you're older. But you'll have to be very determined. Do you think you're very determined?'

'I dunno,' Rose said. 'But I don't want to be like my mom, always sick with having babbies.'

Sarah Whiteley felt tears slide into her own eyes at the thought of women like Dora Lucas with their relentless lives of childbirth and worry.

Rose noticed her emotion and was alarmed. Blimey, what had she done to upset her?

But all her teacher said, quietly, as if to herself, was, 'Well, I suppose if you want to do anything else with your life it doesn't really do to have children.' Then she smiled and looked at Rose. 'Cheer up. You don't need to worry about it yet, do you? And you never know what might happen.'

She stood up and said, 'Come along, your mother will be getting worried. Shall I walk a little of the way with you?'

Delighted, Rose felt her dark little hand being taken by Miss Whiteley's soft pink one. The woman strolled along beside her, pointing out things on the way – a police car, a magpie, white clouds all piled up to one side of the sky – until they reached Catherine Street. Miss Whiteley leaned down and, to Rose's astonishment, kissed her cheek before she said goodbye. Rose couldn't remember the last time anyone had given her a kiss. The walk had made the afternoon feel very warm and special.

But when she got home her mother was tense and furious and snapping at everyone in sight. She'd hung her sheets across the yard as usual and the younger Pye and Donaghue children had been running muddy hands all through them and flicking water up from the puddles. She'd had to rinse and mangle the lot again, and as a result was behindhand with everything else.

'Don't tread on the floor!' she shouted unreasonably as Rose stepped into the house. 'Where the hell have you been? No – don't tell me. Just get scraping these.' She pointed to a pile of carrots. Grace, confined to a sheet of newspaper on the damp floor, had already started on the potatoes.

Dora bustled about rearranging washing on the backs

of chairs and over the frames of the mirror and their two pictures: one of Sid's mom and dad and one of the king and queen.

'I'll make sure those little bleeders don't get at it this time,' she said. 'Come on, set to it Rose, and stop dreaming.'

Rose picked up the peeling knife in silence and mulled over what Miss Whiteley had said. All I can do, she thought, is try as hard as I can. Try and try and try.

That night, when she and Grace and the boys were in bed, Rose heard sounds coming from down in her mom and dad's room. It wasn't the strange, rhythmic noise she sometimes heard, with her mother gasping, and at the end of it a cry from her father as if he'd stubbed his toe on the leg of the bed. This time she knew it would end differently, because he'd been down the Catherine after raising a few coppers selling kindling.

Sid turned to look at his wife as he undressed in their room on the middle floor. She was lying on her back, her face grey with fatigue. He could see clearly the lines that had appeared and deepened between her brows and round her mouth and he felt a moment of tenderness watching her there. Now she was able to rest she looked a little more like the lovely girl he'd courted and married, with her sheet of chestnut brown hair, thicker then and glossy, which he'd smoothed over his face during their lovemaking like a silk scarf.

Remembering this, he wanted her. She'd be out working the next four nights and he'd have to sleep alone. He always felt sorry for himself when she was away at night. It seemed to reinforce his sense of helplessness.

'Dora?' He pulled himself over to her on the bed and leaned on his good arm. Suddenly he felt nervous, and then angry because of it. She was his wife, wasn't she? He shouldn't have to beg any favours.

'Come on,' he said. He put his mouth to hers, feeling

how rough and dry her lips were. He felt himself harden gradually. In the old days he had only to look at her. This was the one thing he had left – that he could make her produce children.

When she felt him moving against her, a wave of despair came over Dora. How could he do this when he knew she'd be up all the next night? But she always felt guilty when she refused him. It was the only thing which made him happy for a short time.

'I need some sleep,' she said without opening her eyes. 'I'm on again tomorrow night. Some of us have to work, you know,' she finished, rather spitefully.

He always took rebuffs badly. 'That's right – and I'm no bloody good for nothing, am I?' he shouted, sitting up again. 'Your bleeding cripple of a husband. That's what everyone says about me, ain't it?'

'I didn't say that – just don't keep on. Get into bed and let me sleep.'

'Open your eyes.' His voice was still loud and full of hurt and anger. 'At least open your bloody eyes, woman!'

Dora dragged her eyes open and half sat up. She pulled back the covers and patted the bed. 'Just come and lie down Sid, please.'

Sid could feel the great dark surge which sometimes forced its way through him, a violence of anger and despair which he could not put into words. He ached to spend himself in his wife, to feel her body moving under him.

'Dora, please. Do it for me tonight.'

'NO!' Dora shouted.

Then Rose heard her mother's screams as he hit her twice, three times, giving her the bruised cheek and cut lip which would be there for all to see in the morning.

'You selfish bitch!' she heard.

Rose screwed up her eyes tight and pushed her fingers into her ears. But she could still hear the next part – what always came next. The worst part. Her father's remorse, the sobs which burst from his body alongside her mother's own crying, and eventually Dora's voice trying to calm his anguish.

Rose slipped out of bed and fetched the little elephant from its hiding place. She lay stroking it in the dark.

'Try,' she said to herself. 'Try and try and try.'

CHAPTER 4

JANUARY 1935

Dora Lucas was sitting at her table with a cup of mint tea in front of her. Often now, when she had a spare moment she sat, her eyes not fixed on anything, her limbs slack and her mind numb.

She was forty-one and exhausted, like an old woman, yet she was soon to give birth again. Her belly already felt tight and heavy with the child which nudged insistently under her ribcage so that she had to keep straightening her spine to ease the discomfort.

Beside her, three-year-old Violet was clattering pebbles on the tiled floor, involved in her game and singing quite tunefully.

'Do it a bit quieter, can't you?' Dora snapped at her, without really having intended to. Weariness and irritation seemed to be all she could manage.

The others would soon be home from school. And Sam – bless him – from work. After the four grimmest and most despairing years of Dora's life they at last had a regular wage coming into the house. How she would have got by without the neighbours she'd never know – Theresa and Gladys especially. The final humiliation had come when they had been forced to go on the Parish. First there was the gruelling session in front of the board. Dora's innards turned just thinking about it. She'd remember the cold, gimlet-eyed woman there till her dying day. The board, which executed the Means Test, decided whether she was worthy of their meagre allowance of food and coal.

Sam, Rose and Grace had become familiar, sad little figures outside factories as far away as Cheapside and Moseley Street, greeting the men who came off shift with persistent cries of 'Have you got a piece for us?' They'd run after the men until they handed over any leftover portions of bread from their lunches.

On Saturday nights they would hang about in Smithfield and the Market Hall until the stallholders were packing up, and then walk home exhausted, carrying a piece of knockdown meat and bags of bruised fruit and veg. Rose would fall asleep with her head full of visions of pyramids of apples and oranges lit by the the naphtha flares which hissed next to the stalls.

The shame and desperation of those years had nearly finished Dora. When Violet was born she had haemorrhaged so badly that she'd been ill for weeks and had had to give up her night job in the metal stamping factory. They'd had Sickness Benefit, and by the time that finished she was pregnant again, but she miscarried in the third month. Again she was left weak and drained.

Dora had been desperate not to get pregnant again. She tried to fight Sid in bed, and kick him off. But even with only one arm he was stronger. He begged her and then slapped her about, and most often now pushed into her with a force which frightened her and left her sore, sometimes bleeding, and with an overwhelming sense of shame as if she had done something wrong. When she had the strength, she crept out in the dark afterwards and fetched a pail of cold water to wash herself with.

As soon as she realized she was carrying this child, for the first time in her life she tried to abort it. She had tried castor oil and Penny Royal syrup and even water which she'd boiled pennies in. She had trembled at the sin she was committing – however ineffective it proved – but even more at the thought of what Sid would do to her if he ever found out. His one remaining source of power was his and Dora's fertility.

'Think yourself lucky,' he said to her one night in an ugly mood. He was lying on the bed naked from the waist down, his member lolling to one side on its nest of dark hair. 'I saw a fella in the army with it all blown away. Where would that leave you, eh?'

She had been brought too low to feel anything for Sid now. Even pity had been drained out of her. Now when his dreams drove him to cry out in the night she turned away and pushed her fingers into her ears. She had pity now only for her children, and admiration for their pluck and spirit.

She leaned back into her chair, folding her arms over her swollen stomach and thinking of her kids one by one.

There was Albert, over in Erdington, whom she hardly ever saw, and Marj, rather smug with her two kids in Sparkbrook. She realized that these two, who could just remember the life before the war, despised what their parents had become. If that was their attitude they could keep away.

As for Sam, he was a good solid lad. She knew he'd stick by her and look after her. Sticking by people was one of the codes by which Dora lived. Disloyalty figured high on her list of human failures, along with thieving and cruelty to children. She felt Sam had inherited that loyalty from her.

'Don't worry, Mom,' he'd kept saying, while he was waiting out his last year at school. 'I'll get myself a job soon. I'll look after you.' It was a promise he'd kept. He was bringing in ten bob a week which was a start and they made up the rest with odds and sods.

Then there were the two girls. Dora smiled at the thought of Grace. She was so transparent and shared things with her mother. She used to climb on Dora's knee and show her the latest picture she'd found of her great passion – the royal family. She was straightforward somehow. Like herself, Dora thought.

But Rose was more of a mystery. Dora had never worked out why that posh vicar's daughter Diana wanted to be so friendly with her. She must have had pals with knobs on up at her public school, but she and Rose were still as thick as anything. And she didn't even seem to mind coming and slumming it down Catherine Street now and then. It was the neighbours who acted suspicious and said, 'What's she doing down here again?'

Dora couldn't help liking Diana, even if she hadn't been sure at first what she was after. Her mother's family were something titled, it was said, and she'd married beneath her. But Diana didn't put on airs. She always said 'Mrs Lucas' so politely. And she was such a pretty lass with all that curly hair round her face. But Rose went up to the vicarage more often than Diana came down here. Rose didn't want the neighbours gossiping about her or Geraldine Donaghue deliberately messing up Diana's dress out of envy.

Rose worried Dora though. She knew her daughter's contact with the Harper-Watts had shown her a kind of life that would never be within her grasp.

'Don't get big ideas, will you?' she warned sometimes.

Sid put it more brutally. 'You needn't bring her round here and get all toffee-nosed. You was born a slum kid and you'll die a slum kid so you needn't go expecting any different.'

It was already getting quite dark. The lamplighter would soon be out on the streets. Dora was about to stir herself when she heard the girls outside, and George came crashing into the house shouting, 'Rose's had the cane! Rose's had the cane!'

As was her way, she didn't ask questions immediately but pulled herself to her feet and lit the lamp. Then she turned to her daughters. Rose was still the taller of the two and bone thin, with long black hair down her back. Her face was puffed up from crying and her cheeks streaked and red. Grace, who was wheezing heavily, also looked tearful. Instinctively, Dora moved across to boil some water for her.

'What's been going on?' she demanded.

'It's that Miss Smart,' Rose burst out, her voice high

with tears and anger. 'She's a wicked, horrible bitch, she is.'

'Rose!' Dora started. But then, seeing how distressed she was, said, 'Turn round.'

Rose turned, and very tentatively pulled her ripped bloomers down to show her bare bottom. It was raw and red with stripes of blood and vivid purple welts, so many that they had all merged together in a hot, angry mass.

'God Almighty,' Dora gasped. 'What the hell has she done? What brought all that on?'

It had been the last lesson, Rose explained. They'd been sitting in the classroom, and she was next to the heavy green curtain that separated her class from Grace's. She knew Grace wasn't feeling too good that day. The weather was damp and cold which always brought on the asthma. She'd been struggling to get her breath even on the way to school. A day in the building, heated by the one feeble stove, had not helped.

As Rose sat through her arithmetic lesson, Miss Smart was teaching Grace in the next section of the room. Suddenly she became aware of Miss Smart's usually abrupt and tetchy voice saying quite clearly, 'Pull yourself together! I've had quite enough of your malingering.'

'I can't help it, Miss Smart,' she heard Grace trying to protest. 'It's me chest. I've got—'

'Be quiet,' Miss Smart shouted. 'You make that horrible noise once more and you'll feel the cane across your behind. I'm not putting up with any more of your excuses.'

Through the curtain Rose could hear Grace's wheezing becoming louder and more agitated. She could picture Miss Smart's angry, spiteful face as she stood over her sister, and suddenly she felt all restraint leave her.

She glanced up at Miss Phipps to check she wasn't looking. Then she lifted up the bottom of the heavy curtain, pushed her way underneath it and ran to Grace, flinging an arm round her frightened sister's shoulders.

'You cruel bitch!' she shouted at Miss Smart. Her voice

sounded surprisingly strong. 'Why don't you pick on someone your own size? Just because you can't keep a bloke for five minutes doesn't mean you have to take it out on my sister. She's got a bad chest, as you ought to know bleeding well by now!'

Grace's face almost mirrored her teacher's in its look of horror. Miss Smart grabbed Rose by the wrist and hauled her through the classroom with astonishing strength, bashing Rose's legs and hips against the desks.

'Come here you uppity little scum,' she hissed, her teeth locked together as though she was trying to hold back some of her rage. 'You'll be out of this school as soon as breathe after what you've just said to me.' The woman's body was quivering all over. 'But now I'm going to give you something you should have been given a long time ago.'

Grace watched, terrified, as Miss Smart grabbed Rose again by the shoulders and forced her round so she was facing the window. She pulled Rose's skirt up and yanked on her bloomers so that the entire class heard them tear.

'Bend over and empty the wastepaper basket,' Miss Smart shouted, only just able to get the words out.

Rose knew the drill. She turned the basket over, tipping out scraps of paper and some balls of fluff, and leaned down on the dusty weave of the base.

Miss Smart thrashed her with the cane as no child in the school had ever been thrashed before. She lost all control as her voice screamed out her frustration and loathing. 'D'you think I like standing here day after day looking at your ugly – ignorant – faces? I hate it. I hate it – do you hear? You stupid – scummy little – slum kids . . . You'll never – do anything – or be anything. I could be married and out of this cesspit by now, but I'm stuck here for ever. Stuck – stuck – stuck!'

Rose's whimpering broke into screams as Miss Smart brought the thin cane down and broke the skin. The lashes shot through her, making her feel weak in the legs and dizzy. She was aware only of the pain and of the saliva gathering in her mouth.

'Helena! Helena Smart – what in God's name are you doing?' It was a deep voice, from the large body of Miss Phipps, who had been teaching arithmetic next door. The beating stopped abruptly as Miss Phipps grabbed the younger teacher's arms and took the bloodstained cane from her trembling hand.

Rose slowly turned the waste basket over and retched miserably into it. She heard Grace's loud breathing beside her.

'Rose? Rose – are you all right?' Grace was crying. A thin trickle of vomit began to ooze out through the wicker and across the floor.

Miss Phipps was holding Miss Smart by one of her wrists. The younger woman was sobbing uncontrollably. 'I'll see you later,' Miss Phipps said in a low voice. 'For now I think you'd be wisest to get out of my sight.'

They all watched Miss Smart, her head sunk down and her shoulders heaving as she left the room.

Miss Phipps came over to Rose. 'Go home and get your mother to dress those cuts,' she said gently. 'Grace, you go with her.'

Rose tried to straighten up. Her behind and the lower part of her back were a tight wall of pain.

Miss Phipps guessed what was painting the worried expression on the girl's face even through her obvious distress. 'It's all right,' she assured her kindly. 'You'll be coming back to school again.'

As Rose was finishing off her story, Sid lurched into the house on his crutch, slamming the door as he always did. Dora tensed.

He looked round the room. Grace was sitting at the table with George, breathing noisily over a bowl while Dora held her hair back. Rose was standing holding a cup with a face as long as Livery Street and not a sign of his tea on the go.

'What's going on?' His voice was ugly.

'Rose got caned down at the school for sticking up for our Grace,' Dora said. 'Her behind's red raw with it.'

Sid looked at Rose's tearstained face. It was rare for

him to see Rose crying. She was a proud cow, in front of him anyway. Strong, independent Rose. Rose, who had all the aspirations he had had and probably even more, going about with that kid from up the vicarage. He felt a moment of identity with her, but he pushed it aside. For once she wasn't giving him that serious, knowing look of hers, that seemed to say, 'Sod you, Dad. I'm going to get out of here and do something with my life.'

He began to enjoy her humiliation. 'I s'pose you asked for it,' he said. 'You're a cheeky little bugger.'

'I didn't ask for it!' Rose shouted. She felt like someone with nothing to lose. 'She was carrying on at our Grace and I stuck up for her. Like Mom could do with someone to stick up for her when you're down there knocking her about of a night. I've listened to you since I were a babby with your bullying and your carrying on, and your – *crying*.' Rose spat the word out with all the contempt she felt. 'You're disgusting, Dad. So don't go telling me I asked for it.'

She stood unflinching as Sid lurched over and hit her round the head with both sides of his thick hand again and again.

'Stop it!' Dora screamed. Grace and George sat quite still as if paralysed with fright. 'Don't you dare hit her! Don't you ever hit my kids.' Her voice dropped to a snarl. 'I've put up with you knocking me about, but don't you ever lay a finger on my kids again or I swear I'll lay you out for good.' She was looking round wildly for something to use as a weapon when Rose simply took a step backwards and Sid lost his balance, falling to the floor heavily, on his side.

With all the dignity she could summon Rose stood over him. 'I shouldn't bother getting up, Dad.' She left Grace and George gawping and went to her room.

Rose lay with her stomach flat against the bed in the dusk light of the attic.

Dora was bathing the sores on her daughter's behind

with warm water and dabbing iodine on the cuts. One side of Rose's face was swollen and shiny and beginning to darken into bruises. Sid's outburst, as much as the treatment she had had from Miss Smart, had created a bond between the mother and daughter stronger than any that had existed before.

'I hate him,' Rose said, banging her fists on the thin mattress, and wincing whenever Dora touched her. 'I hate, hate, *hate* him. He ought to want better than he's had for his kids. He's never cared about us.'

Dora sighed. Rose became aware that her mother was stroking her hair with a new gentleness that she was unused to. She kept very still in case any movement made Dora stop.

'If it were a few year ago I'd've said that's not the truth.' Dora paused for a moment, breathless with the baby pushing up her lungs. 'Now I just don't know. He's turned sour on everything and there's no getting near him. And you can't blame him when you stop to think about it. But that don't make it any easier for the rest of us. There've been times . . .' She stopped.

As if reading her mind, Rose said, 'You'd have been just as well off without him, wouldn't you?'

'No,' Dora said briskly. 'That's not my way. You make your bed and you lie on it, and that's that, whatever happens after.'

Rose turned her head to look at her mother. In the poor light from the window she could see the outline of her scrawny neck and her thinning hair which looked lanker and more faded every year. Her skin was pasty and tired looking. She thought of Catherine Harper-Watt's rosy complexion and her thick, healthy hair. She started to cry again because her mother's life seemed so sad, such a waste.

Dora, not knowing the real reason for Rose's sobs, stroked her back in a way that surprised both of them. 'Ssssh,' she said. 'You'll feel better soon, don't you worry. Hang on a minute – I'll go and get you another nice cup of tea.'

CHAPTER 5

A month later Rose and Diana were walking to the Bull Ring. As soon as Diana had called in for her at Catherine Street Rose grabbed her coat and was off.

'Better get her out of here before she catches anything, hadn't you?' Geraldine called out spitefully as the two of them sped out of the court. They were followed a short distance by George, who was becoming a right tearaway, and Violet, lisping, 'Thweets, Diana – bring us back some thweets!'

The two girls soon left them behind. Rose was never comfortable when Diana came to her house and it didn't happen very often. She couldn't help feeling ashamed of the cramped, filthy conditions they lived in. Whenever Diana came the smells drifting from the toilets in the yard always came over stronger than usual.

Diana was always very polite. Rose had never seen her bat an eyelid at the newspaper instead of a cloth on the table or the cockroaches scuttling busily about on the floor and walls, their antennae twitching. She'd only once jumped and squeaked when one landed clumsily on a slice of bread she was eating. Dora had nearly turned herself inside out apologizing.

'Don't you hate coming to our house?' Rose asked her. 'Why would you want to with us being so rough and ready?' She felt humbled by Diana's tolerance, whereas if her friend had been haughty or critical Rose would have leapt like a wildcat to defend her family and how they were forced to live.

'Come on,' Rose said as they scurried towards town. 'It isn't half a relief to get out, I can tell you. My mom's been on at me all morning: "Rose – blacklead the grate; Rose – Violet's gone and wet the floor, get down and wipe it up will you, Rose; Rose – go and get us some fish and chips for our lunch!" Anyone'd think there was no one else in the house 'cept me.'

It always took the two girls a while to get used to being together.

'We could go on the tram,' Diana suggested breathlessly as they rushed along.

'You mad?' Rose looked shocked. 'What d'you want to go wasting money on that for? It's not much of a walk.'

'All right.' Diana smiled. 'I'll treat you to a cup of tea then.'

'You don't know you're born, you don't.' But Rose was delighted. It was a huge treat to go to Charlie Miles' in the Market Hall or one of the places in the Bull Ring market and sit drinking tea like two grown-up ladies.

'Eh, I haven't told you,' Rose said as they turned into Bradford Street. 'Mrs Smith from number three – you know, Mrs Cut Above – they had to take her to the hospital a couple of days ago. They found her swigging back a bottle of bleach at her kitchen table. Her sons walked in and saved her, before she could take' – Rose struggled to remember the right words – 'the whole lethal dose. That's what everyone said. She had to go and have her stomach pumped out. They put a great thick rubber tube in your mouth and pour water into it till you bring it all back. Mrs Pye told us 'cos it happened the once to her brother.'

'Gosh, how horrible!' Diana said. 'Is she all right?'

'She's home now. She had a bit of a go at Geraldine's mom this morning. Called her an Irish trollop, so I think she's back to her usual.'

Diana stored up this information to tell her father, who waited for the latest instalment of life in Catherine Street with great interest and shook his head in a concerned sort of way whenever she told him anything.

The long street swept them downhill towards the bustling heart of Brum. On either side of them loomed the tall, soot-coated sides of factories from which came all kinds of sounds of hammering and drilling, and the churning of machinery and shouting filled the air round them.

'Let's see if we can spot Sam,' Rose said.

They stopped by the grating over the basement factory where Sam had found his first job. The firm produced galvanized buckets and baths, and all day the sounds of banging and clanging went on as if they were fastening on manacles in hell.

'It's so noisy!' Diana exclaimed.

'Hell of a row, isn't it?' Rose peered down, trying to spot her brother's brown hair and pale, stolid face, but she couldn't see him.

'C'mon Di,' she said, straightening up again. 'Let's get to Jamaica Row for the cag-mag and then we can go over to the Market Hall.'

Bradford Street was crowded with horses and carts and motor vehicles, some stopping for pick-ups or deliveries outside the factories or moving to and from Smithfield, the main meat market at the lower end of the street. You could see the sides of meat hanging up there as you went past. In the road, piles of horse manure steamed in the cold.

Carrying the bag of cag-mag, the cheapest off-cuts of meat, the girls gradually pushed their way through the chaos of the Saturday afternoon crowds into Spiceal Street, past the slim spire of St Martin's and into the Bull Ring.

Diana took hold of Rose's sleeve. 'Better not lose you,' she said. 'Go on – you lead the way.'

Rose felt the usual excitement that welled up once she was inside the market. There was so much to look at. She could hear a band playing, and the delicious smell of roasting meat wafted from the eating houses across from the stalls. Their windows were lit and the glass all steamed up, so you could only see hazy figures moving about inside or sitting at the tables. Outside one a sign said, 'Beef & 2 veg. 11d.'

The market was packed with people swarming around the stalls heaped with fruit, vegetables and flowers. The vendors were competing to see who could shout the loudest to sell their wares.

'Only a penny the cabbage!'

'Get your oranges here – fresh juicy oranges!'

They got tangled up in a knot of people all standing round some attraction. It was the strong man. He had been tied up tightly in his chains and a sack dropped over his head. They could see him struggling inside like an animal in a snare.

'He always gets out, you know,' some know-it-all in the crowd was saying.

'There's got to be a trick in it somewhere. I don't believe in all this rigmarole,' another voice said.

But mostly people stood gasping with admiration watching the man emerge, panting and red in the face as he tore the sack off his head, his face and bare arms shining with sweat.

When Rose looked at Diana she saw that her friend's cheeks had turned quite white and she was taking in fast, shallow breaths.

'I could never do that, never. I can't bear anything over my head. It makes me want to scream and kick.'

'Come on. Forget it,' Rose said, pulling her away. 'Let's go and find something a bit more cheerful for you.'

Round the statue of Nelson in the middle of the market was the place where people always arranged to meet. Probably because they knew this, the Sally Army had set up with their brass band and tambourines. In the background somewhere a man's voice was shouting, 'He who is without sin – he, and only he – shall cast the first stone!'

From the other side of the statue Rose heard the music which she always enjoyed most in the market.

'Come on.' She took Diana's arm. 'If this don't cheer you up then nothing will.'

It was the accordion players. There were two of them,

trying hard to compete with the Sally Army, and by the look of things succeeding. The men had a certain snappiness of style even in their old black trousers and jackets, and their black hair shone with oil even in the grey winter light. One of them had a moustache. As they played they both tapped their feet and the one with the moustache sang to some of the numbers.

'Can you hear what he's saying?' Rose shouted in Diana's ear.

'No,' she shouted back. 'It's Italian. They're from Italy.'

'You know bloomin' everything, don't you?' Rose bawled back at her with a grin.

The two girls stood for quite a time watching the players. Rose thought nothing could ever make her feel so happy as the sound of those dancing tunes. They stood there so long that in the end the one with the moustache danced over to them, inclining first one shoulder and then the other as his fingers carried on playing with astonishing ease and speed. Rose saw the hairs of his moustache, and his shining brown eyes. He sang a long note on some word that sounded like 'mar-ee'. Rose and Diana put their hands up to their mouths and moved away giggling.

They were carried along by the crowd, smelling potatoes baking on a cart and crushed cabbage leaves under their feet and cigarette smoke which seemed stronger on the cold air. There were hundreds of stalls in the Market Hall, selling everything under the sun. They liked to go and see the great crabs and lobsters, bright and astonishing in their shells, and all the piles of toffee and peanut brittle.

'Oh look,' Diana said. She pointed to a big banner. 'It's a hundred this week!'

'Market Hall Centenary Celebrations', the sign read. 'February 11–18', and on each side in bigger print, '1835–1935'.

But it was Diana's turn to see her friend turn pale and serious. At the foot of the steps, leaning against the brick banister, was a man. His face was dark with several days of stubble, and round his neck, hanging from a length of cord, hung a cut-out tray made of cardboard. On it lay a few boxes of Swan Vesta matches. Rose stared at his face, tears stinging her eyes at the despair she saw written in every sag of his rough cheeks. His clothes hung limply, one sleeve of his greatcoat pinned away at the back. Many a night that coat had provided an extra cover on Rose and Grace's bed. The rough, familiar crutch stood against the wall beside him.

Rose stood watching her father, the tears running slowly down her cheeks. Bruises from the beating round the head that he had given her were only just fading. But now, seeing him here away from home, she pitied him for what he so obviously was – a wreck of a man. Her pity was partly for the squalor, the monotony of his life, but mostly it was for the way he had been broken by things too terrible to tell of, that only spoke themselves night after night in his dreams.

'Rose, what's the matter?'

'Nothing.' Rose turned away quickly, realizing he might see them.

'Come on. You were grinning like a Cheshire cat just a minute ago. What's up?'

'I'm not going to turn round again in case he sees,' Rose said sniffing. 'But look, by the steps. It's my dad.'

Diana turned her head and saw Sid's desolate figure. Then she took Rose's hand, and her friend felt a coin being pressed into it.

'Let's go and get the poor old sod a cup of tea.' The two girls smiled at each other, Rose more in surprise at Diana's unaccustomed language than because she thought it was a particularly good idea.

She approached him with the tea, feeling nervous and awkward, and handed it to him saying, 'Here y'are, Dad. You must be cold.'

Sid roused himself, looked at her without any apparent surprise and said, 'Aar. Thanks Gracie.'

'I'm ROSE,' she yelled at him. 'You silly old sod.' And she pulled Diana away, the moment of pity swept away by her anger.

Diana followed her as she stamped her way across the Bull Ring in her worn-out boots. 'Hey, Rose,' she said, running behind to catch up. 'You didn't have to go and tell him what I said about him to his face!'

Rose turned, for a moment still annoyed, and then burst out laughing. The two of them linked arms and moments later Rose was crying with laughter instead of vexation.

'Well, that's the last time I try and do anything for him,' she said defiantly. 'Now, how about that cup of tea we was going to have ourselves?'

CHAPTER 6

Dora's labour pains began in the middle of a cold night in March.

She called up the stairs, 'Sam, Sam! Go and fetch Old Joan – the babby's coming!' Sam shot out of bed and down to the outside door.

Rose scurried around. Her heart seemed more awake than her head and it was beating noisily. As she threw slack on the fire, which had almost gone out, Grace and the other children trooped in and Grace started to get them all organized.

'You come and sit here George, and Vi can sit on my lap. You can see all my pictures. Now, this one's Queen Mary in the royal box at Ascot . . .'

'Oh, not again,' George groaned.

Sid was still asleep and Dora said she couldn't see much use in waking him. She and Rose prepared Rose and Grace's bed in the attic together. They stripped off the bedclothes so the sheets wouldn't spoil, tucked the crackly newspaper round the mattress and spread sheets of it out on the floor.

'This one's a boy,' Dora said as she finally pulled herself up on to the bed. She looked exhausted already.

'How d'you know?'

'I just do,' she said, leaning her head back against the wall so the tendons stood out in her scrawny neck. 'I always know, by the end.'

Rose suddenly felt shy, helping her mother with something so intimate. Before, she'd always been whisked off out of the way like the younger ones, and Old Lady Gooch or Gladys Pye called in to help.

Dora watched her daughter's brisk, practical movements and her serious face as she tucked the paper in neatly round the mattress. She knew Rose had recently started to come on of a month and had therefore become a woman.

'D'you want to stay and help with this one?' she asked. 'I think you're old enough. And Mrs Freeman'll need someone to give her a hand.'

Rose nodded. 'All right then.'

The labour progressed swiftly. Old Joan, who was not in fact very old but enormously fat, puffed and panted around almost as much as Dora. She pushed Sam off downstairs saying, 'This ain't no place for a lad. Go and make us all a cuppa tea, eh?'

'Just help yourself, won't you?' Dora said sarcastically. She knew she needed this woman, and she didn't want to fork out for the doctor as well. But the midwife was notorious for being lazy and sponging off people. She also laid out the dead on occasion and it was rumoured that things had gone missing from the rooms where the bodies were lying.

Rose at first found the sound of her mother's cries frightening. She started to sweat and she felt sick. She had only heard this from at least one floor away before. But between each bout of grunting and moaning Dora got back to normal and said, 'It's all right Rose. The babby'll not be long now.'

Rose ran up and down with water and cloths and alternated between her horrified fascination with the shadowy glimpses she kept getting of her mother's private parts and with the great coils of fat embedded round Joan Freeman's neck and arms and waist. Every inch of her looked as if she was padded with lard.

Joan seemed completely unmoved by what Dora was going through. She sat down on the edge of the boys' bed, her huge lap spreading across much of it. She drew her knitting out of her bag and sat in the candlelight with her head resting on her chins, pulling the brown wool round her stubby fingers.

'Ain't you got any more light than this?' she said to Rose. 'I can hardly see what I'm doing.'

Rose swallowed down her retort that she wasn't being paid to sit and do her knitting and went downstairs to find the small paraffin lamp that they hardly ever used.

'How's she getting on?' Grace whispered. She was very pale with circles under her eyes. Violet had fallen asleep on her lap.

'All right,' Rose said, feeling a bit superior. 'Shouldn't be long now.'

When she was half-way up to the attic she wished more than ever that she could retreat back down again. She heard her mother's cries, louder and more anguished than they had been so far. She had to force herself to climb the rest of the stairs.

'Please don't let me ever, ever have to do that,' she whispered to herself. 'I'll work as hard as I can, I'll get the best job I can. But don't let me have to have babbies!'

When she reached the top the light showed her Dora kneeling now on the bed on all fours like a dog. Her head was hanging down between her shoulders and she was panting and gasping. When she heard Rose she lifted her head. Her face was soaked with sweat. Joan was still knitting complacently on the other bed.

'There's something wrong,' Dora moaned.

Rose hung the lamp on a hook on the wall and went to bathe Dora's face, her hands trembling. Her mother's nightshirt had ridden right up at the back so her behind and legs were on view and she could see her great swollen belly and her breasts dangling beneath her as she knelt on the bed. Rose felt sweat break out all over her again as well.

'The babby – should be – coming down, but he's not – budging,' Dora panted, starting to cry in desperation, moving her body restlessly on the bed. Rose made helpless movements with her hands.

'You'll be all right,' Joan said, switching needles to begin on a new row. 'Just give him a good push.'

Dora heaved again. 'Help me – oh God, help me!'

Unable to do anything to help, Rose felt like crying herself. In the end she went to stand in front of Joan.

'Look, you old cow,' she shouted as Dora writhed on the bed beside them. 'You're s'posed to be here to help, not knit jumpers for the whole British bleeding army.'

The midwife waddled over to Dora in the shadowy light and said, 'You'll have to watch this one, Dora. She's got too much of a gob on her.'

'And you've got too big an arse on you,' Rose retorted. She was suddenly feeling exhausted.

'It's stuck,' Dora screamed. 'It won't come. Get it out, for God's sake. It's killing me.'

'You ought to get a doctor,' Rose hissed at Joan. 'You're not up to this.'

'Cheeky little sod,' Joan said. 'I've done hundreds of these.'

She bent down behind Dora, breathing heavily. Rose watched, horrified, as she pushed two of her thick, lardy fingers into her mother. Dora groaned, and Rose saw frothy saliva dripping from her mouth on to the crumpled newspaper. She was making whimpering animal sounds that turned Rose's stomach.

'The babby's ready all right,' Joan said. 'Must have an arm caught awkward.' And with no warning she forced her entire hand up inside Dora and began to manipulate the baby inside her, trying to free it. Dora's screams rose to a single high-pitched shriek like a creature caught in the iron teeth of a trap. Joan pulled her hand out, slimy with blood, and Rose squeezed her eyes tight and pushed her fingers into her ears, unable to stand it any longer.

When she opened her eyes a moment later, Dora was still screaming, but now it was more of a yell.

'Now you've woken up you can come here and give me a hand,' Joan said.

Still sick and dizzy, Rose just managed to peer under her mother, who was squatting again. Bulging out from her she could see the top of a little head covered in dark, wet hair.

'I can't – I CAN'T!' Dora shrieked.

'Just push,' Joan shouted down her ear. 'One more'll do it.'

With an almighty cry, Dora pushed the child's head out and Rose saw the blood spurt from her ragged vagina. Another push and the little body slithered out covered in blood and a white pasty substance. Dora collapsed forwards on to the bed.

'What is it?' Rose said, all her faintness of a moment before quite forgotten.

Joan's meaty hands picked up the little body and turned it to tie the cord.

'It's a boy, Mom!' Rose said, as Joan wrapped him in an old white cloth. 'You were right.'

'Told you,' Dora said faintly. 'Give him here.' She held out her arms, the palms of her hands grey with newspaper print, and took the little boy to her. 'Go on,' she said. 'You can go and tell your dad he's got another son. And Rose,' she said, as the girl headed for the stairs, 'thanks, our kid.'

Rose wasn't at home when it happened.

George ran across the court in his bare feet as if his breeches were on fire.

'Mom, Mom! Come quick!'

'What?' Dora's heart started pounding as she pulled off her apron. '*What?* Tell me.'

'It's our Violet,' George panted. 'She's gone under a horse.'

Dora was out of the court in front of him and into the street. At the top of Catherine Street by the main road she could see a small crowd of people and she tore along the pavement towards them.

Silently they let her through as if she were royalty. She heard someone say, 'It's the child's mother, the poor cow.'

A man was standing in front of his cart holding the bridle of a heavy black horse. Dora always remembered from that day the smell of the sweating animal, its damp heaving flanks in the sunlight and the stunned expression on the man's ill-shaven face.

At his feet lay the shape of her child. Even in the few moments since it had happened someone had run into their house and brought out an old torn net curtain and laid it over Violet, covering her completely.

Dora saw the ghostly features of her little girl's face through the two layers of net and the blood soaking into the slippery material. 'What d'you go and cover her face for?' she shouted.

She knelt down quickly and pulled back the soft curtain. Her face was expressionless as a stone as she saw the deep wound in Violet's skull and the shards of bone sticking out at grotesque angles. She was dead. Clearly, from the second the horse's hoof had smashed into the right side of her head she had had no chance of being anything else.

The man with the cart was distraught. 'I hadn't a chance, Missis. She was just there, under the horse. I never even saw her till it were too late.'

Dora nodded at him numbly. She felt no anger towards him. At this moment she felt nothing. She had no idea why Violet had been there when she should have been in the yard. Gladys Pye appeared and led her home. Someone else carried the child's body back to the house.

When Sid came home he stood looking down at her as she sat unmoving at the table. He put his face close up to hers, his breath stinking of beer.

'Can't even look out for your own kid now, can you?'

Three days later Rose was banging hard on the door of the vicarage.

When Catherine opened the door and saw the girl's pinched face and the look of desperation in her eyes she immediately led her inside and sat down with her. Ronald arrived as well, back from conducting a baptism service.

'It's me mom,' Rose said, starting to cry as the words

came out of her mouth. All the anguish of the past days started to pour out of her. 'Our Violet was killed by a horse on Wednesday.'

Catherine and Ronald looked at each other, appalled, but something stopped Catherine from following her instinct to put her arms round the girl. Rose was a warm person, but there was still a self-contained, dignified core to her that they'd seen in the small child they had carried in from the rain.

'I'm so sorry,' Ronald said. He knelt down beside her. Catherine watched, fascinated. For once she couldn't think what to do and Ronald, gentle and sympathetic, knew instinctively.

'But it's my mom,' Rose repeated. 'She hasn't said a word since Wednesday when it happened. She just sits there as if something's gone – you know – in her head. My dad's blamed her for Violet going. She ran out of the court when she wasn't s'posed to, on some prank or other. Dad says her getting killed's all Mom's fault. But she won't say nothing. She'll hardly move or eat or anything.'

She cried harsh, frightened tears.

Ronald suddenly stood up as if something had been decided. 'I'll come down and see her,' he said.

'*You?*' Rose and Catherine spoke exactly together.

'Yes, I,' he said and smiled wryly at their astonishment. 'After all, I'm supposed to be a messenger of the Good News, remember. And I presume you came to us for some sort of help, Rose? Well, this is the best I can do.'

Rose, who was suddenly terrified that Sid might be in when they got home, had no idea how much inner turmoil the vicar was experiencing as once again they walked together along the road towards town and Catherine Street. Rose's head reached above his elbow now, but she still had to make little skips to keep up with his long strides.

Ronald knew this was going to be a decisive morning in his life. He had realized gradually over the past years that he was in the wrong place. That his work in his present parish was not where his heart lay. He had encouraged Rose to tell him more and more about her life in the courtyards, of the conditions they lived in. Now he was going to visit the kind of place which drew him. Of course he could have chosen to walk round the Birch Street area at any time, but something had inhibited him. He would have been merely a voyeur. Now he had a real reason to go.

When George opened the door, Dora saw Rose standing outside with an enormous man, his dark clothes topped by a dog collar. She knew at once who he must be. At any other time she would have felt like giving Rose a good hiding for bringing him at all, let alone with no chance to get the place spick and span first. But at this moment she couldn't have cared less.

Dora stood up silently. She looked more gaunt and pale than ever. Ronald saw just how small were the houses in which so many large families had to live, how mean and cramped.

'Mom,' Rose said. 'This is the Reverend, Diana's dad. I told him about our Violet and he wanted to come and see you himself.'

Dora looked at this stranger whose head nearly touched the ceiling, and uttered her first words for days. 'You'd better make a cuppa tea, Rose,' she said. 'Kettle's boiled.' And then to Ronald: 'Have a seat.'

Ronald sat down on a wooden chair at the table, carefully avoiding a blob of congealed porridge on the side of it. 'I don't want to intrude.'

He felt foolish as he spoke, knowing that apart from death itself and the Means Testers from the Parish he was the greatest intrusion they'd had for years. He could hear the baby crying upstairs.

Dora folded her arms across herself as if to hide her breasts. 'Go and get him, Rose. I'll have to feed the babby, if you'll excuse me,' she said to Ronald in a flat, lifeless voice.

Rose carried Harry down. He was a bonny four-month-old who looked as if he'd taken all the nourishment from his mother. He was beginning to look rather like Sam.

'Now,' Dora said decisively to Rose. 'You can take this lot outside and leave us.'

She sat down with Harry on her lap, covering herself modestly with an old cardigan as she fed him. Rose, bemused, shoved Grace and George out of the door.

When the children had closed the door behind them Ronald said, 'I'm so sorry to hear about little Violet, Mrs Lucas.'

The moment he spoke he saw her eyes fill with tears. 'All I can think of is how all her life I've been that worried by everything I've hardly had a kind word to spare for her.'

She felt very shy, sitting feeding her child and blarting in front of this huge, educated stranger. But she could also feel an enormous sympathy emanating from Ronald Harper-Watt. And he had two things that she needed: distance from her own situation, so she could talk to him, and time. His job allowed him the opportunity to sit and listen.

'You'rc a good mother, Mrs Lucas,' Ronald said gently. 'You mustn't think otherwise. Rose often talks about you – fondly.' He'd noticed that more and more recently. 'And it's easy to tell you always do the best you can for your children. I know things haven't been easy for you. I'm sure Violet knew you cared for her very much.'

Dora looked up at him, at his wide, handsome face, the brown hair swept back from his face and his kind, grey eyes. He was the first truly gentle man she could remember meeting.

She began to talk. She had sat in her house for three days feeling she was losing her mind. She had been afraid to speak for fear of what might come out – mad, raving gibberish so that she'd have to be locked away and never let out again.

For about twenty minutes Ronald didn't speak at all. He sat listening attentively, watching Dora as she talked while the baby sucked and sucked at her breast.

She told him everything, from the early, happy days of her marriage to the present, how her once loving husband forced himself on her several times every month and she had almost no feeling left for him in her heart. She spared nothing, talking entirely out of her own need as if it was her last chance.

Finally she stopped and prepared more tea, lying Harry down on a chair. He had fallen asleep with a streak of milk still wet on one plump cheek.

'So that's my life, Mr Harper-Watt,' Dora said, pouring more water into the pot. 'Not much to show for it is there? Sorry you had to listen to it all, but it's been a relief to have a talk.'

'No.' Ronald sat forward to emphasize what he wanted to say. 'You don't realize. It's been a privilege.'

She noticed suddenly that his large hands were trembling, and she felt disarmed by it.

'In fact,' he went on, 'you've probably helped me more than I could ever help you. You see, I've been feeling very – out of place, shall we say? – in my work. I'm thinking of moving to work in a parish such as your own – like St Joseph's.'

Dora stared at him. 'You're coming to St Joseph's?'

'Well, no. But I'd like a parish near the middle of the – a – city. In places which aren't quite so . . .' He was lost for tactful words.

'In the slums, you mean. Well, if you're asking me, I'd say do it. I'll be frank with you, Mr Harper-Watt. I'm not a churchgoer myself, but I've been to more than the odd wedding and funeral at St Joseph's and that Reverend Gasbag, or whatever he calls himself, he ain't living in the same world as the rest of us. We could do with someone a bit more human like you.'

Ronald sat back, feeling he'd received a great compliment.

'And by the way.' Now Dora had found her tongue

again she couldn't seem to stop using it. 'I've never thanked you and your wife for all your kindness to my Rose. You've done a lot for her. And your Diana's a good kid. I thought it wasn't on at first, them two being pals, but now I'm glad it's happened.' And she almost smiled.

'We think Rose is a marvellous girl,' Ronald said, sipping his cup of extremely sweet tea, and to his surprise enjoying it. 'We're all very fond of her. She's a bright child, you know. Given the right opportunities she could go far.'

Even as he spoke, Ronald realized that he was talking out of a different world. Opportunities were not things that had arisen much in Dora's life. She just nodded at him.

When he got up to leave they shook hands, warmly.

'Thank you for talking to me,' he said. 'And for the advice.'

'It were good of you to come,' Dora said bravely. 'I know I can't sit moping here for ever. Life has to go on, and I've got my young genius to look out for!'

In silence Rose watched his tall figure walk across the court. Just before disappearing through the entry he turned and waved to her. At that moment she really thought he must be an angel.

CHAPTER 7

JULY 1936

'I've got a job!'

They were Rose's first words as soon as Diana opened the door.

'Jolly well done.' Diana beamed at her. 'I'm so glad.'

Catherine came into the hall to add her congratulations, looking as stately as ever. She was wearing a cool, cream dress that flattered her curves and her thick hair was pinned up in a fashionable style round her head.

'Come and have a glass of home-made lemon,' she said to Rose. 'We were just sitting outside.'

They went out to the back of the house where there was a blue-brick terrace facing the old walled garden. Tendrils of wisteria hung down from the house and the garden felt warm and languid as bees buzzed round the hollyhocks and tiny yellow roses climbing the garden wall.

Judith looked up from the book she was reading on her lap. She was quite unlike Diana and William, with a smaller frame and dark hair and eyes. 'Hello Rose,' she said. 'I suppose you're all going to talk now.' She slipped off the chair and went to lie with it on her stomach on the grass.

'Come on, tell us about the job,' Diana said as she sat down. 'Was it the first one?'

'Yes,' Rose said proudly. 'My first interview. It's at Lazenby's Butcher's Remnants Company near the market. They deal with all the bits of the animals that people don't want to eat. The whole name of the firm is

Lazenby's Butcher's Remnants Co. and then in brackets, Skin, Hide, Fat, Wool etc.,' she recited proudly.

'Goodness, that sounds a bit gruesome,' Catherine said. She was afraid Rose had jumped impulsively into the first job that would employ her simply because she was so anxious not to go into service or on to the factory floor. Which was in fact not far from the truth.

'It does stink round there a bit,' Rose admitted. 'But I'm their new office girl. I start on Monday. And the offices are ever so nice. They're upstairs above the yard.' She was all puffed up with pride.

'So what did you have to do?' Diana asked, dipping shortbread into her glass. She saw Catherine frown at her.

'There was two lads up for the job as well,' Rose said, starting to enjoy herself. 'And Mr Lazenby – that's the gaffer of course – he said we had to show him how we could read and write. So I said to him, "I bet I can read and write better than either of them two." And he made us write a few things down, addresses and that. And then we had to read him a bit out of a book.'

Rose had stood and read as well as she possibly could, remembering not to drop her aitches, which she could do when she thought about it, and trying to put expression in her voice.

'And when I'd finished,' she giggled, 'Mr Lazenby said to me, "It's all right, we're not here to put on a Shakespeare play, you know. We just want a kid for round the office."'

But one of the boys had scarcely been able to read and write at all and the other, who seemed to be terrified of Rose, had read slowly, stumbling over the words. And Rose knew she had left school with an excellent reference from Miss Whiteley.

'So he said the job was mine!' she said. She didn't tell them the last part, that Mr Lazenby had said, 'Right. You can start Monday. You'll be getting eight and six a week.'

'Excuse me,' Rose said politely. 'But I thought it was ten shillings you was offering.'

'Oh yes.' Mr Lazenby stretched his jowly face into a smile. 'But you're a lass. We've only ever taken on boys before.'

Rose was a bit put out, but eight and six seemed a good amount to be taking home. Besides, she was proud to be the first girl that Lazenby's had ever employed.

'And I was thinking,' she chattered on, not noticing in her excitement that the others were very subdued. 'Just because I've left school doesn't mean I can't go on learning. You can teach me about all the things you're learning at school, can't you?' At this moment, Rose felt she could do anything.

Diana was looking lovely in a pale blue dress, her wavy hair tied up in a bouncy ponytail. Her skin was tanned from playing tennis and sitting out in the garden. But Rose suddenly noticed her miserable expression. Emerging from her own preoccupations she looked across at Catherine and saw she too had a solemn face.

'What's the matter?' She tried joking: 'If I ever saw two people looking as if they've lost tuppence and found a farthing, you're the ones!'

'Rose,' Catherine said, smiling kindly at her. She held her glass on the wood of the tabletop and slowly circled it round. 'Don't think we're not delighted that you've found a job – and so quickly. It's marvellous news. It's just that we have some news as well, and we're not sure yet whether it's good news or not.'

'You may not be sure,' Diana said, scowling. 'But I am.'

'Well go on – what is it?' Rose spread her long dark fingers on top of the table as if preparing herself for a shock.

Gently Catherine explained that Ronald had been looking for a new kind of job, and that as the diocese had not been able to place him in Birmingham he had accepted a post in Manchester.

'Manchester?' Rose was completely knocked for six. It might as well have been Australia. She wasn't even precisely sure where Manchester was. 'But what about your school, Di? And your pals? I'll never see you again if you all go up there.'

Rose's eyes filled with tears, and Diana was already crying.

'It's really rotten,' she sobbed angrily. 'Daddy decides he wants a different job and the rest of us have to change everything.'

'Look darling,' Catherine said to her outraged daughter. 'I know you think it's not what you want, but you won't know until you've gone and tried it. And when you've settled in, I'm quite sure you'll make friends every bit as good as you've got here.'

She wasn't aware of the appalling tactlessness of her last remark and its effect on their visitor.

But Diana said, 'It'll be beastly. And I'll never find another friend like Rose. How can you even think it?' She got up and put her slim arm round Rose's shoulders. Rose's lips were trembling with the effort of not crying.

'Oh, goodness, Rose,' Catherine corrected herself, horrified. 'I didn't mean – oh my poor child, I'm so sorry. How awfully rude of me. But Diana will be able to come down on the train in the holidays and visit.'

'What, and sleep at our house?' Rose asked, her voice heavy with sarcasm.

Catherine chose to ignore the girl's tone, knowing she was upset. 'Not necessarily. There are other friends of ours whom she could stay with.'

Rose stared into her lap. A tight, mutinous feeling was rising up inside her. She wanted to scream and throw all the glasses off the table. Horrible things were happening again that she couldn't do anything about, just as she thought she was beginning to get somewhere. Her joy at having found her job was for the moment completely wiped away.

'Listen girls,' Catherine said, looking at the two sullen and tearful faces in front of her. She leaned one of her plump elbows on the table. 'I know it's bad news and none of us is pleased about it. Judith and William are upset as well. But we've all got to make the best of it.

And it's not happening for a couple of months yet, so let's all be brave and enjoy the time we have got here together, shall we?'

Catherine changed the subject, talking about the civil war that was breaking out in Spain, and how she felt that Mr Stanley Baldwin was not doing any better than the Labour Prime Minister Ramsay Macdonald had at tackling the problem of people out of work. Both the girls realized she was trying to say how small their problem was compared to some of the big things going on in the world. But of course that didn't make them feel any better. Already it felt as if things were not the same. And Rose had a feeling that now they never would be.

It took the employees at Lazenby's a few weeks to get used to having a girl in the office. There was Miss Peters of course, but she was old enough to be most people's mother, if not grandmother.

Rose became a familiar figure, running errands to and from the traders on the balcony of the huge meat market, delivering statements and cheques and invoices. At first they ribbed her because she was a girl, but after a few weeks she often heard, 'Hello Rose! All right Rose!' from the lads as she made her way round between the office and the trading area.

One part of the job she didn't like was running messages down to the yard at the back of Lazenby's. She found she was surprisingly squeamish about what went on down there. She'd already seen the slaughter yard at Camp Hill. Groups of kids often gathered there to watch when they did the killing early in the morning and she'd been dragged along once by Sam. The dogs chivvied the cows or sheep a dozen at a time into the pen which was open for all to see behind a fence of palings. The slaughterers caught the animals one by one as they shrieked, sweating in terror and running at the fence trying to escape. They drove a sharp stick like a poker into their heads through whichever orifice they could reach to penetrate the brain of the flailing, screaming animal. In through the eyes or ears until the damage inflicted on them reached their whole bodies and they writhed and twitched and finally lay still.

In the yard of Lazenby's they dealt with everything leftover that could be sold. When Rose went down there the first time the stench turned her stomach. Slightly sweet and putrid, it was a smell she never got used to. The brick floor of the yard was covered with piles of cow hides which had to be examined to see if they had been holed by warble fly. Then they were rubbed over with salt and stacked in piles graded according to size. Sheep fleeces were dealt with in the same way.

Each time she went down there she had to contain her revulsion for the place and put up with the constant gibing of the yard men. The first time she stepped out into the yard they all straightened up from what they were doing and stood staring at her in their rubber boots and aprons, giving each other mischievous grins and making smart alec comments. One of them was hideously disfigured. His head and neck ran into each other and a goitre was slung like a squashed pig's bladder right round to the back. A cluster of bristles sprouted out of his nose.

'What're you doing here then?' one of them called to her. 'Come to do a turn for us have you?'

'I've got a note for Mr Freeman actually,' Rose said timidly. They were gawping like idiots as she stood in the navy skirt and soft pink blouse that Catherine and Diana had bought for her – new! – as a present for starting work.

'Ew – ectually!' they mimicked.

Rose slowly walked across the yard where there were small pieces of gristle and fat and furry bits stuck on to and in between the bricks. She slipped and nearly fell on a lump of something yellow and greasy.

'Watch your step,' they sniggered.

'This is where we keep some of the, er – accessories of the job,' the goitre man said mockingly.

The smells and the fatty lumps on the ground and the

great mauve bulge on the man's neck were already getting all mixed up in her mind. He took her forearm with his huge hairy hand and led her towards a row of bunkers at one side of the yard. Inside two of them she could see roughly picked bones piled all together, and in the other, glutinous mounds of fat. Shiny green flies were buzzing round greedily.

'And this one's where we keep the salt for the hides.'

Rose could hear the goitre man's heavy breathing as he stood beside her. She looked into the end bunker at the off-white heap of salt. Immediately she became aware that the pile was moving. It was a mass of maggots rubbing ceaselessly against each other's bodies and between the large granules of salt.

Rose knew what the man wanted. She wouldn't give him the satisfaction of looking squeamish, even though the sight sickened her. 'Well, thanks for the guided tour,' she said pertly, keeping her face quite calm. 'Now, which of you gentlemen is Mr Freeman?'

The man pointed his thick arm, letting go of Rose with the other. 'Him over there.'

As Rose made to walk off he said, 'Oi, just a minute. What part of town d'you come from then?'

'Birch Street, near by there,' Rose said.

'So you are one of us then. You look a bit poshed up in them clothes, that's all.'

In the office, though, it was different altogether. There were three main rooms where they worked. Mr Lazenby's office was up at the far end, shut off from the main workroom. You didn't go into Mr Lazenby's without permission and he sat with the door shut.

Rose sometimes knocked and crept in with messages. But she found Mr Lazenby disconcerting, although he was always polite to her, and even seemed to take an interest in her. He sat at his desk with its scratched leather top, all his things arranged on it extremely neatly: the blotter, penholder and account books or whatever he was dealing with. He was in his early fifties with a balding crown and soft, loose-looking cheeks. Rose expected them to slither down off his face at any moment. He had watery blue eyes and a rounded shiny nose. His manner was always quiet and courteous and he often asked how she was settling in with the firm and whether there were any problems.

Once, when she had come in with a message from the meat market, he thanked her and then said, 'Now, you just come round here a minute. I'll show you a picture of my kids. My youngest daughter is about your age.'

Rose walked obediently round the desk and leaned forward a little to look at the photograph. She suddenly felt Mr Lazenby's breath close to her ear and jumped back abruptly.

'It's all right,' he said. 'Don't be nervous, my dear.' And he put his arm round her waist for a moment in a fatherly sort of way to reassure her.

The photograph was another of the items placed neatly on his desk.

'There, you see,' he said. 'My two sons and my little girl.'

Three faces smiled rather stiffly out of the grey photograph. They all looked very well dressed and one of the boys closely resembled Mr Lazenby.

'Thank you,' said Rose, blushing. Mr Lazenby was staring at her and she didn't like being this close to him. He always smelt rather stale and sweaty. 'It's very nice of you to show me.'

'You're a good lass,' he said as she escaped out of the door, her feet sounding too loud on the lino floor.

At the other end of the long office space there was a storeroom for stationery, next to the stairs, and the office in between was where Rose spent most of her time. She dealt with the post and record cards and the stencilling machine. In the same office Miss Peters did the main secretarial work, and Michael Gillespie, the clerk, kept the books.

Michael was seventeen. He towered over Rose, his black hair slicked back very smartly and his blue eyes full of warmth and fun. To Rose, Michael might have been a whole generation older than herself. He seemed so grown up and knowing about the world, and he was already learning a proper skill which he could take on to other firms.

'I don't want to be stuck as an office dogsbody for the rest of my life,' he told her. Rose could hear the very slight Irish intonation in his voice even though he'd been born and brought up in Birmingham. 'There's all the world waiting out there . . .' He moved one of his strong fingers along the frayed edge of a ledger with a grin on his face, pretending it was a plane taking off. 'Lazenby's is just my runway to greater things.'

'What greater things?' Rose asked curiously, franking a pile of letters that Miss Peters had completed.

'Well now, little Rosie, let me see.' Michael sat back in the chair with the air of a tycoon surveying his latest acquisition. 'There's all sorts of things. One of these days I'm going to be running my own business. With a big office. And I'll be able to sit at my desk and send someone running for cups of tea. And I'll tell you what: you and Miss Peters can come and work for me!' He sat forward again, laughing loudly. 'What do you say, Miss Peters?'

'I can hardly wait,' Miss Peters said, looking across at him over her round, black-rimmed spectacles. 'Rose, are those letters going out this week – this month even?'

Rose smiled wryly at Michael, who jumped up and went to lean impishly over the back of Miss Peters' black Remington typewriter.

'You know what a wonderful woman you are, don't you?' He smiled appealingly, bending his head down towards her. 'So efficient, so correct, such a sense of humour. You're an example to us all.' He sensed that Miss Peters was coming round to his charm in her prickly way. 'Sure,' he said, bouncing back to his desk. 'I'd have you to work for me any time!'

Miss Peters made noises of exasperation and gestured at Rose to get off to the post. She ran down the stairs, laughing.

Rose was happy. She treasured the thought of Dora's

proud face as she set off, all dressed up on her first morning, and then when Rose had brought home her first wages. Even the pain of saying goodbye to Diana the week before seemed lightened by the fun she had in the office.

She had been at work on the day they actually left, so they said their goodbyes on the Sunday before. Ronald and Catherine had both embraced Rose as well as Diana, and even William shook her by the hand, rather stiffly, and said, 'I hope we shall see you again, Rose.'

'You'd blooming better,' Rose said, being all joky so she didn't start crying. 'I'll expect you down here to see me as soon as you can, Di.'

'Oh, I shall come, I shall. But you must write to me very, very often. I shall miss you so much.'

They'd given each other a long big hug. They didn't want to let go, and promised each other all kinds of things: above all, letters. And Rose had waved goodbye as she started for home, choked with sadness. When she reached her house she cried and cried.

Later she told Geraldine Donaghue that Diana had left. The girl's face lit up maliciously. The two had spent a lot of time together at school, but Geraldine had always remained jealous of Diana, knowing that she and Rose shared something very special.

'Going to lower yourself to speak to the rest of us now are you?' Geraldine said.

'I've always spoken to you,' Rose said impatiently. 'You know that very well. And if you hadn't always been so green round the gills about Diana we could've been better friends all the time.'

'Hark at her,' Geraldine said. 'Miss High and Mighty.'

Rose knew Geraldine was sore because she hated her boring factory job, and her dad had been laid off again. She knew the Donaghues were struggling, and none of it did much to improve Theresa Donaghue's temper.

But Rose was not very bothered about Geraldine. She had only to be in Michael's cheeky, vivacious company for a few minutes and she felt renewed and lively herself.

She had been attracted to him from the first day there, though she was not thinking about courting. She knew Michael was a regular on the Stratford Road monkey-run and had had a succession of dates. She was very childlike and innocent still about relations between men and women, although she knew that sometimes she was flirting with him. Mainly he provided a figure for her to look up to, who had an infectious kind of drive and wanted to put a lot into his life and get a lot out of it. He made her feel more alive.

'You're a funny kid,' he said to her one day as they were working together. Miss Peters, despite her crustiness, was very tolerant of their conversation so long as she knew the work would be done.

Michael looked appraisingly at Rose. 'You come down here from Birch Street all dressed up in nice clothes that would set anyone back a bit. And sometimes you talk common like the rest of us, and other times you can turn it on and put on your aitches and sound quite posh. What's your secret, eh, little Rosie?' He grinned at her. 'Are you a foundling from Buckingham Palace or something?'

'That'd be telling, wouldn't it?' she said rather pertly, and she knew once again that there was a mild flirtation going on between them.

She had come to Lazenby's with enormous hopes, to learn, as a way of getting experience for better things and eventually moving on.

But not yet, she thought. I'll stay and enjoy it while it lasts.

CHAPTER 8

The summer ended. Rose walked to work on fine days in the rich slanting light of autumn. When it grew colder she put on Diana's coat – one of a number of pieces of clothing that the family had left for her – and walked more briskly.

Though still small and thin Rose was not as painfully bony as she had been during the poorest days of her childhood. She was of a different build from Dora, more rounded, and her breasts had begun to fill out. With her dark wavy hair cut to the level of her chin and softly brushed back from her face and wearing Diana's well-cut clothes she looked surprisingly elegant for someone so young. Her brown eyes shone with vigour and intelligence.

Twice every day she passed builders working on a nearby warehouse whose scaffold extended out across the pavement so she had to skirt round piles of bricks and a cement mixer. The lads working on the site, their boots dusted grey, gave appreciative whistles as she walked by.

It didn't take her long to notice that one of the young brickies had taken quite a shine to her. As the days passed he seemed to be waiting for her, watching quietly. He wasn't one of the whistlers. He was a thin, pale lad with spiky brown hair that looked as if no amount of Bryl or any other creem would force it to lie flat.

Then he began to smile at her and say hello whenever she walked by. Once, when she had almost passed them, she heard the others egging him on, 'Go on – go and ask her name!'

Suddenly the nervous boy was beside her. 'Er . . .' The words stumbled out clumsily. 'I just wondered – I mean – what's your name?'

'Rose,' she replied, amused. 'And what's yours?'

'Alfie,' he said. 'That is – Alfred – Meredith.'

'Oh,' Rose said. 'Hello then, Alfie.'

Alfie seemed to be quite struck dumb and as Rose was still hurrying on down the road he said, 'Tara then.'

'Tara,' Rose said smiling, attaching no real importance to the meeting.

She was still smiling when she reached Lazenby's and walked into the office. Michael was already sitting behind his desk and he looked up and grinned when he saw her. 'All right, little Rosie?' he said. 'Don't you look a picture this morning? Had some good news or what?'

'Yes I have.' She took her camel coat off and hung it up. 'A letter from Diana.'

Rose had gradually told Michael about Diana and her own hopes to get on and do something with her life. She was rather afraid at first that he'd laugh at her and tell her she'd not got a hope. Sometimes she couldn't make Michael out. He could be as kind and generous as anyone she'd ever met – even Diana – and innocent as she was, she realized that the hunger for life they both shared resulted in an electric kind of attraction between them. But there was also a wild streak in him. She knew he was already beginning to drink heavily, and he had come into the office a number of times with his face cut and bruised from fights.

When she told him her greatest ambition was to become a teacher of young children he looked at her and gave a low whistle.

'Well,' he said. 'You're quite a girl, aren't you? Can't quite see you as one of them blue-stocking women though – let alone how you're going to get there. But good luck to you all the same.'

She knew it was not an ambition he could really

understand, but she was grateful to him for not making fun of her.

And hearing from Diana was always encouraging.

'I can't wait until Christmas when I come down to see you,' Diana wrote.

> I miss you and Birmingham so much. My school is all right I suppose, but I haven't really made any friends properly yet. The school is rather a long way from where we live, as we knew it would be. So William, Judith and I all have to go to school on the bus every day. Mummy says it's good for us! But I don't like Manchester as much as Birmingham.

She told Rose that her father was enjoying his new job and Catherine was getting stuck into things as ever.

> Missing you ever such a lot. With love from your good friend,
>
> Diana. xxx

Things were looking less cheerful for Dora. She was pregnant again. At nearly forty-three she'd hoped this kind of sickness was something she'd seen the back of. And this time it came with an intensity and violence that she recognized from nearly twenty years earlier. It could mean only one thing.

'It's twins, I'm sure of it,' she wailed to Rose and Grace as they helped her back up the stairs to bed. 'I've only been sick this bad with babbies once before and that was with Sid and Percy. What the hell am I going to do? Twins at my age!'

'It might not be twins, Mom,' Grace tried to reassure her as they helped her on to the bed, so weak from the incessant retching that she could barely stand. 'It might just be your age making it worse.'

'Ooh,' Dora groaned. 'I feel as if someone's trampled all over me ribcage.'

'Look Mom,' Rose said. 'There's no need to worry.

You don't have to do anything. The money's coming in from me and Sam and our Grace'll be out at work next year when the babby's born. We'll do everything round the house. You just take care of yourself for a change.'

'What about Sid's dinner today? You know how he carries on . . .'

'Let him get it his bloody self for once,' Rose snapped, exasperated that her father's needs were as usual the thing that overrode everything else.

Grace shushed her. 'It's all right, Mom,' she said to Dora. 'I've got a few minutes before I go to school. I'll sort out something to keep him quiet. You just have a sleep and you'll feel better. Rose – you'd better get off to work or you'll be late.'

Rose could feel her sister's stoical calmness beginning to pervade the room. She realized it would be better if she went. She left Grace methodically tidying her father's things in the bedroom and tucking the covers round Dora so that only her grey face, creased in discomfort, was visible.

It was the first time Dora had been able to take to bed during a pregnancy. The sickness left her weak and wretched, and it was several weeks before she was able to be up once the worst was over.

The day had begun well. It was a frosty November morning. The builders on Rose's walk to Lazenby's had almost finished their work, and this fact had stirred Alfie Meredith to new realms of courage. He thought Rose was the best-looking girl he'd ever seen. He longed to ask her out and spent almost all his time rehearsing what he might say. Rose, though she smiled and waved at him, never gave him a thought the rest of the time.

When Alfie approached her that morning, Rose turned to him with her usual smile and said, 'All right, Alfie? Job's about done, isn't it? I s'pose you'll be moving on soon?'

'Yes,' he said, walking alongside her. 'That's it – yes. Er, Rose. Just stop a tick will you?'

She stopped and waited, looking at him.

'I wanted to ask you . . .' He ran his sandy hand through the already wayward hair and it stuck up even more. 'Would you think of coming out with me – on a date like?'

Rose decided in a split second what approach to take to this. She wasn't keen on the idea of walking out with Alfie, though flattered by the question. She decided to let him down gently by keeping up a joking banter. She started to walk on again slowly.

'Well – I'm not sure about that,' she said. 'I'd have to think about it, wouldn't I?'

Alfie immediately took this as a refusal. He ran after her awkwardly in his cement-caked trousers. 'Well tell me your address then – or I might not see you again. We finish here today, see.'

'Court eleven, Catherine Street,' Rose called over her shoulder to him. 'Got to go or I'll be late. Tara, Alfie.'

It was a tiring day. She ran back and forth to the markets with messages amid the seething activity in the echoing building hung with the skinned sides of animals. There were so many invoices and bills to be sorted out that she was not much in the office until the afternoon. When she finally came back the short distance up Bradford Street and along the side street to Lazenby's she saw that the lights were on and the place looked quite warm and inviting.

Upstairs Mr Lazenby was standing in the main office with Jo Perks from the meat market. Miss Peters had already left, her desk cleared and immaculate. Michael still seemed to be concentrating at his desk.

'Hello stranger,' he said, looking up. 'They've certainly kept you on the go today haven't they?' He closed the ledger and tidied a few sheets of paper. 'Well – that's me done. I'm off to the Adam and Eve for a quick one.' Rose smiled as he smoothed back his shiny black hair and put his jacket on. She knew it would be more than a quick one. 'Tara. See you in the morning, kid!'

'Bye,' Rose said, smiling after him. She watched him walk jauntily to the top of the stairs. Just before he disappeared down them he turned and raised his thumb to her with a smile, and she grinned and waved at him.

Jo Perks and Mr Lazenby were standing sorting through a pile of slinks – the hides of unborn calves which Lazenby's also purchased from the markets. They went to make fancy wallets and purses.

Rose looked at her table to see if there were any jobs that needed doing, and then began to get ready to leave. Her feet were very chilled and tired and she thought longingly of soaking them in a pail of hot water when she got home.

But as she made to go Mr Lazenby called over to her. 'Rose – if you wouldn't mind hanging on a minute till I've finished with Mr Perks. I've got a couple of things need sorting out.'

Rose nodded and waited as Mr Lazenby showed out the dapper figure of Jo Perks, carrying a couple of the rolled up slinks that hadn't come up to scratch.

'Come here a minute, Rose,' Mr Lazenby said in his polite but brisk business voice.

He stood back to let her into his office, where the light was already on, making it look completely dark outside. He closed the door behind them.

With rather odd enthusiasm he said, 'I tell you what. Since we're out of hours, you sit in the boss's seat. Go on, for a bit of a joke like. Yes, that's right my dear. Go along and sit yourself down!'

Rose walked round to the big chair behind Mr Lazenby's desk. It had wooden arms and a shiny leather seat. She looked uncertainly at Mr Lazenby, who stood the other side of the desk. His worn black jacket was unbuttoned and as he leaned down to rest his weight on his hands on the desk, the flaps of the jacket swung outwards making him look enormously wide.

Rose began to wonder if he'd been drinking. She'd

never seen Mr Lazenby looking so animated. But he was normally a very abstemious man – known for it in fact. His soft cheeks had more colour in them than usual and he kept tapping his fingers restlessly on the top of the desk.

'There are a couple of invoices I'll need first thing,' he said once Rose was seated on the slippery chair, which smelt rather sweaty, like Mr Lazenby. 'Since you're so good at writing, you can write these ones out yourself. How about that?' he said.

He opened one of the desk drawers and produced a wodge of forms, then handed Rose a pen. 'This one's for Clark's, so write in the name up there – you know how to do it,' he said, pointing with a grubby finger. He gave her details of the address and Rose slowly wrote them on the invoice sheet in her very neatest handwriting. Mr Lazenby watched over her shoulder.

'Very good,' he said, and Rose jumped because the voice sounded so close to her.

'Now – the next bit,' he said.

Rose sat with her heart beating fast. She was beginning to sweat under her arms. She didn't know what Mr Lazenby was up to but he was making her most uneasy. She just wanted to get the job done and go home.

As she was listing the items on the form she suddenly felt Mr Lazenby's hands moving round her and cupping her breasts. She gasped out of shock and discomfort because he was pressing her quite hard. She sat quite still, completely unable to think what to do. What on earth had come over him? This was a mistake – a terrible mistake. Mr Lazenby must realize it in a minute and stop touching her. She thought her heart was going to burst it was beating so loud, and her hands had gone clammy.

'Stand up,' Mr Lazenby ordered. His voice sounded polite still, but had a hard, unfamiliar edge to it. He pulled her up by moving his hands under her arms and he steered her away from the chair. Rose obeyed, bewildered. She was very afraid, but she couldn't think what else to do. The building around them had gone quiet.

After that, quite silently except for his breathing, which sounded loud and fast, he pulled her against him. She was still facing the desk, the impassive blotter, the penholder and the set, smiling faces of his children. He moved up and down against her buttocks, fitting himself close to her.

He began grabbing at her clothes, the green cardigan and soft white blouse. He lost patience with the buttons and she heard the blouse tear apart at the front. The image of Miss Smart's face as she had ripped Rose's bloomers that day filled her mind for a second. At least then she had understood what was happening.

'Stop it, Mr Lazenby – please,' she begged, her voice turning high like a little girl's. 'I don't like this. Please stop and let me go home.'

She turned her head and felt a plunging sensation of revulsion at the sight of him behind her. He didn't look like Mr Lazenby any more. His eyes were half closed and seemed to be rolled up into the lids so he looked all peculiar, as if he were in a trance. And his tongue was sticking stiffly out of his mouth towards her ear.

'What are you doing?' she shouted. 'Help me somebody – please. Please!'

She tried to get his hands off her, but as if prompted by her cries, Mr Lazenby shoved her to the floor, cold against her breasts and stomach as she writhed and kicked. She felt his knee in her back pinning her to the floor, and twisting round she saw he had unbuttoned his trousers and was rubbing himself with his hand, fast up and down. He pulled off her underwear and stockings, pausing to caress himself with one hand as he did so. She knew she didn't have the strength to get away from him. She put her arms flat on the floor and laid her head down so she didn't have to see his face with its self-absorbed expression or his horrifying, swollen member.

He pushed her skirt up and made her move her legs apart. She had never taken her clothes off in front of a man before, not even a doctor. She pressed her eyes shut at the shame of it. Tears squeezed from her lids on to the floor. She thought at least she hadn't got her monthly to add to the humiliation. She knew that what Mr Lazenby was doing must be what she had heard her father do so often to her mother, but it didn't prepare her any better for what happened next.

He gradually forced one of his fingers up inside her so that she squirmed and cried out in shock and pain.

'Oh . . .' Mr Lazenby gave a low groan. 'Young, tight.'

They were the only words he spoke until he'd finished. Quickly he climbed on her and forced hard up into her from behind and she screamed and then whimpered at his repeated movements. Each time he pushed into her she felt a terrible stab of pain somewhere deep in her guts. Her hipbones and ribs were grinding hard against the floor with the weight of him on top of her and she was finding it hard to breathe. She lifted her head, sobbing and trying to take in gasps of air so her mouth dried out. It took some time before he managed to finish, and he came at last with a loud, relieved cry.

When he had stumbled off her he buttoned himself up again and watched as she slowly pulled herself off the floor and found her clothes. The wet ran down her legs as she stood up and her tears wouldn't stop coming. She didn't look at Mr Lazenby when she was clothed again. She began to walk mechanically to the door.

Mr Lazenby gave a little cough. 'Er – Rose, just a minute,' he said.

She forced herself to look round and saw he was bringing his wallet out of his jacket.

'I've been thinking. You've done you best since you've been here,' he said in his normal courteous voice. 'But I'm not sure this is really a job for a lass. I've decided to let you go and get a lad in like we've always had. It'll be for the best I think.'

He was holding out a pound note to her.

'Here – take a couple of weeks' pay. And if you need a decent reference you can rely on me, you know that.'

He came a little closer, holding the money out as if he was trying to tempt a dangerous animal. Rose quickly snatched the note, backing away from him again.

He unlocked the door and she went slowly down the stairs and out into the freezing evening, holding in her hand a larger sum of money than she'd ever earned at once before.

CHAPTER 9

12 MAY 1937

Coronation day. All over the nation there were excited preparations to celebrate the crowning of a new king – George VI. Red, white and blue bunting rippled and flapped along Catherine Street in the bright spring morning. Union Jacks billowed out from the sills of some of the houses, and as it was a day off work for everyone, the road was more full of people than usual. Already the inhabitants of the street were setting up trestle tables along the pavements, to be laid later with white cloths and heaped with plates of food for the street's celebration party. George and his little band of followers were tearing in and out of the courts in their draggle-arsed shorts, pretending to be aeroplanes with a lot of roaring sound effects and getting under everybody's feet.

In Court 11 most of the women were inside hastily icing platefuls of tiny sponge cakes and slicing bread for the little triangular sandwiches which would grace the tables later on. Old Lady Gooch declared, breathing heavily as she went to inspect what was happening in each house, that she'd made a 'rich fruit Dundee – one of me best'. Her large bloodshot eyes ran over every contribution to make sure everyone was doing their whack and that there'd be enough to go round in the afternoon. She was still wearing her working clothes. The dressing up would come later and the pawn shops had been rifled for suitable clothes, some of which had not seen the light of day for months or longer.

The happiest person in the court that day was Grace

Lucas. Not only was she to leave school that summer, but she was ecstatic that there was another coronation so soon after the last. Now she'd got over her grief at the death of her beloved King George V and the startling abdication of his successor Edward VIII, she was ready to throw herself wholeheartedly into the occasion. She had trimmed the edges of her frock by hand with strips of red, white and blue, and decorated a straw hat in the same colours with elaborate ribbons and bows. With it pulled on over her straggly brown hair, her pale, sweet face was almost pretty. Even Sid had noticed and commented that he'd never seen her looking such a 'fine lass' before.

'Rose – you can't miss coming this afternoon,' Grace entreated her sister, who was scraping the last hardening crust of white icing out of a mixing bowl. 'It wouldn't be the same without you. You're not thinking of the neighbours are you?'

'Bit late for that isn't it?' Rose said sourly. 'I'm just not in the mood, that's all, and I need a rest. I cleaned that blooming pub from top to bottom yesterday and I could do with a lie down. I don't feel right.'

Grace's and Dora's eyes met and Grace shrugged. She couldn't get close to Rose any more. She felt like crying when she looked at her older sister standing by the table. She was wearing an old dress of Dora's which they'd shortened together and tucked up at its wide, loose waist. Her belly was straining forward with the unmistakable curve of pregnancy. She was having to lean more than usual towards the table to accommodate the shape of the child. Her hair was hanging limply down her back and around her face. Grace couldn't help thinking – with the realization of how aware Rose must be of it too – that she looked just like a miniature, black-haired version of her mother.

'Leave her,' Dora said rather irritably. She was tired, being now seven months pregnant herself, as well as having had to deal with all the goings on over Rose.

'I'm going to go and see how they're getting on

outside,' Grace said a bit huffily. Her mother and sister had an understanding nowadays that she definitely was not part of.

She went out into the street to look up and down at all the busy preparations. She saw someone coming towards her along the street and for a few seconds she couldn't place who it was. Then she was back across the court to the house as fast as she could move.

'Rose!' she shrieked. 'He's here again!'

Rose looked up lifelessly. 'Who?'

'That bloke – Alfie – the one who come before. He's got flowers this time.'

'Oh no,' Rose said. Dora and Grace could both hear the panic in her voice. 'Don't let him see me, for God's sake.' She was wiping her hands so hurriedly that she fumbled and dropped the cloth. 'Go and tell him I'm not here again. Tell him I've gone away or something.' And she was off upstairs.

Grace managed to reach Alfie as he was coming into the court. 'You looking for Rose again?' she asked, thinking what kind eyes he had and how funny his hair looked all sticking up like that.

'Is she here?' Grace could hear the combined hope and nervousness in his voice. 'I'd really like to see her – if she'll let me.'

At that moment young Harry waddled up and stood staring at this strange man who had appeared. He had wide blue eyes and a fat tummy. And he had nits and was forever scratching busily at his head.

'E-yo,' he said to Alfie.

'Hello.' Alfie smiled down at him. 'Doing all right, are you?'

'That's our Harry,' Grace told him.

'Nice kid,' Alfie said. 'Anyway, is Rose in today?'

'Rose . . .' Harry said, turning towards the house, and Grace could tell he was about to point at it. Hurriedly she grabbed his hands and picked him up, wishing someone would pursue her with flowers and obvious admiration, because she'd make better use of it than Rose.

'Rose ain't here,' she told him. 'She's gone away for a bit – to stay with Mom's sister down Alcester way. She won't be around for . . . well, we don't know how long really.' She didn't like lying to him, but she felt it would save both his feelings and Rose's.

'Oh,' Alfie said despondently. 'Only I was hoping – you know, as it's a holiday today . . .'

'Well I'll let her know you 've been round – when I, er, write,' Grace said. 'It was nice of you to call.'

'Here,' Alfie said, holding out the bunch of pink and white flowers to her. 'You might as well take these anyway. You have them, or give them to your mom.'

As he turned to go he pointed at number five. 'That your house then, is it?'

'Yes,' Grace said shyly. 'That's us – number five.'

'Tara then.'

Glancing up at the dark windows, Alfie felt sure he caught a glimpse of a pale face edged with black hair, before it ducked down below the sill.

He walked away angrily. What's got into her? he thought. I s'pose she thinks I'm not good enough for her or something.

There had been a number of changes in Court 11 during the past six months.

First, Rose had been faced with telling Dora she had lost her job. When her daughter walked in that November evening, Dora had only to look at her to realize something had happened. Normally she came in from work tired, but quite animated, and often full of stories of things that had happened during the day. But that night she was quite silent, as if something had been tied up tight inside her.

'Had a bad day?' Sam casually asked Rose as he polished his boots. 'Aren't you going to tell us what wonder boy's been up to today?' Sam got a bit browned off with Rose's adoration of Michael Gillespie.

Rose didn't answer him. She took off her coat and hung it up behind the door and then went to go upstairs.

'Grub's ready so don't go disappearing again,' Grace said. 'You're late enough as it is.'

Rose ignored her.

'Did you hear your sister?' Sid shouted after her, throwing the newspaper down. 'We've all been waiting for you as it is. You ought to be thankful our Grace lets you off so much of the work around here, you uppity little cow.'

Dora and the others held their breath as they waited for the explosion from Rose which would set off another of the increasingly bitter fights between them. Grace had had to intervene to pacify Sid on a number of occasions when Dora wasn't up to it.

But Rose just said, 'I'm not hungry,' and went to her room.

She sat painfully on the bed, feeling the damp still on her clothes. Her mouth twisted for a moment with revulsion. Then she lay down, curling herself on the mattress like an unborn child. The pain throbbed inside her. She pressed her hand on her bruised private parts, and clamped her legs tight together with her hand still between them, trying to dull the ache of it. What she wanted overwhelmingly was to wash every part of her over and over, but she knew there was no chance of that with all the family sitting round down there. She screwed her eyes tight shut and wished she could fall down, down somewhere very dark and safe where she could be held and comforted. No tears came to begin washing away the shame and despair she felt.

And as she lay there she was overcome with loathing for herself. All the smells of Lazenby's seemed to seep out from her clothes and her body. She smelt the foul stink of the hides, the bunkers of bones and rancid fat in the yard. She saw the maggots squirming among the grains of salt, the frantic greed of the flies; she saw the discoloured bulging shape of the goitre man's neck and the soft, floppy cheeks of Mr Lazenby. She could see him kneeling with that horrible, trance-like expression on his face, his trousers unbuttoned and his hand busy on his penis.

She rushed over to the bucket in the corner of the room and retched over it, feeling the muscles in her bruised stomach heave painfully. She didn't hear Grace coming up the stairs.

'Are you bad, Rose?' she asked sympathetically. 'You should've said instead of just going off. I could've brought you a cuppa tea. Dad just thought you was being awkward.'

'I'll be all right,' Rose said weakly, and she sounded so wretched that Grace said, 'I'll get our mom.'

Dora slowly climbed the stairs holding a candle stuck on to a saucer. She wasn't feeling too good herself.

'What's up with you then, miss?' she demanded roughly, sitting down on the bed, panting from the climb.

Rose had only intended to break the news that she'd lost her job, but when she began talking the tears started pouring down her cheeks again. She had to tell Dora what had happend. She couldn't hold back.

The second she heard what Rose had to say, Dora was on her feet. With more energy than she'd summoned for weeks she slapped Rose hard on each cheek.

'What did you do?' Dora shouted at her, before remembering that on no account must Sid or the neighbours overhear this conversation. 'You must've encouraged him,' she hissed at Rose. She stood with her hands clamped to her waist, her elbows at sharp, hostile angles. Her shadow in the candlelight looked huge and menacing. 'Going off to a place like that in all them clothes of Diana's. You must've given him ideas, you silly little cow.'

'I didn't!' Rose wailed. 'I didn't know what to give him ideas about, did I? He just went for me – held me down on the floor!'

Dora stood over her, her mind trying to take in the implications of what had happened. Then, as if bracing herself, she said in a matter-of-fact voice, 'We'll just have to wait and see if you're having a babby. If not, then there's no harm done. You can go and find another job.'

'A babby?' Rose sat up, horrified. The thought hadn't occurred to her.

'If you didn't know where they come from before, you do now,' Dora said drily. 'God help you if your dad finds out. I'll tell you one thing though. Whatever he says I'll stick by you. You'll not be sent out on the streets like some. But you'd better start praying hard, Rose, that there ain't no babby come out of this. Because you're going to need all the help you can get.'

She gave Rose's quivering body a rough pat. 'When your dad's off to the Catherine again I'll send Grace up with a pail of water for you. We'll just tell her you're a bit feverish. It'll have to be cold though – I can't spare the slack for the fire this time of night. But if you want to wash a man off you that bad you won't be bothered how cold the water is.'

'So you're nothing but a bloody little tart after all!' Sid's harsh voice ran through the house. 'Even that Geraldine Donaghue ain't poking out at the front and she's been working down the factory. But you've been nothing but cowing trouble ever since you learned to open your gob.'

Rose noticed again the perverse triumph that came over him when he saw her put down. But she rode her father's attacks more easily than anyone's. She was used to them. And as she had promised, Dora stood like an immovable wall between him and Rose as he ranted at both of them. But even his insults felt as if they were true, she was in such an emotional state.

It was telling Grace and Sam that came hardest. One afternoon they went with George and Harry to Calthorpe Park. The two young boys ran on ahead as soon as they were released into the green space, little Harry trying to keep up with his nine-year-old brother. Sam, Rose and Grace walked behind, keeping them both in sight.

'How could you, Rose?' Sam demanded, rigid with indignation. He immediately fell into what Rose was beginning to recognize as his role of responsible citizen. His shoulders were pulled back and he clasped his hands behind his back, walking along with a rather ponderous stride. For a split second Rose wanted to giggle hysterically. She had only got as far as telling him that in five months' time she'd be having a baby.

'How could you lower yourself like that?' Sam lectured. Beside her, Rose sensed, Grace had gone rigid with distress, but would not of course be judging her. Not Grace.

'I've always had my suspicions about that Michael Gillespie bloke,' Sam went on. 'Always sounded like trouble to me. You shouldn't be taken in by things that glitter, Rose. All that glitters is not gold, you know. And where is he now you're carrying his child? That's what I'd like to know.'

'It wasn't Michael!' Rose cried, bursting into tears. She was completely horrified that that should be Sam's first thought. Sobbing, she told him who the child's father was.

'You must've given him some encouragement,' Sam said. 'That Mr Lazenby sounded like a respectable feller. You said yourself he lives in a road in Edgbaston, not a street like the likes of us round the Birch. You should be ashamed of yourself.'

'Of course I'm ashamed of myself,' Rose sobbed brokenly beside him. 'D'you think I've felt anything but ashamed since the day it happened?'

'Sssh, for goodness sake,' Sam urged her. 'People're staring at you.'

Grace put her arm round Rose's shoulder and with the other pointed across the park to the two boys. 'Go and get them, Sam,' she said icily to her brother. 'And take your time.'

The two sisters sat down on one of the benches. Rose, beyond caring that she had chosen to tell them in such a public place, leaned on Grace's skinny shoulder and cried and cried. From the evening she had left Lazenby's she had felt only a leaden depression so that some days she could hardly drag herself around. But now the pain released itself from the deepest part of her. The tears wouldn't stop coming, and Grace stroked her hair gently. Sitting there so close, as Rose finally grew quieter, her body still shuddering from the sobs, she could hear the pull of her sister's lungs.

'Why didn't you tell me sis?' Grace asked her. 'I'd never've blamed you, you know. This is the worst thing that could happen to anyone and I know you're not the type to go looking for it.'

'I couldn't.' Rose gulped. 'I mean, I had to tell Mom – about why I'd lost my job at Lazenby's and everything. But telling the rest of you – it made it real somehow. And I didn't know about the babby at first. If there'd been no babby I could've tried to put it out of my mind and just got on with it. But now . . .' She began to cry again, weakly. 'I can't do anything ever again, can I, except be like Mom and have kids trailing after me. Oh Grace – sometimes I could just finish myself, I really could.'

'You mustn't think that!' Grace gripped Rose's shoulders with surprising strength. 'Don't you ever think anything of the sort.' She was crying herself now, and the two of them sat there frozen on the bench on that icy March day as Sam stood in the distance with his back to them, staring across the park.

Little Harry toddled up and stood there gazing worriedly at them, so the two girls picked him up and cuddled him to reassure him.

'Can you feel the babby?' Grace asked timidly.

'I think so. Just a bit of a bubbly feeling at the moment, like wind!' Rose said. She was grateful to Grace for being so matter of fact and kind. She only wished Sam could find it in himself to overcome his principles and be good to her.

'Are you afraid it'll look like him?'

Rose thought about it for a moment. 'It's a funny thing – it doesn't seem to be anything to do with him somehow.

As if the two things don't tie up. It's my babby.' Suddenly she was speaking in a surprised, wondering tone. 'Mine. I'm the one stuck with it inside me. As for him, I hope he falls under a bleeding bus. This babby's nothing to do with him.'

They sat in silence for a while. A touch of warmth from the sun came and went as small clouds passed over its face. They watched families out walking in the park, some of the mothers pushing heavy black prams. It was as if Rose's fate was being paraded in front of them.

Finally Sam headed towards them with George in tow and fell self-consciously into step next to Rose.

'I've been thinking,' he announced as they walked to the edge of the park. 'I won't say anything else, but I'll say this. I may not like what's happened or how you've behaved.' Suddenly he sounded rather bashful. 'But you're my sister and I'll stand by you. The neighbours'll no doubt have their say and none of us'll like it. But you can count on me, Rose.'

'I'm glad you said that,' Grace said, and Rose was surprised to hear the strong edge of anger in her voice. 'You've been a right preaching old gasbag lately and we're all getting blooming weary of it. If you hadn't said you'd stand by our Rose, I'm not sure as I'd've had much to say to you again, whether you're my brother or not.'

Rather stiffly, Sam linked his arm through Rose's, and they walked home close together along the cold streets.

The gossip threaded round Court 11 in a matter of an hour or so. There were two events competing for attention. Number two, otherwise known as Moonstruck House, was again standing empty. Like so many of the former tenants in that house, the Donaghues had vanished, lock, stock and barrel in the night and no one knew where to. Things had been bad for a while, but whether they'd sit it out or do a moonlight to dodge the landlord was anybody's guess. Now the front door was swinging open and there were still a few things left inside from the hurry in which they'd had to load up the cart.

But even this piece of gossip paled when Gladys Pye put it around that Dora Lucas had told her Rose was expecting. Dora made a shrewd choice in telling Gladys first. While Dora knew Gladys would tell everyone the news as fast as breathe, she was also Dora's friend. They had helped each other at the birth of their children and shared their worries day after day. Gladys, while full of twittering speculation with the other women in the court, would in the end come down on Dora's side.

'So who's the father?' Gladys whispered. The two women were standing in the brewhouse.

'I'd rather not say,' Dora hissed back. 'It were a case of him forcing himself on her. There ain't no airy-fairy feelings on her side, you know. She's been bad ever since.'

Gladys saw Dora's eyes fill with tears, and she made sympathetic noises. 'And Sid . . .?' Gladys looked the picture of concern. She was a tiny woman, made even smaller by the bent bones in her legs.

Dora shrugged in reply to the question. 'I stick by my own,' she said. 'He can moan and mither as much as he likes, but Rose is staying home and we've got to make the best of it. But I've hardly had a decent night since it happened, I can tell you.'

Gladys tut-tutted, saying, 'As if there ain't enough to worry about. I saw you was looking anyhow lately, but I thought it was just the babby.'

'Babbies,' Dora corrected her.

Gladys gasped. 'No! You Sure?'

'Sure as I've ever been,' Dora said. 'And I can feel them both now. But I always know, and I'm just as sure our Rose is carrying a lad.'

When Old Lady Gooch heard the news from Gladys she said, 'Well I never. That'll take the little madam down a peg. Strutting about here with her airs and graces. Now she'll find out a thing or two. I should send her off to the Church Army. She'd soon find out what happens to girls who ain't careful with themselves.'

On the afternoon of the coronation, Rose lay on her back in the bedroom, seeing little white clouds move across the pale blue sky outside the window. She could hear the excited hubbub from the street as the party got into full swing. All the kids would be sitting along the tables with the grown ups standing round, everyone in little hats and all enjoying the food and the rare day's holiday. She knew this was a day of all days for Grace, who would be almost counting the minutes until the evening paper came out carrying the pictures. And then tuppence for the *Weekly Illustrated* on Saturday. A breeze blew through the open window and she heard snatches of a band playing somewhere.

Wish I was like you, Grace, she thought. Grace, who could live off other people's exciting lives and not expect to have much excitement in her own.

Rose lay, not wanting to sleep but feeling tired and muzzy. The further the pregnancy progressed the more remote she felt from her life as it had been. Even her sense of despair, which had been most acute when she first knew she was to have a child, had dulled. She felt she was living in a kind of trance which would only end with the birth.

How could she have had dreams of becoming a teacher, of being a friend, let alone equal to someone like Diana? How could she keep in contact with her now? She wasn't even equal to Geraldine who had, after all, held down her job. And when she thought of Michael Gillespie, sometimes she wept with shame. What would he say if he knew what state she was in?

She put her hand on her belly and felt the light twitching of the child inside her. She had no bad feelings towards it. It just seemed unreal and, as she'd told Grace, not part of Mr Lazenby at all. But its presence, its inexorable growth in there, and the certainty that one day she must experience what her mother had gone through, frightened her. She felt so helpless.

'You were a stupid little fool,' she said to herself. 'Thought you could do great things with your life, didn't you? Do better than your mom?'

She listened bitterly as a loud cheer rose from the street, and another and another.

CHAPTER 10

There was a moment of complete silence as the three women waited. Then a snuffle and a cough, and finally the baby let out its first anxious cry.

'He's all right!' Gladys cried. She was tying the cord as the baby lay between Rose's legs. 'You may've got here a bit too soon, my lad, but you're going to be all right!'

Dora was sitting next to the head of the bed, suckling one of the twins. The other lay asleep in a drawer on the floor. They had been born only three weeks earlier and Dora's face sagged with exhaustion.

'Well – you've done it,' she said to her daughter, suddenly feeling choked with emotion. 'So now you know.'

Rose lay back, hot and worn out. The labour had come on early and had been painful but not too prolonged.

'Reckon you didn't have it too bad,' Gladys said. 'Specially for a first. No need to've had old Joan in after all, was there?'

Despite Dora's pleas, Rose had flatly refused to have 'that old cow' anywhere near her.

She lay looking at her tiny son lying curled in her arms. His hair was very pale, even though still damp from the dunking Gladys had given him. He turned his wrinkled little face and began to snuffle at Rose's body.

'He knows what he wants, anyroad,' Dora said. 'Give him a bit of titty, Rose.'

Rose was startled by the force with which the tiny baby

sucked at her, and the pain which gripped her innards as he did so.

She looked down at his face. His eyes were tightly closed and he was already completely absorbed in feeding. 'I'm going to call him Joseph,' she said. 'He looks like a Joseph.'

It took several days before she began to feel much for the child. He was very small, with the tiniest limbs Dora said she'd ever seen on a baby. Rose gradually understood just how much her life was tied to him, so that his slightest sound would set her heart pounding and wake her from sleep or make her leave whatever she was doing to attend to him. It was his fair hair and skin that at first had made him seem such a stranger. She had never seen a baby with such fair hair in the family, and it took some getting used to. But by the end of the first week she could look at him and find tears running down her cheeks at the realization of how beautiful he was, how small and helpless.

'Let me nurse him,' Grace would say, when she was home. 'He's a lovely babby, Rose.' And sometimes Rose felt reluctant to hand him over, but Grace would take him and cuddle him close, singing softly to him until he cried to go back to his mother.

With three babies in the house, Dora and Rose were both sleeping downstairs on makeshift beds on the floor. One night as they were getting settled down, Sid came in and lurched awkwardly over to Rose. She looked up warily at him.

'It's all right, I'm not going to bite you,' he said roughly. And then out of his pocket he pulled a small wooden object. 'I made this for the kid,' he said. 'Here. Come on – take it.'

Rose found she was holding a little wooden horse, rather rough and misshapen, but still obviously a horse, with a little spot of black paint on each side for its eyes.

'Here Joseph, this is for you,' she said to him. His blue eyes were open, staring over at the gaslight on the wall.

'Your grandad's made you a little horse. Are you going to say ta?' It was a relief having Joseph between her and Sid, to use the child as a way of communicating with him. Since Joseph was born he had been gentler with her, as if he could cope with her now she was doing what a woman was intended to do.

'Thanks Dad,' Rose said, feeling unexpected tears fill her eyes.

'No need to make a fuss,' Sid said awkwardly, going to the stairs.

Mother and daughter spent most of the night up and down feeding the babies. If it wasn't one it was another.

'I've had enough of this,' Dora said one night. It was well into the small hours and she was sick with fatigue. 'These two babbies are going to have to do everything at the same time or they're going to finish me.'

The boy, Billy, was yelling loudly for food. Dora woke the little girl, Susan, and latched the two of them on, stuffing a couple of pillows under her arms for support.

'Pour me a drop of milk, will you Rose?' she said. 'I could do with something on my stomach.'

Joseph was asleep, so Rose got up and handed her mother a cup of milk in the candlelight. 'I hope he's all right,' Rose said, frowning down at Joseph where he lay tucked up on the floor. One of his hands was clenched in a tiny fist next to his cheek. 'He's not feeding as well as he was.'

'Can't say the same of these two,' Dora said wearily.

'Here,' Rose went over to her. 'Give one over here. Joseph's not interested yet and I've got enough spare.'

She took Susan off her mother and held the unfamiliar body of the little girl. Even being a twin she felt rounder and heavier than Joseph. Having been able to rest more than she had during any other pregnancy, Dora had carried the two of them almost to term. They were good-sized babies. Rose sighed and looked over at her little son.

'Be right as rain in the morning,' Dora said. 'He's just tired I s'pect.'

By the end of the night they managed to get some sleep. Rose lay down next to Joseph with her nose against his soft scalp, hearing his quick little breaths. Now her life before him seemed even more like a dream. The days and nights felt almost indistinguishable with the round of feeding and changing his napkins and waiting for him to sleep. Joseph had happened to her, and he was not just a part of her life – everything she did was connected inextricably with this tiny person next to her.

Rose was dreaming. Dreams came rarely with all the broken nights, but this one burst in on her, vivid and clear.

She was with Diana on the tram which ran south along the Bristol Road out as far as the Lickey Hills. They had done that ride together a few times, Diana treating her at weekends. The tram lurched along the tracks down the middle of the road with the hedges separating them from the traffic on either side. When they had travelled that way in reality the tram had been crowded full of people, but in her dream it was empty. She and Diana had seats right at the back, looking down the deserted carriage. When they swayed through Bournbrook the tram passed the red bricks of the university, its pointed clock tower standing tall and elegant above the buildings around it.

'I'm going to go there,' Rose said. And then suddenly she was chanting,

> Pussy cat, pussy cat, where have you been?
> I've been up to London to visit the Queen . . .

And Diana sat beside her, her pink cheeks streaming with tears. 'I don't want you to go, Rose,' she begged. 'Stay and be my friend, Rose. Please stay.'

And then they were both crying and holding on to each other and the tram rolled downhill, down and down, and they didn't know or care where it was going any more.

Rose woke, tears wet on her cheeks. Diana had felt so close to her again, and she knew with a physical ache how much she missed her and how ashamed she felt. All the letters Diana had sent, full of hurt, begging Rose to write and not to forget her, were upstairs, lying unanswered in a cardboard box beside the little wooden elephant which had put the seal on their friendship. How could she reply to those letters now?

As she lay wretched in the grey dawn light, one of the twins started stirring and began to cry. she saw Dora pull herself up off the floor, still stunned by tiredness.

Perhaps Joseph would eat a little better this morning? During his first week he had thrived, but over the last fortnight he had sucked at her breast for a time and then given up to lie listlessly, as if the effort was too much.

She turned to him to enjoy lying with him while he was still asleep, trying to forget the memory of Diana's distraught face in her dream. Very gently she stroked Joseph's soft baby head with one of her dark fingers. His skin was so much paler than hers! He felt cold and anxiously she searched out his hands. They were chilled.

'Come here,' she whispered, and turned him to cuddle and warm him.

His tiny body was stiff. Looking at his face, she saw his lips were still and blue.

Rose jumped up as if she'd been bitten, her lungs constricting so she could hardly breathe. 'Mom!' she gasped. 'Something's wrong with him. Quick – come here!'

Dora hastily put Billy down and rushed over. She picked Joseph up and Rose saw her face tighten. She listened to his chest and rubbed him vigorously. Then she put her mouth over his tiny one, breathing into him again and again to rouse him. Finally, with her head down, she laid him on Rose's bed, instinctively drawing the covers over him. Very slowly she turned to her daughter, who was standing still as a rock beside her.

'There's nothing else I can do, Rose,' she told her. 'He's gone.'

*

A man had died in a neighbouring court and Dora arranged for Joseph to be carried on the hearse the next day. When the horse clattered to a standstill outside, Rose was still holding the little body to her as if her arms would be fixed for ever in that position, even after he was taken away from her.

'For God's sake get him off her,' Sid said to Dora upstairs as they readied themselves for the funeral. 'I can't stand to see it any longer.'

'D'you think I'm enjoying it?' Dora snapped. 'She's just parting with the child in her own time.' She remembered how her own dead children – the twins, Violet – had been snatched speedily away from her by everyone around, who thought it for the best.

Downstairs, Marj had arrived from Sparkbrook, dolled up in a smart black dress with a full skirt and a hat with a wide sloping brim. 'Make us a cuppa tea, Grace,' she said, sitting herself down with exaggerated relief. 'I'm worn out already after carting all the way over here.'

Sam turned his head in surprise as Grace replied, 'There might be a drop left in the pot, and if there is you can get it yourself.'

Marj pulled herself to her feet, murmuring huffily about what a welcome she got in her own home nowadays.

'You've not been so keen to look on us as your family when it didn't suit you,' Grace replied.

'Now, now,' Sam said. 'That's enough of that.' He looked at Rose. She didn't seem to be listening to the conversation at all. She sat with her eyes fixed on her little son, as if she was intensely afraid that she would forget what he looked like.

Grace went up to her timidly. 'They're here, Rose,' she said. 'The undertaker wants to know if he can take him.'

For the last time Rose slowly kissed the boy's cold cheek. She ran her finger along the line of the tiny nose and soft lips.

'I'll take him,' she said, and the others moved back to let her through.

She walked outside and handed him over to be laid in a small box that Sam had nailed together for him. The undertaker placed it on the step of the hearse, close by his feet.

A crowd was gathering in the street. The coffin lying on the hearse was draped with a Union Jack; the dead man had served in the war. As the horse began to move off, Sid solemnly saluted it, standing as straight and upright as he could manage.

The children started spitting on the ground and chanting,

> Catch your collar, never swaller
> In case you catch a fever;
> Not for you, not for me,
> And not for any of my family.

Rose stood tearless and in silence. She thought of all the times as a child that she had joined in the superstitious rhyming. And what good had it done her? Every step the horse took seemed to tear her further apart.

Suddenly she heard Marj's voice in her ear. 'It's all for the best you know, Rose,' she said in a knowing whisper, as if imparting a morsel of gossip. 'You'll get over it soon enough. And who really wants a babby at your age? Now you can get back on with your life, can't you?'

Marj would not easily forget the look of bitter hatred that her young sister turned on her that morning, or the adult hardness that she suddenly saw in her brown eyes.

A very thin, subdued Rose Lucas went back to her charring job at the Dog and Partridge. She could easily fit back into all her old clothes, although she felt like an impostor wearing them.

She started work at nine in the morning, walking into the smell of stale beer and smoke. When she got home she helped Dora, handing over all her meagre wages. She shopped and cooked, gave a hand with George and Harry and, as she had continued to do since Joseph died, she helped to feed the twins. They were the main comfort in her life. Her body was still poised to do all the things for which nature had prepared it. At least she could sleep next to Billy or Susan, cuddling up to them, and hold and feed them.

'She's lost her spirit, Mom,' Grace said one day. 'She could get herself a better job again now. She don't want to be charring all her life. I mean I knew I was going into service, but our Rose always had her eye on something better, didn't she?'

Dora sighed. 'It's early days yet,' she said. 'Give her time.'

Grace tried getting through to Rose, but never felt she got very far.

'I'm earning a wage, aren't I?' Rose would say woodenly. 'What more's anyone s'posed to want? What's the use of having dreams of doing something else? It'll only bring trouble.'

And in her head a voice kept saying: I'm not worth it. I'm cheap and dirty. I'm a slum kid with a dead bastard baby.

Grace looked at her reproachfully. 'You're still cleverer than me,' she said. 'You could do better for yourself.'

Rose just shrugged.

As autumn came round again, Alfie appeared once more in Catherine Street. He'd tried going out with other girls, but none of them could erase the image in his mind of the dark, vivacious girl he'd seen the autumn before walking to work. He had to speak with her, and he decided to give her the benefit of the doubt. Maybe she had another sister and it was her he thought he'd glimpsed looking out of the upper window that day?

He came on a grey Saturday afternoon, with rusty leaves whirling along the pavement.

This time it was George who saw him and came

running into the house as Alfie approached, slamming the door behind him. 'It's that Alfie again – the bloke that's after Rose.'

Rose automatically fled to the stairs.

'Mom.' Grace said. 'Ask him in. He seems a good bloke, I reckon. I'll go up and talk her round.'

She found Rose sitting nervously on the bed. 'What're you doing hiding up here?' Grace demanded.

'Well, I can't let him see me, can I?' Rose replied with nervous irritation.

'Why not? You're not expecting any more are you? If you straighten yourself out a bit and put a decent frock on you'd look a picture again. He's all right that Alfie. So why keep yourself hidden away? If I had him following me around I'd jump at the chance. You could do a lot worse.'

Rose sat thinking for a moment. Grace's last words had hit home. What was she really hiding for now? Waiting for a prince to come along? Grace was right. She could do worse, and she wasn't likely to do any better.

'Tell him I'll be down in a minute.'

Grace gave a little skip and ran smiling downstairs. She found Dora handing Alfie a cup of tea. He was talking rather bashfully to her.

A few moments passed before Alfie finally saw the thin, beautiful girl he remembered emerging slowly, almost reluctantly, from the stairs. She'd brushed out her hair and pinned it back loosely so that it waved softly round her face, and she had on a cream dress of Diana's with a pattern of navy dots on it and a swinging skirt.

She came towards him and gave him a rather stiff smile. 'Hello Alfie,' she said.

CHAPTER 11

1 SEPTEMBER 1939

The long line of children standing in pairs snaked along from the gates of the railway station and curved around the wall outside. They stood in almost eerie silence as the teachers counted and recounted them to make sure there was no one missing. In one hand they each clutched a bag of the most basic belongings; round every neck was tied a piece of string to which a large luggage label had been tied bearing its owner's name. The children waited to be loaded on to the carriages which would take them to places which few of them had even dreamed of. Many of them had scarcely travelled any distance from the streets where they had grown up.

Rose stood near George, anxiously watching his tight-lipped, mutinous face. She was glad that Alfie stood reassuringly beside her. He was seeing off his younger brother and sister, Tom and Bessie, both still at school.

'Some of them think it's just a spree,' he said. 'Look at their faces.'

'Not George,' Rose said. 'He's played hell over being sent off. It's a good job they only announced it yesterday.'

The van had come round the day before, the big rectangular loudspeakers like wide, merciless mouths crackling out the announcement. All children of school age were to be evacuated to places of safety, away from the centres most likely to be bombed, when – and it now seemed to be when and not just if – war broke out.

Immediately the mothers in the court banded together

for mutual advice and support, on what would ordinarily have been a beautiful late summer day.

'Not the kids!' Dora cried. 'They can't split up families like that. How do we know where they're sending them? We'll never have a wink of sleep worrying.'

'What if Adolf Hitler starts throwing bombs down on us?' Mabel demanded grimly, leaning her meaty arm up against the brewhouse wall. 'Then you'd be bad with worrying about them all being killed in their beds. It's for the best, you know.'

'There's not going to be bombs, surely?' Gladys asked, puckering up her face in concern.

'Don't kid yourself,' Mabel said. 'What about Czechoslovakia last year?'

'And now they're after Poland,' Mabel went on. 'Things ain't going to get any better I don't reckon, so you might just as well get used to the idea.'

The rest of that day the families could think of nothing else. For the first time in years Dora turned to her husband for advice when he came in. 'What're we going to do?'

'Asking me are you, all of a sudden?' he said sourly, swinging his good arm back and forth to relieve the muscles after supporting himself on the crutch. 'If they say send them, then do it. They're best well out of it.' He sat down heavily. 'We should've finished them off properly the first time round, when we had the bloody chance.'

'I'm NOT GOING!' George shouted.

Sid took off his cap and flung it over on to the table. 'If we say you're going then you'll go!'

'What about Harry?' Dora said. She turned to put the kettle on, trying to steady herself. 'I can't send him away – or the twins. Not that young.'

'Couldn't Edna have Harry for a bit?' Rose suggested. 'After all, most of hers are grown up and gone now. We'll club together for some money for the fare.'

Dora's sister in Alcester seemed, out of the few choices, the most reassuring one. Dora got Rose to write to her straight away.

'But the twins stay with me,' Dora said. 'And that's that.'

They'd got George ready the next morning. He soon realized there was no point in arguing. Dora tidied him up to go down to the school, tugging his collar straight and giving his face a wipe.

'Go on,' she said to him, rather roughly, to stop herself blarting there on the step. 'Don't give anyone any lip and make sure you write and tell us how you're getting on.'

As soon as he was out of the court, walking with bravado beside Rose, Dora sank down at the table, laid her head on it and wept.

Now George stood at the station in front of the two Meredith kids, all with their little paper parcels of 'iron rations': a small can of corned beef, a packet of biscuits, a pound of sugar, a tin of evaporated milk, a quarter of tea and – George's eyes had lit up for the only time that day – a half-pound block of Cadbury's chocolate.

'Still warm from the factory,' one of the teachers joked.

As the kids piled into the railway carriages, Rose tried to give George a goodbye hug, but he pushed her away with his wiry arms. 'Don't go getting all soppy, Rose.'

And Rose, like her mom, held back her tears until they'd waved goodbye to the children, all crowded up by the windows of the train, some looking excited, others forlorn and bewildered. The train gave a loud shriek and puffed out of the station, the smoke and smuts rising in clouds to the wide arching roof. Rose waved her hanky at the little dot she thought was George until the train was out of sight, and then used it to wipe her eyes.

'They'll be well looked after, you be sure,' Alfie said. 'And he's got Tom and Bessie for company. He's a tough lad your George. He'll be all right.'

'It's so horrible not knowing what's going to happen,' Rose said as they walked out of New Street Station. 'I know it's an awful thing to say, but if there's going to be a war, I wish they'd just get on and get it over.'

'Some of the lads got their call-up papers today,' Alfie said.

Rose went quiet. Alfie and Sam were both nineteen and had not yet been called, but the shadow of war, of families being split up even further, hung over all of them.

'Come on,' Alfie said. 'It's no use getting all down in the mouth. I'll take you for a cuppa. Lyons or the Kardomah?'

'Whatever you like,' Rose said. She always let Alfie make the decisions.

'The Kardomah then.'

He took her arm and led her along New Street. It was as busy as ever with trams and buses and people shopping or standing at bus stops. But there was a different atmosphere. The news from Europe was on everyone's lips. Everything felt precious, Rose thought. As if the threat from Germany had made the things they had always known sparkle and shine.

Along the street they could see preparations going on in the offices and shops for blacking out the windows – assistants trying the large black rectangles for size against the panes of glass. And already groups of people were filling sandbags and stacking them against the sides of buildings. They heard the raucous newsvendors' voices shouting, 'Germans overrun Poland! Get your *Mail* here!'

'Blimey,' Alfie said. 'He really means it, doesn't he?'

Rose felt her stomach tighten with a mixture of dread and excitement.

'I should get back to work,' she said, as she and Alfie found a table in the Kardomah amid the comforting smells of roasted coffee and warm rolls.

'They gave you the morning to send off the kids, didn't they?' Alfie said. 'Come on – have a cuppa tea and calm down. The Co-op'll survive for half a day without you!' He grinned and, leaning across the table, chucked her lightly under the chin. 'That's my girl.'

Rose smiled back dutifully and sipped the tea he'd bought for her.

Alfie sat back in his seat, looking at her. As usual he felt pleased with himself for just being with Rose. Even though he'd been walking out with her for almost two years now he still couldn't believe his luck, that this beautiful girl wanted to be with him. He'd heard some gossip about her of course, but that was all in the past and he preferred not to know about it. He was going to believe the best of her. And she seemed to have quietened down since he'd first seen her, which was no bad thing. Who wanted a loud mouth on a woman? She was his girl and he was dead chuffed with her.

Alfie himself had filled out over the past two years. His hair was just as unruly above his pale face, but he looked less lanky and more substantial. His shoulders had grown broader and stronger from his heavy work. And the fact that he'd been luckier than many in the trade and had been in work more than out of it had done wonders for his sense of himself. His blue eyes looked directly at people now and he was much less hesitant when he spoke – especially with Rose on his arm. What a picture she was in that red frock she had on! Soon, when he'd maybe managed to save a bit, he planned to make her his wife.

Alfred and Rose Meredith, he thought. That sounded truly grand.

Rose stood preparing butter in the Co-op that afternoon dipping the wooden pats in the jug of cold water and teasing the yellowish lumps into shape. She was partly mesmerized by the movement of her hands and by the rhythmic click and whirr as the money cup shot along its overhead wire to the little cash office at the back of the shop.

'Come on Rose, wake up! We need three pound of sugar over here!' the woman in charge of her called over. 'I dunno what's got into that girl today.'

Without speaking, Rose moved over and began to shovel out the sugar into the blue paper bags. Then she went back to sort out the butter and bacon again.

What had got into her was that she had, for the first time since Joseph's death, begun to allow herself to think properly. It was not something she decided to do; the thoughts just seemed to come upon her, long-buried feelings nudging for her attention.

She had been grateful in one way for the problems in Europe, for the looming war. Since they had waited tensely through the last threat, the crisis in Czechoslovakia the year before, it had all helped to take her mind off her own sorrows. And, she thought, it's brought me closer to Alfie – hasn't it?

They had things in common to talk about now, important things. Before he had talked about football or the latest murder trial.

'Have you heard about the one they're doing at the Old Bailey this week?' would have been the conversation before. Then he'd give her a long and gruesome description of the crime.

They'd shared a lot of experiences over the past months: the flicks and walks and family meals. Changing jobs. But had they shared the experience of falling in love? The question wouldn't leave her alone that afternoon, try as she might to put it out of her mind. Was what she felt for Alfie what people would call love?

From that day when he had turned up again in Catherine Street, she had tried to close her mind to everything that had gone before – to Joseph, Diana, Michael and everything about Lazenby's. To her dreams. She tried to be someone with no past. From now on she was going to be sensible and down to earth and take whatever came along.

He's made me feel better, there's no doubt, she thought. He's kind and generous and he loves me. What more could I want from anyone? I've already got more than me mom.

When she first went out with him she had felt relieved and grateful. Here was someone who wanted her and thought highly of her – she who at fifteen felt so old and soiled and washed up. And she was especially grateful to him for not probing into her past. He was prepared to accept her just as she was.

Those feelings she had had for Michael, the electric excitement in his presence – that was all airy-fairy nonsense, not real life. What she had with Alfie was real, like married people had if they were lucky.

She knew one day he'd ask her to marry him. That was another thing she'd tried not to think about. As long as they stayed as they were she didn't have to decide or face up to things. But the threat of war was overturning everything. For a moment she had an overwhelming feeling of panic. All her life – forever – spent with Alfie. Nothing else? Then she pushed the feelings away.

What's got into me? she thought. He'd make a good husband and he wouldn't knock me about. That's what matters.

Of course it made sense to marry Alfie, she said to herself. Perfect sense.

In early December the government extended the call-up age to men between the ages of nineteen and forty-one. Both Alfie and Sam received their papers almost immediately.

'At least I'm sure of a job now!' Sam joked. 'So you can keep the wireless.'

After they'd heard the soft voice of Prime Minister Neville Chamberlain crackling out of the Pyes' old wireless set, Sam had rashly gone out and bought one for their own house, with its battery and accumulator. Now, at almost every news bulletin, some member of the family was listening in.

When the broadcast finished that Sunday morning, the distant voice informing them that 'consequently we are now at war with Germany', Sid had pulled himself up abruptly and left the house.

Grace watched him out of the window. 'What's got into him?' she said.

'Leave him,' Dora said.

Out in the brewhouse, Sid Lucas stood propped on his crutch next to the old stone sink, his whole body trembling. The build-up to another war had set his fragile nerves on edge. Breathing in shuddering gulps of air, he tried to steady the emotions aroused by memories of the last war that suddenly sprawled out in front of him like fresh corpses. After the war to end all wars, here it was beginning all over again.

Dora looked out and saw the shadow of her husband's hunched figure. She could guess what was going on in his mind, but she had her children to think of now, their survival and their future. That was what mattered.

It was Grace who slipped outside and went to him. As she walked quietly into the brewhouse she knew immediately that her father was weeping. All through her childhood she had heard this sound through the floorboards from her parents' room, but she had never seen him with tears on his face before.

'Dad . . .?' She went and put her work-roughened hand on his heaving shoulder. He didn't throw it off. He didn't move or turn to her.

'I'll be all right, Gracie.'

'It's the war, isn't it?'

He nodded. After a moment, he said, 'I'm fit for nothing. The last war saw to that.'

'Don't say that,' Grace said. She took his arm. 'Come on. I'll leave you if that's what you want, but it's best you come in. We've all got to stick together now there's a war on, haven't we?'

Sid took out his grubby handkerchief and wiped his eyes in a way that made Grace's own fill with tears. At that moment he looked so much like a child.

'Come on now, Dad. Come in and have a cuppa tea.'

The evening before Alfie was due to leave, he and Rose walked slowly back from town in the blackout darkness that had overtaken the city. They had been to the flicks at the Scala and then Alfie had treated them to a hot pork sandwich from the Market Hall, so despite the freezing evening they felt quite warm and well fed.

Now and then people loomed up out of the cold, foggy darkness, close enough to touch almost before you could see them. A few were carrying small torches so you could make out little lines of light moving towards you.

'I can't get used to the dark,' Rose said. 'If it wasn't for this mist you could see the stars.'

'I s'pose it's a bit daft making you walk instead of catching the tram,' Alfie said. 'But then we'd have got there too quick. I wanted to spend all the time I could with you.'

Rose felt her stomach plunge at the thought that Alfie would be gone the next afternoon. She kept forgetting, and then something reminded her again, like the muffled lights on the few cars that passed them, which gave you a tiny glimpse of something before the darkness fell back over everything again.

'It feels like the end of the world,' Rose said.

Alfie grinned in the darkness. His Rose said the queerest things at times.

'Nah,' he said. 'We'll show that Adolf Hitler feller in no time. They'll get us all trained up and it'll be time to go home again. The lights'll be back on and we'll be right as rain, you'll see.'

Rose said nothing, wondering how much Alfie believed of what he was saying.

He peered at her, trying to make out her expression. 'You're not scared, are you? Here, stop a tick.'

Alfie pulled her arm and guided her over to the dark factory wall. He pulled her close to him. She looked up, just able to see his eyes and the outline of his angular face.

'I'll miss you,' he said. 'You know how much I love you, don't you?'

She looked guiltily up at him. 'Yes. Of course I know.'

She knew he was waiting for her to tell him the same, how she would long for him to be there, how she couldn't live without him. But the words wouldn't come. It would be stepping over a cliff if she said more than she meant tonight of all nights, when things were so serious. Once the words were spoken, she could not take them back.

Alfie leaned forwards and began to kiss her. She felt his soft, familiar lips on her mouth, and all the warmth and sincerity going into that kiss. She kissed him back, trying to summon up all her gratitude to him. She had got over his touching her reminding her every time of Mr Lazenby. Alfie had always been very gentle and never demanded anything more of her. She didn't feel revolted by him. She didn't feel – the thought came to her like a cold shock – anything. And inside, her heart was pounding with a sense of panic she could not explain even to herself.

'Rose – I wasn't going to ask you yet. I'd planned to save it. But now things are different – you know . . .' He stumbled over the words, unused to expressing his feelings. 'What I mean is, would you – will you marry me, Rose? We could have a wedding when I come home next. There's bound to be some leave in a few weeks around Christmas, and it'd give you time to get sorted out a bit . . .' he babbled on nervously.

Rose felt an almost unbearable sense of tension inside her, as all the feelings she'd been keeping at bay for the past months flooded into her in conflict and confusion. Should she be content, accept what was being offered by a good, kind man whom she could at least like? Or should she listen to that part of her which as a young girl had clamoured for fulfilment?

In utter vexation with herself she dissolved into tears.

'Hey, Rose,' Alfie said tenderly, holding her again. 'There . . . don't upset yourself. I know I'm asking a bit sudden like, what with going away in the morning. But I've put a lot of thought into our future, you know.'

'I know,' Rose said sobbing. 'You're so good to me. I don't deserve it.'

Alfie stroked the soft, dark head that was pressed against his chest.

'What d'you mean? How can you say that? My God,

you're the most fantastic girl I've ever seen in my life, and it was a miracle when you said you'd come out with me. And now you're saying you don't deserve me?' He laughed. 'You're a case, Rose Lucas, you really are.'

Rose calmed herself and stood sniffing and wiping her face. After a few moments she said with unexpected resolve, 'We'll have to ask my dad.'

'Right,' Alfie said, and she could hear the jubilation in his voice, so at odds with the flat sense of inevitability she was feeling herself. 'It's not too late. I'll come and ask him now.'

'No. You can't.'

Rose and Alfie looked at each other, dumbfounded.

'But—' Alfie said.

'But nothing. You heard what I said.'

'What the hell's got into you, Sid?' Dora gasped. 'You've always said Alfie were a good lad!'

'And we're promised to one another,' Alfie said, his voice starting to tremble.

'You can promise what you like,' Sid shouted, slamming his newspaper down on the table and standing up. 'But you're not marrying my daughter one day and going off to get yourself blown to buggery the next.'

'But—' Alfie said again.

'Look at me!' Sid's voice rang round the walls of the small room. 'D'you want to give your wife a husband in a state like this, who can't keep his family and's no bloody good to anyone? Do you? I'm not making one of my kids a war widow or marrying her off to a wreck like me, so you can forget it.'

Rose and Dora stared at him, both rooted to the spot. Sid seemed bigger and broader than they'd ever seen him. And Rose was aware, while feeling sorry and angry on Alfie's behalf, of a warm sense of relief spreading through her.

'Get married after the war's over if you come back in one piece,' Sid was saying more quietly. 'But don't ruin her life by rushing into things 'cos you think you're going to be a hero. There ain't no heroes in a war, lad – only blokes getting killed all around you.'

There seemed no more to be said. Alfie whispered to Rose, 'I'll come round and say goodbye tomorrow if I can.'

And she watched him walk, crestfallen, out into the darkness.

There was silence except for the clock ticking on the mantelpiece and Dora's coughing. Rose was still standing where she had been since they started talking, and Sid sank down into the chair again.

'Anyroad,' he said, looking up at her with defiant eyes. 'You didn't really want to marry him, did you?'

CHAPTER 12

MAY 1940

Rose sat, bleary-eyed, drinking a very welcome mug of tea as Winston Churchill's gruff voice growled at them out of the wireless.

'I speak to you for the first time as Prime Minister in a solemn hour for the life of our country, of our Empire, of our Allies, and above all, of the cause of freedom . . .'

'Well – he sounds as if he might know what he's on about. Not like the last one,' Jean said, stirring sugar into her tea.

Rose was sitting in her brother Albert's house in Erdington with her sister-in-law Jean, a plump, rather plaintive woman who Rose was quite glad she only saw for limited parts of the day. Jean was about to give her full opinion of Neville Chamberlain, but Rose raised her hand to quieten her.

'Ssh. Let's hear the end of it.'

'Today is Trinity Sunday,' the voice was saying. 'Centuries ago, words were written to be a call and a spur to the faithful servants of truth and justice: "Arm yourselves and be ye men of valour, and be in readiness for the conflict, for it is better to perish in battle than to look upon the outrage of our nation and our altar."'

'Ah,' Jean said, shifting her wide hips on the chair. 'Ain't that nice? He can string together a good lot of words, can't he?'

Rose had felt a thrill, a sensation which raised goose-pimples on her flesh on hearing the commanding speech. With all the grimness, the increasingly terrible news which greeted them daily from Europe, she had been unprepared for the exhilaration she felt at the challenges with which war had presented her.

At least I'm doing something, she thought. She felt free for the first time in years. She pitied Jean, and all the other women left to fend for themselves with nothing changed in their lives except for more struggles to feed their families, and more worries to carry in their minds about their loved ones. Rose smiled across at Jean. Her sister-in-law, with her long blond hair tumbling untidily over the crumpled blouse she was wearing, smiled back, rather startled.

'You heard from Teddy?' Rose asked her, reminding herself that Jean, like Dora, was going through the hell of being separated from one of her children. Teddy, who was seven, had been evacuated out of the city.

'I just can't stop fretting about him,' Jean said. 'He says he's all right, but I don't know if it's true, do I? And after what happened to your George I can't sleep nights thinking about it.'

'Oh, I s'pect he's all right,' Rose said, laying one of her slim hands over Jean's plump one. 'Not much chance of the same thing happening to both of them, is there?'

January had been one of the coldest anyone could remember, the city clogged up with deep snow so the traffic could barely pass along the streets. It was a strange time. It felt as if everything had frozen up: the arteries of the city, the food supplies, which began to be officially rationed, and even the war itself. It had not begun to affect Britain with the intensity anyone had expected. The strange blanket of quietness brought to the streets by the snow, and the houses muffled at night by the white blanket outside and the blackout coverings inside, all added to the air of peculiar unreality.

Rose stayed at home through the winter. She saw Alfie briefly at Christmas. He had long got over the shock of Sid's outburst and was all for looking on the bright side.

'We're engaged anyroad, aren't we?' he said.

He chatted on about army life and the pals he'd made, and while Rose enjoyed his company and was glad to see him looking so full of it all, she felt even more distanced from him.

Sometimes she popped over to Small Heath to see Mrs Meredith, who always gave a gasp of delight when she opened the door, crying, 'Rose, come on in, bab! I was just making a little cake, so you can take a few slices back with you!' She always tried to feed Rose up like a turkey cock on whatever she had to hand, and always seemed to remain astonishingly cheerful.

The same was not true of Dora. Rose had been worried about her all winter. When the weather hardened against them, Dora's chest became infected and her lungs ached agonizingly as she coughed, bringing up terrible amounts of green phlegm. Rose and Grace nursed her as best they could, though Grace wasn't at her best either during the cold, with her asthma.

Christmas had been difficult. Edna managed to get over from Alcester with Harry. They put up a little tree and did their best to make it a jolly day, especially for the little boy's sake and for the twins. Dora burst into tears at the sight of him when they arrived and wouldn't let him out of her sight, holding and stroking his plump, healthy looking limbs in a way which Rose never remembered seeing her do with any of them before.

'I can't let you take him again,' she said to Edna. 'I know you've looked after him as if he were your own, but I'll not part with him again. Not unless things start to get bad.'

Edna nodded, understanding how she felt.

But the worst was that they hadn't heard from George at all since the middle of October. He'd written three sentences saying he was with a family in Wales and he was all right. Then they'd had an equally brief note from a Mrs Beamish saying that George had moved from her care to work on a farm near by. Dora looked lined and tattered with worry.

'He's probably living the life of Riley,' Grace said, without much conviction. 'He said he was all right, didn't he?' They all tried to blame his silence on the bad weather.

As usual it was the neighbourliness in the court which helped them all pull through. They compared the best ways to make the food rations go as far as possible. Mabel's corned beef hash was voted one of the best dishes.

'I fried the potatoes,' she told everyone darkly. Though quite what in she wasn't prepared to say.

When the snow came, everyone who was around came out into the court and built a snowman for the little kids who were left and Gladys and Mabel built a fire outside from an old door out of Moonstruck House, which was now in bad repair and boarded up. Everyone chipped in a lump of coal and they managed to bake a few potatoes for the kiddies. The twins, Billy and Susan, both stood wide-eyed and pink-nosed by the fire, cramming the warm potatoes into their mouths. Rose had dressed them up in so many clothes to come out that they looked quite rotund.

'All right, you two?' she said, smiling at them. She leaned down and gave them each a kiss on their round, cold cheeks. They both nodded, mouths full. Rose looked wistfully at their lovely trusting little faces, and stood with a hand on each of their shoulders, wishing she could hold them for ever and protect them from all harm.

Afterwards they all had a snowball fight. It was a memory Rose knew she would treasure for ever. She remembered Dora's face smiling at the window, still not recovered enough to be out in it, but cheered by the sight. And Old Lady Gooch trotting with her swaying gait across the yard in pursuit of Gladys Pye, gleeful as a twelve-year-old, with a huge ball of snow ready in one hand. Soon Gladys was flat on her back on the snow, helpless with laughter.

'I can't get up!' she shouted, trying to get her bandy legs in a position so she could stand up. 'God Almighty, look at the state of me – I'm caked in it!' And she collapsed into more helpless giggles.

As darkness fell, everyone was getting cold, and they all went in for a hot drink feeling more cheerful than they had for months.

By the time spring came and the snow turned grey and slushy in the streets and gradually disappeared, Hitler had progressed across Europe. Czechoslovakia, Poland, and now Norway and Denmark had fallen, and the forces of evil and destruction were pushing up against France, the Netherlands and onwards as if this was their destiny.

One evening in April, Rose and Grace sat in their bedroom talking. It was a rare moment of leisure shared together, and they were taking it in turns to brush each other's hair as they had when they were little girls. Through the window Grace saw Sid come shuffling in across the yard.

'Dad's back.'

Rose began to sing softly: 'The day thou gavest Lord is ended,' and both of them fell back giggling on the bed. It was a relief to get rid of some of the tension they all felt.

'You are terrible,' Grace said, wiping her eyes.

'Well,' Rose started to unpin Grace's brown hair. 'He always seems to be on at me.'

'You always answer back.'

'I can't help it. I know he's got some good in him really, and a lot of what's happened hasn't been his fault, but I just wish we'd had the chance to see him before and know what he was like.'

'I think you're quite alike. He was stubborn and determined to get on in them days. Like you are.'

'Like I *was*,' Rose corrected her. She stopped brushing and sighed. 'I don't know what's happened to me,' she said, hesitating to say what she was thinking.

'You mean you don't want to do all them things you used to talk about when we was at school?'

'Yes. Well, no. It's just . . .' She sat down next to Grace and spoke very seriously. 'When Alfie was here and we were together and everything, I felt as if I was in a kind of dream all the time. I didn't have to think for myself, and after all that happened with Joseph and Lazenby's I was glad not to have to. You know what blokes are like – they always think they have to do all the thinking for you. So I just let him. It was easy. Nice in a way. Like having a rest.' She smiled rather wistfully at Grace who watched her sister's brown, troubled eyes, rather puzzled at what she was getting at.

'You miss him, don't you?' she said, thinking this was the right response.

'I miss his company,' Rose said carefully. 'And I want the best for him of course, for him to be safe wherever he is. But now he's gone – I don't know.' She looked at her sister.

Grace saw that her eyes had the life back in them that always made Rose so striking as a child.

'I feel as if I've just woken up or something,' Rose said. 'Now that I can't just lean on him. I know it's an awful thing to say with the war and everything but I suddenly feel happier than I have in years.'

'But you do love him, don't you?' Grace asked, bewildered. She longed to have a young man of her own to walk out with.

Rose looked away, down at the floorboards. 'I like him of course. But I can't honestly say I know whether I love him or not.'

Grace made tut-tutting noises. 'You don't half get yourself into some messes, you do.'

Rose was silent, trying to think of some way in which she could express the overwhelming sense of restlessness she had felt since Alfie left. The past, before Joseph, had welled up, and she found herself thinking about Diana and the Harper-Watts with an aching sorrow for what she had lost.

Suddenly she said, 'You know those women we saw in town today?'

'The recruitment lot you mean?'

As they'd walked along Colmore Row, a long line of women had marched past, many of them carrying placards which urged: 'We have the Work – We want the Women!'

They were employed by many of the industries round the city. Some of them were wearing dresses and skirts, but a large number of them had on baggy dungarees in dark, heavy materials. Rose had been startled at the sight of them, but also warmed and excited. How strong and capable they looked! She had always known women who worked in factories, of course – Dora had for years. But she could never remember seeing them marching together like this, looking as if they really belonged in the world.

'I want to do something for the war effort, something really useful. I've been thinking about it all day. There's that new place they're recruiting for – the Nuffield over near Albert's place. They need a lot more workers. I thought what with Albert being away and Jean on her own with the kids, she'd be glad of a bit of company. And I could do war work in the factory.'

'I'll miss you,' Grace said.

Rose laughed. 'I was only talking. I haven't done anything about it yet!'

'No – but I know you when you've decided on something. And Mom was only saying the other day how sorry she feels for Jean. She'll let you go as long as you come home now and then.'

'Course I will,' Rose said. She began to feel excited.

Suddenly they heard a shriek from down below, then Dora's voice yelling up the stairs, 'Rose! Grace! Get down here quick! Quick!'

'What's got into her?' Grace said as they clattered down the stairs into the dusk light of the kitchen. They found Sid and Dora both standing by the Morrison shelter, the top of which was laid up for tea.

Warming his hands by the stove was George.

Both the girls fell on him, trying to hug and kiss him.

'George! Where've you been?'

'How on earth did you get here?'

Their delight soon wavered and turned to concern. George pushed them off roughly. As they looked at him properly they started to take in the state he was in. He'd always been a skinny kid, but now he looked gaunt and hollow round the eyes. His legs, poking out of a filthy, torn pair of shorts that they'd never seen before, were stick thin, making his knees look pathetically bony. His skin was grey and shadowy with deeply ingrained grime and his hair, dull with filth, was sticking out in tufts all round his head. But the worst was his eyes. The expression in them was blank and hard, making him seem a person quite strange and alien to them.

As she stood looking at him, Dora burst into tears.

'What's happened to you?' She went to him and squatted down, putting her hands on his shoulders.

George pushed her away as if she were some kind of monster. 'I want some grub,' he said. 'NOW.'

'Don't talk to your mother . . .' Sid started to say, but Dora gestured at him impatiently to be quiet. Sid himself looked shocked at the sight of his son.

'I'll get you some broth. And here's some bread to be going on with,' Dora said gently, slicing a huge chunk off the loaf. 'And you can tell us in your own time.'

'Fat lot you care,' George snarled. 'You'd have left me there to rot – the whole effing lot of you.'

'George!' Dora cried, her cheeks still wet. 'Oh George, that's not true. It wasn't like that. They told us you had to go. Because of the bombs. And we was told you were all having a marvellous time. I didn't want you to go.'

George gave her a look of complete contempt and then started on the soup. He ate like a starved animal. He flung chunks of bread into the bowl and pulled them out soaked in soup, cramming them into his mouth apparently quite unbothered by how hot they were. The family were silenced by the sight. Rose felt her insides tighten with anger and sorrow. George only paused to scratch his head every now and then with soupy fingers. They could see the nits moving between his clogged hairs.

When he'd finished he pushed back his chair and said, 'Now I need some kip.'

'Leave him for now,' Dora said as he went upstairs. In the short time since George had returned, her face seemed to have fallen into even heavier, darker lines. 'I s'pect he'll talk to us after he's had a sleep.' And her face crumpled in distress again, her lips pulled back as she cried, showing the dark gaps between her remaining teeth. 'I only wanted to do the best for him!' she cried. 'I knew it was wrong to send kids away to strangers.'

When she crept up later to look at her own little stranger of a son, he had thrown himself just as he was on his old bed and pulled the blanket over him. In the candlelight she watched him for a few moments as he slept. His frail body was never still. His eyes and his arms twitched about and he kept moving his head, painful whimpering noises breaking out of him.

What his life had been over the past seven months emerged only gradually as he began to adjust slowly to being at home again.

So far as they could gather, the first month hadn't been too bad. The Beamish family who had picked him out originally had been quite decent. They lived in a village near Llanelli in South Wales and regarded taking in evacuees as their contribution to the war effort. Unfortunately, in their enthusiasm they had taken in three at once, including George. As they already had four children of their own, they quickly realized that introducing into the family three city kids with their strange ways was too much. The children of the house had rebelled and turned against the newcomers, and in particular they disliked George, the only boy of the three.

Eventually George was told that they were going to pass him on to a Mr Evans who owned a farm some distance away from the village, who wanted a boy old enough to lend a hand on the farm.

George had not felt at ease in the first house, but at least there had been company and, as he said, 'They gave you as much grub as they could spare.' Now his problems really began. Mr Evans was a short, burly man with a gingery-coloured beard who lived alone on the farm. He had no idea about children and no ambition to learn. George had spent most of the past six months almost entirely alone, except for the surly, religious-minded Mr Evans, a few chickens, a dog and fields full of sheep.

He had not been allowed in the house except for his meals which Mr Evans supplied when he remembered – at best once a day. In the evening he usually brought him into the cold, stone-flagged kitchen for some kind of soup or stew. The rest of the day he went without. In the beginning, as it was the end of September, George had found a few blackberries. As the winter drew in there was nothing. He slept in the barn where Mr Evans had supplied him with one filthy blanket stinking of dogs. During the day he had to help on the farm – herding and feeding sheep when there was work to be done, and being sent round with the dog to catch rats.

George woke in the morning often before it was light, to a hard prod from the farmer's boot and a gruff 'Get up now', which was often Mr Evans' longest utterance of the day. He communicated more readily with a cuff or a kick, as if George was just another of the sheep or dogs from the farm.

Once the snow came, George lived wrapped permanently in the stinking blanket and an old pair of boots of Mr Evans' that he wore over his own shoes. The snow cut the farm off from everywhere, so there were no letters, there was no one to talk to, not a word of kindness or of even the most basic communication. He lived like the animals: waking, sleeping, eating only when given the chance.

Some time after the thaw came he walked away from the farm one night and reached Llanelli by the morning. From there he jumped trains to Birmingham. He hid his wiry, emaciated body in any cranny necessary to escape the guards on the train, sometimes ducking and dodging as they moved along between carriages. And a couple of days later he was home. They may have abandoned him, but where else did he have to go?

His one remaining, overriding emotion was that of anger towards his family. They had sent him away to this place, left him for months now without a word of contact, as if they didn't care whether he was dead or alive. And for that he would never forgive them.

CHAPTER 13

Rose moved to Erdington at the end of April and was taken on the night shift at the new 'shadow' factory, as the extra factories built to extend wartime production were called, at Castle Bromwich, right on Birmingham's northern edge. They taught her to use a rivet gun for attaching the metal plates which made up the wings of the Spitfires.

When she first walked through the gates of the huge works she felt so frightened that she nearly turned back and went home again. The rows of long production sheds where they turned out the Spitfires and Lancasters stretched further than she could see. There were people walking about briskly in overalls, all looking as if they knew exactly where they were going.

Workers were needed from any possible source, and Rose found herself working among a wider mix of people than she'd ever been with in her life before. Alongside her stood a girl called Maureen from Londonderry. They worked just far enough apart for there to be little opportunity to chat, but the two of them often sat together in the canteen at break times and became quite friendly. Maureen came from the Catholic side of Derry, and like Rose was from a large family.

'I'd most likely have come to England anyways, even without the war,' Maureen told her. 'But now they're giving out jobs like First Communion cards, I thought I'd take the chance while it was offered.'

Maureen was a thin, anaemic-looking girl with terrible

spots. She was kind and soft spoken and Rose found her easy enough company. She was also very homesick, and spoke with special affection for the baby of the family, her four-year-old sister Josie.

'It's not the same without little ones about,' Maureen said. 'I'd give anything to see her.'

One day when she was sitting under the bright lights of the canteen with Maureen, Rose noticed the man with one arm.

'Hang on a tick,' she said. 'I'm going to have a word with him.'

The man was older than many of the employees, and when she got up close to him, Rose saw that on one side of his face the skin was shiny and puckered up as if from a severe burn.

'Excuse me,' she said. 'I hope you won't think me rude for asking . . .'

The man turned and smiled with the half of his face that worked. He had one vivacious blue eye; the other was missing. The injured side of his face remained still, as if dead.

'What's up love?' he asked.

'It's just when I saw you I thought of my dad. He's without one arm and a leg from the last war and he hasn't been in work for years.'

'Well now's his chance,' the man said chirpily. 'Doesn't he know they'll take anyone on nowadays? They've found me a little job I can do with one arm – with the petrol tanks. If your dad asks, you can bet they'll find him something – even if they turn him upside down and sweep the floor with his head!' He gave a long chesty laugh and Rose couldn't help joining in.

Within a week Sid was taken on by the Birmingham Small Arms Company, which in peacetime manufactured bicycles and motorcycles. It had reverted to turning out bombs, rockets and guns and all the ammunition needed to feed them. They found him a job packing bullets.

The day he left the house in dungarees to catch a bus to a proper job for the first time in over twenty years, Dora watched him as he pulled himself on his crutch out of Court 11. She reflected with some pride and more bitterness on the irony that her husband who had been so shattered by the last war, might only begin to feel useful to anyone again now there was a second one in progress.

At the end of May, France fell to the Germans, and a huge flotilla of British boats evacuated all the troops they could transport from the French coast at Dunkerque.

On 2 July, Hitler ordered the invasion of Britain.

'The Battle of France is over. I expect that the Battle of Britain is about to begin,' Churchill told the House of Commons. 'The whole fury and might of the enemy must very soon be turned on us.'

And the country waited, as if holding its breath for a long descent into deep, dark water.

One night, at the beginning of August, the first bombs to fall on Birmingham dropped on Erdington, in the streets around Albert and Jean's house.

When she came in from work the next morning, Rose found Jean in a proper state. She was sitting on the old sofa in her dressing gown, with a tearstained face, and clutching Amy and Mary close to her as if she'd never let them go.

'Thank God you're all right,' Rose said, putting her bag down and running to her sister-in-law. 'You poor things, you must have had an awful night. We heard them come down. We were all in the shelters as well.'

Jean sat and sobbed helplessly. The Anderson shelter down the garden had a puddle right along the middle and it had grown even damper with the condensation from their breath. It had been horrible sitting there all night, cold and scared stiff.

'I wish Albert was here,' she cried. 'He'd know what to do. I hate being here without him. I can't stand it. And he might never come back!'

'Look,' Rose said firmly, wishing Albert had married someone with a bit more to her. 'You should try and keep things normal for the kids' sake. Get them dressed and send them out to play.'

'No!' Jean protested. 'I'm not letting them out of my sight – either of them. Them planes could come back any time!' Her face was getting puffed up with tears.

Rose sighed. 'Look. Get the kids dressed. Then you give me the ration books and I'll take them down the shops. That'll give you a bit of time to pull yourself together and get some things done, won't it?'

On the streets and in the shops everyone was saying 'Wasn't it awful?'

'We're not going to stand for that,' Rose heard a woman say as they queued in the butcher's. 'Coming over here and knocking people's houses down. Who does he think he is?'

They were comments that would recur many times as the bombing intensified. The raids became so much heavier and more frequent that the journey to work in the evening was often hazardous. And then in the morning Rose travelled home, her stomach churning with worry that Jean's house might not be still standing, and wondering about Dora and the others in Catherine Street.

Every time she got the chance, Rose caught a bus over there. One afternoon in late August Dora's first words were, 'Have you heard – the Market Hall's gone up?'

'What?' Rose said, stunned. It seemed impossible that a building she'd known and loved all her life should have been hit.

'The middle of town's a right mess,' Dora said, brewing up tea for Rose. She was delighted to see her, though less likely to show it. 'Didn't you see it when you came across? I took the kids in this morning. The Market Hall's a shell. The roof's gone – the lot. And what a stink! All burnt and musty. And there was flaming rabbits and guinea pigs running about all over the place.' She sat down, laughing slightly hysterically. 'I know I shouldn't laugh, but I saw this great fat bloke chasing his rabbits all round the churchyard . . .' She sobered up suddenly. 'And there was Union Jacks all stuck in the mess – that's the British for you.'

Rose could see Dora was in a state and trying not to show it. 'How's everyone?'

'All right.'

Rose looked at the worn face in front of her. Dora didn't look well. She had never really thrown off her cough from last winter and the strain showed in every line of her face.

'I hope you're looking after yourself,' Rose said.

'I'll do.' There was a pause. 'Could do without spending the night in this thing though.' She patted the Morrison shelter.

'What about Dad?'

'Oh, he's all right. Better than the rest of us as a matter of fact. He's palled up with some bloke from the BSA who's got an allotment over that way. Your dad helps out how he can. Digging for Victory and that.' Dora smiled, reluctantly. 'Gives me a bit of peace anyroad. I even heard him whistling the other evening. No, he's not the problem . . .'

Rose saw her mother's face cloud over again. 'George?'

'He's started thieving. I found him with a clock this morning and he wouldn't say where he got it. Next thing is he's sold it and put the money in his pocket. I reckon it came from one of the houses that got it last night. I'm ashamed of him – I really am. But it don't seem no good saying anything.'

'I wish I could do more to help,' Rose said.

'You're doing what you can. And it can't be a picnic for Jean over there either.'

As Autumn came, Dora was taken ill again. Grace gave up work to be with her and take care of the family. The bombing began in real earnest in November. On the fourteenth the centre of Coventry was burnt to the ground, and it seemed only a matter of time before the attention of the German Luftwaffe would be turned more fully on Birmingham.

A few days later it began. Night after night the waves of bombers came over, dark, malevolent shadows in the sky. All night searchlights criss-crossed the darkened buildings and the ack-ack guns rattled out their fire.

Across the city fires burned and the water supply was disrupted. In the quiet mornings, after the all clear had sounded, exhausted people emerged blinking and sick with nerves out of the shelters or from under their staircases to the smell of damp, charred masonry, wet plaster and the sour smell of the incendiaries.

One morning, after another heavy raid, Grace arrived just as Rose was about to go to bed.

'What's happened?' Rose shouted down the stairs, seeing Jean letting Grace in. She was down in an instant. 'What're you doing here? What's wrong?'

'It's Mom,' Grace said. She looked pale and exhausted. 'She's been taken very bad. We had to get the doctor in after the all clear. He says it's pneumonia.'

'Oh my God,' Rose said. She just stared at Grace, stupid with tiredness.

'I can look after her,' Grace assured her hurriedly. 'Only she's fretting about the kids. It was so bad last night she wants Harry and the twins over at Edna's till it's all over. She's sure Edna'll have them.'

Rose felt a momentary pang at the thought of Billy and Susan being sent away, but she knew it was for the best. 'What about George?'

Grace gave her a look which implied how stupid the question was. 'I need you to come and stay over a night at Mom's while I take them over. It'll be too much to do it in a day.'

Rose thought for a second. 'I can get Maureen to swap with me for tomorrow. She'll do anything for kids. I'll get over early. Do me a favour and don't go till I've had a chance to see them.'

Grace nodded, knowing Rose felt they were almost her own. 'Make sure you're over sharpish though.'

*

As Rose made her way home the next day she was horrified at the extent of the damage wreaked on the city. She sat in her old grey coat, looking out of the window of the bus. Some of the solid edges that had outlined her existence were gone. It was shocking, impossible, as if the very foundations of life were shuddering underneath her.

Two of the houses at the end of Catherine Street were down. The house next to them had been shattered in half, some of it still intact, with a chest of drawers with clothes spilling out and a picture still untouched on the inside wall. It seemed indecent: the details of the private parts of people's lives hanging there on display.

Grace hadn't told her how bad it was. She must have wanted to avoid worrying her any more.

She gave the little ones as cheerful a send off as she could. Dora was upstairs in bed and had already said her goodbyes.

'Why do we have to go?' Susan raised her dark eyes to Rose with a puzzled frown.

'Well, it's because of all the big bangs you keep hearing in the night,' Rose told her.

'We don't like the bangs,' Billy whispered.

'No. Well, it'll be quieter at Auntie Edna's. And there's a lot more space to run about. And Harry'll look after you – won't you?'

Harry nodded, holding on to a very old rag doll that had been Violet's.

'I tell you what,' Rose said. 'I've got something for you two to look after for me.'

She ran upstairs, and when she came down after a few minutes she put into Susan's hand a small wooden elephant and into Billy's the roughly carved little wooden horse. Both of them beamed with delight.

'I'll put him in bed when we get there, 'cos he'll be tired,' Susan said solemnly.

'That's right. You look after them for me until I see you – all right?'

Rose found Dora in a bad state. She was very weak

and her breathing through her one good lung was laboured and noisy. She had a high fever and was drifting in and out of consciousness. Rose sat beside her most of the day, offering her sips of water, bathing the hot, sallow skin of her face and rubbing camphorated oil on her chest. When Rose became so tired she could no longer stay upright, she lay and slept beside her.

In the early evening, when Dora opened her eyes and seemed fully conscious for the first time, Rose said, 'They've gone off all right.'

Her mother nodded and whispered, 'Best out of it.' Then she said, 'Grace is a good girl.'

Rose smiled.

'And so are you,' Dora went on in her rasping voice.

'Don't talk if it hurts, Mom.'

'No – I wanted to say—' Dora went on, and then started coughing, her body curling in pain as she held her side tightly. It was some time before she had enough breath to speak again.

'You've had some bad things happen to you – before you should have—'

'Don't, Mom—'

'No . . .' She stopped to get her breath again. 'It's as rough as it gets losing a babby. And your friend – Diana . . .' She saw Rose look at the floor. It was the first time anyone else had mentioned Diana, and hearing her name suddenly was more painful than she expected. 'All I was going to say was – I'm proud of you – how you've come through it. Alfie'll make you a good husband. And you can have some more of your own kiddies then.'

For a moment Rose couldn't think of anything to say, she was so moved by the fact that her mother understood how bad she still felt about Diana. And at the same time she realized with a wave of guilt how seldom she worried about Alfie.

She just said, 'Thanks Mom. Shall I get you some camomile tea now?'

As she was preparing the hot drink, George came back into the house carrying a bag of trinkets which he'd rifled out of another of the houses bombed the night before. He laid them out quite brazenly on top of the shelter.

'You ought to be ashamed of yourself,' Rose said.

'Oh yeah? How's that?' he said, insolently. His little pinched face was hard and bitter.

'Look,' Rose said, infuriated, her hands on her hips. Small as she was, she looked forbidding in her anger, her slim curving figure outlined by the red dress. 'I know you think you're a special case and everyone's got to apologize to you for the rest of your life. But you're not. Mom sent you away because she wanted the best for you, and there's no excuse for you acting like a thieving litle urchin and taking advantage of other people.'

'Aw, sod off,' George said.

Rose marched up to him and gave his face a sharp slap. She turned, shaking with anger, to begin preparing their rations of food for the evening meal.

'You're a selfish little bugger,' she shouted after him as he went out of the door.

He left the door swinging open so that the forbidden light streamed into the yard. Rose went and slammed it shut.

'We'll have the ARP lot round carrying on next,' she muttered to herself. Despite her anger she saw in her mind George as a tiny child forever running to her to be picked up. She felt sorry for being so hard on him. But all their nerves were on edge and he'd become so distant and infuriating.

Soon Sid came in with a cabbage and a handful of carrots in a bag dangling from his crutch. 'You can throw these in the pot,' he said proudly. 'How's your mother?'

'She's just had some tea,' Rose told him. 'She's about the same, I think.' She took the cabbage and started to clean it up. 'How's it at the BSA?'

'Hell of a mess up there,' Sid said, easing his coat off. 'The whole of the new building went up. Awful lot of blokes went with it. We're carrying on the best we can.'

While she finished preparing the meal, Sid went round the house and checked it was properly blacked out. She heard his voice upstairs as he said a few words to her mother. It was odd getting used to seeing him differently. Now he was someone with things to do, with a role. Like a proper dad, she thought.

When he came down, she said, 'How do we get Mom into the shelter?'

'She won't come,' Sid said flatly.

'Is that what she said?'

'She didn't need to say. She hasn't been in there since she was taken bad.'

Rose gaped at him. 'You mean . . .? Well, who's looked after her?'

'Our Grace has stayed up with her. Your mother told her to go down and leave her, but Grace wouldn't hear of it.'

'Grace? You mean all these nights they've been bombing the guts out of us those two have both been . . .' She pointed towards the ceiling. Sid nodded. 'Why didn't you make them come down?'

'Don't you think I've tried?' His voice was loud with guilt and worry. 'She just won't hear of it.'

'Good God,' Rose said. 'Our Grace is tougher than you'd think. Well' – she looked defiantly at Sid – 'if she can put up with it, so can I.'

Sid shook his head. 'I thought you might've been the one that'd talk her down. I just wish there was something I—'

'It's all right. Save your breath,' Rose said irritably, and then added more gently, 'It only takes one to see to her, doesn't it?'

Her father sat down, quiet for a moment. Then he said, 'Grace is very like your mother used to be. She was always one for looking after people.'

'Good job really, wasn't it?' Rose retorted. She was finding being alone with her father for the first time in years strange and uncomfortable. She suddenly realized that Dora had always stood between them so they had seldom talked to one another without someone else to mediate.

'You can be a hard bitch, you can,' Sid said matter-of-factly. He stared at the plates Rose was laying on top of the shelter as he spoke. 'Whatever you think, I do love that woman up there.'

Rose turned away, knowing that whatever tender feelings she'd ever had towards her father, or might have now, she was damned if she'd ever be able to show him.

The raids began early that night. Rose spent part of those long hours lying in Sid's place in the bed beside Dora's restless, feverish body. The rest of the time she sat up or stood by the window, frozen in spite of the blanket wrapped round her.

The seemingly endless groups of planes droned past overhead, ack-ack defences hammered at them, and finally there came the crump of bombs landing at a distance or a much louder explosion if they were nearer. Then the planes roared away again. She peeped out from behind the blackout curtains and saw the searchlights moving over the city and the sky orange from the reflected light of the burning buildings. She thought she could smell smoke, but wasn't certain if it was her imagination.

She thought of Jo Pye out there helping to put out the fires, and Gladys and the kids all crushed into their shelter.

I should have volunteered for the ARP or something like that, she thought. Where I could have been out helping people.

Suddenly there was a huge explosion, so close that the house shook and the windows rattled. Rose found that she was lying flat on the floorboards without having thought about it.

Dora stirred. 'Grace . . .?'

Rose crawled shakily over to the bed. 'It's me – Rose.'

'Oh. What was that?' Dora sounded very drowsy.

'Don't know. Wasn't us, anyway!' It could only have been a street or two away though, she thought. Astonishing that the glass was still in the window. Good job they'd taped it across. If she hadn't had her mother to look after she felt she would have panicked, her nerves were stretched so taut.

'D'you want a drink?' she whispered.

Dora accepted a few sips of water, with Rose supporting her arm. She was so frail, her face and limbs pared right down to the bones. Feeling the ghostliness of her mother's body, Rose knew that she didn't have much time left to her.

'D'you remember those nights we spent together up with the babbies?' she asked Dora.

Her mother nodded her head very slightly. 'It weren't right – you losing yours like that.'

'I miss him still – terrible sometimes.'

'Course you do – mine too – it never goes.' The coughing took her over again, and the attack seemed to go on for a long time. Rose was quite oblivious now to what was going on outside. Dora seemed to doze off again when the coughing eased up, but suddenly she said, 'You'll always have Billy and Susan.'

Rose knew she was saying, look after them, keep an eye on them for me. She reached out and took her mother's hand gently in her own.

'Sod them out there,' she said. 'I'm coming in to lie down.'

When she returned wearily to work the following night she noticed that the space beside her where Maureen usually worked had been filled by another girl, whom she'd never seen before.

'You done a swap have you?' she said, puzzled. 'What's happened to Maureen?'

The girl said she didn't know because she'd been asked to move over from another block. Rose saw Madge, an older woman who worked in a position near by, moving quickly over to her.

'You'll have to know, Rose,' she said. 'Maureen was killed last night on the way to work. One came down when she was going for the bus. House came down on her. She never stood a chance.'

Hurriedly someone fetched a chair for Rose, who had turned a sick-looking white in the face.

'You all right love?' Madge asked. 'I never meant to give you such a shock. Only I didn't think you two that close.'

Rose sat under the remorseless lights of the vast factory, her mind a collage of confused thoughts. Maureen walking out for her bus from her lonely digs, the bomb coming down like a great slug in the darkness, and a small Irish girl called Josie, little Josie whom Maureen adored and whose heart would break.

A fortnight later, on a frozen, gusty December afternoon, Rose, looking pale and exhausted, stood between her father and sister at Dora's funeral. They walked back from the graveside under an iron sky, between the leafless trees, Sid, Rose, Grace and George. They hadn't called the little ones back. With Sam away, this, for now, was the family.

But as the wind murmured in between the skinny branches of the trees that bleak afternoon, Rose glanced back to the spot from where they had walked. And she knew that the centre of the family, the person who had kept them together, now lay buried beneath the fast-freezing ground.

PART TWO

ITALY

1943–1945

CHAPTER 14

MARCH 1941, BERKSHIRE

The truck swayed along the narrow country lanes, its huge khaki bulk looking out of place between hawthorn hedges and elms. From the half-open back of the truck women's faces looked out at the early spring countryside and they waved at people they passed. They all held on to anything they could to keep from falling on top of one another. Deeper inside the truck, where it was almost too dark to see, someone was singing 'My Bonny Lies Over the Ocean' in a loud, tuneless voice.

'So this is the British army,' a voice piped up over towards the daylight end. 'You can see why they call them cattle trucks, can't you! I say – you've got your foot on my case. Move it, would you? There's a dear. Mustn't have my things crushed before we've even started.

'You won't be needing crêpe de Chine where we're going!' someone shouted over the growling engine, and the others round her tittered. The voice had come from a large woman with peroxide blond hair. 'And stop that bleedin' racket, will you?' she yelled down at the singer. 'Me head's thumping something awful already.'

Rose, who was standing near her towards the back, silently agreed. As the afternoon had worn on a tight band of pain had stretched between her temples so she felt almost unable to think, exhausted as she was from all the newness and strain of the journey further away from home than she'd ever been before. She could hardly feel her feet in her old down-at-heel shoes and she was hungry. The few sandwiches Grace had packed for her were long gone. The day seemed to be going on for ever.

'Here . . .' She realized the blonde was speaking to her through the gloom of the truck. 'You deaf or something? I said pass us me bag will you? Yeah. That one.'

Rose bent down unsteadily and got hold of the heavy carpet bag. She pushed it to the other woman along the floor of the truck.

'Ta. Where'd you come from then?'

'Birmingham.'

'Ooh ar!' the blonde squawked. 'Yow'm a Brummoy then – orroight are yer!' she mocked.

'That's all right with you is it?' Rose snapped at her. She couldn't place the woman's own accent.

'Now girls,' a voice called from the light end. 'No point in being cattish. We've all got to get along and live together. There's a war on, remember.'

The blonde said, 'Oooh, yes. I'd almost forgot!' and rolled her eyes round in such a comical way that Rose couldn't help grinning.

'What's your name then?'

'Rose. What's yours?'

'Gloria. From Deptford. That's London to you. This is a lark innit?' Gloria stood with her solid legs braced apart as far as space would allow. 'Could do without the old school tie brigade though.'

While they had waited for their transport at Didcot Station surrounded by piles of army supplies, the women had gathered instinctively into two groups. The old school tie group, as Gloria called them, looked much better dressed and cared for, and one of them even had a fur collar on her coat. From the loud conversations in their posh accents, Rose gathered that several of them were bound eventually for the élite Intelligence Corps. There was a rather mousy, timid-looking girl with reddish brown hair who Rose noticed because she seemed to be constantly on the point of bursting into tears. She didn't seem to be sure which group she belonged in, and hung around the posher ones as if hoping to be taken under their wing.

The second group, which Rose and Gloria had fallen into, looked scruffier, mostly togged up in second- or third-hand clothes and lumpish old coats. Gloria seemed the most brashly confident. A couple of them looked pale and unhealthy and terrified. One clearly had nits, so everyone shrank back from her.

The journey from the station to the camp was roughly four miles.

'I say – I think we're here!' someone soon called out. Others pushed towards the back end to get their first sight of the camp where they were to spend their first three weeks of initial training. Rose could see nothing at all.

'Golly, sentry boxes,' one of the posh girls said. 'Those chaps look jolly cold, don't they?'

'Look at all that barbed wire. Makes it look frightfully serious, doesn't it?'

'Let's hope they'll let us have a cup of tea now. I'm quite parched.'

The truck stopped abruptly at the reception hut and they scrambled out with their bags, those from the dark inside screwing up their eyes as they reached the daylight. The March afternoon had turned damp and windy. They all looked round at the camp which extended along the edge of the Berkshire Downs. There were row upon row of Nissen huts with corrugated-iron roofs, and round the camp stretched the spiky border of the barbed wire. It was a bleak scene, with no trees and few bushes between the huts, and the rounded greyish hills curving away beyond. Rose experienced the same feeling as on her first day at Castle Bromwich, an urge to turn round and run home. But home was much further away now, and there wasn't much to run back there for.

After they had filed into the reception hut they were each given a printed postcard to fill in saying they had arrived safely and where they were. Rose addressed hers to Grace.

A brisk officer with an Eton crop introduced herself to them as Lieutenant Waters. 'I'd like to welcome you to the Auxiliary Territorial Service. I know everything must seem very new and strange to you now, and I'm sure you're all rather tired and cold. But you will get used to us and our ways here and, before long, our ways will of course become your ways.'

She went on to say that they were part of Platoon 4, and that later that day they would be issued with ATS uniform, of which, she assured them, they would become very proud after a few weeks. Rose listened rather blankly, sitting on a hard wooden bench beside the girl with nits, who kept fiddling with her head.

Then a plump woman in uniform came in and announced herself their corporal.

'Right!' she shouted at them. 'Outside in threes!'

Carrying their cases, they slouched and stumbled out of the hut into the cold and stood in rough lines, three abreast.

'Let's see you begin on some marching,' the corporal yelled. 'When I say march you lead with your left foot. Ready? Right – march! Left, right, left, right, left . . . left . . . left . . .'

And the line of women, tall and short, plump and skinny, in as great a variety of clothes, tried to discipline their tired legs and march, heavy cases swaying in hands, to their huts. Rose heard Gloria give a snort of laughter at the sight.

Hut J, into which Rose was ordered, housed twelve women in beds with black iron frames, six down each side. Along the middle of the floor ran a very shiny strip of brown lino, and in the centre of the hut stood a stove, its rather rusty pipe angling up and out through the roof. It was not lit at the moment and the hut, with its drab greenish walls, felt cold and cheerless.

Rose sat down, slipped her shoes off and rubbed her slim, icy feet. She closed her eyes for a moment, wishing she could lie down on the bed and sleep straight away. She opened them again at the sound of a voice next to her.

'Gawd! This is the first time I've ever had a whole bed to meself.'

A skinny girl with a pale, rather rat-like face, her lank greasy hair held back by a couple of kirby grips, was unpacking her things on the next bed. 'How about you?' she asked Rose.

'Me too,' Rose said wearily. She was tired and didn't feel like talking. The girl had an accent rather like Gloria's. Her name was Tilly and she came from Canning Town. Rose realized she meant London as well. Between all her actions Tilly kept biting furiously at her rough nails.

Rose got up slowly from the bed and started to open her case. As she glanced down the long room she saw that Gloria was up the far end, and she recognized the mousy girl who'd been hovering round the posh group at the station.

Standing by the bed on the other side of her was a girl with wavy brown hair and round, healthy-looking cheeks. For a second Rose was startled by how much she reminded her of Diana.

The girl smiled at her. 'You look done in,' she said. 'Come a long way?'

'From Birmingham,' Rose replied. 'It's felt like a hell of a long day.'

'Yes, I'm lucky. My people only live over near Oxford, so it hasn't been too much of a chore for me. My name's Muriel, by the way.'

Rose warmed to Muriel. She was well spoken, but without a trace of the stand-offishness she'd sensed in some of the others.

'We'll be able to help each other out, won't we?' Muriel said. 'Did you know that these funny mattress things are called biscuits? Odd, isn't it?'

Rose saw that the mattress on the iron frame was made up of three thin sections: – the 'biscuits'. They also had two sheets each and four blankets.

Suddenly there was a to-do at the other end of the hut. The mouse was in tears.

'What's up with her?' Tilly asked, with more curiosity than concern. 'Can't see there's much to have a crying match about. S'like a boarding house here I reckon!'

The mouse, whose name turned out to be Gwen, had promised to write to her mother the instant she set foot in the camp and had just realized she had lost her writing paper.

'Oh for heaven's sake, wrap up,' Gloria said to her. 'Someone'll give you a bit of paper. And you've already sent her one of them cards, so what're you fussing about?'

'But the card didn't *say* anything,' Gwen sniffed. 'And Mummy worries so. She's a widow, you see.'

Rose thought for a moment of Sid, and of Grace left to look after them all. She thanked her stars Sid had the BSA job to keep him occupied. And Grace had told her that in a few weeks when she had reached eighteen she was going to volunteer at a first aid post. 'That way I can stay home with Dad and George and still do something useful,' she'd said stoically.

Now Rose wished overwhelmingly that her sister was there with her. It would be so good to see a familiar face.

Muriel found Gwen a sheet of paper and an envelope, but the moment she sat down to write they were all ordered out again. The rest of the afternoon and evening was spent rushing from one thing to the next: getting fitted into their stiff khaki uniforms and peaked caps, pulling at skirts and tunics to make them fit over hips and busts, and collecting a huge mound of kit: steel helmet, greatcoat, groundsheet, respirator . . . And clothes and more clothes, the shirts and slacks and gloves and everything you could think of except, for some reason, handkerchiefs. There were shrieks of laughter at the sight of the heavy underwear and thick khaki stockings.

'Cor – look at them passion killers!' Gloria cackled, waving a pair of stockings round her head.

Then there was bed making and a quick meal of poached egg on toast in the Naafi canteen and, finally, bed.

*

Rose lay under the sheet and heavy army blankets. A couple of girls were crying. It was very dark in the hut, but Rose guessed from the direction of the sound that one was Gwen. She wondered if she ought to get out and try to comfort her, but she couldn't think of anything to say and wasn't sure Gwen would want her.

The hot cup of tea she'd drunk earlier had begun to ease her headache, but she could still feel her heart thumping too fast. Unable to sleep in this strange new place, she thought over the peculiar day she'd had and back to one event in particular.

That morning when she had left Catherine Street, she told Grace she'd rather say her goodbyes at number five. 'I'd sooner think of you here when I'm gone,' she said. 'And you've got enough on your plate without traipsing into town with me.'

Grace had fussed around her like their mother would have done, and Rose couldn't help thinking how much her sister looked like Dora now that her face had become thinner. The two of them packed up Rose's few things in a small, decrepit suitcase.

'I'll miss you like anything,' Grace said shyly, with tears in her eyes.

'D'you think I'm deserting you?' Rose asked. She had felt many pangs of guilt at going off and leaving Grace at home.

'We'll be all right,' Grace said. 'I've got used to you being over at Jean's, and if you was here with Dad the pair of you'd do nothing but fall out anyhow. It's best this way – specially with Alfie being stuck out there and everything.' Grace still persisted in her fantasy that Rose was pining dreadfully for Alfie.

Sid had said a gruff goodbye to Rose before he left in the morning. 'I don't s'pose they let you lasses get anywhere near the action like the blokes. Just make sure you don't give 'em lip and you'll be all right.'

George just said, 'Tara,' as if Rose was off down the shops for the morning.

'You'll let me know how Billy and Susan are, won't

you?' Rose begged Grace. 'And Harry of course,' she added quickly. 'It's going to be the worst thing, not having any kids around.'

The sisters embraced. The strong grip of their arms round each other said everything. Neither was the sort to make a fuss. Rose walked away from Court 11, past the bomb rubble at the end of Catherine Street.

Sitting on the bus into town, she began to feel this was actually real. She was really going to leave Birmingham for the first time. Her stomach churned with nerves and excitement. It was a bright, blustery morning and she stared hard out of the window as if trying to remember every stone of her city: the dark factories, Smithfield, St Martin's, and all the other less obvious places that were so much part of her. She couldn't imagine anywhere different. Leaving it all was terrifying now she was actually facing it. But this was what she had always wanted, wasn't it? To see something of what was outside? The war had at least given her that chance. She sat hugging the small, battered weekend case on her knees, the one familiar object in a world that was shifting all around her.

New Street Station was seething with people, many of them service personnel in their blue or khaki uniforms. Rose wondered if there were others going to the same place as her. Trains were constantly moving in and out with a great clamour of engines and whistles blowing. The air was full of sharp smells of soot and cinders and acrid whorls of smoke from cigarettes.

Rose picked her way along the crowded platform, saying 'excuse me' and 'sorry' until she was somewhere near the middle. According to the long fingers of the clock there were still twenty minutes until her train to Oxford was due to leave. She wondered whether to go back and try to get a quick cup of tea.

A train slid slowly into the station from Rose's right. She stood on tiptoe to watch. It was a grand sight as it hissed finally to a halt, steam clouding up to the steel beams of the roof. The doors opened and people clambered out on to the already packed platform. Rose, like everyone else, shuffled back to give them room.

She was standing like that, deciding against the tea, when she heard the voice: a strong, well-spoken woman's voice but containing a waver of uncertainty.

'It is, surely – is it? Rose? Rose Lucas?'

Rose turned and found herself face to face with a smartly turned out WAAF officer, her fair, wavy hair fastened back stylishly under the grey-blue cap. Her vivacious face wore an apprehensive smile. In the five years since she had seen her, Diana had matured into a beautiful, poised young woman.

'It is you, isn't it?' Diana exclaimed.

The two of them eased further back into the crowd to let the other passengers past and someone behind said, 'Here – watch who you're pushing, will you?'

Diana made a helpless gesture as if unsure where to begin the conversation. 'Well. Where are you off to?'

'The army. ATS,' Rose managed to gasp out. Her heart was beating breathtakingly fast. She was amazed how Diana could begin chatting as if they'd only seen each other the week before. But then that was her upbringing – politeness, social graces.

'Good for you,' Diana said. 'I'm a WAAF – well, as you can see . . .' And she giggled, looking down at her uniform. For the first time Rose realized that Diana was as nervous as herself. 'I'm just off home on leave. Mummy and Daddy will be thrilled I've seen you!'

Rose found herself unable to speak. Lying remembering it now she thought of all the things she should have said. She should have asked after Catherine and Ronald, said how pleased she was, *something* at least. But she had felt so scruffy and ignorant and overpoweringly awkward, and those feelings were made worse by the memory of how much the two of them had shared and of the way she had cut Diana off so abruptly.

Diana quietened suddenly and looked serious. 'Listen. I'm going to have to be off shortly – train to catch. But Rose, I . . .' She struggled for the right words. 'What happened to you? We were all so worried about you and it made me so unhappy. I couldn't understand why you didn't answer my letters.'

Seeing the tears in her old friend's eyes Rose realized that she was, beneath all the jolliness of her class and of service life, still the same, kind girl she had known.

'I couldn't . . .' Rose's face felt hot and red and she knew that if she tried to explain here she would be unable to stop crying. 'I wanted to tell you,' she stumbled on. 'But you'd have hated me if you'd known . . .'

The sight of Diana's blue eyes so full of concern made Rose feel even more emotional. 'Look. You'll miss your train. Give me your address. I'll write. There's no time now and I'd just make a fool of myself. But I'd like to tell you . . .'

Diana handed her a slip of paper with her WAAF address on it. They reached out and awkwardly gripped each other's hands. And then she was gone, vanished among the other drably clad bodies. Rose was left feeling weak-kneed and suspecting it had all been a daydream.

She tossed and fidgeted on the hard bed. What am I going to say to her when I write? she wondered. More than ever, Diana had seemed to come from a different world. But the only thing to do was to tell her everything, truthfully. She owed Diana that. To finish things off. But as she drifted off to sleep, she couldn't help wondering whether this might also be the beginning of something new in a friendship that had never truly died.

CHAPTER 15

'Oh, these confounded blisters!' Muriel groaned, gingerly trying to squeeze her feet into her slippers.

They were all in Hut J because it was domestic night. Each Wednesday of the three weeks in camp they were expected to scrub the hut and catch up on any cleaning or mending chores. Some of the girls were crowded round the stove, which was lit only in the evenings.

Squatting in front of the glowing coals with her legs apart in a silky confection of a nightie was Gloria. She was holding out a large pair of scissors on which was stabbed a slice of bread she was toasting. Rose, Tilly and a couple of others were sitting round in stiff blue and white striped army pyjamas. Muriel was wearing her own floral cotton nightie, and Gwen sat swamped by a pair of pale pink winceyette pyjamas. Both she and Tilly were dabbing at their feet with blobs of cotton wool.

'Our feet'll be in ribbons by the end of this,' Gwen moaned.

All of them had sore feet but they also had pink, healthier-looking cheeks than when they'd arrived, after the new experience of half an hour's vigorous PT every morning. They tucked into the toast with increased appetites from all the fresh air.

In between the gripes about blisters and arms throbbing from the inoculations they'd had, Gloria was regaling them with tales of her men. She apparently had several in tow at once. To prove the point she'd pinned four photos on the wall behind her bed, and went through a half-joking ritual of kissing them all at length before she settled down to sleep.

'That one's Bob,' she told them, pointing out a dark, moustachioed figure. 'He's my favourite really. It was him who give me this.' She flounced round in front of them in the shimmering, peach-coloured folds of cloth.

'Under the counter stuff,' Tilly said knowingly. 'Has to be. How'd he get it otherwise with rationing on?'

Gloria stood magnificently above her, curling a lock of her pale hair round a finger. 'I'll have you know,' she said disdainfully, 'that my Bob actually owns the factory where they used to make these here gowns.'

Gloria turned to Rose, who was sitting with her army jacket in her lap, lighting matches to burn off the pinkish film which covered the buttons. It was something they all did to make the jackets look more presentable.

You're a looker,' Gloria said. 'Why ain't we seen any pictures of your bloke? Or ain't you interested in fellers?'

'I'm – sort of engaged to someone,' Rose told them hesitantly, still not feeling sure it was really true.

Muriel and Gwen both said, Ah, how lovely.'

'Where is he then?' Tilly asked. 'He in the army too?'

'Yes, but he's in Germany.'

There were noises of horror from the others.

'Picked him up, did they?' Gloria asked, more gently. 'Is he in a Kraut prison camp?'

Rose nodded. 'I just had one of them cards, a couple of months ago. You know, name, in good health and all that. The camp's called Felsig. I think they picked him up in France.'

The others sat silent for a moment.

'That must be terrible,' Muriel said.

'Yeah,' Gloria joined in, trying to cheer things up. 'But at least you know where he is and that he's alive. Eh,' she nudged Rose playfully with her elbow, 'he won't be getting up to much mischief in one of them camps!' She gave her loud laugh. 'So in the meantime you can have some fun, can't you? I mean being engaged ain't the same as being married, is it?' She laughed again. 'I'll tell you one thing. I'll give this army lark a chance, and if I don't like it I'll be over the men's quarters right quick, getting meself a Paragraph 11!'

Paragraph 11, in army regulations, provided a let-out clause for women who were having babies. The others laughed, rather uneasily, at the thought of Gloria going brazenly over to the men's side of the camp to help herself to a pregnancy.

'That's awful,' Gwen said, blushing.

'Oh, ta very much.' Gloria was unruffled. 'I can't see any point in not having a good time when you can – specially with a war on. And I don't know why you're looking so bug-eyed about it. You only joined up to get away from that bleedin' mother of yours, didn't you?'

Gwen leapt to her feet, her face instantly a hot red. 'That's not true!' she cried. 'How could you say something so awful?' And she ran sobbing over to her bed and lay down on it, curled up tight.

Rose put her jacket down. 'I thought I had a gob on me till I met you,' she said matter-of-factly to Gloria, and went to sit on Gwen's bed. The other girl wouldn't say anything, but gripped Rose's hand.

'Time for bed, methinks,' Muriel said, with all the authority of a boarding school prefect, which until a few months before was what she had been.

Gloria grinned, making a thumbs up sign at Muriel and winking at the others. 'Definitely officer material there!' she said.

Every morning they were up at six-thirty and ready for PT by seven. This was made even more of an agony for the first few days by pain in their arms from the injections. Rose felt as if the scab was lifting up and down every time she swung her arm in the freezing air.

Compulsory inoculations had only been one part of the medical when they'd first arrived. They had also had to go through the dreaded 'free from infection' inspection.

'Oh my Gawd,' Gloria had said as they queued up.

She seemed genuinely rattled by it. 'It's the bugs, babies and scabies job isn't it? Do we really have to take our bits off in front of that lot?'

They all stood in line outside the chilly medical hut. Weak sunshine lit the grey camp buildings and a damp wind swept across the downs. Their grumpy corporal kept shouting 'NO TALKING!' and refused to answer any questions.

All of them were anxious. Most had never taken off their clothes even in front of their closest family before. When they had filed inside and Rose was stripped down to her vest and pants, she found herself trembling, and not just with cold. The stale, sweaty smell of some of the girls reminded her sickeningly of Mr Lazenby. She saw with enormous relief that the medical officer was a woman.

She listened to Rose's heart, poked about in her hair and felt along her spine. She pulled out the elastic of her knickers to have a quick, impassive glance down them, and then it was over and Rose was pronounced nit free and fit for duty.

'It's nothing much,' Rose whispered to Gwen, who was standing outside looking pale with fright.

Every day there came another trial: kit inspection. Beds had to be 'barracked' – arranged with the sheets and blankets folded in a very particular way – and then all of the kit had to be laid out in precise order and immaculately folded. Woe betide you if any of it was missing and could not be excused as being in the laundry.

And then drill. They stood in lines, an extraordinarily unformed-looking bunch in the first few days, as one of the male NCOs bawled relentlessly at them.

'Right, you lousy shower. Let's see some discipline around here! You've got to learn in three weeks what we normally take three months of army life to pick up, and I'm damned if any of you are going to let me down! Right. Chests foward, shoulders back, bottoms in. Atten-*shun*!'

Gradually, as the days of marching and saluting and manoeuvring back and forth went by, their bodies creaked and cranked into familiarity with it. They began to look as if they might belong in the army.

After lunch, for which they lined up in the canteen, men and women bantering together, they sat down for a bewildering assortment of lectures and films. One talk on army regiments or history might be closely followed by a luridly educational film about VD or how a baby is born. This was a mixed camp in a mixed army and they were expected to take all this in their stride, but there was many a green, shocked face after they'd seen the festering genitals in the VD film.

And then came the fatigues or camp chores; scrubbing floors, washing dishes or spud bashing.

One afternoon Rose was standing in the canteen hut with Gloria. They both had their khaki sleeves rolled up so they could dip their hands into the freezing, muddy water.

'You know, gypsy Rose,' Gloria teased. 'I can never make you out. What d'you really make of the army?'

Rose was silent for a moment, working on the cold, earthy skin of a potato. She turned her strong gaze on Gloria.

'I don't like being pushed around, except when I can really see the point of it. I mean I'll do what they say if it's right – for the war effort like. And I've always wanted to get away, see a bit more of life than just Brum. I miss home of course, but my mom's died anyhow and I can't stick living with my dad.'

Gloria seemed in an unusually solemn mood. 'Seems like everyone's running away from something when you come down to it, doesn't it?' She grinned. 'Quiet here though, isn't it? We hardly had a wink of sleep back in Deptford. They was bombing the balls off of us.'

Rose pulled back a wavy strand of hair with cold, wet fingers. 'Is that why you joined up then?'

'Not just,' Gloria said briskly. 'They got me brother. He was a rear gunner in the RAF. Went through all the Battle of Britain, right till the end. Then he went out one day and they lost him over the Channel. We was close, me and Jo. It was only me he told how scared he was – brown trousers, the lot – you know. When he went I thought, I'm not going to just sit here with them dropping this bloody lot on us night after night. I'm going to get the buggers.'

Rose still found Gloria an unlikely addition to the army with her peroxide hair, her curl papers and slinky nighties. 'D'you think you'll stick it?'

'Oh, I'll stick it,' Gloria said grimly. 'I'll stick it if it kills me.'

'So all that you said about Paragraph 11 – you was joking?'

Gloria gaped at her in astonishment. 'Course I was bleeding joking! What d'you take me for?' With a broad grin on her pink face she picked up a wet potato and lobbed it over in Rose's direction. 'The very idea, you cheeky bugger!'

It was two weeks before Rose found an opportunity to write to Diana. She sat under the stark light in the hut with her pillow propped against the black iron bedhead. She wanted the letter to be warm and friendly. It was easier to write than she'd feared. Away in this place that was so different from home and Birmingham life, she felt almost as if those terrible years had happened to someone else. She wrote about Lazenby's and, as clearly but briefly as she could, about what Mr Lazenby had done to her.

Yet when she described Joseph's short, fragile life, tears began to pour down her face and on to the paper. It brought back vividly what she tried to keep from her mind: the feel of his soft, downy head, and the tiny frozen hands she'd found that terrible morning. She knew with renewed clarity that that day would be the worst of her life – far worse than the day Mr Lazenby assaulted her and worse than anything she might face in the future.

'I wish now I'd told you, Diana,' she wrote.

Now I think back I know you'd have understood – and your mom and dad. But at the time I wasn't thinking straight. I just felt dirty and ashamed all the time and I couldn't see how you'd want to be friends with me again. I hope you can forgive me. I know you'd never get yourself in a mess like that – much too clever, you are! And I want you to know I never stopped thinking about you and wondering how you was getting on. And your family too. They were all so kind to me. Please remember me to them.

I'd like to see you again some time. Maybe in more cheerful days after this war's over?

She signed the letter,

With kind thoughts from your friend,
Rose.

After that, when she'd wiped her face, she dashed off a quick note home. She usually found herself talking in her mind to Grace as she wrote.

'I miss you ever such a lot,' she finished off. 'When I come home next I want to see you in your nurse's uniform!

'Love to all – Rose. xxxx'

She heard the door open, and glanced up to see Gwen come in looking wet, dishevelled and flustered. She sat down miserably on the edge of her bed without even taking her coat off. After a moment Rose realized she was crying. She put her writing things down and went rather timidly to sit beside her.

'What's up with you?' she asked.

Gwen looked up, startled and rather uneasy. She hadn't even noticed Rose when she came into the hut, and she wished that if anyone had to be there, it had been Muriel.

'You'll think I'm so stupid.'

'Why should I?' Rose asked, genuinely surprised.

'You give the impression of being, well, not exactly worldly, but of knowing a lot about life.'

'Me?' Rose couldn't help bursting into laughter. 'Gwen, you do know this is the first time I've ever set foot out of Birmingham, don't you? Come on – out with it.' She patted Gwen's shoulder.

Gwen mopped her eyes with a delicate lacy handkerchief. 'I went to the Naafi tonight. And one of the chaps – it doesn't matter who – kept making up to me all evening. He seemed quite nice, but then he asked me to go outside with him. It's raining, so it wasn't very pleasant, but he didn't seem to care. He pushed me up against the ablutions hut and started . . .' She paused, her head down, ashamed. 'He kept pawing at me. And then he grabbed hold of me and started sticking his horrible tobaccoey tongue in my mouth. It was disgusting. So I just pushed him off.' Her voice had gone high and plaintive with emotion again. 'I mean it was all wrong! D'you think there's something the matter with him, Rose? Or with me?'

Having so recently revived the memory in her letter to Diana of how she'd had to find out about sex herself, Rose felt her heart go out to Gwen. 'Look,' she said gently. 'I know it seems a bit funny if you've not done it before, but that's just a way of kissing.'

'*Kissing!*' Gwen squeaked. 'That's not kissing. It's . . . it's – insanitary!'

Rose looked at Gwen's distraught face in silence for a moment, trying to work out how to phrase what she knew she had to say next.

'You know that film we saw last week, about the babby being born?' she said. Gwen nodded, eyes wide. 'You don't know how it got in there in the first place, do you?'

'Well, Mummy said they just get sort of planted there . . .' Gwen trailed off. 'No, I don't. She told me I didn't need to know anything about 'that' until I'm married. And she said even then I'd be luckier not to find out. She's very protective.'

Rose sighed, and then, as carefully and clearly as she could, so that Gwen could be left in no doubt what she was talking about, she explained. She watched Gwen's expression change from astonishment to disbelief and horror, and then to a stunned gratitude.

'So when they call us ATS 'officers' groundsheets', that's what they . . .?'

Rose nodded.

'And that's what Gloria meant about Paragraph 11,' she said slowly, her horrified expression returning. 'That she'd actually . . .?'

'It's all right,' Rose reassured her with a wry smile. 'From what I hear in this place she wouldn't be the first to try that way out. But I'm sure she was only joking – honest.'

By the end of the final week of basic training, they had been drilled and barracked and bumpered into something that not only resembled army discipline, but was also becoming second nature. Now it was time to be assigned a trade. They all sat through aptitude tests and interviews designed to help the army allot each of them a suitable job. Rose found most of the tests less formidable than she'd feared.

During the interview with Lieutenant Waters, the question Rose remembered despite her nerves was when the woman, sitting behind her desk, asked in a crisp voice, 'You're from Birmingham, aren't you, Private Lucas? What was your father's occupation before the war?'

'Well, he was an engineer—' Rose began to tell her.

'Ah,' the officer said, jotting something down. 'At last, some mechanical potential.'

Rose didn't have the heart or opportunity to tell her that Sid hadn't worked as an engineer since before the last war.

When she came out of the interview she met Muriel outside.

'So – what was the verdict?' Muriel asked her.

A broad smile spread across Rose's face. 'Driver. I'm off to start at Camberley next week.'

She felt not only pleased and excited but flattered too.

She, little Rose Lucas, being able to drive Jeeps and trucks about!

She walked to lunch with Muriel in the moist April wind, across the open area where they did their square bashing, saluting a male officer they passed on the way.

'Gloria's furious,' Muriel said. 'They've told her she's got to be a cook!'

'Gloria?' Rose exploded into laughter. 'Oh my God, heaven help the poor sods who have to eat her cooking! What's yours then?'she asked Muriel.

'Oh, admin. Predictable, I suppose. I've done a certain amount of helping out in my father's firm. Gwen's doing something similar – or is it wireless operations? And Tilly'll be on the telephones I think.'

So the five of them from Hut J who had been thrown so incongruously together were now to be scattered again.

At the end of the three weeks they waited with all the others for their transport back to Didcot to begin on their new careers. They looked a very different collection of women from those who had arrived, all setting off to equip themselves with skills that a few weeks ago they would scarcely have dreamed of. Except for Gloria, who was vowing furiously that every meal she cooked would be sabotaged until they let her do something else.

'Burnt sodding porridge – that's what they'll get!' she yelled out of the back of the truck.

They parted with more emotion than they would ever have thought possible for such a mixed group of strangers within the space of three weeks.

CHAPTER 16

NOVEMBER 1943, AT SEA

The merchant ship *Donata Castle* slid slowly away from Southampton in a grey choppy sea and under a heavy winter sky.

Those who stood at the quayside saw that the decks were lined from bow to stern with the drab khaki colours of army personnel. Among them, for the moment cordoned off in their own separate section, were three hundred women of the British ATS.

It was a solemn hour for all those on the ship. They knew neither when they would be returning home, nor where the *Donata Castle* was bound. The land receded behind the stern, becoming less distinct until it shrank to a soft line on the horizon like a land in a dream. Then it was gone.

As if released, everyone began to move away from the rails of the ship. They had really left England now, so it was time to look forward instead of back. They needed some immediate purpose, and most made their way towards cabins and berths to sort out the rest of their belongings.

A slim, pale young woman with reddish brown hair and a rather perturbed expression was one of the last to turn away from the rail. As she did so, her eye was caught by another of the khaki-clad figures walking away from her on the gently swaying deck. A short young woman, dark hair curled round her ATS cap, a neat but somehow intensely purposeful walk . . .

'I say – Rose!'

The young woman turned, brown eyes searching out the voice. Then her serious face was suddenly smiling broadly. 'Gwen!'

They gave each other a strong hug, something unthinkable in their early army days.

'I didn't see you when we came on board,' Gwen exclaimed.

'I was late.' Rose was looking Gwen up and down. 'Well – you're a sight more pleased with yourself than when I last saw you!' She laughed. 'I thought there wasn't anyone I knew on board here. I *am* pleased to see you.'

'Oh, me too,' Gwen assured her. 'And I can't get over the sight of you. You look marvellous!'

It was true. The reliable army food and plentiful amounts of fresh air that Rose had had access to for the past two and a half years had improved her looks no end. She had gained weight, so that her cheeks were no longer gaunt, and her complexion a healthy pink. Her petite figure was now curvaceous instead of skinny, her rounded breasts and hips filling her uniform.

'Fancy you signing up for abroad!' Rose said, remembering the anxious girl she had first known at the Berkshire training camp. 'What about your mom? She must've had a fit.'

Gwen's expression suddenly turned stiff and obstinate. She glared back at Rose with blue eyes that held a new conviction. 'Mummy is having to fend for herself,' she said abruptly. For a second she wavered and looked appealingly at Rose. 'You must think me terribly hard-hearted, but it's taken the war to make me see just how much my mother ruled my life.' She smiled. 'Come on. Let's go and get a cup of tea and have a good old chat. I want to know all about where you've been.'

They climbed down to the makeshift canteen and sat together with mugs of tea next to a porthole where the dark slant of the sea kept appearing as the ship rocked back and forth.

For a couple of minutes neither of them knew where

to begin. It was less painful to look to the future, with all its uncertainties, than to look back on the past couple of years of the war.

They had been two of the grimmest years anyone could remember. At home there had been the separation and uncertainty over loved ones, the privations of shorter and shorter rations, bitterly cold winters, and of course the bombing, things precious and familiar being destroyed all around. Across the world, what Churchill had in 1940 called 'the foulest and most soul-destroying tyranny' had swept on relentlessly. Those years had brought defeats on the eastern front in Russia, the Japanese advance through Malaya into Singapore, and the failed invasion of the Allied forces at Dieppe as they tried to get a foothold in occupied Europe.

Then, when things could not have looked bleaker, there was at last one overwhelmingly hopeful piece of news. General Montgomery and the Eighth Army had fought against German commander Rommel's forces in the deserts of North Africa. And they had triumphed at El Alamein in northern Egypt. There was a sense that the tide had turned. British and American forces had landed first in Sicily, then Italy. The balance of the war had shifted, but many of the memories Rose and Gwen looked back on now were associated with the darkest days of 1941 and 1942.

'Do you really drive those fearful trucks?' Gwen giggled. 'Silly question, I know. Girls do it all the time. But it looks so difficult.'

'You just learn it like any of the jobs,' Rose replied. 'But it was hard at first, I can tell you. When we got to Camberley, at the start I'd be at it day and night. When I wasn't driving I was dreaming about it. I'd wake up with the sheets all tied up round my legs with trying to double-declutch in my sleep!'

At first she had been astonished at the responsibilities that the army seemed willing to entrust to her. She had learned to drive anything: army pick-up trucks, fifteen hundredweight Bedford wagons, and the huge canvas-covered three-ton trucks. It seemed absolutely normal now that she should.

'So where were your postings?' Gwen wanted to know.

'Oh, all over – all HAA Batteries. First it was Lancashire, Widnes. I was driving the supplies, messages. At one place I even had to empty the lavs, oh my God! You needed to be patriotic to put up with Lancashire that winter. It were enough to freeze the balls off a brass monkey! In the March I went down near Winchester for a few months. And then it was Essex for the rest of the time. Tillingham Marshes, another ack-ack battery, trying to get the planes before they got to London.

'Then they asked me if I wanted my name down for abroad, so I thought, what the heck? I'm not at home anyway and I feel like a cuckoo in the nest when I'm back there. So I might just as well be even further away.'

'My feelings exactly,' Gwen agreed.

She told Rose that she had been sent to Sussex originally to do clerical work. But she had found it very tedious and had proved lucky in applying for a change.

'Once I'd managed to break away from home I thought I might as well go the whole hog! So I applied to train in Signals and as they were short at the time they agreed to let me go. I'm Royal Corps of Signals now.'

'By the way,' Gwen said, after Rose had fetched more of the warming tea. 'I heard news of a couple of the others we were with. Tilly got pregnant fairly early on and was released after the six months. And Gloria didn't last long as a cook – surprise, surprise. She served up such unspeakable food that they let her change after a couple of weeks. She's on a predictor at one of the ack-ack batteries somewhere round London.'

Rose grinned. 'Good for her. So she's getting the buggers after all.'

When Rose went back to her four-berth cabin, she found to her relief that she was alone. Wearily she sat down on her lower berth, leaning well forward so as not to bang her head on the one above. She rested her elbows on her khaki skirt and rubbed her eyes. The journey to Southampton after a couple of days of leave in Birmingham had been a strain. There had been several delays and she had wondered if she was going to miss embarkation.

The two days she had spent in Catherine Street had not been easy. She felt so changed, so enlarged by her experiences. The army had become her life for the time being. It was closer, more immediate and exciting, and in many ways easier.

She had been greeted like a hero by the neighbours, and she'd managed a reasonably cheery visit to Mrs Meredith, who was as delighted as if she was a physical extension of Alfie himself. Even Sid had seemed openly proud of her. Grace cooked the best meals she could manage on the rations, and the great treat for Rose was that they managed to get Edna over for twenty-four hours with Harry and the twins.

Billy and Susan had grown into robustly healthy-looking six-year-olds who were faring well on fresh eggs, country air and Edna's kindness. Rose hadn't seen them for two years, and she knew they could scarcely remember who she was. She couldn't help crying when they left, especially when Susan, forgetting Rose was her sister, said, 'Bye bye, Auntie Rose – it were ever so nice to meet you!'

'I wish I wasn't missing them growing up,' Rose said wistfully to Grace afterwards. 'They'll be so used to Edna when the war's over that they won't want to come home!'

Grace frowned. 'That's the best thing really, isn't it? No good having people swanning in and out of their lives. They want someone who's always about.'

Rose swallowed the reproach in silence, hurt but knowing she was right.

Grace was also growing in confidence. She had trained as a nursing auxiliary and worked several nights a week at the first aid post in the local baths. Rose knew without seeing her working how good she'd be at it. She was outwardly just as kind and warm a person as she'd always been, but Rose knew there was a new distance between them. They could not at present share the kind of closeness achieved by living with each other and sharing the same concerns.

George was still causing them worry, going off for several days at a time, although he always came back, and Grace told Rose she'd learned to live with it.

Being back in Catherine Street also brought back sharply Rose's grief at Dora's death and the huge gap it had left in her life. She could sense her father's loneliness even though he seldom spoke. Away in the army the loss felt less real.

With all the shadows of the pre-war years crouching round the house, and her feeling of being an outsider in her own family, she was glad to leave again, even with the sadness of not knowing when she would be back.

She sighed, sitting there in the half-light of the cabin. Other reminders of the past were tucked into her kit-bag. She drew out two more of the standard cards which she had received from Alfie. He was still in Felsig POW camp, apparently in good health. There were no other details. Rose stared for a long time at the two cards. They seemed to bear no relation at all to the Alfie she had known four years ago in Birmingham. She tried to picture his pale face, his kind expression, which she could only remember rather sketchily. She wondered in what ways the war would have changed him, as it had changed her. And suddenly she wished, for the first time in months, that she could see him. At least then maybe she could make up her mind how she felt about him. She still told people she was engaged. Partly because strictly speaking she was, and also because it was useful to avoid getting involved with all the forces men from whom she was constantly receiving attention and offers. Little of it was welcome. After Mr Lazenby she still found it hard to trust men, or even like most of them.

She had trusted Alfie. Memories of the good times

they had had together filled her mind. It was not easy, after all that had happened since, to remember the passive, dependent state she had fallen into when she was with him. She felt anything but passive and dependent now.

She put the cards aside and took out the other envelope that she was still carrying with her. Inside there was one letter on thin, wafer-like blue paper, and the beginning of another on a thicker, cream-coloured sheet. Rose lay down on her side, resting on one arm, and read them both again.

The blue paper letter gave only the central WAAF mailing address and the date: 2 September 1941.

> Dear Rose Lucas,
>
> I hope you won't mind my writing to you, but I felt it right that I should, and am sorry not to have done so sooner.
>
> I'm afraid that what I have to tell you will come as a terrible shock. I am writing as a friend of Diana Harper-Watt. We were fellow WAAFs and mostly recently I have been posted with her. Diana was killed last month when she was travelling up to London from our base. The train received a direct hit before it pulled into Waterloo and only about half the passengers aboard survived.
>
> Diana's mother has requested that as a close friend I look through her things down here to see if there was anything that needed tying up. In the course of doing so I found your letter dated 30 March this year, and also the enclosed letter that Diana had obviously started to write in reply. Knowing that you were also a friend, may I send my condolences for the sorrow we all share at her death? She was a marvellous person. I'm sure I don't need to tell you.
>
> With my kindest regards to you and apologies for bearing such ill news,
> Celia Ravenscroft.

Diana's own letter consisted of only a few lines.

My dear Rose,

Thank you so much for writing to me. I shall truly treasure that letter. My apologies that I've taken so long to reply – WAAF life is so hectically busy. I'm sure you know from your own service life. Your letter made me feel so, so sad, I can't tell you

It broke off there as if she had been called away. And that was all. It was so tantalizing, this minute taste of her thoughts. If she had finished the letter, at least Rose would have had a fuller picture of her, of the person she had become. The letter and their brief meeting gave her just enough to know that things could heal. 'My dear Rose', she read over and over again. 'My dear Rose'. She had long ago written a brief note of condolence to Ronald and Catherine and had received a brief, though warm letter in reply. She knew her own letter explaining herself would have reached them among Diana's possessions.

She read the letters again, and then climbed back up to the deck with them in her hand. The ship was travelling at a steady speed now, and she stood looking out over the water with the rush of the cold wind against her cheeks. Standing by the rail, she thought of the first time she had seen Diana in her bedroom at the vicarage. Her beautiful, curly-haired, generous friend who had accepted her immediately and without hesitation. And of that last time, her blue eyes hurt and questioning, on New Street Station. And she remembered for a moment Diana's face that day when she saw the strong man in his chains struggling to loose himself inside the heavy sack. She closed her eyes against the pain of it, hoping fervently that Diana's death had been instant, that she had not lingered there, trapped and suffocating in the railway carriage.

She wanted to open her mouth and scream and scream into the wind. Instead she tore the letters into tiny cream and blue pieces. When she opened her hands the wind whisked the light fragments away instantly towards the stern of the ship.

'They've taken the ropes down between the quarters,' an excited voice announced at the door of Rose's cabin. 'Now we'll see some fun!'

They were a week into the voyage and until this point the male and female troops had been kept firmly apart. The ropes across the passages separating the two were guarded at night, and fraternizing was strictly forbidden.

Now everything suddenly became more relaxed. The sky was a pale, clear blue and, though not hot, the sun was shining and it was a great deal warmer than it had been in England. The sea had turned a rich green-blue, its surface ruffled by a strong breeze. Conditions for the voyage so far had been perfect. Now they were allowed the run of the ship, and romances started to blossom in every nook and cranny. Promises were made, weddings planned, and it all felt like a fantastic holiday reprieve after the dark winter of war they had left behind.

But of course the war was never far away.

'I wonder where we're going,' Gwen kept saying as she and Rose paced restlessly up and down that morning. They spent most of their time on the ship together.

'I think it's Australia,' Rose said. 'I mean they've given us all that lightweight uniform, haven't they? Must be somewhere hot, wherever it is.'

'It could be quite a number of places, couldn't it?' Gwen said, staring rather absently out over the endless water. 'But it's awfully unsettling not knowing.'

They were to find out sooner than they realized. Just as Gwen, screwing up her blue eyes, had said to Rose, 'I say – it's not my imagination, is it? That is land over there?' an order came that they were all to assemble on the deck where Rose and Gwen were already standing.

When the three hundred women were standing smartly

to attention in the bright sunlight, their new Company Sergeant Major Marjorie Keaton told them she had an important announcement to make. She was a tall, thin, pleasant-faced woman with large teeth that made her look as if she was permanently on the verge of smiling.

'Some of you may already have noticed that we're sailing pretty close to land,' she shouted, trying to make her voice carry as far as possible. 'I am now authorized to tell you where we are to be posted. Later today we shall pass through the Straits of Gibraltar – between the coast of Spain and the north coast of Africa,' she explained carefully to those whose geography was not what it might be. Three hundred pairs of eyes gazed at her intently.

'We shall then enter the Mediterranean. From there, if conditions stay as they are, it will take us approximately six days to reach our destination. The ship will dock at Naples. The orders for our company are that we staff the new Allied Forces Headquarters which have been transferred to Caserta, seventeen miles to the north of Naples.' They all saw her smile. 'Evidently our work is to be housed in a royal palace. That'll make a change for some of us, won't it?'

A wave of appreciative murmurs and laughs passed through the crowd.

Then CSM Keaton's face grew solemn again. 'Enjoy the rest of the voyage,' she said. 'There will be a great deal of work to do when we arrive. Every effort will be needed in order to help the progress of our forces northwards.'

The women's assembly broke up, all chattering excitedly as they moved off to different parts of the ship.

'So much for Australia!' Gwen teased.

'Italy?' Rose seemed completely bemused by the news. 'We're really going to be living in Italy? I hardly know a thing about the place. Doesn't seem real, does it?'

That afternoon, the ship slowly negotiated the Straits of Gibraltar. People lined the rails of the decks pointing out the famous Rock, monkeys and all. And there were constant cat-calls from the men to the ATS on board: 'Come over here!' 'Give us a kiss girls!' 'Go on – get your knees brown!'

As soon as they were through the straits they all noticed a number of small boats peeling off from the Spanish coast and homing in on the *Donata Castle* before she had a chance to pick up speed again. As they drew in closer everyone leaned over the rails to watch, and started cheering and whistling when they realized what was going on. In the painted boats dark Spanish men stood up unsteadily, their legs braced against the sea's movement.

'Stockings!' they shouted up in accents which sounded strange to English ears. 'You buy stockings – silk, nylon – very good?'

Silver coins, half-crowns and shillings, started to rain down from the *Donata Castle*. The Spaniards passed up the stockings on long thin poles. There were squeals of excitement from some of the ATS on board as the goods were examined for their colour, length and lack of holes.

'Here – let me treat you to a pair, may I?'

Rose and Gwen turned to find out who the rather smarmy voice belonged to. A strongly built, red-haired fellow was standing behind them smiling. Openly he looked the two of them over and targeted Rose as the more obvious looker of the two with those sultry dark eyes.

'Let me buy you some of the merchandise they're offering?'

Rose returned his stare quite indifferently and said abruptly, 'No thanks.' She turned back to watch the noisy, hectic scene on the water below.

The man smiled knowingly at Gwen and winked at her. 'Well, what about you?'

Gwen, flattered by the attention and rather embarrassed by Rose's lack of grace, nodded, smiling and blushing.

'My name's Brian by the way,' the young man said. He pushed between them and called out, 'I say – over here!'

One of the vivid blue and red boats sped over on the bright water, the boatman rowing eagerly.

Brian tossed a half-crown down and the boatman reached up, trying to snatch it from the air. When he'd passed the nylons up on the pole he made off again at high speed.

'Well, that is kind of you,' Gwen said, beaming at him.

She held up the stockings to admire them, and Rose turned to watch. She saw Gwen's smile drop into an expression of horror and embarrassment. The stockings only had one foot between them.

Brian grabbed hold of the one and a half nylon legs he had just bought, shouting, 'Of all the damned cheek! Come back here, you thieving, cheating . . .'

He disappeared along the deck yelling helplessly down at the boatmen between everyone else's shoulders. If he had been listening, he would have heard Rose's unrestrained cackles of laughter.

Gwen, one hand clapped over her mouth, started to giggle too.

'Oh – his face!' Rose cried, straightening up and wiping her eyes. 'I'll never forget it as long as I live!'

When they had stopped laughing, Gwen said to Rose, 'You don't like men very much, do you?'

'Oh – some of them are all right.' Rose's black eyebrows pulled into a slight frown. 'I just can't stand the ones who think they can buy a favour before they even know your flaming name.'

Rose sensed they were approaching land even before she was out of bed. It was only five-thirty in the morning, but she found she was completely awake, her heart pounding, and she knew she would get no more sleep.

When she'd dressed, very quietly so as not to disturb the other three in the cabin, she went outside into the bright, chilly morning.

There it was, nearer even than she had expected. The

curve of the bay was blurred as yet, so that she could not make out any clear details. She could only form an impression of the brightness of it, the buildings near the top of the slice of land must be dazzling white. She stared, quite mesmerized, as the *Donata Castle* inched nearer and nearer.

There were only a couple of other people out on the deck at that hour. She noticed a young private standing not far away, staring with fascinated attention in the same direction as herself. She was struck by the concentrated look of interest on his face as he gazed towards the land, unaware of her watching him. She saw that his short hair, just showing round the edges of his army beret, was very light brown, almost blond. He was slim, not especially muscular in build, and he stood gracefully resting his weight on one foot as he leaned on the rail.

He turned suddenly and saw Rose watching him. Without smiling or changing his expression, he walked slowly along the deck and stood beside her.

'Incredibly beautiful, isn't it?' he said. He had a soft voice, his accent southern, she thought, and quite well spoken.

'I've never seen anything like it,' Rose said. She spoke quietly and rather correctly, affected by his serious presence.

He turned and pointed back to one of the open arms of the bay. 'That's Vesuvius,' he told her, indicating the grey, cone-shaped mountain rising up from the sea. 'The volcano. Quite spectacular. I hadn't realized just how near it would be.'

'How did you know about that?' she asked.

'I've done a bit of reading, that's all. I've always been fascinated by volcanoes. I didn't know we'd end up here of course.'

For the next hour the two of them stood side by side, almost entirely in silence, watching the lines of Naples slowly grow clearer. The city seemed to tumble down to the sea in layers, made up of a hotch-potch of terraces, with houses and trees stepped at different levels down the cliff. The vivid blue sea lapped at its feet and, above, a few puffs of white cloud were the only marks on the sky.

The white brilliance gradually turned to more ambiguous greys and yellows. They could see trees, and roads like nail scratches zig-zagging down the steep cliff. Gradually, drawing into the port, the briny sea smell became obscured by the stench of sewage. Any illusion that they were entering a shining, pearl-like city melted away rapidly as the *Donata Castle* nosed towards the remnants of the heavily bombed port area of Naples.

CHAPTER 17

'Blimey – what a pong!'

'See Naples and die, smell Naples and you *will* die. Not far wrong!'

'What the hell must it be like in August?'

Kit-bags slung on shoulders, they all made their way down the plank walkway from the *Donata Castle*, a long stream of khaki-coloured movement in the warm air of what was now almost midday in Naples. They walked briskly away from the sea to the trucks which were waiting to transport them to their new billets. Everyone was glad to bc back on land.

Around them the stench suggested a city festering like a corpse left for days in the sun. The Allied bombing of the port area, before the Germans had finally given up the city in September, had wrecked the sewers and cut off the mains water supply. The two hundred thousand already impoverished Neapolitans the bombing had left without homes were camping out where they could among the rubble of bricks and unrecovered bodies. It was a city stinking not only of charred wood and sewage, but also of disease, starvation and death.

It was early enough in the day for the transport to take them straight to Caserta.

'You ought to be driving us,' Gwen teased Rose as they climbed up into one of the trucks. Rose didn't reply.

'By the way, who was that feller I saw you with this morning?' Gwen chatted on in the back of the truck. 'He looked awfully nice, I thought.'

For a moment Rose stared blankly at her. 'Oh – you mean when we were coming in? I never asked his name.'
'You're hopeless,' Gwen told her.
Rose wasn't in the mood for talking. She had made sure they had been almost the last to get into the truck so as to be near the back. She didn't want to miss a single opportunity to take in this new place.
As the trucks rumbled further into the city, Rose saw people in the streets, some shouting and waving, standing in front of the rubble or the dusty husks of houses. Some were hawking a selection of their posses ions on the pavements. Dark-eyed, scrawny children, wearing only the filthiest remnants of clothes, ran after them for a few yards yelling things they couldn't hear. Faces looked pinched and pallid even under the dark skin. In contrast, the Allied servicemen on the streets, who came from many different countries, looked well fed and full of muscular energy.
There was little traffic. The Neapolitans had been starved of petrol along with everything else, and the trucks passed only some bony mules pulling carts and a couple of very decrepit old cars with patches riveted on to the tyres.
There was a lot to take in at once, but one detail which didn't escape anyone's notice was that across the entrance to each side street off the main road was strung a wire bearing a bold army sign: 'OFF LIMITS – OUT OF BOUNDS. VD AREA'.
'That inspires no end of confidence, doesn't it?' someone said.
Most of the comments were adverse.
'Of course, they don't live, in places like this,' a voice said close to Rose. 'They merely exist.'
Rose turned and saw a fair, milky-skinned face, freckled and healthy looking. She shouted over the noise of the truck, 'What part are you from the ı?'
'Me? Oh – Buckinghamshire,' the young woman shrilled.
'And you know all about being poor, obviously,' Rose

bawled back at her. Even under those conditions the sarcasm communicated itself quite clearly.

The young woman looked very taken aback. Rose felt Gwen nudge her hard with her elbow. 'D'you have to be so damn prickly all the time?' she yelled in Rose's ear.

Her touchiness was part of a more complicated emotion. Almost from the moment she had caught sight of the Italian coastline, and with increasing force since they had docked, she had felt drawn to the place. As she looked out at the old, splendid buildings of central Naples and saw at the same time the plight of its people, a powerful sense of kinship came over her. These hungry, downcast Neapolitans seemed, astonishingly, part of her. She didn't even know yet whether she liked the place. All she could be sure of, instinctively, was that she was meant to be here.

As they reached the northern edge of the city Rose caught sight of a huge cemetery which overlooked the Bay of Naples, containing some graves the size of small stone houses. Then they were away on the road north to Caserta. They passed small villages with crumbling tile roofs, fields showing a down of tiny green growth surrounded by fig trees and vines which had fingered across and clung on to the trunks.

It was slow going. There had been rain in recent days and the road suface was covered with a slippery layer of mud. The journey took over an hour and a half, and on the way they saw several Jeeps overturned in the ditches by the side of the road.

'Goodness, someone needs driving lessons!' Gwen shouted when they'd passed the third Jeep.

'They're all American ones!' Rose called back with a grin. Now out of the city, she was exhilarated by the new countryside, which even in winter looked so much lusher than England, with the dark shape of Vesuvius behind them pushing steam clouds into the sky.

Caserta was a small town of faded red roofs and cream and yellow paint peeling from the fronts of old buildings. Rose took in the wooden shutters on the windows, the tiny wrought-iron balconies, the slim square tower of a church. But the town itself seemed completely dwarfed in size and significance when they caught sight of the palace. There were gasps of astonishment from those who could see out.

'Is that where we're going to live?' Rose asked.

'I don't think so,' Gwen said. 'That's the headquarters, I think, where we'll work. We're going to our billets now.'

It was during their first viewing of the inside of the eighteenth-century palace the next day that they were to discover the full extent of its majesty. The vast central block of rooms was the royal apartments. It was possible to walk through those for a long time without finding a room that looked in the least commonplace. Every floor and doorway was a work of art in different colours and textures of Carrara marble; the ceilings soared above, resplendent with gold and rich-coloured oil paintings and intricate designs of paintwork and stucco. Each room was different, and each magnificently designed. At first the sight was impressive and awe-inspiring. But after walking round for any length of time it cloyed and overwhelmed.

'It's like hogging a whole plate of cream cakes all at once, isn't it?' Gwen commented wearily. 'Rather indecent really.'

'Out the back's the best bit,' Rose agreed. 'Now that is beautiful.'

From the back entrance to the palace an enormous landscaped garden extended as far as the eye could make out any detail. A narrow road ran straight through it, thinning to a pencil width as it climbed the tree-covered mountain in the far distance.

The real glory of the garden lay in the fact that from a far point up the mountain water rushed in cascades over the rocks. The water was channelled into a long line of stone tanks, from where it fell splashing into a green pool. Watching over this stood a semicircle of stone statues. As a recreation ground for the huge number of forces people who were to be living in the area it could not have looked better.

Their billet, a mile from the palace, had previously been a hospital. It was a stark white building, housing groups of sixteen of them in blocks which each extended off a long central corridor. Rose and Gwen made sure they took beds in the same block, along with the young freckled blonde Rose'd had words with in the truck.

She latched on to them straight away. 'My name's Wilhelmina,' she announced.

Rose grimaced and said, 'Oh my God,' flinging her kit-bag on the bed.

'Is she always so rude?' Wilhelmina asked Gwen.

Rose grinned repentantly. 'Only when there's an R in the month. But for heaven's sake, we can't carry on calling you Wilhel— whatever it is. What in God's name did they call you that for?'

'Most people call me Willy,' the girl said apologetically.

'And what's your name?' Gwen asked the solidly built young woman who had taken the bed on the other side of her. She had dark brown, rather greasy hair, cut in an abrupt bob round the bottom of her ears.

'I'm Madge,' she said gruffly. 'And before you ask, I'm a driver, and I come from Leeds.'

'Rose is a driver.' Gwen pointed her out.

Madge put her hands on her broad waistline and stared at Rose. 'Where you from, then?'

When Rose told her, she said, 'You look all right. At least you're not from down south – well, not quite, anyway.'

'Glad I qualify for the human race,' Rose quipped. She took to Madge straight away with her straight talking. Eyeing her up and down she asked, 'Do they use you to jack up the trucks when a wheel needs changing? You could do it with one hand I should think!'

Gwen and Willy looked anxiously at Madge to see how she'd take this. She gave a great snort of laughter. 'They just call me in when the blokes can't get their nuts undone!'

Everyone else joined in the shrieks of laughter.

After they had returned to their unpacking there was a sudden squeak from Willy. 'This is blood here – look!'

They went over to where she was kneeling by the bed, peering anxiously at some reddish brown stains on the wall. 'Doesn't that look like blood to you?'

'It does rather,' Gwen said. 'Goodness, what a thought!'

'Well, what do you expect in a hospital?' Madge said. 'That's why the beds still feel warm.' She gave her great bellow of laughter again. 'Don't worry. I think some American WACs have stayed here already. You won't catch anything!'

Life soon began to settle into a routine. Rose was assigned a three-ton truck and was soon occupied in taking people from their billets to the palace for work and back, bringing in the loads of rations from the Divisional Headquarters and transporting the laundry and all the other requirements of the huge community they lived in. It was often her job to carry the German prisoners from the POW camp near by to the compound where they worked. And there were nurses to transport to the hospital, lifts to be given to officers in pick-up trucks, and messages to be relayed. All day she was in and out of some vehicle or other, refuelling them, sometimes repairing them, but, more often than not, on the move.

She wouldn't have changed her job with anyone in the service. At the beginning of the day she climbed up on to the hard bench seat of her truck to handle the big steering wheel, with a load of passengers in the canvas-covered area behind. The seats in the trucks were high, but she still needed to add a firm cushion to give her a good view out. Even though most of the journeys were fairly short, she was exhilarated seeing this new place, the villages around Caserta strung together by muddy tracks, the ragged *contadini* working the fields, mules pulling carts and hens bustling in consternation across the road in front of the truck.

Though it was winter the weather was better by far than it would be at home. The cool, often sunny days were more like an English spring, so there was not the struggle to wield a spanner with hands she could barely move for the cold. She felt no envy at all of Gwen, who spent her shifts on duty receiving the coded messages from her wireless set deep in the cavernous basement area of the palace.

'It's odd, isn't it,' Willy said to Rose and Madge one day, 'how whenever we go out anywhere for fun we have to be chaperoned to the hilt, yet you two go driving off all over the place on your own.'

'Typical army logic I'd say,' Gwen commented.

At Christmas they did the best they could to brighten up their sleeping block. They hung home-made coloured paper streamers across the bare white walls and brought in cuttings of greenery from outside to decorate the corners and windows. Some of the German POWs had also made little wooden Christmas trees which they put on the windowsills. The place still looked pretty bleak, but the decorations did something to soften the hard angles of the room.

'I think it's going to be a good Christmas,' Gwen said the day before Christmas Eve as they were all getting ready for bed. She sat down on her bed beside Rose's. 'In fact, I have to admit I much prefer Christmas in the army to being at home.'

'It's not the same without the kids around,' Rose said sadly. 'That's what I really miss. But they're not even at home any more.'

Gwen reached over and took Rose's hand. 'Come on – let's try and be cheerful,' she said. 'I know it's not the New Year yet, but let's talk about resolutions. What great things are you going to do in 1944?'

Rose, her chin set in her determined way, and just waiting for Willy's look of bewilderment, said, 'I'm going to learn to speak Italian.'

CHAPTER 18

By the beginning of January 1944 the Germans had established a defensive line across the shin of Italy known as the Gustav Line. At its central point was the Benedictine monastery set in craggy isolation on the peak of a high mountain called Monte Cassino. The Allied troops, made up of British, American and many other nationalities, found themselves unable to progress further north. They were enduring a gruelling winter camped out among the sharp ridges and muddy gullies of the Abruzzi Mountains.

In the middle of the month the Allies, convinced that the Germans had taken possession of the monastery as an observation post, began to bombard Monte Cassino. It was the beginning of a long, mainly futile and mutually destructive battle. And on 22 January, Allied forces landed on the coast at Anzio, a point north of the Gustav Line, as a way of trying to break the stalemate. However, instead of moving immediately north from there, they delayed, became trapped by German forces, and were once again unable to make progress. The destruction of Monte Cassino continued.

In Caserta, in the Allied-occupied south, things remained relatively peaceful. It was possible to work each day at the royal palace and almost forget that there was a war going on.

One morning in late January, a REME engineer, Tony Schaffer, was walking across the open area at the front of the palace, enjoying the feel of the sun through his cotton shirt. He noticed a three-ton army truck pull up in front of the building. The small figure of Rose Lucas jumped from the cab. Tony smiled and headed over to her. She flexed her legs, stiff after sitting for several hours, and reached up into the cab for her canvas bag.

'Hello Rose,' Tony said. 'Buzzing about as usual?'

She turned to look at him and a smile transformed her thoughtful face. 'Hello Tony. Yes, I've been trying to keep the army fed again.'

Since she had been in Caserta she had a number of times run into this young man with whom she'd had her first sight of Naples on the *Donata Castle*.

'I'm just off for a cuppa,' she said. 'You got time for one?'

The more Rose saw of Tony, the more she liked him. Her automatic caution in relating to men had been allayed by his own obvious shyness. He wasn't one of those cocky sods, she thought. He didn't put any pressure on you. He wasn't like some of the other blokes who wanted to kiss you the minute they'd said hello, if not before. He seemed to want friendship, and he was interesting to talk to.

They strolled down the curving path to the palace which ran along the front of one of the stable buildings. Rose was telling Tony about where she'd been. He liked the directness of her conversation, the spontaneity which had not been curbed by too much education, but which made her seem to him somehow vulnerable. He felt very protective towards Rose, unlike a number of other chaps around who were put off by the sharpness of her tongue.

'You really enjoy your job, don't you?' he said. 'It's good to hear someone who's not constantly full of complaints. That's the trouble with institutional life – the way it leads to this constant carping about everything.'

'I do like it,' Rose agreed, thinking suddenly what a solid person Tony was. He reminded her with a pang of Sam, though he was less stodgy. 'I never thought I'd do something like this,' she went on. 'I mean what other job gives you the chance to—?'

She stopped talking abruptly, with a gasp that made Tony look round, concerned that she was in pain.

'What's the matter?' he asked. She didn't answer.

In front of them, a tall figure had turned out of one of the stable doorways close to the palace and was walking towards them. He was dark haired, with wide, muscular shoulders which looked constrained by the khaki tunic top. Rose noticed he was walking with a slight limp as he came forward whistling 'Run Rabbit Run' with extra flourishes and patting his breast pocket as if in search of cigarettes. Despite the limp, she would have recognized the jaunty, slightly bow-legged gait anywhere.

As he reached them he nodded, interrupting the whistling to say 'Morning', and was clearly going to carry on past.

'Michael?'

He stopped and turned, clearly not having any idea who she was.

'Michael Gillespie.' It was not even a question. She knew it was him.

He stared at her. 'You sound like another Brummy but who the—?'

Rose said just one word: 'Lazenby's.'

She saw Michael register the word. Then he slowly pointed a finger at her, still unable to believe it. 'Jesus – if it's not little Rosie!'

And to her astonishment he came forward and picked her up easily by the waist, swinging her round and laughing, and Rose laughed with him, completely delighted to see him.

'Oh, Michael,' she said breathlessly as he finally put her down. 'You always were a mad sod!'

Suddenly she remembered Tony and introduced him. The two men nodded at each other. Tony muttered, 'Pleased to meet you,' and Michael said, 'All right Tony?' and they all stood together in the bright morning sunlight.

'Well,' Michael laughed. 'Lazenby's. That's real old times now, isn't it?' His memories gradually began to come back to him. 'You did a bunk from Lazenby's, didn't you? What got into you? Old Lazenby came in blinding away one morning, saying you'd gone off without a please or a thank you and he'd have to get someone else.'

'Did he?' Rose said drily. 'Well it wasn't quite like that. Let's just say me number came up. Anyhow – what on earth are you doing here? Got time for a cuppa?'

'No – 'fraid not. I'm late already. I'm after having a bath – the first in a long while I can tell you. And now I'm clean and fit, and this is sound again' – he stamped his left foot – 'I've got to rejoin my unit pronto. I've had sick leave. Smashed me ankle up jumping off a wagon soon after we got here. Not much of a war wound eh?'

'What division are you?' Tony asked him.

'Infantry,' Michael said. 'One of the poor buggers who goes up front and cops all the shit – 'scuse me, Rosie. These bust-up bones down here have got me out of quite a bit of it so far. There's no putting it off now though.'

'You're not going to Cassino are you?' Rose asked, horrified.

'Not Cassino, no. Further east along the front somewhere. Dodging the mines.'

Rose's eyes showed her dismay, so that Michael bent down and kissed her on the cheek. 'You're a sight for sore eyes,' he said. 'Look at you in that uniform – you're a picture. I've got to go now, but don't you worry, Rosie. I'll see you in Corporation Street when it's all over!'

And he backed away, clowning around and singing 'We'll meet again, don't know where, don't know when!' with a flourish of his arm, and then he was gone.

'Mad sod,' Rose said again, and realized suddenly that she had tears in her eyes.

'Are you all right?' Tony asked. 'You look a bit shaky. I take it Michael is an old flame of yours?'

'Oh.' Rose was startled. 'No. No – not really. I worked with him. It's just – things keep happening like that. Bits of the past and bits of home blowing in when you're somewhere else and not expecting it.'

As they sat drinking a cup of tea Rose found herself

telling Tony about Lazenby's and Michael and the sort of work she had done there. She didn't explain why she'd left. Tony sat listening, his grey eyes attentive, his large hands curved round his mug.

'Sorry,' she said after a while. 'I'm running on again.'

Tony smiled. Rose liked the way his wide mouth with its generous lips made his smile look completely wholehearted.

'That's all right,' he said. 'I was enjoying hearing about it. Your life's been so different from mine.'

Tony had already told her that he came from a village in Sussex and that his father had died when he was five. He and his brother and sister had been brought up by their mother. Tony had been an apprentice engineer when the war started.

'You've had a decent education, haven't you?' she asked him.

'Well – we had a good local school,' he agreed. 'I think I educated myself really. I was the sort of child who sat reading *Encyclopaedia Britannica* and filled my mind up with a whole collection of apparently useless snippets of information. It's surprising how often they come in handy though.'

'We never had books in our house, except a few a friend lent me now and then. I remember reading *Treasure Island* out in the lav to get a bit of peace. Someone always came knocking on the door sooner or later though. I thought I was going to surprise them all and become a teacher. Some hope.'

'But just because you haven't had all the chances doesn't mean . . .' Tony saw Rose was watching him very seriously as if hungering to be given assurance. 'I mean intelligence just shines out of you. Look – there are a lot of well-educated ATS here, but how many of them are taking the trouble to try and learn Italian like you?'

Rose shook her head. 'I dunno. I don't understand a lot of the people here. We've been given the chance of a lifetime really, haven't we? To come and live in this country, which is fascinating – to me anyway. And all most of them can think about is the next social and what bloke they can get hold of . . . It's not the only thing is it? They all live as if they're still in England. I mean, what the hell's the point of that? We'll be back there sooner or later and none of them'll be any the wiser.'

'Oh, I agree – although my goodness, it can be a harsh place.' Into his mind flashed the uncomfortable image of a warehouse in Naples where a misguided friend had taken him a couple of weeks before. All around inside, women waited impassively to give their bodies there and then to any man, in return for tins of army rations. The men had queued awkwardly at the door. Ashamed and revolted, Tony had put down some food and left. He didn't feel he could tell Rose about this so he just said, 'You need to be careful.'

'Yes, but I want to see a lot more,' she said. 'More of Naples for a start. Get to know people. I've found someone to help with the Italian already.'

She told Tony she had got to know an old woman across the other side of Caserta who did tailoring.

'She's called Signora Mandetta. She's making me a skirt at the moment – you know, she's only got that black stuff like the old ladies wear. Anyway, she said she'd help with my Italian. I think she likes the company, so I pop down whenever I get the chance.' Rose sighed as they stepped out into the sunshine. 'Touble is, to get anywhere much there's all this ruddy chaperone lark.'

'Well . . .' Tony looked at her shyly. 'Would I do?'

Suddenly Rose felt full of confusion. She had seen Tony as a friend. Was he now asking her on a date? What did he expect from her?

'I . . .' she stumbled over the words and then decided to cope with anything that happened when the time came. 'Thank you. That'd be very nice.'

'Right,' Tony told her. 'If you want to see Naples, there's going to be transport over on Friday evening. Let's go, shall we?'

Rose nodded, excited, noticing with relief that unlike most people he didn't refer to the leisure transport as 'passion wagons'.

It took them just over an hour to reach Naples. The sun was setting over the bay as they wound through the evening clamour of the city's streets. The uncertain light, and the familiar stench, to which was added a smokiness as evening fires were lit among the rubble, made them hurry towards the familiarity of the Naafi to spend the evening drinking and dancing.

Even over that short distance they were surrounded by a gaggle of children, their hair caked in filth, most wearing the meagrest of rags. The boys gave out gruff adult cries, 'Ey – ey!' they shouted, bony hands prodding at the well-fed foreigners, fingers snapping for attention. They wanted food, cigarettes, anything that was on offer.

'You come!' one of them shouted at Tony. 'My sister pretty! *Mia sorella molto bella* – ey, jig a jig!'

Some members of the party, in slight panic, threw cigarettes and coins. The children scrambled for them like wrangling birds.

'My God – they're starving!' Rose said, horrified, once they had entered the relative comfort of the club. She had been moved almost to tears by the sight of them.

One curly-haired boy who could only have been two or three had stood silently, his huge brown eyes staring, his small hand stretched out to them. He had been covered from head to foot in filth. 'Oh, I wish I could've taken that little one back with me and looked after him!' she said.

Tony smiled at her. 'There must be thousands out there like him,' he told her. 'You can't feed them all. Let's just try and enjoy the evening, shall we?'

Rose was beginning to look disgruntled. 'We're not going to see a lot of Naples sat in here, are we? Home from bleeding home again.'

Couples sat round the tables laughing and drinking. A

band was playing songs of home: 'The Lambeth Walk', 'There'll Be Bluebirds Over' and, as ever, 'In the Mood'.

As Rose sat beside Tony they were joined by another fair-haired lad who Tony introduced as Alex. He was a fellow engineer and the two of them were soon chatting beside her. Opposite them, a chap called Stan from Huddersfield was trying to entertain everyone by telling jokes. The ATS girl with him kept snuggling up like a kitten, resting her head on his shoulder, giggling. After a quarter of an hour of this Rose could have happily socked the pair of them.

Lightly she nudged Tony, who turned a little apologetically from his conversation with Alex.

'I'm just going to find the Ladies,' she murmured.

She walked towards the front entrance where there was a small reception desk, as if to enquire. Then, casually glancing back towards the table to check none of them was watching her, she walked to the door. A moment later she was standing alone out on the street.

CHAPTER 19

She knew she needed to move fast. Her eyes adjusted quickly to the dark of the unlit city. Now that the Germans had moved out of Naples it was their turn to bomb it, so the inhabitants were still constrained by a curfew and blackout. When she reached the end of the street the Piazza Municipio opened out in front of her. In the gloom a huge building loomed up, round, dark turrets at its corners, and she remembered having driven past it. It was the Castel Nuovo.

She made the mistake of stopping for a moment to get her bearings. The sea was a whisper to her left. From somewhere else she could hear a wheezing, squeaking sound as if someone was playing a very old and asthmatic concertina. She heard carts go by, creaking to the exhausted clop-clop of the mules' hoofs, and a number of shadowy figures passed her in the darkness, some of them in uniform.

And then she felt a hand grip her. She jumped, giving a loud gasp, feeling bony fingers clasping her lower arm. She turned to see a minute old lady standing beside her whose body was bent forward so that her shoulders were rounded into a grotesque hump and she had to twist her head round to look up. Her mouth appeared like a terrible empty hole in the darkness and Rose could make no sense of the cracked whimpering noises she was making. In revulsion and panic of which she was immediately ashamed, she jerked her arm down to rid herself of the goblin-like figure beside her and walked away very fast. She began to hear other voices calling out to her from people she could barely see.

Rose knew she had no definite way of finding her way back once she left the main square. But she had been taken over by her old drive to press on and explore, and it would not let her turn away. She turned her back on the sea, her stomach churning with fear and exhilaration, and walked quickly towards the dark, mouth-like openings of the side streets. She could just make out a pale OFF LIMITS sign over her head, suspended in the smoky air. She felt as if she was watching herself from the outside and not really responsible for what she was doing: an ignorant, reckless foreign woman heading into the blackness of the slum streets; and thought, I must be off my head.

And then she was inside, or that was how it seemed: that these streets were the real heart of the city. It was even darker here, the sides of the buildings looming on either side of her very close together, so that looking up she could just make out a ribbon of sky above her head between them. There were a couple of stars showing their minute clear light. Around her the shadows were thick and menacing. She had no idea whether anyone was watching her, but ahead she could see a faint flickering light which must have come from a candle burning in one of the *bassi*. Further along the street she became aware of an orange glow playing on the outlines of the buildings. She could hear voices, women shouting, and somewhere a man was singing.

There was no chance of walking very fast. There was too little light and the thick paving slabs underfoot were littered with rubble from the destruction wrought by the bombing and such rubbish as the Neapolitans could spare lay rotting and urine soaked on the street. Among the stones and chunks of wood, Rose felt her foot slide on something rounded and yielding and nearly cried out in revulsion.

As she moved along, now and then she felt hands clutching at her. She held her bag clutched tightly to her chest, cursing herself for bringing it. She pushed people away with a roughness born of fear and panic. She was beginning to realize just how foolish she had been to come.

I'll just go a bit further and then I'll get myself out of here, she said to herself. She was breathless with fright.

As she drew nearer the glow of the fire she saw that it was burning in the shell of what had once been a tall building like the rest around them. Some lower sections of the outer wall were still standing. Inside was a chaos of stone and timber with beams jutting across at odd angles to the floor and heaps of rubble. In a space among the obviously dangerous ruin, what looked like two or three families were clustered round the darting flames. The stench of drains was even worse here. She watched the circle of people crowded round the fire over which a large cooking pot was balanced on a makeshift support.

She stopped for a few seconds, only to find herself surrounded by clamouring children. The shadows of the fire wavered over their faces, and Rose felt herself unable to move from fear and helplessness.

'I haven't got anything for you,' she shouted. 'Go away – leave me alone. *Va te!*' Adults, attracted by the noise, were joining the children. She was crowded in by stinking bodies, all shouting and groping at her, moving in like vultures.

'Leave me alone,' she cried again. 'Let me go!'

Only once before had she felt such fear: that November evening in Mr Lazenby's office. But here she was also aware that she could disappear and never be seen again in this dark, fetid warren. An image pressed on her mind of the crowd carving her up and roasting pieces of her on sticks by the fire.

She tried to back away from them, hitting out in panic at the grabbing fingers. Someone wrenched her bag out of her hands and made off fast into the darkness. She found herself pressed up against the crumbling stones of the building opposite the fire. In despair she clamped her arms across her chest and shut her eyes tight.

She sensed a ripple of movement and the clamour around her quietened. She opened her eyes just as strong, male fingers gripped one of her upper arms and another hand reached roughly round her back and wrapped tightly over her mouth so that she had no chance to make a sound. The man shouted a few rough words to the people around who stepped back to let them through. Without loosening his hold on her, the man half dragged her along the street and round a corner.

They stopped, and still gripped by one arm, she heard him opening a lock. In the dim light she could make out a huge wooden gateway. Then a small door set into it swung open and she was pushed over the step and inside. She heard the dull slam of the door behind her and his key turning again in the lock.

He released her slowly, and she could hear him breathing heavily beside her. He stood in silence for a moment, and then uttered one angry word: '*Pazza!*'

Madwoman.

From then on it was like a dream. Rose realized they were standing in the entrance to an inner courtyard. There was a scratching sound as the man lit a match. He handed her a thick, white candle.

'Follow me.' Bending down to pick up a bundle wrapped in newspaper which had been lying by the outer door, he walked across the courtyard.

They came to a doorway which led to a flight of stone stairs. At each level the side of the building that looked over the courtyard was partly open to the air through high, rounded arches like huge windows without glass, with a low protective rail to stop anyone walking off the edge. In some of the arches Rose saw the wilted shapes of plants in heavy pots.

On each floor, doors opened off the stairway. She followed the young man's legs in their dark trousers, bewildered, but sensing that he meant her no harm. They climbed three floors and then he turned off and walked to one of the doors. As she held the fat candle near the wall, Rose saw that on the greyish green of the plaster were painted in rough white letters the words *IL RIFUGIO*. The man knocked briskly three times on the door.

'Where are we?' Rose asked timidly, praying that her Italian might be good enough to understand at least some of the answer.

The man turned and she saw his face properly for the first time, a smooth, surprisingly aristocratic face with a long aquiline nose and thin lips. His curly hair was clipped neatly round his head and he had large eyes which he kept directed at the door as if he was listening.

'Don't worry,' she thought he said to her, rather absently. 'I'll take you back.'

Then they heard a woman's voice calling softly through the door. 'Francesco?'

Impatiently he replied '*Si, si,*' and they heard the door being unlocked inside. A young woman with a round, gentle face and black hair curling over her shoulders was looking out at them with anxious eyes. 'Thank God,' she said. And then, 'Who's this?'

As they went inside Rose heard Francesco explaining how he had found her in the next street. He unwrapped the parcel he was carrying and showed the young woman what was inside, though Rose couldn't see what it was. The two of them conversed in the sort of quiet voices Dora had used when there was a baby asleep near by. She noticed that Francesco had seemed more relaxed the moment he was inside the place.

Rose looked round her as they talked. They were standing in a sizeable square hallway off which led four doors. On three of the walls there was nothing but bare, crumbling paintwork. Against the fourth stood a small shrine where a tiny candle burned in front of a statue of the Madonna, casting shadows over her gaudy face and robes. Around it hung carefully placed strands of flowers and leaves.

The young woman moved closer to Rose. 'Who are you?' she asked cautiously. 'Are you American?'

'No,' Rose said. '*Un'inglese*. English. A soldier.' She

tried to explain that she had been lost, and the young woman smiled suddenly.

'You have learned Italian?'

Rose nodded. 'A little.'

One of the doors in front of them opened and Rose found to her further confusion that she was suddenly face to face with a short, plump nun, her heavy black clothes reaching to the floor. Cradled in her arms was a young child. The nun smiled, a rather odd gnome-like smile as she had a bad squint in one eye, and her expression suggested someone without all their mental faculties.

'She needs water, Margherita,' she said in a high, lisping voice.

The younger woman disappeared, returning a few seconds later with a small china cup and put it to the child's lips.

Rose felt herself drawn towards them. She could see the child's black curls resting on the nun's arm. She reached out and stroked the dark mop of hair. It felt stringy with dirt. She knew all their eyes were on her.

'You like children?' Margherita asked her softly.

Rose nodded. Margherita looked questioningly for a second at Francesco, who gave a slight nod.

'Then come.' She beckoned Rose forward. 'I will show you.'

Still holding the candle, Rose followed her to the door from where she had seen the nun appear. She came with them now, the scrawny child in her arms. They walked through the dark doorway into a long room which must have extended along the back of the building. There was one other candle in the room. Beside this other fragile light a second nun was sitting on the floor, her face in shadow.

After a moment, Rose took in that the little bundles of rags of varying sizes in rows along the floor were the bodies of children. There must have been twenty or thirty of them. She became aware of the sound of their breathing as they lay in exhausted sleep. Despite the size of the room she could smell the dirt on their bodies, and realized that the pungent stench of excrement was coming from a tin pail which stood near the door.

Looking first at the others for permission, Rose walked slowly along between the sleeping children. Some of them lay on mattresses which appeared to be stuffed with something coarse like straw. Others had only an arm crooked under their heads for a pillow. A few of them twitched and stirred in their sleep. They reminded Rose of George, how he had slept without really resting when he came back from his months in Wales.

Her mind was alive with questions about these people. As she drew near the seated nun, she saw that she was watching over a young girl. The nun's face was pale and thin, with prominent cheekbones, and she looked up at Rose through thick black-rimmed spectacles.

Seeing the tenderness in Rose's eyes as she looked at the girl she said in a whisper, 'This is Maria Grazia.'

Rose smiled and nodded, looking at the little girl lying asleep on her side, her face half hidden by long, straight hair. She had to struggle to understand the next part of what the woman said.

'*E gravida,*' she said sorrowfully. '*E ha solo dodici anni.*'

Rose frowned. The girl was only twelve. She had understood that. The nun made a graceful gesture, a curving movement out from her stomach.

Rose gasped, pointing at the girl's belly. '*Un bambino?*'

The nun nodded, watching the horrified pity spread over the stranger's face. 'Her father is dead,' she explained. The woman spoke so fast that Rose could understand only snatches of what she said. She gathered that the girl's mother had also recently died and that to survive she had 'pleased' the soldiers. 'All these children,' the nun went on, 'they have seen terrible things. Some of their families are so poor they even try to sell them.' Gesturing round the room she indicated that though they could only take in a few, they tried to create a home for them.

Rose was aware as she listened that Francesco and Margherita were watching her and discussing something in low, urgent voices. They beckoned her to come out of the room with them. Rose noticed that Margherita looked almost excited, as if in anticipation.

Now she spoke slowly and carefully. 'What is your work in the army?'

Rose couldn't think of the word and mimed turning a steering wheel and changing gear. She saw the two of them exchange glances.

'I see by the way you look at the children that you have a special feeling for them. We have decided to ask you if you can help us.'

The dreamlike peculiarity of Rose's evening was increasing even further. 'I don't understand.'

Francesco made as if to answer, but Margherita gestured at him to be quiet.

'We need help here from wherever we can find it,' she said, still speaking slowly. 'Our refuge is linked with the Church, but it's not official.' Seeing Rose frown she said, 'Francesco and I were members of Catholic Action when we were students. We are also anti-Fascists. The Fascists banned Catholic Action, a long time ago, from any sort of involvement which was not Church related. We stayed in Catholic Action but we carried on our other activities outside. You understand?'

Rose nodded. She had picked up most of it.

'Now that Mussolini has gone things have become a little easier.' Margherita continued. 'But our bishop has confused feelings about us. We are loyal Catholics, but we are also seen as troublemakers . . .'

'You mean the Church supported Mussolini?'

Margherita sighed. 'At first, no. Later – yes. Mussolini did deals with the Church, offered bribes . . . presents for them,' she explained. 'Anyway, because of who we are we cannot get official support from the Church for our orphanage. Not in the form of money. This building belongs to the Church. We do not have to pay rent. And the sisters, Magdalena and Assunta, help us with the work. And candles.' Her mouth curved into a wry smile. 'A lot of candles! But we have to feed the children from the black market like everyone else. There is hardly any water. Sometimes it is dangerous because people try to steal from us. They are hungry too, of course.'

Rose was struggling to keep up with her. 'I'd like to help,' she said, cursing her slowness in the language. 'I like children. What do you want?'

'Anything you can bring,' Margherita told her. 'Food, soap, blankets, clothes. We can use anything or we can sell it. I know you cannot come here often. But you come how and when you can. We cannot give you anything in return.'

'Yes,' Rose smiled, 'I think you can. A refuge, perhaps.'

And the two women laughed for the first time. Rose had taken to Margherita straight away. She felt that they could be friends.

'I will come,' Rose said. 'I promise. But you must show me the way back. My friends will be worried.'

'What were you looking for here?' Margherita asked.

'I wanted to see Naples,' Rose said. 'Even at night!'

Francesco indicated that he was ready to leave and Rose went out with him. 'You were very foolish to walk here alone. It is dangerous for us, but even more so for you.'

As they walked down the stairs again they heard hasty footsteps coming towards them and a man appeared, with something stuffed under his jacket. He looked startled as he saw them.

'Evening Enrico,' Francesco said. 'What's that? Bread? Rosa, this is Enrico – he is a magician. He finds bread from the stones.'

The man was staring with wide eyes at Rose and she saw sweat on his pallid skin even though it was a cool night. He had brown hair and a thin, stubbly face.

'This is Rosa,' Francesco said. 'An English soldier. She is going to help us.'

The man gave her a long, intense stare, fearful or hostile she was not sure, and then ran on up the stairs.

'He does not speak,' Francesco explained to her. 'We know almost nothing about him except that he has shown he can be trusted. We think perhaps he is a little—' Francesco tapped a finger against his head. 'But he has connections and from somewhere he brings us food.'

He walked with her, back to the edge of the dark square, from where she said she could find her way.

'When you come again, you will remember,' he said. 'We are in the street next to Via degli Spagnoli. You will help us?' For the first time he smiled, rather appealingly.

'Oh yes,' Rose said. 'I will.'

'Good. Then you will need this. It's for the outer gate.' She felt a large key being pressed into her hand.

Then he turned to go, saying '*Arrivederla.*' And disappeared into the darkness.

'Where the hell have you been?'

Tony was standing outside the club, rigid with anxiety and anger. 'God knows what might have happened to you!'

'Why?' Rose asked stupidly. She had just returned as if from another existence and didn't have her wits about her. She'd only just remembered that she was without her bag. Fortunately there had not been much in it.

'Why?' Tony shouted, and then lowered his voice to an infuriated whisper, not wanting anyone else to her. There was no one standing near them. 'You walk out and disappear for almost an hour and a half and you ask me why I'm worried! For God's sake, I thought you had a brain, woman. And besides,' he added rather petulantly, 'you've made me look a proper fool.'

Rose was astonished at the strength of his anger. He was usually so gentle and soft spoken. She looked at his thin face and felt sorry she had let him down so badly.

'I'm terribly sorry,' she said, reaching out to touch his arm. Instantly he pulled away from her. 'I just wanted to have a look round the place. It was so boring in there and—'

'Oh – I apologize for being boring. I was under the impression you liked my company until now.'

'I do, Tony. But you were talking to Alex and that Stan was carrying on and getting on my nerves. I never meant to stay out for so long – honestly I didn't. I don't know what came over me.'

She was very surprised to find it was now only ten-twenty. It felt as if she had been away for hours, and she realized that it had not even crossed her mind to worry about being stranded here if they'd left without her. The passion wagons were due to start back for Caserta at eleven.

The two of them walked a short distance down the slightly misty street.

'Look,' she appealed to him again, glancing at his dejected face. 'It was stupid of me. I'm sorry. But I'm all right – see?' She did a mock curtsey to try and make him laugh. 'I just didn't think you'd be that bothered.'

'Well you were wrong then, weren't you?' he said grimly. Rose realized to her consternation that the young man beside her was not far from tears. 'Just because I don't—' he stopped abruptly.

Rose stepped closer and went to touch him on the shoulder, moved by the emotion she seemed to have aroused.

'Don't,' he said savagely. He turned to her, his white face looking strained, the lick of fair hair falling down over his forehead. 'It'll be wrong. We'll just get each other all wrong.' He stood in silence for a moment, hands thrust down hard into his trouser pockets, looking away from her. A few people passed – the shadowy figures of other servicemen, some with women on their arms, laughing and necking together after an evening's drinking.

In the end he said almost formally, 'I just want you to know I do have feelings for you, Rose. That's all.'

'Well, I'm fond of you too,' she said helplessly, thinking how strange he was.

'Come on,' he said impatiently, as if unsatisfied by what had been said. 'Let's go and have a last drink before it's time to go back.'

CHAPTER 20

MARCH 1944

By the third week in March, Rose had only managed one brief visit to Il Rifugio. She felt she had failed them badly. The first time she had tried to go back, in February, she had only managed to get together a few bars of army soap, some cigarettes and a few tins of food. She had a lot to learn. Naïvely, as she realized afterwards, she had packed the supplies into her army bag, which was instantly recognizable even though she was dressed in mufti herself.

After the truck from Caserta had dropped them off and she and Tony had parted, Rose walked quickly into Via degli Spagnoli looking around her anxiously. She had just begun to take in the full destitution of the place in daylight when she felt a hand hard on her shoulder. Thinking it was someone begging for food she tried to shake the grasping fingers off.

'And where do you think you're off to?' an English voice said sternly.

She turned to find herself staring into the mocking eyes of a Red Cap, the Military Police. She couldn't think of anything to say.

'Open the bag,' he ordered from under a little ginger moustache.

'You from the Midlands?' Rose appealed to him as she unfastened the bag. She thought she heard a familiar ring to his accent.

'Coventry,' he snapped. 'Though I hardly see that's

any concern of yours.' He took a notebook from his breast pocket and bent over to look into the bag.

'What have we here? Army soap, army rations – cigarettes. Hmm. I see. Got your legs under the table in one of the *bassi* have you? My God – I thought it was only the chaps who played at that sort of game. You want to watch you're not rounded up with all the other prostitutes in the VD wagons.'

'I beg your pardon!' Rose shouted at him, absolutely livid. 'Don't be so bloody rude! Who d'you think you are talking to me like that? You and your poxy little notebook.'

The young man glared at her, infuriated.

'And a fishwife to boot,' he said. 'Now, let's see: being found in an area designated out of bounds to service personnel, unauthorized use of army property . . .'

'But that's all *my* stuff,' Rose argued. 'It's none of your business what I do with it!' She was wild with frustration.

'. . . and insubordination to a senior officer.'

'You're only a ruddy corporal!'

'Which makes me senior to you, doesn't it, *Private* Lucas?'

As a result her leave was cancelled, she was ordered to return to Caserta immediately, and spent a substantial part of the day waiting for transport. As well as that, she was confined strictly to the limits of her working area for a fortnight.

'Well, what were you doing in Naples?' Madge asked, standing by her bed and attempting to squeeze her large waistline into a non-uniform skirt. 'I should've thought you'd have had more sense. Anything for a quiet life, I say.'

'Oh, I was just nosing around.' Rose bent to undo the laces of her heavy black shoes, evading Madge's curious eyes. If that was army rules, she thought, then they were made to be broken.

As soon as the fortnight was up, Rose went to Signora

Mandetta in Caserta, who had made her a skirt. The widow sat at her old sewing table, her gnarled hands working on the intricate seams of a wedding dress.

'I need to look like an Italian,' Rose said.

Signora Mandetta smiled indulgently at her. She was a woman of about sixty with faded hair and a large wart on her left cheek. But her eyes were like those of a seventeen-year-old – a little watery, but still dancing with life.

'Rosa . . .' She held out her hands, palms up, and shrugged as if to underline Rose's eccentricity. 'You already look like an Italian – your hair, your eyes . . . Tell me the truth. Your father – he is really a Neapolitan?'

Rose laughed, enjoying the signora's teasing. 'Not wearing these clothes I don't,' she said, pointing at the khaki. 'I need to look really Italian. I want black clothes made of old material.' Her Italian was coming more easily now through use at every possible opportunity.

The signora narrowed her eyes with shrewd curiosity. 'You have a boyfriend? An Italian *amante*?'

'No.' Rose wondered how she could possibly explain. It might be easier if Signora Mandetta thought she was disguising herself to meet a lover. She giggled with as much coyness as she could manage. 'Well . . . it's a secret. You'll make me the clothes?'

'Of course. Whtever you want.'

'Marvellous. *Grazie*. Now look what I've brought.'

She often brought a cake or two from the Naafi with her and shared a snack with the signora. This time it was a couple of rock cakes. Signora Mandetta chewed on hers thoughtfully, pouring out tiny tumblers of rough red wine.

'Better if they leave them for the rocks next time,' she commented.

Rose grinned. 'Next time I'll bring doughnuts.'

Within a few days the signora had produced a black outfit for Rose, cobbled together out of some other old clothes. To top it off she offered her a threadbare cardigan and some worn black mules of her own for which Rose paid as well.

'These look just right,' Rose told her as she tried them on.

Signora Mandetta cackled unrestrainedly when she saw Rose in her 'new' clothes. 'Now you just need a fat belly on you to look like a true Italian signora with at least four children!' she cried, wiping her eyes. 'Holy Mother, what a transformation. I only hope he doesn't go off you, *mia cara*!'

When the leave day finally came round Rose brushed a drop of olive oil through her hair. She also bought herself a couple of string bags in which she carried the objects, well wrapped, that she was going to take into Il Rifugio. She changed in the Ladies at one of the Naafi clubs, slipped out the back entrance and walked briskly across the square towards the Via Toledo.

The black market was flourishing on almost every street corner, and she identified with some amusement the array of army goods laid out to be sold on the streets. The food, cigarettes, soap and many other objects which were spirited away from the docks with the collusion, quite often, of army officials and sold openly to the locals. Rose approached one of the little makeshift stalls and bought another handful of packets of cigarettes so that Francesco or Margherita could sell them and buy something they really needed.

Then she made her way through the filth of the Via degli Spagnoli, startling fat green flies with her feet as she walked. She let herself quickly into Il Rifugio. Francesco and Margherita greeted her with admiring hilarity.

'You should have been a spy,' Margherita cried, kissing her with real warmth. 'Oh, look at this! Soap, Francesco, and meat. When can you come again?'

'Soon,' she told them. 'At the beginning of April I get two days. Can I stay here and help you? I will try to bring more things with me.'

'Come when you can. Stay as long as you like,' Francesco said with a shrug. Then he grinned at her. 'You're welcome – *pazza*!'

She spent a few hours there that day, talking with Francesco and Margherita and playing with some of the children. The oldest of them, Margherita told her, was fifteen and the youngest only just over a year old. The routine seemed surprisingly relaxed, and they sat outside in the late afternoon after feeding the children and giving a few of them as much of a wash as was possible with the limited supplies of water which had to be fetched from a pipe outside. Some of the children played out in the courtyard, watched by a couple of the elderly tenants occupying lower rooms in the building. Sometimes they sat out and talked to the children, but mostly they kept to themselves.

Rose picked out the figure of Maria Grazia trailing round the courtyard, her pregnant belly protruding from her pitiful, stick-thin body. She had long straggling hair, and deep-set, myopic-looking eyes which held a sad, dreamy expression. She and another little girl were playing with a filthy cloth doll.

'What will happen to her?' Rose asked Margherita, who had sat down wearily on a stool beside her in the courtyard.

'She will stay here. We can help her care for the baby.'

'But after . . .?'

Margherita shrugged. 'What will happen to any of them? We shall have to see what God intends for them.'

Rose was silenced by this. Her practical upbringing had not accustomed her to leaving things up to God to decide.

After a while Francesco came out, stretching and yawning from a long siesta. He sat beside them on the ground in the pale afternoon light, his arms round his legs.

Margherita smiled and rumpled his curly hair with her hand. 'My husband would sleep all day if there was not work to be done,' she said affectionately.

'Husband?' Rose said, wondering if she had heard right. 'I didn't know you were . . .'

Both of them laughed, so much that Rose wondered

whether she had said something hilarious in Italian by mistake. They laughed even more at her astonished face.

'You are not a Catholic, are you?' Margherita gasped out eventually. 'You think the Church would even give us candles for this place if we weren't married? Can you imagine the bishop, Francesco!'

That afternoon Rose learned as much as she could about everyone at Il Rifugio. Margherita told her that Francesco came from a wealthy Neapolitan family who had a large house at Vomero, the affluent suburb high up on the cliff overlooking the bay. He was evidently something of a rebel. When Italy entered the war he had been completing his studies in political history at Naples University. His family knew where he was but left him to follow what they saw as his bizarre inclinations.

'He calls you mad,' she said, 'but the family think he is truly . . .' She tapped her head with one finger. 'For them, madness is to live here and to identify with the poor. To make their troubles one's own.'

Francesco silently shook his head as if what he was hearing made him sound too heroic. 'But,' he said, jumping up suddenly, 'I have not given away all my possessions to the poor. Let's have some music.'

In a moment he was back with an old wind-up gramophone which he set down on the pale paving slabs. He wound the small machine and fed it with his thick records, songs in Italian and French, most of which were strange to Rose.

'The soul must have music,' Francesco pronounced, in the solemn manner which made Rose unsure whether he was taking the micky out of himself. 'I will sell my body to feed the poor, but not my gramophone.' He saw Rose looking at him rather quizzically and laughed. 'She takes me very seriously this Englishwoman.'

While the tinny sound of the music played cross the courtyard, Rose asked Margherita whether the two of them had married as students.

'No, only when we came here,' she said. She told Rose that her family came from a village near Torre del Greco, and that she had met Francesco while studying literature. 'My family are much poorer than his,' she said. 'We got married very quietly.'

'But you're happy, I can see that.' Rose was impressed by the pair of them, by the degree of freedom they seemed to have with each other along with a respect and commitment matched only by their devotion to Il Rifugio.

The two nuns, Assunta and Magdalena, had also made her very welcome during the visit. Magdalena, for all her soulful appearance, proved to be a very down-to-earth woman in her thirties, who could always be relied upon to get things done.

Assunta, who tended the shrine in the hallway as lovingly as if it were another of the children, spent her life waiting for miracles to happen. All her conversation that day while they were preparing food for the community was of the flying monk at Pomigliano. He was said not only to have demonstrated the stigmata, bleeding from hands and feet, but also to have left the ground and soared up to rescue an Italian pilot from a burning plane. Assunta was completely convinced of the truth of this. But for Rose, who nodded politely as she listened, hearing these bizarre claims from Assunta's pallid, cross-eyed face made them seem only more barmy than they would have done otherwise. The children, however, seemed to adore her, and whenever she was not busy with some task she sat cradling one of the younger ones in her plump arms.

The only discomforting presence was the brooding Enrico, who stood at the edge of rooms, silent, always watching. Then he would disappear without even indicating to anyone that he was going. Rose could not quite make out what was odd about him but he made her feel very ill at ease.

The day passed far too quickly, but seeing the children, getting to recognize some of them and realizing at the mealtimes just how little food they had to live on was a spur to her to think up more ways in which she could help.

'You see the problems?' Margherita had said to her while they were eating, all sitting round on the floor of the long room where Rose had first seen them asleep. 'We can manage to feed them – just. But it means we spend so much time finding food. We have so little time to give them any teaching or the love they need.'

Rose looked round at all the dark faces, wolfing down the tiny portions of sloppy army meat and vegetables that she had brought in tins, mixed with macaroni. She would have liked to put her arms round every one of them, dirty and ragged as they were. She felt as if she had found herself a family in Italy. And she was damned if she was going to let them go hungry.

As spring progressed the temperatures grew quite hot. The country was at its most beautiful, with oranges and lemons hanging heavy on the trees. During off-duty periods the men and women stationed at Caserta spent more of their time outside in the grounds of the palace. The last long tank into which the cascades fell was large enough to land a light aircraft on. It was certainly big enough for a swimming pool and already people were making use of it.

One evening Rose and Tony were strolling towards the cascades in the uncertain light of dusk.

'I always forget what a long way it is,' Tony said. 'It must be a couple of miles I suppose.'

Rose just said, 'Umm.'

Tony turned to look at her. Her thoughts were obviously elsewhere. For a moment he enjoyed looking at her face, the soft line of the cheeks and her dark, pensive eyes.

'Sorry,' she said suddenly. 'I was just wondering if there's going to be any more bombing tonight.'

A couple of nights ago they had heard heavy raids on Naples and, knowing that most of the raids were concentrated on the port area and Il Rifugio was not very far from the sea, Rose was concerned. Her mind was constantly occupied with thoughts of how she could help them further. It had ocurred to her that Bill, Gwen's young man who worked in supplies, might be prepared to help. Most likely not. He seemed a bit of a stuffed shirt. Bccause what was she really thinking of? Stealing from the army? On a large scale? The thought frightened her. Of course odd things were going missing all the time – but more than that . . .

'That Virgin parade in the town,' she said to Tony suddenly. 'Those costumes the girls were wearing. A lot of that was army mozzie nets wasn't it?'

'Certainly looked like it,' Tony said, bemused.

Rose snorted with laughter at the memory. 'Virgin parade!' she said with her deep chuckle. 'God Almighty, have you ever seen anything like it?'

The young women in the town's parade had been wearing an astonishing collection of clothes, many trimmed with netting dyed in dazzling colours. They marched through the streets of Caserta to display their chaste beauty.

But as these 'virgins' passed, voices of Allied soldiers had piped up in the crowd, 'Eh – that's Rita (or Theresa or Maria); I was with her last night!' which caused raucous outbursts of laughter all round.

Seeing Tony look rather embarrassed at her forthrightness she asked, 'D'you think it's wrong to steal from the army?'

'I suppose it's wrong to steal from anywhere really. But you can't help thinking when you see some of the poverty around this place that we probably wouldn't miss a bit. Why – thinking of joining the black market?'

Rose laughed rather nervously. 'When d'you think I'm going to find time to do that?'

They passed the rows of tanks until they were at the bottom of the cascades, where white water rushed down over the stones. It was possible to scramble up the rocks alongside the water, but on the hillside round behind the cascades, pathways had been cut on both sides, zig-zagging up steeply until they rejoined at the top. Up there, where the water gushed out of the ground, the spring was covered by a great rock, carved round and hollow inside like a shell, so that it made a small cave.

Rose suddenly felt full of energy and mischief. 'Tell you what, I'll race you to the top. You go that way and I'll go up here. Go on, I dare you!'

'Are you joking?' he asked. Clearly, this time it was his mind that had been elsewhere.

'No, course not. Come on.'

Tony roused himself. 'All right then. You're on.'

They set off, each taking a path on opposite sides of the cascades. Immediately she lost sight of him and stared up the path, Rose began to feel frightened. There was a gate behind the cascades which opened on to the rest of the mountainside. There was no knowing who might be wandering about up there, and the darkness was falling fast. But she enjoyed the sense of danger, scrambling up in the half-light smelling the sweet scents of herbs and plants by the path. All her senses were alert and her body felt strong and capable.

She reached the top a fraction later than Tony, her lungs heaving, and stopped beside him panting and laughing.

'Oh, thank God!' she gasped. 'I thought I was going to get caught by bandits down there and never make it to the top!'

Tony laughed, leaning over to get his breath back. She could see the sheen on his honey-coloured hair in the last of the light.

There was something about the scented warmth of the air, the loneliness of the place, that allowed feelings to come to the surface. Rose knew she was not in love with Tony. She had not come out of herself as far as that yet. But she was aware from the evening they went to Naples together, as well as from many small acts of kindness and affection, that Tony cared for her. And she felt that, given time, she could love him. His very reticence had broken through her fear and mistrust. But there was never more from him. Never a touch, any other sign, except for his quivering emotion when she had disappeared in Naples. What was it? Was he afraid of her? She felt very strongly that she needed to understand.

Tony straightened up and saw her dark eyes watching him. It was a look he had never seen on her face before. Whether serious or full of fun, he knew that Rose had strong defences, usually showed you herself only at one remove from what she was feeling. Now her expression was disarmingly naked. Even in the half-light he could read bewilderment, sadness and a kind of hunger. It was a moment he had feared would come.

'Shall we go up on top?' he asked softly. A short flight of steps led up to the flat top of the rock, which gave a marvellous view of the palace, the town and over to Naples and Vesuvius. Tony let her climb up first and they stood together in the light breeze looking at the gleaming ribbon of water below, and the sky still rimmed with light. Over the volcano the light deepened to a pink incandescence.

The pressure for one of them to speak increased every moment. Rose struggled to find words that would not sound complaining or critical.

'Tony, can I ask you something?'

'Of course.' He didn't turn to look at her. 'I think I can guess.'

'Can you?' This confused her even further. 'I just feel muddled up about . . . well, how to feel about you. I feel a lot for you, as a friend, but—' She broke off, feeling that each of her words sounded more clumsy and unfortunate than the last. 'When we're together we're not like – well, like a man and a woman can be. Oh dear. I can't say this properly. I'm sorry. You must think I'm ever so forward.'

'You mean I don't hold you or try to kiss you?'

'Well I don't mean you should,' Rose said hastily. 'I mean I don't want . . . mostly I don't want men touching me.' She could feel her cheeks burning with shame and embarrassment in talking like this, but she knew Tony well enough to be certain she could confide in him.

'Because you're supposed to be engaged?'

'No. Not really. That's what I tell people. I mean I *am* – supposed to be. But it's not that.'

Taking a deep breath she told him quickly about Mr Lazenby and Joseph. When she'd finished she saw he had turned and was watching her, his sensitive face full of emotion.

'My poor Rose.' He stepped close to her and took one of her hands in his and stroked it. His hand was very warm and reassuring and surprisingly soft.

'You really pick your men,' he said, and she was startled by what sounded like anger in his voice.

'What's the matter?' she asked, her own voice turning high and tearful. 'I just don't understand you.' She felt tears running down her cheeks. 'I don't know how to feel about you!'

And then to her distress she realized that he too was weeping.

'Tony,' she cried. 'What is it?' She moved forward to comfort him. To her surprise he accepted, and for the first time they held each other. She felt his slight body in her arms, smelt the familiar salty smell of him, and she could feel his heart beating against her.

'Please tell me what's the matter.'

'I'm afraid to.'

He was silent again and she reached up and stroked his face with her hand. He removed her arms until he had hold of her hand again and wiped his eyes. He led her to the low parapet which ringed the rock and they sat down, leaning against it.

'Rose – I want you to know that I feel a great deal for you. Much more than I ever believed I could—' He broke off abruptly. 'You're a marvellous person, so bright, so full of life. I can't express very well what you mean to me. But I can't . . .' He stopped again as if he simply could not bring the words out of him.

'You can't love me?'

'I do love you. That's what I'm trying to say.' His voice grew louder with frustration. 'But not . . . You have to understand. I can't love women. Not like a man is supposed to love a woman.'

He loosed her hand and lowered his head nearer his bent up knees as if to shelter from a blow.

'You mean . . .?'

'I mean that, sexually, I love other men. Only men.' He spoke very deliberately and slowly. 'Ever since I can remember, Rose.' He paused. 'I'm sorry.'

She was silent. Eventually he looked up, interpreting her silence as disgust or disapproval.

'You won't tell anyone. Please?' She shook her head. 'Rose, I'm so sorry if you feel I've been deceiving you. I do love you, in a way which is very important. But I can't make love to you. It's not in my nature.'

'It's all right.' She looked up at him and he saw how powerful her gaze was even in the poor light. 'I'm just trying to think about it. It's the first time I've ever known anyone . . .'

'Homosexual?'

'Yes.' She could feel herself, like a sea anemone that had begun to reach out slowly and tentatively towards love, touched by something unexpected and shrinking back. But her thoughts were more objective. Those very occasional knowing looks when she was young, hushed talk of 'queers'. How different it was when it was real. When it was someone you . . . liked.

'I'm glad you told me. I wanted to understand, and now I do. You got me confused, and the reason I liked you to start with was that you left me alone – you know – like that. But now I know where we stand I won't do anything stupid. We can be friends without spoiling it, can't we?'

Tony watched her. 'I don't disgust you?'

Rose considered this for a moment.

'The father of my son disgusted me. What he did to me had nothing to do with love or kindness or anything good. I know you better than that. No – you don't disgust me.'

The conversation stopped and started with patches of thoughtful silence.

'D'you have anyone. A bloke, I mean?' she asked after a while.

'I think perhaps, yes. It looks like it. You don't know him. He's an American. His name is Lewis.'

'And you care about him too?'

'I don't know him as well as you. But we have certain things in common.'

'Like both going for other blokes.' Rose cursed herself immediately for her sarcasm.

'You're right to be angry.'

'I'm not angry. I'm sorry. Anyway . . .' She hesitated. 'I've just thought. You can help me out.'

'Me? Of course. How?'

Suddenly excited, she confided to him her discovery of Il Rifugio. 'It's perfect,' she said. 'If you don't want people to know about you and Lewis, you can carry on letting them think you're going about with me. If you're my chaperone to Naples on leave weekends, you can meet Lewis and that way I'll get left alone as well and I can go and help with these kids!'

Tony burst out laughing in pure astonishment. 'My God, Rose Lucas, you're one of the most extraordinary people I've ever met! You mean to say you've been wandering about in the slums of Naples dressed up as an Italian because you've fallen in love with an orphanage?'

She nodded happily. 'That's where I was, that night I went off. I'm sorry I didn't tell you before, but it all seemed like a dream at the time. And I hadn't realized I was going to get so involved. But you should see the kids, Tony. They're poor little mites who've been left on the streets by their families. Some of their moms and dads are dead, but not all. Some of them were even sold into prostitution. I want to find ways of getting more food for them. We've got more than enough here and there must be some way . . .'

'So that's what that was all about. Now wait a minute.

Just wait a minute. Are you talking about diverting army supplies? Because if you are, you could get yourself into one hell of a lot of trouble.'

Rose looked down at the ground, away from him. 'I don't know what I'm talking about really. I haven't thought it through enough. But it's not right that they're hungry and that Margherita and Francesco have such a struggle. It's not the kids' fault there's a war.' She was becoming quite emotional, trying to convince him.

Tony sighed. 'You're right, of course. Relative morals, I suppose. You can count on me to help – I think. And yes, the Naples weekends are a grand idea.' He touched her shoulder gently. 'You must believe that I wish with all my heart I could marry you Rose, if things were different.'

She reached up and stroked the hand on her shoulder and they sat in comfortable silence.

As they did so they became aware of a strange sound, a distant roaring as if a massive beast was roaming somewhere in the sky behind them.

'What the hell . . .?' Rose said.

Tony was on his feet instantly, looking back towards Naples. 'Good Lord!' he cried. 'Look! She's going up!'

The sky round the volcano had turned blood red, and from the top of the crater they could see what looked like great clumps of fire being hurled into the air, with giant orange sparks, as Vesuvius spat fury and venom out into the night sky. From lower down the sides trickled bright streams of lava, bleeding down the volcano's flanks from points like giant stab wounds.

There was nothing they could do except stand watching in petrified silence. A massive belly of cloud had gathered over the volcano, the eruption a low, growling roar beneath it. Every now and then they heard a louder sound, like a great hoarse voice, and a pillar of fire shot up from inside the cone, hurling itself up towards the cloud and the terrible sky.

They watched for a long time as the night air around them grew colder. It reminded Rose of the nights of the

Birmingham blitz: such complete helplessness when faced with destruction all around.

'Will Naples be all right?' she asked, and Tony knew immediately whom she was most afraid for.

'It's quite a way round the bay, so it should be. But God help all those towns and villages underneath it.'

After a while he said, 'It's enough to make you want to pray, isn't it?'

And Rose nodded. Prayer did not come naturally to her, but she was praying with her whole heart tonight.

CHAPTER 21

By the time she returned to Il Rifugio in April – this time for a whole precious weekend – the force of the eruption had abated. While it was going at full strength, the sky had stayed grey and soupy for days, and soft grey ash fell to a depth of at least half an inch for miles around. Walking through the streets of Naples, Rose saw that even the graffiti of the multitude of political parties, and the large black letters proclaiming 'DUCE! DUCE' (now often crossed out with blacker paint), were dusted over by a layer of ash which clung to the crevices in the walls.

Naples, now convalescing from its days and nights of fear and prayer, had been spared the full destruction of the volcano. Many of the population were convinced this was due to the beneficence of their patron San Gennaro, who had watched over them for fourteen centuries since his martyrdom in Pozzuoli, just along the coast. His protection had, however, been of no help whatever to the inhabitants of the towns and villages strung along the fringe of coast between Vesuvius and the sea, many of which had been engulfed once more by the lava.

Francesco opened the door to her, and she saw at once the strain and exhaustion plain in every line of his face.

'Are you all right?' she asked anxiously. 'You look terrible.'

'It has been a terrible time.'

Rose searched around with her eyes. 'Where's Margherita?'

Francesco pulled one of his hands through his unruly

curls. 'She's gone to visit her father. He had found a place to stay. He was away from home when the eruption started. Her mother and sister – both gone.' He made a wiping motion with his right hand, his face full of pain and bewilderment. 'The house was destroyed.'

'You're saying that . . .?'

'Now she has only her father and one sister. She has two older brothers who are in the army.'

In English, Rose said, 'My God. How terrible.'

She wanted to comfort Francesco somehow, but felt shy of him. After all she barely knew him. If Margherita herself had been there it might have come more naturally.

They were still standing in the gloom of the hall, Rose holding her two parcels of rations. From the big room, where Magdalena and Assunta were keeping the children occupied, came the sound of singing.

Francesco seemed to rouse himself. 'There is something else I need to tell you. Another person has come to live here. A friend of ours called Paulo Falcone. We were at the university together. He is a bit older because he was a medical student. He arrived two days ago from Rome – God knows how, across the lines. He says he has been with a group in the resistance, but he will not talk to me any more about it. Perhaps if Margherita were here . . .' His expression seemed to sink further into tiredness and pain. 'I am telling you to warn you that he is not easy to be with at the moment.' He pointed to the small room to the left of the big room, where they stored and prepared food for the community. 'He is sleeping in there now, but we can go in. He won't wake.'

Francesco suddenly reached out and touched her hand in an unexpected gesture of gratitude. 'I'm glad that you have come, Rosa.'

She smiled sadly at him, picking up the parcels which she had put down while he was speaking. 'I hope I can relieve you all a little. You must be so tired.'

They carried the food parcels to the storeroom. Rose felt how small and inadequate they were. How could she do better?

She could hear the man's deep breathing from where he lay in shadow under the window on two poor straw mattresses laid end to end. He was lying very straight as if sleep were a duty rather than a relief. She went and looked down at him, intrigued to encounter another of their educated friends. The young man was sleeping with a slight frown on his face. He looked well built, though thin, but his naturally rounded jawline had prevented his face from turning gaunt. The closed eyes were fringed by long dark lashes, and his black wavy hair had grown untidily down to his shoulders. The lower part of his face was shadowed by several days of stubble. It was hard to picture him as a doctor, reassuring and authoritative, perhaps smartly dressed. He lay vulnerable as a child battered by the hurts of the day before. Rose surprised herself with an impulse to reach down and stroke his brow, to smooth the perturbed expression off his face, but she held back.

'Come,' Francesco whispered, surprised by her attention to the stranger. 'Let's go.'

She went and joined Magdalena and Assunta, who greeted her with delighted though tired smiles. On seeing her arrive, one of the boys, a three-year-old waif called Emilio, ran to Rose crying, '*Bacio! Bacio!*'

She knelt down to take his small form in her arms, giving him the kiss he wanted so badly. She sat with him on one knee, and on the other a younger girl who sidled up to her shyly. She pressed her face against Emilio's, and against the plumper cheeks of the little girl, enjoying the feel of cuddling children again. Emilio turned and put his skinny arms round her neck.

Magdalena finished off the session by saying the Angelus with the children, and then it was time to prepare something to eat.

'Let me help tonight,' Rose offered. 'You should all sleep. I do little enough here. I'll sit up to watch the children.' They took it in turns to perform this vigil, partly to comfort any children who woke up disturbed in the night, and also to make quite sure no one else found their way into the building.

Magdalena nodded in response to Rose. 'It is good that *il dottore* Falcone has come,' she said. 'He can help us with Maria Grazia. That child needs every help we can give her.'

It was not until they were settling the children down for the night that the doctor woke up. He stumbled out from the small room carrying a cup of water in one hand, his expression entirely bewildered, as if he had woken to find himself in another country. The eyes which looked round at them were large, dark, fringed by the long lashes Rose had noticed as he slept. She saw his gaze settle curiously on her and linger there for a moment.

'So Falcone – you feel better?' Francesco called to him.

Falcone nodded absently. Now he was standing, Rose could see he was a powerfully built man, though, like almost all Neapolitans she had seen, too thin for his build. His dark grey trousers and green shirt were dirty and extremely worn. The shirt had only two or three buttons remaining near the bottom, so that it fell open in a V, showing the dark, curly hair of his chest. He stood watching them all from the doorway as they settled the children, covering them with a strange array of old curtains, army blankets, tablecloths – anything they had managed to get hold of.

Some of them wanted comforting before they could sleep, and when they were all settled Assunta stayed in the room for a while, sitting in a ring of candlelight with her rosary beads held between her fingers.

The others went quietly into the room opposite the kitchen storeroom, where there was a thin rug on the floor and an assortment of old chairs.

'Rosa has brought some English tea,' Francesco announced, perking up for a moment. 'The life-blood of the British army.'

'I'd better make it then, hadn't I?' she laughed. 'Goodness knows what you might do to it!'

As she stood in the dim light of the kitchen, waiting

for the flame from the gas cylinder to heat the water, she heard knocking on the outside door. She realized Francesco was letting Enrico in and she felt immediately uneasy. He sloped in behind her, laying a number of wrapped loaves of bread on the table. She jumped slightly when she turned and found him watching her, his pointed features accentuated by the candlelight.

'Good evening,' she said coolly.

Enrico nodded, still staring hard at her, and for a moment she thought he was about to speak. But he turned and went out of the room again.

The place seemed strange and empty without Margherita. Rose sat drinking the black tea with the strange assortment of people who were left: Magdalena and Francesco both seemed stunned by exhaustion, Enrico, whose eyes carefully watched everyone else, and the troubled figure of Falcone, who despite Francesco's attempts to rouse him was often wrapped in his own thoughts.

'Should I take Assunta some tea?' Rose asked.

'No, leave her. She is saying her rosary every night. For the liquefaction,' Magdalena said, yawning, her eyes straining to keep open behind her spectacles.

'The what?'

Francesco explained. 'It is a miracle which shows us that there will be good fortune for our city. The blood of San Gennaro which is kept in a phial in the Duomo liquifies. Assunta is very worried that too many bad things are happening. The war, the eruption. She's frightened that there will be no liquefaction this May, so she's saying a special rosary every evening.'

Rose nodded solemnly, glad that she had managed to bite back the words, 'Thank God for that – I thought it might be something really important.'

After a moment Magdalena said, 'What are we going to do about Maria Grazia? Margherita thinks she should be taken to the cemetery before the child is born and I think she is right. She should be able to see her mother's grave. Her mind has nothing to settle on.'

'But when?' Francesco asked wearily. 'We have so little time and transport is impossible. It would take us all day to walk up there. I don't even know when Margherita is going to come back.'

At the thought of Margherita they fell silent again, so Rose took her opportunity. 'I've been thinking,' she started timidly, gathering courage when she saw they were all paying attention. 'I don't come here very often, and when I do I bring very little with me. You asked me for help, and I think I have disappointed you. I should be able to do more. After all, I'm a driver. I could transport almost anything, except I don't know how to get hold of it. I can't think who to ask.'

Francesco nodded. 'It's always a question of making the right connections.'

Suddenly, to everyone's amazement, a voice said, 'Why the bleeding hell didn't you say you was a driver before?'

Everyone looked round for the owner of this English voice. Enrico.

'If you've got a truck,' he went on, addressing Rose, 'then that's all I need. I can get the rest of the gear. Blimey – I've been trying to get hold of a driver who can shift the stuff free for months but no one'd cough.'

'What did he say?' Magdalena pulled on Rose's sleeve impatiently. 'He's English too? Who is he?'

Falcone and Francesco were both looking astonished. Especially when Rose burst out laughing.

'So that's why you've been giving me those queer looks every time I've seen you! You're a deserter, aren't you? D'you think I was going to blow the whistle on you or something?' She laughed again. 'We all thought you had a screw loose!' The others watched, totally bemused. 'Enrico, my foot,' she said. 'What's your real name then – Fred?'

'No. Henry,' he said, looking rather sheepish. 'I'm from Bromley. Couldn't stick the army. When they moved on through here I just stayed. There's quite a few of us in Naples you know. Scared the arse off me – all them mines every time you moved a foot forward. I can fight a better war helping to feed these kids than anything I could ever do with that lot. But I couldn't work you out at first. I had to size you up and make sure you wasn't trouble.'

'So – come on, then. How d'you get hold of the food?'

'Easy. The depot. When they've taken the stuff in from the docks it all goes into the warehouse. I've got a couple of mates there. They can make a packet selling the stuff, but they'll give me the odd load free – in a good cause.' Henry winked at her. 'Anyhow, I've managed to get hold of a bit of petrol, which makes a good price, so they don't do it all out of love. Problem is, I've never had proper transport. If you can get yourself over here a night or two in the month, we can get these kids fed up like turkey cocks.'

'Excuse me.' Magdalena gripped Rose's arm, no longer able to contain herself. 'Please – what is he saying?'

Rose explained. 'Don't you speak Italian?' she asked Henry.

'Nope. But I can tell what they're going on about as long as it ain't too involved.'

Rose could feel her breathing going shallow from excitement and anxiety. In Italian she asked, 'D'you think it's right that I take my truck and steal for you from the army?'

There was silence for a moment, and then Francesco said, 'Of course. Already we eat their food, their bread. You know, even the fish in the city's aquarium have been eaten by now. What choice do we have?'

Suddenly they were all startled by Falcone's voice, low, but full of conviction. 'We have to do what is good for the children,' he said. 'What use are the laws of peace during a war? Our Lord tells us to feed the hungry, so that is what we must do, even if we have to take a little from the rich.'

'You sound like another Lupo,' Francesco teased, referring to the Robin Hood figure of Domenico Lupo who travelled in the south with a small gang of bandits, raiding the army and the black market to feed the poor of his people. 'You'll have us holding up trains next.'

Falcone said nothing, but sat staring at the ground between his knees.

Henry pressed Rose further. 'We'll have to be on the spot about times and meeting places. No hanging about. It's a risky business. So – d'you think you're up to it?'

Rose took in a deep, fearful breath. 'I'll have to find a way, won't I?' she said.

CHAPTER 22

It was a night Rose would remember all her life. The sisters and Francesco gratefully accepted the chance of rest and soon all of them were fast asleep. She sat up watching the children with Falcone.

At first it looked like being a long, hard night. Rose was very unsure of this silent, scruffy man who sat leaning against one side of the doorframe smoking cheap cigarettes. For a while she busied herself by walking round the room with a candle to check on each of the sleeping children. As she turned at the far end of the long room and her huge shadow leapt up the wall behind her, she realized that he was watching her. When their eyes met he moved his solemn gaze to the wall opposite him.

When she had exhausted all the activity she could think of, Rose offered to make tea. She sat tensely on the floor at the other side of the door, drinking the watery brew, unsure whether to try to talk to him.

Eventually she said, 'You are an old friend of Francesco and Margherita?'

He pulled the cigarette out from between his lips and said, not ungraciously, 'Yes. We studied together.' Then he added, 'That seems a very long time ago.'

After another silence he said, 'You are English. You do not look English. Why are you here?'

'I wanted to help.'

Suddenly he turned his whole head to examine her fully. Shyly, she turned also and looked into his large brown eyes with a hint of challenge in her own. But in his she read sorrow and vulnerability. Francesco had hinted that Falcone was holding back a weight of feeling that he could not communicate and in that moment she knew it was so. That exchange of glances between them after such brief conversation seemed to carry an intimacy which went a great deal further than their words.

But they could not find any more to say, and Rose began to resign herself to the fact that the rest of the night would be like this.

After about half an hour they heard the sound of planes overhead, followed by a number of bangs. Rose saw Falcone jump, shocked out of his thoughts. Several of the children began to cry. Glad of some diversion to keep her mind off the bombing, Rose went round whispering comforting words to the little ones who, only half awake, were only too happy to sink back into sleep again.

There was another wave of explosions from outside, evidently from the port, as the Germans sought out Allied supply ships. As she sat holding her breath it brought back vividly to Rose the night she had spent watching over her mother while the blitz raged outside.

She heard another shrill voice calling 'Rosa! Rosa!' It was Emilio. She went to sit beside him. To lull him to sleep she sang 'Golden Slumbers' in English because she didn't know any lullabies in Italian.

There was one more wave of bombing and then it seemed to go quiet. A brief raid, thank heaven. Rose stayed by Emilio, humming to him and rocking her slender body in time with the tune until she began to feel quite sleepy herself and closed her eyes.

A shadow moved in front of the candle. When she opened her eyes, Falcone was squatting down opposite her looking at Emilio. Curious, she watched him. As he gazed into the child's face she saw in his expression an extraordinary sympathy and tenderness. Emilio, barely awake, smiled up at both of them and she saw Falcone smile for the first time, lighting up the dark eyes with a warm, mischievous light. Emotions she could barely identify stirred in her.

He said softly to her, 'You must love children very much. You could be resting in comfort away from all this.'

As she looked up at him she too felt trusting as a child, and spoke without hesitation. 'My own little son died when he was three weeks old. I never saw him at this age. If he was alive now he would be seven this year.'

Falcone looked a little puzzled. 'You have a husband?'

She shook her head. 'I was raped. By the man who employed me.'

How strange that she should make this confession to this stranger whom she had sat with for only a couple of hours. That she should feel able to trust him as much as anyone in her life before.

Falcone said sadly, 'That is a terrible thing. And to suffer the death of your child as well. Now I understand why you long to be with children.'

'I don't usually tell people,' she said. 'I felt you wouldn't judge me.'

He let out a sharp rush of breath as if she had said something outrageous. 'I am not fit to judge anyone.'

Suddenly he sat down facing her and scanned her face. 'You do not look English,' he said again. 'Perhaps your face does not look quite Italian, but your colouring, the clothes – one could almost think . . . You are very beautiful.'

Rose smiled, looking away from him to deflect the compliment. 'Your name – does it mean, like the bird? Is it the same?' she asked.

'Yes, *falcone*, the bird with the sharp, vicious beak. I hoped that I wasn't like this bird but I'm not sure what my nature is any more.' His face took on the sad, troubled expression it had worn for most of the evening.

'Why are you here?' she asked gently.

He replied slowly, as if he had not spoken the words before but had been thinking for a long time how to say them. 'I'm here to wait for the end of the war. Until it's finished I have to be like someone without a real home. A wandering soul.' Seeing Rose frown at this rather abstract notion he went on, 'As soon as the war's over I shall enter the seminary of San Domenico Maggiore. I'm going to be a priest.'

'A priest?' Rose cried, then lowered her voice again, looking round to see if she had disturbed any of the children. 'But you can't do that. You're a doctor.'

'I was a doctor.' His voice was bitter. 'Actually I only practised for a short time after I qualified. I don't have a lot of experience.'

'But being a doctor is one of the most important things you could do,' Rose argued. 'Honestly, you people with an education don't know you're born. All that work to become a doctor and you want to give it up and be a priest? You must be mad.'

Falcone didn't rise to her anger. 'You didn't have an education?'

'Not much, no. It was what I wanted, badly. To be a teacher. But . . .' She shrugged. 'Dreams.'

'I would've thought you were educated. You're a very intelligent woman. And you speak my language well.'

'Thanks.'

'You're right though. It's a great privilege to have an education. But you see, to be a doctor – a doctor is supposed to have reverence for life, to cherish and preserve life.' Falcone cupped his hands as if holding up a large and delicate egg shell. 'And I'm tainted. This war has given me a feeling of guilt, of loathing. Whatever I try to do for the best, I'm pursued by death, by destruction. You see?'

He saw that Rose's eyes were full of sympathy and interest. He knew she would not condemn him, that he could lay on her the weight that was pulling his mind down, sometimes it seemed, towards madness.

Rose indicated that they should move back to the door so as not to disturb the children. She fetched them each half a cup of water, and they sat each side of the door again, surrounded by their shadows and the sleeping children.

'When Italy became involved in the war I was still finishing my studies,' he began. 'I felt it right to stay because I was doing something dedicated to giving life instead of working to destroy it.'

'Didn't you have to join up?' Rose asked. She had wondered the same thing about Francesco.

Falcone smiled wryly. 'The Italian army does not even have enough socks to go round. We steal them from the dead when they have finished with them. No – not everyone joined the army.

'When I finished it was 1941. By then we were occupied by Germany. Things were very hard. Naples was growing hungrier by the day. I went home to my family in Cellina, north of Caivano and Acerra, not all that far from Caserta. My father was the town's doctor. Perhaps I would've simply taken over his role. Who knows? For about eighteen months I helped him in the practice. It wasn't difficult work. I enjoyed it, using the skills I had been trained in. Even under occupation a job like that brings a lot of satisfaction.

'Then everything changed. It was December forty-two. I had been out on a late call and I was still in bed. That was why my father was the one to open the door. The body of a German soldier had been found in a side street off the main square. He'd been stabbed in the night and bled to death there. Naturally no one would admit to such a crime. When the Germans found out they had to have their revenge. To teach us Italians a lesson. They are a people who carry out vengeance with mathematical precision. For each German, the life of ten Italians. The ten most prominent men in the town. The mayor, Signor Pacelli, the postmaster – and of course they came to the house of the doctor. They took my father.

'The same morning, they made them stand—' Falcone made a slow pointing gesture with his finger. 'A line of them against the wall of the post office. They made sure there was a big crowd to watch the spectacle. They didn't even blindfold them. I stood there in the piazza as they shot my father. One moment he stood, looking so old suddenly, so frail. He was looking for me, I could tell. But his eyes did not find me among the crowd before the guns went off. And then they were all on the ground. The wall of the post office is broken open with holes. We were allowed to take them for burial.'

Falcone paused for a moment to light another cigarette. Rose sat very still, not wanting to interrupt now that his story had begun to flow out of him.

'For a time I stayed at home alone. My mother died when I was a small boy, and my sisters and brother are all married and live elsewhere. I tried to keep the practice going, and for some time I succeeded. But all the time I was corrupted inside by anger and guilt. If it had been me who opened the door that morning my father wouldn't have died. It would have been me. For the first time in my life I experienced the power of real hatred. I'd felt it touch me when our country was invaded. I'd known disgust and loathing against the Fascists. But nothing which approached this bitter need for action, as if I was possessed. It lay inside my intestines like a poisonous snake. I wanted to join the resistance, to fight back, but there was no organized resistance in the south. Nothing that I could find.

'It was when they threw out Mussolini in July last year. The army was taken over by General Badoglio. All through the winter before there had been signs that Fascism was collapsing. There were even strikes, up in the north – Milano, FIAT at Torino, many other factories. This was unheard of under Mussolini – people like that speaking with their own voice. Such signs gave me hope that it was possible to achieve changes by direct, personal action. So I left Cellina and went to Rome.

'At first I suppose I was filled with an enormous kind of joy, of euphoria at being able to join the resistance at last. I made contact with the Gappisti – GAP is Gruppi di Azione Patriottica. The groups work in many cities to subvert German and Fascist operations. They – we – planted bombs. We attacked columns of soldiers on the move. Assassinated prominent German officers. We attacked the prison, Regina Coeli, the opera house when it was full of German soldiers . . . One of the first actions

I was involved in was to plant a bomb in a petrol depot for German trucks. Everything went up – the drums on the trucks, the storage depot itself. What a feeling that was! We destroyed more than two thousand gallons of their gasoline that afternoon.

'The life we lived was very hard. For those of us without many contacts there was nowhere to sleep except in stone cellars with their cold, hard floors. Often we shared them with prisoners who were trying to escape, English, Canadians, Poles. And we became sick living like this. But the extraordinary thing was that the atmosphere among the people was such as I had never met before. The unity of feeling against the Germans. I was brought up in my faith to believe that people are unified by the love of God. But I discovered there how strongly people are brought together by hatred.

'I lived this life of destruction for eight months. Then, only a few weeks ago, I was ordered to be involved in an ambush against a column of German forces. They weren't just an arbitrary collection of soldiers. We'd heard they were training on the streets of Rome specifically to search out and destroy partisan cells both in and around the city. Our attack was to show that we were not prepared to be intimidated. It was really just a statement, of course. Already they had executed more than half the partisans in Rome.

'The plan was to ambush the column as they passed down the Via Rasella. It's a narrow street with a tunnel at the end. It would be hard for them to turn back or escape. I wasn't one of the key operators. There were members of GAP with much greater nerve and skill. But I was involved as surely as one brick holds up the others in a wall. My job was to watch the column approaching along the route and to signal to Pietro, the next in the chain along the way. In the Via Rasella, one of our women was waiting to give the signal to a man called Bentivegna who was disguised as a rubbish collector. His cart was loaded with explosives. Others were ready to throw mortar bombs.

'We all waited. How can I tell you how it felt that day? It was as if my body was pumped full of electricity. One touch and I would explode. The Germans were over an hour late. We were wondering whether to give up the attempt, all terrified that the police would search Bentivegna's cart. Then they came at last, marching perfectly – beautifully, though it is horrible to say it – the way German soldiers do. The attack went according to plan. The mortar bombs went off, Bentivegna lit the fuse, and we all began to run towards the Via Nazionale.'

Falcone stopped talking for a few seconds. Rose looked at him and saw him take several deep breaths.

'The whole place was in chaos. The bombs blew thirty-three of them to pieces and wounded a great many others. The Germans were there within minutes and we heard gunfire in the streets. While we were escaping, scuttling like rats to our cellars where we hid, the SS were rounding up civilians, door to door, dragging out anyone they could find and loading them on to their trucks.

'The mathematics was the same. That night they took at least three hundred and thirty people – from the gaols, ones they had pulled out of their homes – almost anyone to make up the numbers. Ten Romans for every German soldier.'

His breathing became shallow as he talked, and he was having difficulty taking the air in.

'The orders came direct from the Führer. They drove them to the catacombs, the Ardeatine caves. You must have heard of them. The German soldiers who took them had been drinking. They were blind with drink, taking it like an anaesthetic. Blind enough to lead the prisoners inside, five at a time. They had lit torches so that the shadows shuddered in the caves. Then they made the people kneel and shot them in the back of the neck. It went on until dawn. The last ones had to climb over the dead to be shot. Then they sealed up the cave and blew it up inside.'

Falcone's shoulders were heaving so violently that Rose thought he might vomit. His strong frame was shaking with the horror of those memories. Through chattering teeth he said, 'It was inaccurate. The German commander was very angry. They shot five too many.'

Rose fetched a blanket and wrapped it around his shoulders. He trembled under it as if he had a fever. She handed him some water, and when his hands were shaking too much to take the cup from her, she raised it to his lips herself, so moved she could not speak.

When he was a little calmer he said, 'I haven't talked about it before. It's made it come alive again.'

'Could you not tell Francesco?'

Falcone shook his head. 'Francesco was part of my life when I was a different person. I did not know what destruction I was capable of. I can't bring myself to speak of it to him, or Margherita, though she is so kind, so well meaning. Although they work in this place and it's hard, their lives have been smooth until now. They haven't even known the suffering that you've known. I find I can talk to you.'

'I think Margherita is suffering now.'

'Of course,' Falcone corrected himself.

Their eyes met again with the peculiar tenderness which communicated itself between them, the more so after their shared confidences.

'I knew I should have to tell someone, or such memories would corrupt me even more.'

Though it was the small hours of the morning they continued to talk for the rest of the night. When Falcone had recovered he seemed eager to listen. In those hours Rose talked more than she had ever done, disclosed more about herself than she ever had to anyone in her life. She found herself telling him about her family, about Diana, about Lazenby's, and finally about Alfie. And Falcone talked more about his father, of his rather distant respect for him, and of the little he could remember of his mother. He tried to explain his motives for entering the priesthood, a point on which they could not even begin to agree.

'To be a priest is the highest service you can give to

God,' he told her. 'If you were a Catholic you would understand.'

'Just because I'm not a Catholic doesn't mean I'm stupid,' Rose replied heatedly. 'I just can't see the good of you wasting all you've learned by going off and saying prayers all day.'

'I feel strongly that my life has become corrupted. As a priest I can dedicate my life to the truth. To repentance. Perhaps even to holiness.'

'But why not as a doctor?'

'This is my calling now,' he told her. 'I feel sure of it.'

After they had talked and argued through the night, the light gradually seeped over the city as dawn broke. They saw daylight round the edges of the shutters, and after a time, Magdalena appeared looking surprisingly fresh and rested.

'I will sit until they wake,' she said. 'You go and sleep.'

Falcone thanked her. 'But first I want to go out and see what damage they did last night.' He looked at Rose. 'Do you want to come?'

Early morning light washed over the weary, battered city. Already, as they set out through the smoky air towards the sea, people were coming in the opposite direction carrying pails of shellfish which they could try to sell for a few lire. Voices echoed through the streets and children squatted to relieve themselves among the refuse. They crossed the Via Speranzella and headed for the square. One of the narrow side streets behind the Via Toledo was completely blocked by rubble where buildings had collapsed, making it impossible to pass or even see much light along it. People were digging frantically among the rubble looking for loved ones. Somewhere a dog was howling.

The dead were already being laid in rows away from the rubble, to be loaded on to carts. Among them were several children, and into their cold arms the survivors had thrust huge, pink plastic dolls, their gaudy splendour probably far superior to any toy the children had possessed when alive.

Falcone gently steered Rose by the elbow back in the direction of Il Rifugio. 'It was a mistake to come,' he said. 'There's only so much any of us can do, and the authorities are doing their work. We should sleep.'

'I don't want to sleep,' Rose protested. 'I haven't come here to sleep.'

'Sleep!' Falcone commanded as they climbed the stairs. 'We don't want any martyrs here. You must sleep!'

CHAPTER 23

'Who d'you think you are, Gracie Fields?' Madge demanded, astonished.

Rose had walked into the dormitory singing. All the ATS girls were getting ready for an Easter dance to be held in the ballroom at the palace. The contrast of all this colourful gaiety with the doleful Italian Holy Week was striking.

'She's in lo-ove!' Willy sang as she rubbed cream into her already perfect skin. 'I never thought I'd see you looking this half soaked over a man, Rose!'

'That Tony's obviously doing something for you that no one else can,' Madge teased.

Gwen, looking up from flattening out the skirt of her floral dress, said with a bright smile, 'Are you two really getting serious? I'm so happy for you. I've never felt so good in my life as I have since I met Bill. It's marvellous, isn't it?'

Rose just smiled and unfastened her uniform belt.

'Oh heavens, why are you always so flipping secretive?' Willy asked, frustrated.

Rose looked round at them all, bewildered. Was it so obvious? Had she changed so much that they could read it in her face? 'There's not a lot to say really,' she told her inquisitive room mates. 'Tony and I are just very good pals that's all.'

She knew she had changed. She also knew that she was in love with Paulo Falcone. It was as if the feelings that Tony had stirred in her had found their completion in him. She did not think what this might mean for the future. Falcone determined to become a priest and herself engaged to Alfie. It made no sense. While the war, the agonizing crawl of the Allies towards Rome continued, it was not possible to contemplate the future. For the moment the newness of her experience of passion – of her excitement at the thought of seeing him, of the way they could confide in each other, and the expression in his eyes when they rested on her – these were enough. She was also rather enjoying the way Gwen, Madge and Willy were all jumping to the wrong conclusions.

The dance was already warming up when they arrived at the palace ballroom. Rose walked in beside Willy, who was wearing a shimmering emerald green strapless evening dress, her blond hair fastened immaculately on her head. Willy always looked very pure, freshly washed, every line neat and crisp. Beside her Rose felt dark and rather gypsyish. Willy was immediately surrounded and taken off by a circle of admirers.

Tony was waiting by the door for Rose. 'I say – what a stunning dress,' he told her. 'Is that one of the signora's creations?'

Rose nodded, smiling, and Tony was startled by the ecstatic glow of her face. The plain, close-fitting black dress she was wearing was not cut from expensive cloth, but Signora Mandetta had tailored it perfectly to the shape of Rose's curving figure. She had brushed her hair up into a simple knot at the back, and the smooth, unfussy style emphasized her large brown eyes and the fine shape of her face.

She danced with Tony for as much of the evening as she could, though other partners frequently tried to cut in and split them up. Rose's radiant looks and Tony's admiring, affectionate expression gave all the impression of two people who were strongly attracted and perhaps falling deeply in love.

The ballroom was huge, its beautiful floor inlaid with brown and white Carrara marble, the walls and ceiling encrusted with rich gold ornamentation, and warmly lit by lamps suspended from wall brackets and crystal chandeliers which hung on long chains from the ceiling. The centre of the ceiling was covered by a vast mural of what looked like courtiers, dressed in rich reds, blues and greens. At one end of the room was a low, red-carpeted dais on which a low gold throne upholstered in maroon cloth usually stood. Tonight it had been shifted to one side to make room for the band.

'You're not really the impoverished little child you've told me about, are you?' Tony teased Rose as they danced, holding each other lightly. 'You're really an Italian contessa in disguise.'

'Oh, if only!' Rose laughed. 'You don't reckon I'd be driving for the British army if I was do you?' Her eyes wore a mischievous expression. 'How's Lewis?'

'For heaven's sake keep your voice down. He's fine, thank you, since you ask. And we're all right too – together I mean – if that was your next question. We haven't fallen out or anything.'

'Good,' Rose replied, rather taken aback by his flustered response.

During the next dance she could not resist murmuring to him in a low voice, 'It's tonight, by the way.'

'What is?'

'The first drop.'

Tony nearly stopped dancing altogether on hearing this. 'You're going to Naples – tonight?'

She nodded serenely back at him, as if they were talking about a day's pleasure trip to Sorrento or Capri.

'I'm driving the midnight shift over. Then I'm off. Sorry to desert you.'

'But what about the truck? You'll be so late back.'

'Oh, I've got it OK'd – special delivery. They don't ask too many questions as long as it's back for work the next morning.'

'I'm coming with you,' he said heatedly. 'You can't go wandering round the countryside at night on your own. Let alone in Naples. God knows what might happen.'

'No you're not, Tony,' Rose said, still smiling, and

rather enjoying the sense of danger inherent in discussing her plans while surrounded by all these people. 'Henry and his mates are meeting me. And then Francesco, or someone else from the refuge.'

To his puzzlement, Tony was sure he noticed a blush seep across her cheeks.

'They'll carry the stuff in. I've got to do this on my own.'

At half past eleven Rose said goodbye to him and slipped out of the ballroom to go and change. Twenty minutes later she had signed the truck out of the compound for the shift drive and was on her way to the palace again carrying a group of signallers and other administrators.

'Thanks Rose!' they called as they jumped out. 'Sorry you're missing the dance.'

She backed the truck up and then drove along the sweeping curve at the front of the palace. Turning into Caserta, she took the road for Naples.

Henry had briefed her that afternoon a fortnight ago at Il Rifugio. He had given her details for 'the drop' as he insisted on calling it. He gave her a plan of where to find the supply depot in Naples.

As she sat in the cab her mind ran over the instructions again. From the yard behind the depot to the Via Toledo and as near as she could get to the Via degli Spagnoli. Her mind kept leaping forward to delivering what she had picked up. Who would come to help fetch it in? And what if the truck was raided while they were doing it? Who would come to help? Would Falcone come? Would she see him? She forced her thoughts back to concentrate on the driving.

She left the sleeping town of Caserta and headed out across country. It was a dark night with no moon, and the lights of the truck were half muffled by blackout shields throwing the light down on to the road. It was fairly warm, and she was not chilled by the air rushing past the open sides of the cab. She drew a couple of squares of chocolate out of her bag and sat chewing them. Cadbury's, all the way from Birmingham. It was so dark that the truck created its own little world of light and she could not see anything other than the road immediately ahead.

During the journey to Naples she passed only a couple of *contadini* who were trudging wearily along at the side of the road, another with a mule and cart and, at one terrifying moment, an army Jeep coming towards her. But as it rushed past she realized it was an American one. They pipped their horn briefly and sped on towards Caserta.

Approaching the outskirts of Naples, she pulled up for a moment to study the map again. Following the northern road from Caserta into the city she memorized the main junctions of the first part of the journey. It was not too complicated, though it was an area she was not familiar with. She looked at her watch. A little after one o'clock. She had got there even faster than she expected. So long as she didn't get lost she should arrive just about on time. Suddenly aware of all the darkness around her now she was not moving, she hurriedly pushed down on the clutch and pulled the long gear lever into first.

The road came into the city from the north-east, and she found herself muttering the directions out loud as she went along, very nervous now, every fibre of her body awake and alert. She could already smell the city, that fetid, urine-soaked smell. Supposing she got lost and let them all down?

'Turn into the Via don Bosco,' she told herself. And then she kept saying 'don Bosco, don Bosco' until she had found the turning and was looking out for the next one. She had to take a turn off to the left, which seemed an impossible task in a strange street with no lights. A church on the corner, Henry had said. Not a big one – need to keep your eyes peeled. Once along that road she should find herself eventually in the Piazza Nazionale. After driving in frustration down several streets which might or might not have been a continuation of the same one, she saw the square open out in front of her. It was already one-fifteen. A few more turnings and she would be there.

Finally, after ten minutes, she had located the depot, and drove quickly round into the street behind. At once the doors of the yard swung open and she reversed inside.

'Get your engine off quick,' Henry hissed at her as she slowly negotiated the space between the high gates. He flashed a torch into the cab. 'There could be trouble. We've had wire cutters out here. I've only just managed to get shot of them.'

'Wire cutters?' Rose turned off the engine as they swung the gates shut behind her, and in the darkness and sudden quiet she realized how hard her heart was pounding. She sat taking long, deep breaths.

'They nick the telephone lines to sell the copper wire. Anyway – you all right?' Henry suddenly appeared beside her with the torch. 'Any problems?'

'No, not really. It was a hell of a lot harder than I thought in this pitch black though.'

'Better get cracking then. Open up will you? Johnny's started bringing the stuff through. Best not to use the torch unless you really have to.'

By the time Rose had got out and unfastened the tarpaulin at the back, Henry was already on his way over with the first load from the gate at the back of the yard.

'What's in there?' Rose asked.

'Christ alone knows,' Henry said, grunting as he hauled it up into the truck. 'They'll have to sort that out when we get it there. Imagine Margherita's face when she sees this lot though, eh?'

For half an hour the two men ran back and forth with boxes, and threw in a few extras like blankets and mattresses for good measure. Rose found herself smiling at each new item that was brought across. How good all this would be for the children – for everyone at Il Rifugio!

When the floor of the truck was covered inside and part of it stacked up at the sides as well, Henry told her to close up again. He called Johnny to come and lock the gates behind them, and jumped into the cab beside her.

'Let's go then.'

As soon as they reached the arranged place on the Via Toledo, where they could not take the truck any further into the narrow streets, Francesco melted out of the shadows and came towards them.

'Any trouble?' he asked anxiously.

Rose and Henry reassured him.

'Now we've got to be quick,' Henry said. 'You stay with the truck, Rose, and we'll make sure there's always someone else here too. Take this.' She found a rifle being thrust into her hands. 'Chances are most people are asleep, but you never know. I'll take a few bits over and bring Falcone and Magdalena back with me. The others are staying with the kids.'

'How's Margherita?' Rose asked Francesco.

'Back with us at least. What else can we do but carry on?'

Rose nodded, and they stood in silence until the others came back. As they emerged from the complete darkness of the side street Rose could feel her heart beating faster. First she saw Magdalena. Falcone was behind her. When he came up close to the truck she saw that his hair was shorter, clipped round into his neck.

Dark though it was, she easily caught his smile and it lifted her, filling her with happiness. He looked slightly amused to see her wearing army trousers and tunic but with her hair still arranged as it had been for the dance.

'*Buona sera*,' he said softly, and she smiled back and said good evening to him and Magdalena.

After that, one of them always stayed while the other three carried the supplies back to the courtyard at Il Rifugio.

Only once, briefly, were she and Falcone left together.

'Are things going well for you?' Rose asked.

'Il Rifugio is a very peaceful place to live – even with all the children. You understand what I mean? It's one of the few places to make something good out of this war.'

'Yes, I suppose that's true. In England I felt I was doing something. Everywhere was under threat, you see. But when I came here, at first the army seemed so peaceful – such an unreal life. I suppose I'm fighting the war through the children.'

'You've done well tonight. It will make Margherita very happy.'

'We've done it together. I'm surprised. I thought there would be trouble of some kind.'

Falcone smiled in the darkness. 'So perhaps God is on our side after all. When are you coming next?'

'I have a weekend. May the sixth and seventh.'

'You know the sixth is the day of the liquefaction, at the Duomo?'

'That business Assunta was on about?'

'The blood of San Gennaro. Why don't you come with me? You'll learn a lot about Naples. Make sure you dress like an Italian.'

Rose agreed happily as the others came into view from across the road.

'Rosa?' Francesco approached her. 'Margherita sends her love and says thank you a thousand times for all this. But she has another request. We need help to take Maria Grazia to the cemetery. Since Margherita has lost her own mother she feels . . .' He didn't need to finish the sentence.

'Of course,' Rose said. 'But it might have to be at night.'

'OK, if it has to be. The child will be born in June, so we have some time.'

'We'll arrange it,' Rose said. 'I'd better go. See you all in a fortnight.'

Magdalena gave her a kiss before she climbed up into the cab, and Falcone took her hand for a second.

She started up the great growling engine, which sounded horribly loud in the street, and waved as she moved off.

'*Ciao!*' she called through the window. She could just see them all waving.

During the drive back along the deserted road she was fully awake and elated. It had worked! She had really managed to bring in something they needed. It made her feel more a part of the place. And he had been proud of her – that was what seemed to matter most of all. She shivered, half with cold, half with excitement.

Soon after four-thirty she was undressed and in bed.

CHAPTER 24

As usual they were discussing and arguing almost from the moment they were together. Rose drove the truck through the darkened city on the way to the cemetery. Beside her in the cab, Falcone sat with Maria Grazia on his lap. And in the back was Henry, who had volunteered to stay and guard the truck.

'But how can you say that?' Rose demanded, her hands tight on the wheel. 'Which way now?'

'Left,' Falcone instructed. 'And it's not me that says it. The Church teaches that it's wrong ever to destroy life.'

Rose snorted. Sod the Church, she found herself thinking, but fortunately could not have said it in Italian even if she'd wanted to. Maria Grazia, about whom the conversation had started, sat holding a bunch of flowers and looking dreamily out at the shrouded streets. Occasionally she stared wonderingly up into Falcone's face. He had been looking after the health of all the children in Il Rifugio, and hers in particular. She seemed to have formed a strong bond with him.

'But what have they done to stop all this destruction?' Rose asked. 'What about Cellina? What about what happened in Rome?'

'You don't have to remind me,' Falcone said bitterly.

'OK, but apart from the war, how many women have you seen die from having too many children? You're a doctor. You know what happens. My mother's life was destroyed by having too many kids.'

'But it is against nature to prevent it. Against God.'

Rose was growing ever more exasperated. 'If your God says you should spend your life miserable, and exhausted and sick even if you can do something about it, then I don't think much of him.'

Falcone was silent.

'After all, it's not the effing Pope who has all the babies, is it?' Rose muttered in English. She often felt frustrated in Italian because she spoke more slowly and correctly. It didn't feel natural.

'What did you say?'

'I just mean, what have all these rules to do with real people?'

'It's an ideal we're supposed to try to live up to, however miserably we fail because we are human.'

'You're so sure about it, aren't you?'

Falcone gave her a surprised look. 'It's all I have left. I don't really know if I'm sure about anything any more.'

It had been the same when she went with him to the liquefaction. She had come to Naples with Tony that morning.

Summer had truly begun. The fields were full of ripening plants with chaotic vines twining along the edges. In Naples blinds were being pulled down over windows, and the street hawkers stood with newspapers draped over their heads.

'You sure you'll be all right?' Tony asked. He was going to meet Lewis.

'Perfectly, ta. Once I've changed out of this garb anyway. Go on. Have a good weekend.' They kissed each other on the cheek.

By the time Rose and Falcone arrived at the cathedral in the muggy late afternoon, there was a tense, hysterical atmosphere and Rose noticed the Military Police were gathering at the edge of the crowd.

'Do I look Italian enough?' she murmured, half joking, to Falcone.

'Everyone will think we are husband and wife,' he

replied mischievously and, to her embarrassment, Rose blushed.

'But you won't be allowed a wife if you're going to be a priest.'

'True. So you see, priests don't have everything their way.'

They stood among the garlic-fed, sweating throng, Rose sickened by the stench of unwashed bodies. A few yards away, an old woman collapsed and Rose watched, helpless, as she disappeared under the feet of the overwrought crowd.

'She'll be killed!' she shouted to Falcone, pointing to where the woman had fallen.

They tried to elbow their way towards her. They had nearly reached her, when two men lifted out her body, the face still and dry as parchment.

'*Morte! Morte!*' they yelled. Most of the faces did not even turn to look, their eyes fixed in rapt expectation on the Duomo.

'Perhaps she died as she fell,' Falcone said.

'This crowd's enough to finish anyone off,' Rose called back. She felt shaky at the way death was taken so lightly.

At the edge of the crowd someone had started smashing shop windows and the police moved in, arms swimming through the bodies. Several people seemed to be in a trance-like state, rushing here and there where space permitted and shouting out in strange, high voices. Rose saw a crinkled old man shrieking in a shrill, unearthly tone. A yellowish froth spewed from his mouth.

She indicated to Falcone that she had something to say and he bent his ear close to her mouth. For a second she longed to kiss his dark, stubbly cheek.

'This is horrible!' she said. 'Why do people believe in this?'

'In what?'

'In this saint who's supposed to stop the lava flowing and keep everyone safe.' He hadn't saved them from the bombs after all, she thought. 'And all these great big churches. Why don't they use the money to help poor people?'

Falcone bent close to her and said, 'If there weren't any churches there'd be nowhere better for the poor to go. People need somewhere to shelter their dreams, their hopes. These people have been through so much. First the Germans, now the British and Americans. At least the Church is something constant for them to hold on to.'

'I can see that,' she yelled back. 'But why not give them something better to believe in than a little bottle of blood?'

'Sssh!' Falcone said urgently. 'Not here of all places. You'll get us lynched. This is the Neapolitan way. Just watch and see, OK?'

She heard the defensive note in his voice and was ashamed of sounding so critical. After all, she loved the place, but she also wanted to understand.

It was impossible to see any of the ritual. Only the earliest and most privileged had a place inside the Duomo. The crowds in the streets could do nothing but wait for the news.

Bursts of shouting could be heard near the doors of the cathedral. Sometimes a surge ran through the crowd, a powerful ripple forcing them towards the building, crushing the people in front. Sharp elbows dug into Rose. With each terrifying sweep forward she was afraid she too would trip and be swept underfoot. Then everyone would fall into a doom-filled silence again. The liquefaction was a long time coming.

Soon after eight a cry went up. The miracle had taken place! Slowly, reluctantly, as they heard later. But it had happened. A collective sigh almost like a breeze passed through the crowd before voices all around them, cracked and hoarse from thirst and tension, were raised in jubilation and relief.

Rose turned, smiling, to Falcone, and saw to her surprise that he was standing with his eyes closed. She bit back what she was going to say, not wanting to intrude.

The rejoicing of the crowd was in the end fairly muted, and soon everyone began to move away.

'Let me take your arm,' Falcone said rather formally as they set off. 'Otherwise you may get lost.'

Rose linked her arm through his dark-skinned one, intensely conscious of every contact of her flesh with his. She looked up at his thoughtful face, which wore an expression of slight puzzlement.

'So are we safe for another year?' she asked as they walked slowly down the Via Tribunali.

'Only until September,' he replied, looking down at her with smiling eyes. 'The liquefaction happens twice every year.'

'Oh, blimey,' Rose said. In English.

'Don't fall asleep for God's sake,' she hissed at Henry as they climbed out at the cemetery gates. 'It's more than my life's worth.'

'Trust me. Anyway, you're not going to be that long, are you?'

It was a clear night, with a few wisps of cloud covering the stars. The thin slice of moon gave little light. Crickets were loud in the scrubby vegetation as the three of them slipped away from the truck which Rose had parked in the dense shadows outside the main cemetery entrance. Maria Grazia walked between them, holding tightly on to Falcone with one hand, and on to her flowers with the other, her back very straight to balance the weight of her pregnancy. The main iron gates were chained and padlocked, but to one side of them a stiff-hinged wooden door in the wall was left open for late visitors.

Inside the cemetery, Rose became aware of huge shapes around them, the towering old mausoleums of the wealthy with their roofs and doors and plaques. For a few seconds Falcone switched on the torch Henry had given them, and shadows leapt and shuddered up their walls. Rose saw that many of the graves were decorated with pictures of the dead and bright sprays of red and white gladioli.

'Better switch it off,' she suggested. 'The shadows are horrible.'

'Don't be afraid,' he said, extinguishing the torch. 'We'll be all right. We need to go down.'

'Is it far?' Maria Grazia asked in a trembling voice. 'I don't like it here.'

'No, not far, *piccola*,' Falcone said tenderly. 'Come on – you're safe.'

They headed down the hillside, along the terraces lined with graves and vaults. Rose's heart was pounding in her chest. She was trying to keep her thoughts away from ghosts and the stories she had heard about Italian burial traditions. Sometimes bodies were unearthed after being buried for a year. The bones were scraped, then laid in much smaller boxes which were stacked in a chancel house.

She had asked Falcone about it, horrified. 'They don't really do they?'

'It does happen here, but more further south. You have to understand – this isn't a big country and there are a lot of people. In many parts the ground is made of solid rock, so it's difficult to find places for burial. You have to find a way to deal with it. You see?'

She had been amazed by his acceptance of such macabre practices.

'That's why many cemeteries have wall graves, built above ground. It's all to save space.'

Rose had seen them, the coffins inserted into slots in a stone structure like a giant chest of drawers.

She sensed Maria Grazia shivering beside her, so she took off her jacket and wrapped it around the child. They walked on slowly, the sound of their feet crunching on dry earth.

Suddenly they all stopped. There was a strange, unearthly sound in front of them, a high moaning, growing louder, making the hairs rise on the back of their necks.

'My God,' Rose said. She wondered for a second if it was a cat, but the sound was too loud and full. Maria Grazia turned to Falcone and buried her head against him.

Then they heard another noise, a low grunting, rhythmic and urgent. After a few seconds both cries began to die down together. Rose's eyes met Falcone's as the intimacy of what was happening so close by dawned on them both.

Falcone looked away quickly and bent to cuddle Maria Grazia in the darkness. 'It's all right,' he soothed. 'It's nothing to be afraid of.'

Without looking at Rose, he said, 'Lovers meet here during the day. I had not expected them to be here at night too.'

As they continued down the path in silence, Rose was seized by an overwhelming desire to giggle. Tight bubbles of hysterical laughter were welling up inside. She could see herself from the outside, a stranger in a foreign cemetery at two o'clock in the morning, with a prospective priest and a pregnant twelve-year-old, listening to the coupling of complete strangers in the dark. Who would believe her if she told them? A loud snort of laughter escaped and Falcone turned in bewilderment.

'Are you all right?'

Rose began laughing then, and couldn't stop. Maria Grazia, quite unused to people roaring with laughter around her, started to giggle at the sight, and eventually, completely astonished, Falcone joined in as well.

Gradually they got themselves back under control. Falcone reached out and put his arm lightly round Rose's shoulders. 'You crazy woman. Do you English always act like this when things are horrible? I haven't laughed so much since – well, I can't remember.' Quickly he removed his arm. 'Come on – we must go.'

Further on the path became much rougher and more stony under foot. Small pebbles rolled away as they walked.

'This must be the oldest part of the place,' Falcone said. 'I'm lost.'

He switched on the torch and shone it in front of them. The sight that met their eyes instantly wiped away any last traces of laughter. At this side of the cemetery some of the oldest wall graves had been built against the rocky side of the hill. With age and erosion, and perhaps from earth tremors in this turbulent area, most of the graves had collapsed. Among the rubble they could clearly make out the broken shapes of coffins. From some, the shrunken bodies had slid out, white, petrified figures, tossed carelessly about among the ruins. Rose would take away the memory of perfectly preserved fingerbones at the end of an arm, pointing up from behind a slab of stone, the hand bent forward at the wrist as if the person behind was relaxing in a bath.

Maria Grazia screamed and rushed in to Falcone's arms. She had seen the dead before many times, but never in these conditions.

'D'you still want to find your mother's resting place?' Falcone asked her gently. 'Or would you like to go home?'

'I want to see it,' she said, sniffing. 'I want to know where my mother is lying.'

'It must be that way,' Falcone said, pointing.

Once they reached the lowest level it was not difficult to find. All signs of attempts at individual Christian burials came to an end, and in front of them, as Falcone flashed the torch around, was a large area where the ground had been disturbed and refilled to cover one of a number of mass graves. The bombing, the typhus epidemic, the general ill health of the population meant that death carts trawled the streets as if in a medieval plague, and none but the wealthy could hope for a gravestone above their heads. Maria Grazia's mother had been poor. It was a bleak, sad sight. Flowers and trinkets had been scattered among the stones on the rough soil. Otherwise the graves lay unmarked and indistinguishable from each other.

Maria Grazia stood staring at the place. Falcone laid the torch down on the ground.

‘Find a spot for your flowers,’ he said, putting an arm round her shoulders. ‘You can make it hers. You are very near her.’

The child walked miserably forward, a skinny, pathetic sight with her bulging belly, and her half-crushed blossoms.

She found a place where there were no other flowers, and knelt on the dry earth to place them. After a few moments she threw herself forward on to the ground, weeping. Then she sat back on her knees, rocking slowly in what seemed to be prayer.

Rose moved as if to go and comfort her but Falcone stopped her. ‘Leave her,’ he said. ‘It’s good for her to do this.’

They stood watching her, and Rose felt tears come to her eyes at the thought of her own mother, and the freezing day on which they had buried her. How long ago it all seemed: England, her family, everything, as if it had happened in another life.

She knew that Falcone’s eyes were on her, and she turned to look at him as they stood in the shadow behind the torchlight. He moved awkwardly towards her. Then his arms were round her, drawing her to him, and they embraced, his lips seeking out hers. All the tenderness and longing they had seen in each other’s eyes were expressed in that kiss. Falcone stroked Rose’s hair, and then her face, with wonder, and she leaned against him, filled by emotions she had never known before. For the first time she knew what it was to respond to a kiss, to long for the other person.

She did not know how long they stood in each other’s arms. It was only when Maria Grazia finally stood up and walked slowly away from the grave that they parted. Falcone picked up the torch and they went to meet her. Supporting her between them, they began the climb back to the gate.

‘Thank Christ for that!’ Henry exclaimed as soon as he saw them. ‘You’ve been gone blooming ages. What the hell’ve you been doing?’

'It took us a bit of time to find her,' Rose told him vaguely. She had a strange, dreamy sensation of complete happiness, as if nothing mattered, neither the truck, nor geting back to Caserta, nor being exhausted the next day. Everything she needed was here.

They drove back to the city in silence, except for Falcone's directions. She wondered whether he was thinking, as she was, of the night's strange, conflicting moods. He sat beside her, his hand laid on the head of the young mother who had fallen asleep across his lap.

CHAPTER 25

On 4 June, two days before the D-Day landings on the coast of France, General Mark Clark led the tanks and trucks of the Allied Forces along the sweeping, majestic roads into Rome. For many of the troops there was an awesome sense that they were moving along the paths of history. But when they reached Rome there was no decisive battle to determine which occupying force should control the fate of Italy. The Germans immediately shifted north to consolidate another line straddling the country's knee. It felt as if the slow crawl up this long, spiny country would never come to an end.

A week after that, another small but momentous event took place at Il Rifugio. Maria Grazia gave birth to a son, a tiny, fragile creature with only enough strength to snuffle into life. The birth was hard and Falcone was forced to call upon another doctor for help to be sure of saving the child. But enter life he did, and he clung to it. Maria Grazia called him Mauro.

Rose first saw him when he was ten days old, and was entranced by his crinkly perfection.

'He's so beautiful,' she said, smiling tearfully down at Maria Grazia as she let her hold him. 'Isn't it an amazing thing?'

The young girl stared blankly at her. She was very pale, and now she no longer carried the weight of the child it was clear how thin she was. Every effort was being made by Margherita, Falcone and the others to feed her up so she could nourish the child with her barely formed breasts.

Thanks to Rose and Henry's monthly 'drops', which had so far gone miraculously well, the children were all thriving, except for two boys who had fallen ill and been removed to the hospital for fear of infecting the others.

If it had not been for Falcone distancing himself from her, Rose would have spent the summer in a haze of happiness. How many times during those weeks did she regret that kiss! Such a small thing, that moment of intimacy, but it changed everything. It had brought into the open the powerful current between her and Falcone which, once acknowledged, could not be ignored.

But wasn't she committed, at least verbally, to Alfie Meredith? It would soon be five years since she had, in a backhand sort of way, agreed to become his wife, a man from a different life, imprisoned in a country she had never seen.

She had tried to abide by her promise, but her feelings for Falcone overpowered everything else. Who was that person who had bound herself to Alfie back in Birmingham? A sad, fragile girl who had no idea of what she was capable. How could she have foreseen meeting Falcone, or the feelings aroused in her by his presence, of wanting to reach out and touch him each time they found themselves close, to stroke his thick black hair or smooth the back of her fingers down his cheek?

She remembered the kiss with longing, but also with a poignant sense of loss. Her own confusion was simple compared with the tension her presence appeared to have set up inside Falcone. He had been so sure where his future lay! Now when she was at Il Rifugio, they were almost never alone, nor did Falcone create opportunities for them to be so as he had before.

They still talked and argued about things, but usually in the presence of Francesco and Margherita, once the children were all asleep. Often they talked about Italian politics. What should happen once the war was over, now that Fascism seemed to be defeated? Magdalena would join in in her deep, animated voice. When Rose and Falcone were alone she found it possible to express her thoughts in a direct way, but she was intimidated by this gathering of educated Italians. She felt truly at home only when they were dealing with the children. Yet she needed more now from Il Rifugio than her work with the children. She needed Falcone. To talk with him, be alone with him, to understand why he was withdrawing from her, shutting her out.

In every other way her life felt charmed. The country came into bloom. Caserta flowered with red and pink geraniums hanging from almost every window and bright blooms of bougainvillea stained every wall across the town. In the countryside oranges and lemons hung ripe on the trees and the vines were heavy with grapes. The heat of the sun softened the road surface, giving it a spongy feel, and the air blowing in at the sides of the trucks was warm and caressing.

Behind the palace the long sweep of grass turned brown and wiry, and the tanks below the cascades gave off a slightly stagnant smell. The ATS pulled up their light cotton frocks on the grass to sun themselves during their hours off duty. Rose found that she had formed an easy, if not intimate camaraderie with Willy, Madge and, of course, Gwen.

As the temperature rose, Naples steamed and came alive with fat green flies which shimmered in dark clouds and settled on anything damp, heading for the face, mouth and armpits.

'It's beyond me why you spend your weekends over there when you could get out to Amalfi or Capri,' Tony said to Rose. 'God, the stink of the place! Lewis and I get out as fast as we can. Anyway, I thought you were mad keen to see the country round here?'

'But you've never been to Il Rifugio,' Rose retorted indignantly. 'And it's much cleaner there than you'd think. The two nuns spend half their lives cleaning up.' But he did have a point. There were so many places she still hadn't seen.

*

One Sunday afternoon, Rose was sitting in the courtyard with Mauro in her lap while Maria Grazia slept. The baby's tiny hand gripped her little finger as he lay half asleep. Rose smiled down at him. She'd found a spot in the shade on the warm stone flags, her back against the wall, and she could smell the pungent leaves of a geranium plant growing in a pot near by.

She looked up, to see Falcone watching her. He was standing, his hands in the pockets of his blue dungarees, leaning against one of the pillars of the arched entrance to the staircase. He had been talking with Francesco. Now he stared at her in silence, and she saw in his face such a depth of longing and bewilderment that she had to turn her face back towards Mauro.

Falcone pushed himself away from the pillar and turned to walk inside.

'What's eating him?' Francesco asked.

'He's in love with Rosa,' Margherita said without looking up from her sewing at Rose, who started, but kept her eyes on Mauro.

'He's *what*?' Francesco exploded. 'He can't be! He's going to the seminary.'

Magdalena snorted, pushing her veil back over her shoulders. 'Can't be? What nonsense you do talk.'

'Of course he's in love. It stands out a mile,' Margherita told him.

'I haven't noticed anything,' Francesco said rather petulantly.

'What do you expect?' Magdalena was scornful. 'You're a man.'

'Rosa?' Francesco leaned down to see her expression. 'Is this true?'

Slowly she raised her head, her cheeks burning red. There was no need for her to reply.

'And you love him?'

'Of course she does,' Margherita said, biting off a piece of thread. 'It's obvious.'

'So what's going on?' Francesco had the air of someone who has had a fast one pulled on him in a card game.

'You don't speak to each other any more. Falcone is like a mule with a sore bottom. What is the matter with you both?'

'Falcone is trying to decide his vocation,' Magdalena explained, in the kind of patient tone she usually reserved for Assunta and the children. 'Not everyone gets a visit from an angel to tell them which way to go.'

'Do you think he will be a priest?' Rose asked. 'It's all very strange to me.'

'Only God can tell us that,' Magdalena said, smiling at her.

'He's no priest,' Margherita said firmly. 'Two heads on the pillow. That's his vocation, and deep down he knows it really.'

'He won't even speak to me,' Rose said. It was a relief to confide in the others. 'I don't understand him. I never even see him alone any more.'

'Go now,' Margherita told her. 'Assunta is asleep. He's alone up there.'

Rose stood up and laid Mauro in Magdalena's arms.

The others watched as Rose and Falcone crossed the courtyard together and unlocked the gate. Out in the baking streets the stalls were closed down and the usual clamour was muted by the routine of the Sunday siesta.

Not speaking, they walked down to the small strip of parched parkland which edged the Mediterranean at Santa Lucia. Scrubby pine trees offered a meagre shade, and they chose a spot to sit away from the sea, where there were no bodies snoring in the heat. Through the trees they could see the white glare of light on the water, and make out the hazy, grey shape of Vesuvius, quiet now, in the distance across the bay.

Falcone said, 'It's my fault. I'm sorry. When you're not here I begin to believe that I know what I'm supposed to do with my life. As soon as I see you again, I'm thrown into confusion.'

'Sometimes, the way you look at me,' Rose said

haltingly, 'I begin to think you hate me, that I'm nothing but trouble in your life.'

'You know I don't hate you.'

'But it would be better for you if I did not come here – to Il Rifugio?'

Falcone sat leaning his elbows on his raised knees, his head between his tanned hands, staring out to sea.

He shook his head. 'No. That's not true either. You know as well as I do that you're far more help to them than I can ever be.' He picked up a small, dry twig and threw it hard towards the sea. 'I couldn't even manage to deliver Maria Grazia's baby safely on my own. I'm no great asset to them. It's not you that's at fault, Rosa. It's me. I told you: everywhere I go I bring hurt and destruction. I thought things were clear. God's call felt . . . strong, pure. I don't know if you can understand that. And sometimes I can feel it. But when I am near you I don't know which is the right path for me. In the meantime I just bring you pain.'

In the silence that followed, Rose found herself crying. They were mostly tears of frustration, at not knowing how to console him since she was the source of his conflict. She wanted to take him in her arms and hold him, but she knew that for him it would be like being embraced by a thorn bush.

'Rosa?' Falcone said in distress. 'Please. Please don't.' He made helpless gestures with his arms and laid one of them briefly round her shoulders before withdrawing it again. 'Please don't cry, dearest Rosa. It's better for you if you're not near me – I'm so confused, I only hurt you. That night in the cemetery, I allowed my feelings for you to – to sweep me along. I shouldn't have. It was wrong.'

His words only made Rose weep even more. Why was it wrong? Why?

He stood up suddenly. 'When the war's over you'll go back to England and marry your English husband. Think only of that and forget me. Please.'

He turned from her, aghast at himself, and walked away from Santa Lucia and back towards the Via Toledo.

When he crossed the courtyard of Il Rifugio alone, only half an hour after they had left, the others exchanged sad, puzzled glances.

Rose sat for a long time under the dry, bleached pine trees, crying for both his anguish and her own.

She tried to bring down her protective shutters as she had done in the past, to stop any expression of her feelings for him, even to herself. As the autumn came and began to turn to winter, and the fields faded to blander colours once more, she carried on with the drops. She spent her leave weekends at Il Rifugio, but as far as possible she avoided contact with Falcone. It wasn't difficult. They were polite to each other when they had to work together. Rose talked to him briskly and brightly, almost as if he was a new arrival in the place whom she barely knew.

'Could you go and fetch a bucket of water please?' she might ask, or, 'Margherita says she needs you to look at one of the children upstairs.' And Falcone would nod respectfully as if she were in charge and do as she asked.

She stayed just as committed to the place, but her mind began to hunger to see more of the country around. She mentioned the fact to Margherita and Francesco, and they encouraged her to go.

'Perhaps Falcone could take you?' Francesco suggested.

Margherita looked at him as if he were a half-wit.

'I can easily find a chaperone from the army, thank you,' Rose said rather bitterly.

'I'll take a weekend to go some time,' she said to Margherita later on. 'But I'd like to come here for Christmas. Is that all right?'

Margherita gave her tired smile. 'You know you don't have to ask. Just come when you can.'

*

As it turned out, she did not spend Christmas at Il Rifugio. One evening in November Gwen came rushing into the dormitory as most of them were preparing for bed. She looked as if she was about to explode with excitement. 'Bill's just asked me to marry him.'

'And . . .?' Rose said.

'I've said I will.'

'Course you have!' Madge dashed up to supply one of her bear hugs. 'As if you'd have turned him down. We'd've all lynched you after the amount we've heard about your Bill this year!'

All of them went to add their congratulations. Willy had tears in her eyes. 'Oh, it's so romantic,' she cried. 'Are you going to get married at the palace?'

'Yes,' Gwen told them. 'We've fixed it for Christmas Eve. We thought it would be an awfully nice time, when everyone's feeling festive anyway. Goodness knows if we'll be ready by then though.'

'What's the problem?' Madge asked. 'All you need is a bloke and a dress, isn't it?'

Gwen laughed, looking really pretty. 'Yes, I suppose you're right. But wherc shall I get a dress from?'

'Ah – I can help you there,' Rose said. She knew Signora Mandetta would be pleased to have the work, though she would have been more delighted had it been Rose's own wedding dress.

When the fuss had died down, Gwen came and sat on Rose's bed.

'I'm so happy for you,' Rose told her. 'Bill seems a good bloke.'

'Thank you,' Gwen said, smiling again. 'He is, really.' She was watching Rose, her auburn hair curling round her face. 'I wanted to ask if you'd be my bridesmaid. I'd be ever so pleased if you would.'

'Of course,' Rose said. 'I'd be honoured.' She leaned over and gave Gwen a hug. 'I'm really chuffed.'

'I'm not going to tell Mummy,' Gwen told her, looking serious suddenly. 'Not until it's all over and settled.'

'Oh, blimey,' Rose said. 'Don't you think you

should? She could hold it against you for the rest of your life.'

'She'll do that whether I tell her now or later.'

Gwen became Mrs William Charles Crowther in the little blue-walled chapel in the palace, with her ATS friends standing round. They had gone to great lengths to get hold of flowers to decorate the place, which already had its share of marble and ornate white inlay against the blue ceiling.

Signora Mandetta had made Gwen a beautiful satin dress which hung in soft folds round her hips and swept the floor behind her, decorated with tiny mother-of-pearl seeds. For Rose she had chosen a dress in a pale blue material, and both of them held simple bunches of white lilies.

'It's funny, isn't it?' Rose said to her, before they set off to the palace in a specially decorated army Jeep. 'I can't help thinking about the first time I saw you, at Didcot Station that day when we'd joined up. I'd never have dreamed I'd be doing this with you.'

Gwen looked solemn for a moment. 'Sometimes it makes me go cold thinking about how my life would have turned out if I hadn't joined up.' Suddenly she stepped forward and put her arms round Rose. 'I'm so happy,' she said. 'And you've been a real brick the way you've helped with everything.' She looked into Rose's face. 'Maybe it'll be you and Tony next. Maybe our wedding'll give him a push in the right direction.'

Rose smiled back, impishly. 'Stranger things have happened, I s'pose.'

Standing with Gwen as she and Bill made their vows, Rose was glad of Tony's solid presence behind her. Everything went smoothly, and when she danced with Tony at the little celebration afterwards, Rose realized she felt almost light-hearted, glad of a break from Il Rifugio and from Naples.

'I was thinking of going to see Capri on my next leave weekend,' she told Tony. 'Any chance of you sparing some time to show me around?'

CHAPTER 26

APRIL 1945

The letter from Grace arrived two days before Rose's weekend leave. It was the second that fortnight, which was unusual for Grace who never wrote more often than every month or so, and only a brief note when she did. In the first letter she had announced her engagement to a GI called Joe Landers. He had just been posted and she was missing him. Just like Grace not even to mention him until she really had something to say.

The second letter was only a couple of sentences: 'We had a telegram today. Sam's been killed. Thought you'd want to know straight away. Love, Grace.'

Rose re-read the skeleton of a letter, trying to take in the reality of it. She knew its brevity stemmed from Grace's shock and grief, and also from the fact she didn't know any more than that. After all, what else was there to say? But Rose longed for detail. Where was he? How had he died? Suddenly the reality of home poured in on her, of life back in the greyness of England, stuck there, waiting for news. In Italy it had all receded from her mind as if Catherine Street was an old film she had seen years ago and half forgotten. Home. The place she would go back to when this was all over, with no Dora, no Sam. No reliable, pedantic Sam.

Over the next two days she thought more about her elder brother than she had in the whole of the war. Memories of their childhood kept forcing themselves into her mind: of playing marbles with him out in the yard; of Sam rescuing her little cloth doll when one of the Pye children threw it over the wall into the next court. Sam going out to start his first job; his stiff loyalty when he found out she was pregnant.

The next weekend she had planned to go to Sorrento with Gwen and Bill and a friend of Bill's. They'd made up a foursome on the previous leave to see Positano and Amalfi. Tony had taken her to Capri for one weekend, and she had revelled in the rich blue of the sea, the sparkling beauty of the island with its bright white villas and cobbled squares where people lingered and drank and talked, even in winter, as if there was no war anywhere in the world.

Rose had only been to Naples for the weekend once since November. She could not face spending her days so close to Falcone while they were so remote from each other. Now she felt a strong need to talk to Margherita, who she saw as her closest friend in Italy. Several times Margherita had confided in her, breaking down and pouring out her worries about her father, living in a new place surrounded by strangers. Rose knew Margherita was the one person she could allow to see her feelings.

Without mentioning Sam, she told Gwen she would be going off with Tony for the weekend after all. Gwen smiled knowingly at her.

'What is it?' Margherita asked as soon as Rose set foot through the door. She was sitting pounding at some piece of cloth in a bucket of water, her eyes ringed with tiredness. A circle of children stood watching.

Rose burst into tears for the first time. She started to shake and sob. 'My brother is dead.'

Margherita stood up and led her into the little sitting room, indicating to the children that they should not follow. She put her arms round Rose and let her cry for as long as she needed to, as Rose had done for her a number of times in the past. She stroked Rose's hair as she sat beside her, her kind eyes solemnly watching her friend's face.

Then Rose, still shaking, but quieter, was able to tell the little she knew. 'I don't even know where he was –

what country,' she said. 'I know we'll find out in the end. But it seems terrible to die so far from home.'

Margherita nodded, understanding.

'I feel so guilty,' Rose said, starting to cry again. 'I've hardly given my family a thought since coming out here. I've been so wrapped up in the army and this place – you've all been like my family. It's suddenly come home to me all they've been through, and I've been no help at all.'

Margherita sighed sadly. 'I know,' she said. 'Believe me, I have those feelings too. When the eruption came and I lost my mother, that was when I realized I had hardly seen them since the war began. The children had taken all my time. Francesco and I were always so busy, so involved with each other and this place. My family only lived across the bay, and still I did nothing for them. Now I shall never see my mother again. Every day my heart aches when I think of it.'

Holding Margherita around her waist, Rose felt how thin she had become. When they let each other go, she realized they were not alone. Falcone was standing in the doorway, his face full of concern and at the same time surprise at seeing Rose there at all.

'What's happened?'

'Rosa's brother has been killed,' Margherita told him. 'Somewhere,' she added. '*Qualche parte*.' The words hung woefully in the air.

'I'm so sorry, Rosa,' Falcone began.

'You need some time,' Margherita interrupted. 'You shouldn't be working here this weekend, Rosa.'

Rose started to argue, but Margherita silenced her.

'You must go somewhere else, somewhere more peaceful and pleasant. Falcone – you take her.'

'But . . . I—' Falcone started to say.

'You are the person we can spare most easily,' Margherita continued ruthlessly. 'Take her. Look after her.' She sighed, tilting her head on one side with a certain impatience. 'Forget your own struggles for a bit, eh?'

'No!' Rose cried immediately. 'No. I'll stay here. It

will do me good to be working.' A few months ago nothing would have filled her with greater delight than the idea of two days alone with Falcone, but now, the thought of him being forced to take her away for a weekend against his will filled her with panic. 'If I'm busy I won't have to think,' she protested.

'Go,' Margherita said. It was an order. 'You need to think.'

Rose had never heard her so steely and commanding before. It seemed as if she and Falcone would be thrown out bodily if they refused to go. They looked at each other warily for a moment. It was the first time their eyes had met for a very long time. Rose went and picked up her bag.

'Where are we going?' she asked as they stepped out into the warm spring air of the streets. The hawkers were in full throat on the pavements.

'I know a peaceful place I can take you. I used to go with my father. We had holidays there when he needed a rest. You'll like it.'

'I'm sorry you have to do this.'

'You don't have to be sorry,' he said stiffly. 'Margherita's right. I've been too wrapped up in myself. I need to do my duty by other people.'

Quelled by the coldness of the word 'duty', Rose fell silent again. They walked along the majestic Corso Umberto and into the Piazza Garibaldi where they could catch a train. Rose felt her spirits plummeting. The easy friendship, the fire of discussion between them, the tenderness – all this had vanished. Now they were like wooden puppets with each other. She felt despairing at the thought of the cold, awkward weekend ahead.

They took a train for Sorrento. Falcone had money and they each paid for their own ticket. He also bought a newspaper. They sat opposite one another, and throughout the entire journey Falcone read the newspaper. Rose often glanced across at his solemn face, the brown eyes moving in concentration across the print. A stranger's face, she thought. Had she loved him? Who was he? Where was the vulnerable, complex man she had given her heart to?

Determinedly she looked away from him out of the window. She wanted to see more of Italy, didn't she? But she could have been seeing this same place so much more cheerfully with Gwen. She stared out at the louring shape of Vesuvius. The lava fields from the eruption lay greyish mauve, spongy looking, and cool now. Villages, orange groves and vineyards pushed defiantly right to the edges of them. On her side of the train she caught glimpses of the sea, the morning sunlight wrinkling in its deep blue surface. How these sights would have exhilarated her had her mood not been so sad.

The train climbed high along the verdant cliffside, and Rose smelt the pine trees. For a time they looked right across the sea, and then gradually rolled down into Sorrento.

Everyone climbed out at the small station. Immediately the place felt different from Naples. Quieter, with almost a holiday feel. Rose was terrified of meeting any service people who might recognize her, and she was relieved to get away from the station. Walking with Falcone and dressed in her black clothes she was certainly not conspicuously British.

'We have a way to go,' Falcone told her. 'I hope you're not too tired? My friends live on the hillside outside the town.'

'I'm all right,' Rose said, though in truth she felt dragged down and exhausted.

Falcone led her along the cobbled streets, usually walking slightly ahead of her, though she was unsure whether this was through impatience to get there or because her presence was unbearable. As they left the town and toiled uphill, past rough cottages with flowers bright at the windows, the stones burning hot under their feet, she became convinced it was because he could not stand to be near her. That long walk in the heat, bothered by flies, seeing his back in front of her, was the lowest point she could remember since being in Italy. With her head aching and her hand sweaty on the handle of her bag, she could only think about what she had lost and this terrible silence that had grown up between them.

For the first time she found herself thinking, 'I wish I could just go home. Get away and forget it all.' Hot tears stung her eyes and she wiped them away crossly. She was not going to let him, an alien creature, as she thought of Falcone now, see her cry again. At that moment she hated him.

Falcone stopped finally at what seemed to be the end of the road, at a large house, its front covered in pink, crumbling plaster and shaded by two eucalyptus trees. As he went to knock at the door they heard a dog give a moaning bark somewhere behind the house, and two white geese waddled out from among the weeds and stood muttering at them.

Rose put her bag down and wiped the sweat from her forehead. There was a slight breeze up there and, suddenly refreshed, she looked around her. Not far from the house, where the road petered out, a stepped path built from huge, pale stones wound upwards between the trees which covered the higher slopes of the mountain. She longed to walk there and lose herself among the trees, to escape from Falcone and these people she now had to meet.

The door opened and a voice cried, 'Paulo! Is it you, really? How marvellous. Welcome, welcome . . .'

An elderly man, with steely grey hair and a stubbly little moustache, opened his arms wide in greeting. His face was deeply lined and tanned the colour of strong tea.

'Who's this?'

'This is Rosa, Signore Finzi,' Falcone said loudly. 'Rose Lucas. She is English.'

'*Un'inglese?*' Signore Finzi looked puzzled, staring at Rose, who suddenly found herself blushing at the thought of all the questions that must be going through the old man's mind.

Falcone explained briefly what they were doing there, and their host offered condolences while leading them inside to a large cool kitchen.

'Clara, Clara! Look who's come to visit us!'

No sooner had Clara Finzi set eyes on Falcone than he was clasped tightly in her plump arms amid loud expressions of delight, and wasn't he thin and where had he been all this time and, finally, tears, which she mopped from her round, soft-looking cheeks. His father, his father. It would seem like the old days young Paulo being here – but holy Mother, how it made her think of Doctor Falcone . . . What a terrible, terrible thing . . .'

As soon as Rose was introduced as a friend she also found herself crushed against the signora's bosom, and kisses landing on her cheeks from lips with a hint of moustache above them.

'Fetch wine, Angelo – and water,' the signora commanded at the top of her voice. Rose had quickly grasped that Signore Finzi's hearing had almost gone. They sat down at the scrubbed wooden table. On a side table the signora had been cutting long strips of tagliatelle. Her husband sat down with them having brought the drinks and the signora talked and talked while she carried on preparing the food.

'You have come right in time for a meal!' she exclaimed. 'It's so long since anyone has been to stay here. We have the rooms ready, but not even the soldiers come. They don't know we are here, of course, and they want the sea, the bars, the shops. Nothing is like it was in the old days. And we make no money.' She stopped to take a swig of the wine. 'But now I have someone to cook for,' she added, almost like a threat.

'We must drink to your father,' she said to Falcone. Looking at Rose she added, 'Ah – *il dottore* Falcone. What a gentleman. What a doctor!' Her tears started to flow again. 'Of all the places he could have stayed, he came again and again to our poor house. Every year, with his children. From when this one was a small boy. Look – I have a photograph.'

Rose glanced nervously at Falcone, but saw nothing but affection and amusement in his eyes. He had relaxed suddenly, and looked younger, as if revisiting this place of his childhood had stripped some of the troubled lines from his face.

The signora swung herself back to the table after taking a small photograph from a shelf of the dresser.

'There. You remember?'

She held out the picture between Rose and Falcone. Rose saw a tall, thin man with a serious but gentle face, standing rather formally beside two boys. Behind them was the Finzis' house. The three of them were dressed in dark trousers and jackets. The taller of the two boys next to him closely resembled his father, the face thin and hair lighter than his younger brother's. Clearly the smaller of the two was Falcone, even if Rose had not known he was the youngest. Darker and stockier than his brother, he stared out of the photograph with the mischievous expression she recognized and those long-lashed eyes.

Without thinking she turned and smiled at him. 'You'vc hardly changed at all.'

'It's true, he hasn't,' Angelo Finzi said. 'He was always like his mother, God rest her.'

To Rose's surprise Falcone returned her smile, the warmth suddenly back in his eyes. The Finzis exchanged glances.

Signora Finzi put in front of them bowls of delicious tagliatelle with *pomodoro al sugo* and an egg on top, which they both ate hungrily. All the while the signora talked and reminisced and lamented the war, and the tragic murder of *il dottore*, so that neither Angelo Finzi, who sat nodding at what he could hear, nor Rose and Falcone were required to say anything at all. They sat eating beside each other in what now felt a more comfortable silence.

'You need to rest now,' Clara Finzi instructed them.

She led them upstairs and into a small passageway at the top from which led several doors. The first she opened was for Rose. It was a simple, white room, very cool, in the middle of which a huge wooden-framed bed took up most of the space. Wooden shutters were closed at the windows, and when she pushed them open, letting in warmer air and languid flies, she realized the room looked over the back of the house. The Finzis had a small plot of land which stretched out to the point where the trees took over. They cultivated it intensively, and among all the rows of growing vegetables and tomato plants, chickens and geese ran here and there. Rose could still hear the dog, but it was not in sight.

She breathed in the warm air, her headache easing off a little now they were out of the direct heat, and turned to the whitewashed room behind her. Over the bed hung a small wooden crucifix. There was a chair and a rough chest of drawers with a deep porcelain bowl resting on top. That was all.

Well fed and tired enough now for all thoughts to be blocked out, she lay down gratefully on the firm, white bed.

CHAPTER 27

When she awoke, the only sound was the clucking of chickens below the window. She had left the shutters open and the light had grown softer, with the gentle, pinkish tinge of late afternoon. Her watch said four-thirty. Slowly she drank the cup of water by her bed and stood up, stretching her limbs.

There were no signs of life in the rest of the house when she left the room, so she let herself out of the front door. She would walk. It would be good to be alone, really alone for a time. Army life meant always being with other people.

The air outside was caressingly warm, full of the scents of herbs and gorse, and from somewhere the smell of frying onions. Rose turned towards the path which led up the hillside and began to climb, still feeling rather muzzy from her sleep. Every few yards along the sloping path there was a deep step, and she could feel the muscles in her legs pulling hard as she climbed between the greyish olive trees, with salamanders scuttling away from the path and the loud, abrasive rhythm of the crickets and cicadas.

She soon realized this was more than a convenient path up the side of the hill. In fact there were no other houses up there that she could see, nowhere for the path to lead. But at every other bend in the route as she made her way up was a little brick shrine, about waist height. Bending to look inside she found that set into each brick column was a roughly painted picture, each bearing a number. The pictures were the same as she had seen on the walls of the austere Naples churches, the fourteen Stations of the Cross. Jesus receives the Cross, Veronica wipes Jesus' face, Jesus is nailed to the Cross. On the sills of some of the shrines she saw the remains of candle stubs and wilted flowers, perhaps left over from the Easter procession.

It felt appropriate that she should have come walking here to think about Sam. Sam, who had had his own beliefs, in his way, even if he would have staunchly disapproved of the colourful Catholic imagery in this thread of shared belief she was following up between the trees. She tried to concentrate on Sam, to talk to him.

She sat down on one of the cold steps, suddenly overcome by a great welling up of feeling. Hot tears ran down her cheeks.

'I'll miss you. I'll miss you so much.'

Putting her hands over her face she wept for a few minutes, picturing the old, hard life in Birmingham, the way it had all been swept away by the war, changing and displacing all of them. Killing them, one way or another. None of it would ever be the same again. This thought was reinforced by the sight of the worn black skirt pulled tight over her strong tanned legs. It seemed such an alien thing. Who was she now? Who was Rose Lucas? Alone in a far-away country, dressed in strange, foreign clothes, giving her heart to a man who could not love her back. She remembered the smile Falcone had given her as they looked at the photograph together, and it made her cry again. It felt so cruel, that glimpse of how things could have been.

Angrily she stood up and walked on up the hill, trying to work the pain out of herself by physical exertion. She passed the final three stages of the pilgrimage without stopping to look at them, her legs aching.

At the top there was a small stone chapel. Outside stood a pale, bland-faced statue of Mary. The path led on upwards behind the chapel, but it looked less well tended.

She pushed open the door of the chapel quietly. It was gloomy inside, but her attention was drawn straight away to a raised altar where stood a Madonna quite different from the lifeless image depicted outside. She was dressed in heavy blue velvet, and at her breast was pinned a large metal heart, pierced through with a bristling collection of pins, large and thick like nails. One of her arms was outstretched, and her mouth was open as if she was constantly crying out, her grey eyes staring across the chapel in anguish. This was no serene plaster statue, but a woman who had watched her son die a most terrible death and had been powerless to stop it.

In front of her lay all kinds of tributes: garlands of flowers and sacred hearts, offerings of money and rosary beads. And more personal objects: the army cap of someone else's son, a ring and some bracelets, a pair of thick black-rimmed spectacles. Had she been able to save the kin of others when she had failed so completely with her own?

Rose stood staring at her for several minutes. As if sharing the grief of the woman in front of her, she thought of all the people she had lost, Falcone among them. Try as she might to think of anyone but him, he was rarely out of her mind. She remembered that first night when they had talked all through the hours of darkness with the children sleeping round them, how there had been that new sense of herself moving out to him from her very centre, which she later recognized as love.

She turned to look at the rest of the chapel, and jumped violently. As if her thoughts had spirited him to the place, there he was, kneeling at the back of the rows of chairs, looking across at her.

'I'm sorry,' he said gently, standing up. 'Didn't you know I was here?'

'No. I thought I was on my own. Have you been here all the time?'

'I've been here nearly an hour,' he said, walking towards her. 'It's a very peaceful place, isn't it? My father used to come here often and sometimes I came with him.'

He stood beside her, looking up at the statue.

'You know she shares in all our sorrows?' he said. 'When I came and prayed here as a boy I used to remember all my father's patients, those who were suffering great pain, and the ones who had died. It was as if I could commit them all to her.'

'And now?'

Falcone shook his head sadly. 'Now I wonder if even she can comfort all the suffering in the world.'

As they walked out into the early evening light he said, 'The path doesn't end here. Come, I'll show you, it's lovely. No one comes up here except on feast days. There's just an old man who looks after the olive groves.'

Rose climbed beside him. The stones here were further apart, with tufts of wiry grass and weeds poking up between them. Falcone did not rush on ahead as he had earlier, but walked beside her, quite unlike his harsh self at midday.

'Were you thinking about your brother?' Rose noticed with bewilderment that he sounded rather nervous.

'Yes. I was thinking about all my family. How the war has changed everyone. Taken away so much of what was there before. And the way everyone has become someone else.'

'Do you think the people we were are still somewhere inside us?' he asked, in that way she remembered, as if he really needed her opinion. 'That one day we can be reunited with ourselves again?'

'Not the same,' she insisted. 'I know I'll never be the same after being here.' After you, she added in her thoughts.

When they had climbed a little higher the path forked, one branch continuing upwards, obscured by the vegetation around it. The other, which Falcone took, led into a clearing. There was a flat area like a ledge that had been cut into the hill to make a semicircular space, the long, straight side of it against the body of the hill. In the middle of that line stood one more statue, this time of the risen Christ, its stone stained by green lichen. Through the trees he looked out over the town, his arm raised in benediction.

'It's beautiful.' Rose walked to the edge of the clearing.

The air was hazy, but the faded terracotta roofs of the town were easily visible below. She stood trying to absorb herself in the sight, but she was acutely aware that Falcone was watching her. Her body tingled under his gaze. Her heart was beating hard. She knew that something had changed, that the charged atmosphere which had existed between them before had returned, but she did not know how to react, or what to do with the turmoil of feelings inside her.

When she realized that he had come to stand just behind her she said. 'You were very angry with me this morning, weren't you?'

She heard him make a low sound, as if in pain, and turned round quickly to look at him. She was moved by the look of sorrow and desire she recognized in his eyes.

'If you knew,' he said. He looked down at the ground, unable to face her.

'Every step of the way up here as you walked behind me, all I could think of was that you were there, as if your shape was burning into my back, and I couldn't look at you. The train was torture, pretending to read that newspaper when I could only think that you were there, a few feet away from me. I knew if I was alone with you again it would be like this. If I'd looked at you or touched you I would have—' He shrugged helplessly. 'I want you so much. I can't help it.'

Each could feel the other trembling as they moved into each other's arms. They kissed again and again, faces, lips, necks, in a great hurry as if at any second the experience might be snatched away. Rose made little whimpering sounds, almost of distress, at the strength of the emotions he aroused in her.

It did not occur to her to hold back from him. They clung together, exploring each other's bodies with their hands. Slowly, Falcone unbuttoned the black blouse Rose was wearing, uncovering her breasts, cupped in a black cotton bra. His hands were trembling so much as he tried to undo it that she reached round and unfastened the hooks herself. She pulled the little garment out through one sleeve, freeing her breasts with their dark, generous nipples, already peaking at his slight touch.

'You're so, so beautiful,' he said. As his hands moved over her breasts, stroking her, he heard her give a sharp intake of breath at the intense pleasure of it. Never had she been touched like this before. Alfie had not had the imagination to give her more than a clumsy squeeze through her clothes. But this, this stroking, his taking her nipple between finger and thumb sent waves of desire through her body such as she had never even begun to experience before. Her legs were trembling, and the lower part of her body had come alive. She felt a sharp, warm sensation of need rising in her.

'Don't stop,' she said. 'I couldn't bear it if you stopped touching me.'

Quickly they looked round for the softest part of the dry, stony ground. There was not one patch which appeared better than any other, so they knelt down together anyway, unfastening clothes, and they were in each other's arms again, with Falcone's shirt spread out beneath them.

It was awkward, their lovemaking that first time, their unfamiliarity with each other's bodies, the hard ground, but they barely noticed the discomforts of it. At the height of it she called out some words in English and burst into tears at the release. He held her tenderly until both of them quietened, stroking her wet face. He stayed inside her for a long time afterwards.

'I love you,' she whispered into the silence. 'I love you so much.'

She heard his voice, felt his warm breath on her neck. 'And I love you.'

He came to her that night, after they had eaten with the Finzis and talked long into the evening over fish and bread and glasses of wine until the old man fell asleep in his chair, snoring softly, his whiskery mouth hanging open.

As she let Falcone into her dark room, their lips were on each other before either of them had even spoken, their bodies already tight with wanting each other.

'I can't see you,' Falcone whispered. 'I want to see you naked – every part of you. Is there a candle in here?'

'I'll open the shutters,' Rose replied, shivering slightly. 'There's a moon tonight.'

Laughing as quietly as they could manage, they released the shutters, both saying 'Ssshh' with childlike exaggeration as one of the slatted wooden blinds banged too loudly against the frame.

'Well *he* won't hear us anyway,' Rose whispered.

'No. But the signora, she's always had ears like a cat.'

To Falcone's amusement Rose was still wearing her striped army issue pyjamas, not having bothered to get any others. Smiling down at her he unbuttoned the jacket. The solemn, concentrated expression in his eyes made her want to take him to her straight away, but she stood still. He pulled the top away from her breasts and pushed it off down her arms. He slid his hands gently inside the top of her trousers and eased them down over her hips until she could step out of them. She stood naked in front of him, her black hair falling in soft waves over her shoulders, her eyes wide and vulnerable, looking up at him.

For a moment he didn't move to touch her, but stood gazing at her, the moonlight casting deep shadows on her small, curving body, the strong hips and slight curve of her stomach, her full breasts. How many times he had tried to imagine her like this, unclothed, ready for him.

He moved towards her but she raised a hand. 'Wait a minute.'

He had changed into a very worn cotton shirt and frayed shorts. She pulled the shirt off and ran her hands through the black curling hair on his chest, feeling the powerful beating of his heart, aware of his wide brown eyes watching her, a little shy at her taking control. His body was slim but muscular, and she stroked him tenderly across his shoulders, down over his chest and belly. She brought her hands slowly along the soft hair of his thighs, feeling him shudder and flex his legs slightly in anticipation. When he was naked, hard and ready for her, she took him between her hands, caressing him until he gasped and moved to stop her.

'No – wait. Not yet, please.'

And then he was touching her all over, his lips kissing her mouth, her breasts and limbs and then, laying her on the bed, exploring between her legs until she was whimpering with amazed desire, aching to have him inside her. At last she pulled him close, guiding him into her. They both cried out with relief and pleasure and both came almost instantly, first he, then she, and she began to make such a noise that Falcone lovingly laid one hand over her mouth until they both lay back laughing, quietly but slightly hysterically, in each other's arms.

They stayed like that for a time, talking drowsily, sleeping at last on the hard bed. Later in the night Rose woke to feel Falcone's hands moving over her body. The moon had moved and it was darker, but they made love under the covers, more slowly this time, with less urgency, an experience more of touch than sight, both taking longer to climax, but still moved to tears by each other's pleasure.

When she awoke, Rose expected to find him gone. But as the lemon morning light bathed the room through the open shutters, she realized he was beside her still. His face and hair looked very dark against the coarse white linen of the pillow. He was lying with his head resting on his bent arm and she saw his smiling, long-lashed eyes watching her.

Rose half sat up, startled. 'You shouldn't be here! What if they—?'

'They get up very early. I can hear them outside. Don't worry.'

He stroked her hair and kissed her. Then, as they embraced, he pulled her over on top of him, moving against her. The feel of her immediately hardened him, and he lifted her until he could enter her. She sat, both of them moving together gently, his hands stroking her breasts.

'You are a miracle,' he said, rising under her like water until she felt herself come alive again with the tingling at her breasts and his reaching deep into her.

'It feels very good, like this,' she told him. 'I can feel you so far inside me.'

He smiled. 'Good,' he said, 'good.'

She saw his eyes half close as the power of the sensations overcame him, and once more they moved together until they were lost in each other, and every other thought or feeling was taken from them.

CHAPTER 28

MAY 1945

It was over!

On 2 May the German forces in Italy made their official surrender, and the fortunes of Europe had fallen to the Allies. After the long stalemate in the Italian campaign, events had suddenly speeded up during April in a landslide of activity. The Allied Forces finally crossed the enormous span of the River Po, which had long proved such an obstacle, and pushed across the northern plains to the French border. It was a time of sudden reversals, of power overthrown. Mussolini and his mistress, Claretta Petacci, were seized by a colonel in the partisan army in a farmhouse at Dongo on Lake Como to which they had retreated in hiding. The two of them were shot and hung ignominiously by the feet for all to see outside a garage in the Piazzale Loreto in Milan. And on 30 April Hitler and his mistress Eva Braun committed suicide.

The Victory in Europe celebrations were set for 8 May. Caserta was taken over by an air of fiesta and celebration, although the work of administering the army still had to go on. The war was over! They would be going home! Sooner or later they would be back in Blighty with familiar people and places around them. Home, far away and long unseen, was enhanced in the memory and seemed the very sweetest place to be.

But among all the dances, the hugs and kisses and drinking and singing, there were deeply mixed feelings. Some ugly scenes broke out when British soldiers exulted in their victory by taunting the local Italians, whom they saw as defeated. Fights broke out, and at least one Italian in the area was stabbed to death. As it began to sink in that returning home was not just a dream which might be realized some time in the future, memories grew sharper, less softened by nostalgia.

'I'm longing to set up a home with Bill,' Gwen confided to Rose as they walked round the palace grounds. 'Make a real cosy nest, have lots of children. But in some ways I dread going so much. I'll have to face Mummy, and she's going to expect us to live as close to her as possible and I know she'll never leave us alone.'

'Go and live near Bill's family then,' Rose suggested. 'His Dad's not too well, is he? That's a good enough reason I'd've said.'

'Not good enough for Mummy,' Gwen said grimly. 'If I go and live in Bromley she'll never speak to me again. Are you looking forward to going back?'

'No,' Rose said bleakly.

Earlier in the war she had longed to see Grace and the twins and Harry – even George. But so much time had passed that although she did want to see them they felt like strangers. How could she leave Italy now, when the person she loved most in all the world was here? Her mind was already working on how she could arrange to stay. The thought of making her life here with Falcone was the only future she could imagine.

'You and Tony haven't . . . I mean – is there any chance?'

Rose looked at her, frowning for a moment as if puzzled. Then she registered what Gwen was saying. 'Tony? You mean us getting married? No. Tony and me have never been anything but good pals. That's all.'

Gwen sighed sympathetically. 'I'll miss you such a lot, you know, Rose. You've been ever so good for me. Don't know what I'll do without you in fact.'

Rose smiled, her dark eyes warm and suddenly amused. 'We've all been good for each other, when you think of it. Look at that toffee-nosed Willy for a start.

She's almost human nowadays!' They laughed together. 'Anyway, come on. We're not leaving yet. Knowing the army it'll take them months to get round to demobbing us.'

Rose went to Naples a week later. The truck carrying them there could not move fast enough for her. She was almost frantic with anticipation at seeing Falcone, of feeling him close to her again. In her mind a plan had been forming over the past days. It was exciting, frightening, but right. She knew it was what she must do. This was home, the place she wanted to give her life to. When her number came up for demobilization she would not leave. She was going to stay on. Whatever else mattered in her life, there was nothing so important as being here with Falcone.

As they reached the city and rumbled over the cobbles, the usual stench hitting them, she felt like putting out her hand to stroke the faces of the dusty, weary-looking buildings. They had become familiar to her and she knew she was meant to remain here among them.

Napoli, she said in her mind. Napoli, Napoli. My home, God help me. And she smiled so broadly that the barrel-chested corporal opposite her in the truck might have mistaken it for a come on had her mind not been so obviously elsewhere.

She half walked, half ran to Il Rifugio through the squalor of the back streets. She had not bothered to put on her old black clothes this time, and she had gathered quite a bunch of poking, nudging children around her by the time she reached the rough wooden entrance. She opened the gate with her key and locked them all out behind her. She ran up the stone stairs, her heart pounding, and hammered on the door. Next to her on the wall, more faded now, were the rough letters she had first seen: IL RIFUGIO.

Margherita opened the door. Rose saw her look of pleased recognition tighten into one of sorrow, fear almost. Without speaking she took Rose's hand and led her inside, not even kissing her, and she shooed away the children with unusual sharpness. Rose felt her insides turn with dread.

'What?' she gasped. 'What is it? Where is everyone? Where is he?'

'Rosa,' Margherita said gently. She led her to a chair in the little side room and made her sit down.

She went over to the old table and opened the drawer. For a second she hesitated before turning to Rose with an envelope in her hand. Rose saw that she had tears in her eyes.

'He left this,' Margherita said. 'Rosa, I've never seen him more distressed, more frightened of himself.'

Numb, not understanding, Rose took the army issue envelope and opened it, her hands beginning to shake. She realized as she read the short letter, written in bold, black ink, that she had never seen his handwriting before.

'*Mia carissima Rosa*,' it began. 'My dearest Rose,

> What can I write to you that will ever make you understand what I have done? In my mind I can see your eyes filled with nothing but pain and I know that I, and only I, am the cause of it.
>
> As you read this you'll know I am thinking of you, as I begin life in the seminary of San Domenico Maggiore, because I can think of nothing else until I can be sure you have left Naples and I know there is no chance of us meeting again.
>
> Now that the war is over, I know that you will go back to your country, my beautiful English friend, for your life is there. I know that this is what you have to do, that our days together here during the war have been a time like no other that we shall never have again. I have asked myself a thousand times if we could make a life together, but I know that your home is really in England, and that my certainty that I must try this vocation would stand between us. Please know that you take my heart with

you. I am following God's call, but believe me, it's a road of thorns.

I don't have the words to ask you to forgive or to understand. I know only one thing. That I love no other human being as I love you.

Please accept this ring as a bond, a memory of a time like no other. Forgive me. Go well, my love.

Paulo Falcone.

Slowly Rose tipped the envelope and shook it, and into her hand fell a slim, silver-coloured ring. She recognized it as one of the many hammered out and sold as souvenirs in the area after the eruption. Into its rim was engraved 'NAPLES '44'.

For a few seconds she sat staring dumbly at the letter, at the ring, both of which seemed to bear no relation to him, to the man she loved. Then, leaping up, she exclaimed wildly to Margherita, 'Where is he? Where is San Domenico Maggiore? It's on the way to the Duomo, isn't it? I remember. I can walk. I must go.'

Solemnly Margherita held her back, taking her firmly by the shoulders, almost shaking her to make her stand still.

She looked hard into Rose's distraught face, willing her to accept, to understand. 'No,' she said. 'It's no good, Rosa. Even if you go they'll never let you see him when he's just entered. It's the rule.'

She watched her friend's face, so alight with love and anticipation when she arrived, as it crumpled finally into shock and grief. For a long time she held Rose in her arms that afternoon as her heartbreaking sobs filled the room, the sound of a woman beyond hope and beyond comfort.

PART THREE

HOME

1947–1957

CHAPTER 29

MAY 1947

Gradually she came to, feeling sick and muzzy, and opened her eyes, becoming aware of the white room. She saw the edge of a long blue and white curtain hanging beside her, and, above, a light with a white institutional shade over it like a stiff little hat. Wherever was she? She tried to move, and felt a sharp, tearing pain across her stomach which made her sink back on to the bed again.

After a moment a face appeared, smiling down at her. A young woman with blond hair pinned back under a starched white cap.

'What happened?' Rose demanded. 'What's wrong?'

'Wrong? Nothing at all,' the nurse said soothingly. 'You've got a lovely little daughter, Mrs Meredith. Just over seven pounds. You needed a bit of help with her, that's all. Anyway, now you're awake I'll bring her to you. Your husband's waiting outside.'

Soon Alfie walked into the ward following the nurse who was carrying their tiny child wrapped in a white cellular blanket. Alfie was grinning broadly. Rose felt the blanket bundle in her arms and saw the baby's small squashed face, her eyes closed and a shadow of brown hair on her head.

'There,' Alfie said, as if he'd given birth to the child all by himself. 'Meet Hilda Grace. Our firstborn. Ain't she grand, eh?'

Hilda. Rose tried to smile back at him. So he had named her already, before she, Rose, had even come round. They had argued for months about the name.

Rose had wanted Diana if it was a girl ('That's a toff's name,' Alfie had said), or Dora, or Margaret. Hilda was Alfie's mother's name. Though she was fond of Mrs Meredith, Rose thoroughly disliked the name. But it had been said. Once a new baby had been greeted by its name it seemed too late to go back on it.

She looked down at this child, whose birth she could not remember and whose name she had not spoken, with a strong sense of unreality. She was lovely, it was true, healthy and wholesome. But even at a few hours old, so obviously Alfie's child – his colouring, his narrow eyes. What connection did she have with her mother?

Alfie's face wore a delighted, triumphant grin as he watched Rose suckling their daughter, oblivious to the hard, angry expression on her face.

'Ah, Mrs Meredith. You're back with us I see.' A doctor with dark, bushy hair was striding towards the bed, white coat gusting out behind him. 'Feeling all right? Your baby was breech I'm afraid. Feet first, in other words, and very awkwardly positioned. So we had to whip her out by Caesarean section. All's looking good now though, as I can see.' He spoke very fast.

'Just have a quick glance at you.' He pulled the curtain across briskly on one side and gestured at Alfie to move out.

When he'd checked her wound and opened the curtains again, the doctor suddenly turned with a smile. 'By the way, do you speak Spanish by any chance? Or Italian?'

Bewildered, Rose said, 'Italian. Well I did. In the war.'

'I've been hearing about you from my staff,' the doctor told her with an amused grin. 'Believe me, you haven't lost your touch. You caused quite a stir – chatting away nineteen to the dozen in Italian as you came round from the anaesthetic.'

'Oh my God!' Rose was suddenly delighted, and smiled back at him. Then she saw Alfie scowling beside her. He didn't like hearing anything about Italy, about her war. He was jealous of it in ways he didn't really seem able to explain.

Cautiously she asked, 'What did I say?'

'No idea,' the doctor said. 'Afraid none of us speak the lingo. I was out east myself. Picked up a smattering of Hindustani. You must have worked hard at it. Apparently it was quite impressive.'

When Rose was finally left alone and Hilda had been taken back to the nursery, she lay drowsily in bed, trying to take in the existence of her daughter. It all seemed very new and strange. Her body, having recovered sensation, felt battered and sore from the operation, and her breasts tingled with the forgotten pains of feeding. She had not yet experienced much in the way of any stirring of love for her child. But those feelings would come, she hoped with all her heart. That little girl had to be the centre of her life, for what else was there? A baby. A child. Was it not, if she was honest, mainly so that she could have children that she had agreed to change her name from Lucas to Meredith?

Hilda was crying. Again. All afternoon, on and off, she had screamed and cried until Rose, after trying to work out what it was that was distressing her, had now reached the point where she could scarcely bring herself to care. The sound set all her nerves on edge again. Tutting with infuriation, she picked the baby up and started suckling her in the hope that it would put her back to sleep.

As she was gently lying the child in her wooden cot, she heard the slam of the back door.

'Got the dinner ready?' Alfie shouted. Holding her breath, she heard him drop his heavy boots on to the floor one by one. Then she heard him rattling the lid of the big stewpot, the contents of which had been simmering for over an hour, the smell of gravy and vegetables filling the little prefab house.

'Smells a bit of all right,' he called out.

Hilda stirred in her cot and let out a loud, cracked-sounding wail.

Alfie padded through in his dusty socks, daubs of

greyish cement stuck round the ankles. 'Hello. All right, love?'

'You've woken her up again!' Rose snapped at him. 'D'you have to shout about the place every time you come in?'

She had meant it to be different. She was going to try much harder today: smile at him when he came in; make life sweeter between them.

Alfie shrugged. 'Can't have your whole life ruled by a babby. They have to fit in with everyone else. That's family, ain't it?'

He came over to try and cajole her, putting his arm round her shoulders as she picked up Hilda, who was showing no sign of wanting to go back to sleep. Rose flinched at his touch.

'Can't you get changed first? You're filthy dirty.'

'Oh, a dirty frock won't hurt. Not when you hear what I've got to tell you. Got some news. I've got a new job. Bigger firm – not just houses like MacMahon's is, so we shouldn't get buggered about so much. All that on, off, on, off with the government. Don't know if you're coming or going. And it's fifteen bob a week more. How about that?'

'Oh, good,' Rose said, trying to sound enthusiastic.

Alfie kissed her. 'I knew you'd be pleased,' he said. He unfastened his trousers and slipped them down as he sat on the bed. 'You'll see,' he said. 'Half this blooming city needs rebuilding. I'll have me own little firm one day.'

She tried to arrange her face into a tired smile. 'I 'spect you will.'

His shoulders flexed back allowing his work shirt to slide off and revealing his very white, though quite muscular torso. Fishy white, Rose thought, staring at his back. Alfie turned to look at her, deliberately, she suspected, not putting his clean shirt on straight away. Did he really imagine the sight of him would excite her, with a restless baby in her arms?

'We're going places, you and me, Rosie,' Alfie said,

his grey eyes showing his habitual optimism. 'We're going to give our kiddies the best you can get.'

Hilda was now looking up at Rose with eyes that were the image of her father's, and though her face was flushed she was quiet, as if listening to them both. Rose stepped over the pile of filthy clothes her husband had left lying carelessly on the floor and went towards the kitchen.

'Spuds should be ready by now.'

She laid her wakeful four-month-old down to kick on a blanket in the little living room next to the kitchen. Then she went through and strained the potatoes and mashed them without any milk. After all, there was gravy. Something was always in short supply it seemed, and at the moment it was milk. As she pushed the masher through the potatoes, Hilda began to cry again.

Rose stood still, closing her eyes. The cries grew louder and more agitated until Hilda sounded as if the whole universe must be collapsing around her. Rose slammed the lid on the potatoes and marched into the living room.

'What d'you want?' she demanded roughly, Hilda was already in such a state that sweat glistened on her pink skin. Sometimes she screamed for so long and so vigorously that her fine brown hair became drenched and stringy.

Rose picked her up.

'Why can't you just be quiet?' she shouted. 'For God's sake stop this sodding racket. There's nothing to scream about.'

'Don't talk to her like that.' Alfie came in behind her, still smoothing Brylcreem into his wayward hair. 'Here – give her to me. That's no way to talk to a babby.'

'Well, *you*'d soon yell at her if you had it all day!' Rose screeched at him. 'You can't even stand five minutes of it when it's your precious sleep she's breaking into!'

It was true. Alfie would mumble drowsily, 'Can't you do something with her?' as Rose hurried out of bed in the night. She felt permanently tired and foggy in the head. The days seemed to swim around her, shapeless, busy, but tedious. She had no spare energy to do anything but care for Hilda's needs, and for Alfie's, and to take a quick nap in the odd half-hours that Hilda slept during the day.

Mrs Meredith, on her occasional visits from Small Heath to see her granddaughter, was kind and fussing and full of unwanted advice.

'If you have a happy mother, you get a happy child,' she told Rose one day, her plump little frame perched on one of their two old chairs. Rose, hollow-eyed, sat staring at her, hardly listening.

'Your job is to pull yourself together and look a bit more cheerful,' she said. 'Then the babby'll soon perk up, you'll see if she don't.'

Rose did feel everything was all her fault. She had selfishly had a child by a man she didn't really love and everyone was suffering.

Now Alfie was walking round the little square of garden in the late afternoon sun, with Hilda in his arms. Rose sat down and burst into tears. She cried a lot nowadays, and Alfie, at first sympathetic, was growing rather impatient.

'What's up with you?' he'd ask. 'You've got a nice home, and a bonny babby. What more can I give you?'

Then he'd assume that protective, fatherly air which made her want to scream with frustration. But she could not break through it without saying things which would have been far crueller than he deserved.

After a while he came in with Hilda dozing in his arms, went through and laid her in her cot. He kissed Rose on the cheek. 'Come on Rosie, that's me girl. Let's see a smile out of you, eh?'

Rose turned her mouth up into a guilty smile.

'That's more like it,' Alfie said. 'Now – how about some of that stew?'

The stew had cooked too long and the carrots were mushy, but Alfie shovelled the food down without comment. Rose watched him gratefully. He was as uncritical over her cooking as he was over housework, not seeming to notice whether she'd done much or not.

'So,' she said. 'How did you get this job then?'

Alfie looked at her with a rather sheepish expression on his pale face. 'It was just – well, a bloke Eddie knows.'

Rose rolled her eyes upwards. 'Might've known he must've had something to do with it.'

'Look, he's all right. I keep telling you.' Alfie forked his last mouthful of potato into his mouth. 'He's on the level, honest he is. He just has the contacts, that's all.'

'Alfie,' Rose said emphatically, 'Eddie is as on the level as Dr Crippen. He's a horrible bloke. Why did you have to pal up with him of all people?'

Alfie looked across the table at his wife's thin, tired face. A little frown line was beginning to form between her dark eyebrows. He loved Rose, proudly and loyally, and knew that he always would. But he couldn't hide from himself the fact that she'd changed, that his affection for her was stronger than hers for him. He could live with that, provided she was there for him. What was harder was this sharpness, the way she was so critical of people. She hadn't been like that before the war. Tart as an acid drop now.

'If I get this job, money and all, I don't s'pose you'll want to moan about that, will you?' he said, sarcastically.

Rose looked at him in silence, refusing to be drawn. 'If you want the job, then you'll do it. Not up to me, is it?'

'No,' Alfie agreed. 'It isn't.'

As she was pouring the boiling water into the teapot after their meal, Rose heard a hasty tap on the glass of the back door. She opened it into the dusk, the air still warm.

Grace was standing on the step, her hand still raised to knock. 'There's trouble,' she said grimly. 'It's George. He's been arrested.'

Rose gasped. 'What the hell for?'

'There was a big job last week. One of the warehouses over Bordesley way. They had parts in there for one of the bigger firms. I don't know if it was the Austin or what. But it was done over. They shifted a whole load of stuff and one of the blokes had a gun on him. George was in on it.'

'No!' Rose protested. 'He wouldn't. Even George wouldn't go that far, surely.'

'Oh wake up, Rose,' Grace snapped. 'George is as crooked as a bent half-crown – has been for years. I always hoped the army'd straighten him out, but he's come back even worse. Since he's been with that spiv Ronnie Grables he's turned professional. He'll have been in on it, no two ways.'

Rose banged the teapot down hard on the wooden surface. 'Silly little sod,' she said. 'What the bloody hell's the matter with him?'

As they carried the tea through she said to Alfie, 'I suppose you heard all that?'

'All right, Gracie? Yes, I heard. It don't surprise me. He's been heading that way for a long time I reckon.'

'Did they come round to the house to pick him up?' Rose asked as they all sat in front of their cups.

Grace shook her head. 'No, thank God. They found him with Ronnie somewhere.' She was silent for a moment. 'Anyway, it'll be the magistrates next week, and then we'll see, won't we?'

Rose sighed. 'He was such a nice little kid.'

Grace shrugged. 'Weren't we all?'

The war had changed Grace in a number of ways. Though still only twenty-four, the skin stretched over her bony face looked aged, with the kind of lifeless greyness Rose had noticed in most of the people who had stayed in the city during the war. The sweetness which had marked her out in her teens had turned sour. Perhaps we'll just be bitter now, Rose thought, for the rest of our lives, over what we've lost. And as for George, his own bitterness, his damage, had begun even earlier in the war.

Alfie pushed back his chair. 'I'll just go and have a walk in the garden before the light's all gone.'

Rose smiled gratefully at him, knowing he was leaving them alone for a talk.

The two sisters sat on despondently at the table.

'If he goes to prison,' Rose said, 'we'll have lost him, sort of, won't we?'

Grace looked dispassionately at her. 'We lost him years ago.'

'But he's our brother. We can't just turn away from him for all he's done. We've got to stand by him.'

'No,' Grace said. 'He ain't our brother. Say what you like, but it's his choosing. We've all done our best. I stood by him for years while you were off in the army and I've had enough of it. He's made his choice in life and he can go to hell his own way.'

Rose was startled. Was this Grace, idealistic, sweet Grace? 'Well what choices are *you* going to make then?' she challenged her.

'I'm going to train to be a nurse if they'll have me. A proper one. If I'm going to have to work for the rest of my life then I might as well do a job worth doing.'

'Does that mean you'll be living in, at the hospital?'

'How else am I going to get out? Dad can take care of himself when he needs to. You got out – everyone else has, one way or another. Why shouldn't I?'

'No—' Rose held her hands up as if to protect herself from this onslaught of resentment. 'You've got me wrong. I'm not getting at you. I think you're right. I've always felt bad that you've been the one left taking all the flak. I think it's just the right thing for you. In fact I . . .' Suddenly all the frustration of her own life bubbled up. 'I wish I could get a job. I wish I could get out and do anything except being stuck here all day long. Hilda just screams and I can't get anything else done. And Alfie—' She bit back the words. She could not let the truth out, even if they both knew it. Alfie bores me. I have no feelings for him. I should never have married someone so dull and calm, so kind, so limited . . .

Grace watched her sister with anger and disgust written plain on her face, as if she had sucked all the angry, guilty thoughts out of Rose's mind.

'You're a silly cow, d'you know that? Never satisfied, are you? Always have to be off wanting something else than what you've got. D'you know what I'd give to have a kind husband and a home of my own and a babby daughter? You can't see yourself for looking, Rose, and if you don't pull yourself together and act a bit more like a proper wife you're going to lose what you have got!'

CHAPTER 30

Grace had not heard that Joe was dead until weeks after the war ended. A letter arrived one morning on thin, crackly blue air mail paper from a neighbour in Peoria, Illinois, who had been drafted at the same time as Joe. Only then, once he was back in mid-western America late in the summer of 1945, had he thought to write. Grace's hopes of a reunion with the only man she had ever given her heart to were cut to nothing.

It had happened only shortly before Rose arrived home to find what was left of her family still in Catherine Street, shrunken by loss and grief. She felt that she added nothing to it except her own restlessness, her own loss and mourning.

Since she had been one of the first group, with Gwen, to be posted at Caserta, she was also among the first batch to be sent home. Those final three months, before they began their journey across Europe, should have been the sweetest in Italy. The atmosphere had become more relaxed, and there was more opportunity for 'jangling off' on excursions all round the area. For Rose and many others there was a poignant sense of making the most of the warmth and the languorous beauty of the country before the goodbyes began and they all had to head back into new, possibly more difficult lives.

When Rose went for the last time to Il Rifugio, steeling herself to say goodbye to Margherita and Francesco, she found the place depleted. Apart from the one great absence in the house which made it so painful to her,

Henry was gone too. He had hot-footed it out of Naples as soon as the war was over.

'I'm sorry our home has come to be such a sad place for you,' Margherita told her. 'Please don't forget us. You have been a very good friend – to me especially.'

On the very few occasions that she had seen them since May, Rose could never hold herself back from asking, 'Have you heard from him? Have you seen him?'

'Not a word,' Francesco told her each time. 'Truly. If we had I would tell you straight away. You must understand. They have to adjust to a new way, their lives are so disciplined . . .'

She had still been unable to believe it completely; to accept that he would not change his mind as he had done so often before; that he could transfer such feelings of passion into a way of life that she could not begin to understand. Some time before she left, she still hoped he would come back to her.

'I wish I could be angry with Falcone,' she said to Margherita.

'It's true he treated you badly,' her friend said. 'Though he did not mean harm, I'm sure.' Margherita always tried to be fair on the motives of others. 'But no one could blame you for being angry.'

'I'm not, though,' Rose said flatly. 'I just feel . . .' She searched round for the right word and settled for the simplest: '*Triste.*' Sad. A deep, deep sadness which never seemed to leave her, which Gwen and the others attributed to her 'failed' relationship with Tony.

'What will you do, Margherita?' Rose asked. 'Will you stay here?'

'Of course.' Margherita looked as calm and steady as ever. 'And perhaps now the war is over we can persuade the Church to give us some proper backing. After all, there is no British army for us to live off now.'

'Well, God help you,' Rose said, without irony.

The two women stood with their arms round each other for a long time before Rose left. Magdalena and Assunta and Francesco all came and embraced her,

Assunta with tears running down her kindly, cock-eyed face. When Rose handed back her key and heard the wooden door slam behind her for the last time, she held in her hands a beautiful, poignant present from Francesco: the copy of his favourite French song that they had listened to so often, '*J'attendrai – le jour et la nuit j'attendrai toujours* – I will wait . . .'

The journey to England took them several days on trains with hard, slatted wooden seats. Rose and Gwen travelled together, exclaiming when at last they saw the Channel and the white cliffs of Dover, which they seemed to have left a whole lifetime ago, and at how lush and neat and altogether more cosy the English landscape looked than anything they had seen during their years away.

'I say – it all looks bigger, doesn't it?' Gwen exclaimed as they gazed out at the Kentish orchards, and the elder and hawthorn along the railway tracks. 'I suppose we did leave in the middle of winter, but even so, everything seems to have shot up.'

Rose nodded silently. She felt disorientated and strange, as if returning to another foreign country, not her own. The feeling took quite some time to wear off.

Once she and Gwen had been to the army clearing house and were released from the ATS, they said their farewells in central London before catching trains for their different parts of the country.

'You'd better write!' Gwen said.

Rose nodded. 'Of course.' She had already made Tony the same promise.

On her journey out of Euston in a hot, smoke-filled railway carriage bound for the Midlands, she pulled from her bag the letter each of them had been given from the Senior Controller of the ATS.

'As you say goodbye to service life,' it began, 'I am writing to thank you in the name of the Auxiliary Territorial Service for the loyal and devoted service you have given to your King and Country.'

Rose looked up for a moment, glancing at the drab outskirts of north London which were beginning to give way to countryside. The man in the seat next to her glanced curiously at her letter.

'You will be called upon,' she read, 'to make further efforts in the service of your country, and I know that you will make them with the same generosity which has always marked the work of the ATS. Goodbye and the best of luck.'

The train was crowded and a number of those on board were men and women obviously as freshly demobbed as she was. But even amid the hum of conversation and jokes and scraping of matches to light cigarettes, she felt a kind of solitude descend upon her. The letter made the army seem official and impersonal again. There was a sense of it all falling away from her, the experiences of the past four years beginning to recede, dream-like. Now she needed to reshape herself, though how, as yet, she didn't know. She thought of Gwen heading towards her mother's home to wait until Bill was released. What would her reception be? And her own? How would it feel to walk into Court 11, Catherine Street, again?

Birmingham came as a shock to her. Although she had been there during the worst of the bombing, the city had somehow reformed itself in her mind while she was away. She had tended to remember it still complete, with the Market Hall standing and the rows of terraced houses undamaged. But now she saw afresh the jagged gaps which the war had left in the city: the bombsites between the houses, a few levelled off, but many still with rubble in place. Young lads took them over as playgrounds, still plundering shrapnel, and thistles and purple fireweed pushed up between the timbers and bricks.

As she stepped in her solid service shoes across the dirty blue bricks of Court 11, she was struck for the first time by just how small were the houses in which thousands like her had spent their years growing up. She put her hand up automatically to knock at the door, forgetting for a moment that this was where she now belonged. This was life now and she had nothing else. She was home.

Only Sid was in. He was sitting at the old table, a paper open in front of him. He looked up as she opened the door, seeing for a moment a beautiful, neatly dressed stranger in khaki, her hair still arranged carefully under the ATS cap as if she was afraid to take it off.

He looked blankly at her for a moment.

'Rose?'

He pulled himself up, then waited at a loss as she closed the door and came in to stand the other side of the table, putting her bag down on its newspaper surface.

'All right are you?' he said eventually.

Rose could tell he was finding it difficult to think of anything to say, and she was faced with the same problem. She felt tears slide into her eyes. Nothing had changed, although everything had. Sid's face looked thinner, haggard and unshaven.

'You still at the BSA, Dad?' she asked finally, looking for a point of contact.

He shook his head, and she saw how many grey hairs there were among the black. He was fifty-four and he looked an old man.

'They let me go,' he said. 'Back to making bikes now the war's over.'

'Oh. I'm sorry,' she said.

Sid shrugged and then frowned, his pallid skin wrinkling as if he was trying to remember something. 'Where've you come from then?'

'Italy. Near Naples.'

Sid nodded slowly, bemused. 'Have a good journey then, did you?'

Rose knew at that moment that it would be quite pointless trying to talk to anyone at home about her years out of England. It was too far away, too removed from their own experience.

She nodded. 'Got cheap tickets on the train – cut rate if you've just been demobbed.'

She looked around. So far as she could remember, the room was exactly the same as when she had left, almost eerily so.

'Where's Grace?' she asked.

'Up Willett's. She's got a job. On the bedsteads like.'

After a moment he said, 'Fancy making us a cuppa tea?'

And that was that. His sole interest in her war.

The distance was there with Grace too, though the two of them embraced and laughed and looked at each other with tearful eyes when she came in from work. Rose was shocked by Grace's thin, careworn appearance. She felt there ought to be years' worth of things to say, that they should be making up for lost time, yet no one could think what to say.

'How are the twins?' Rose asked eagerly when the two of them were peeling and cutting up vegetables together late that afternoon. 'Have you seen them?'

'Oh, they're full of the joys,' Grace said. 'And Harry. All at school near Edna's. To tell you the truth, she can't bear the thought of parting with them. I asked her if she wanted to send them back here now it's all over. But as she says, they've been there nearly all their lives.'

'I'll have to go over,' Rose said. More people, she felt, who would be lost to her.

As the days and weeks passed after her homecoming, Rose fast began to resent the narrowness of the life she had been thrown back into, and her own lack of independence. How restless she felt! How could she ever settle down to this drab existence of rationing and dreariness after her time in Italy?

It was 'Where've you been? Make sure you're in by ten. Who've you been with?' From Sid, from Grace. Not that she went out much anyway. But Grace had got into the habit of questioning her as if she was her mother. She had completely taken over the role of woman of the house.

Everything seemed shrunken and oppressive. Even the

clothes Rose had left behind when she joined up no longer fitted her new, rounder figure. Number five was like a doll's house, while Rose felt like a giant who had been out striding across the world. Why couldn't they realize that after these four years she was now an adult who could run her life without being questioned all the time?

Once more, when there were important considerations like the family's mourning for Sam and Grace's personal grief over Joe, Rose found herself cast in the role of the restless, selfish one, always looking over the wall for fresher, greener grass.

After a month at home she found herself a job as a delivery driver for Snell's grocery store in Balsall Heath. Of course it had none of the excitement of her Italian driving, but at least it got her out and about and brought another wage into the house.

She would never forget her sister's face that day. Usually when Rose reached the house after Grace she found her sister's skinny form bustling round, tidying, handwashing, the evening meal already in hand.

Opening the door, Rose thought for a few seconds that there was no one in. She put down the few groceries she had bought on the way home – Typhoo and milk and Rinso. A ray of late afternoon autumn sunshine had managed to reach its way through the normally dark court windows and lay in a bright slanting shape on the table-top. Rose was already adjusting her mind to doing the evening meal herself when she saw her sister sitting there, to her right, the horsehair chair swivelled towards the window which looked over the court.

Grace didn't turn to look at her. Rose watched for a couple of seconds, seeing her cheeks drained of any colour, and the tight compression of her lips. She was taking in quick, shallow breaths.

'Are you all right?' Rose asked anxiously. 'Got an attack coming on?'

She stepped closer. Still Grace didn't move. Then Rose saw the letter in her lap, the thin blue paper.

'What's happened?' she asked gently, kneeling down by the arm of the chair, her heart thudding.

Without turning her head, Grace said, 'It's from Joe's mom.'

Rose frowned. Grace knew he was dead. What more could be wrong? 'Poor woman – she must be in a right state.'

'No.' Grace's head whipped round suddenly. 'She ain't in a state. She's got nothing to be in a state about.' Her voice suddenly rose to a piercing shriek. 'Because he's not dead! He's not bloody dead! And he's getting married next month!'

She got up suddenly and moved agitatedly round the room, as if she couldn't think what to do with her body. She picked up the bread knife.

'I could stick this in me!' she screamed at Rose. 'He's stuck enough knives in me to make me feel as if I'm bleeding to death!'

And then the sobs broke out of her. Rose took the knife from her, and drew her shaking sister into her arms.

'I don't understand,' she said softly, after she had let Grace have a good cry.

'That bloke who wrote to me,' Grace gasped out, her head pressed hard against Rose's shoulder. 'He must've known Joe was still alive. They were pals. They live in the same town. Joe must've told him to say he was dead – just to get rid of me.'

'Oh my God.' Rose suddenly saw it as clearly as Grace had done. 'What a bastard.'

'All he's put me through,' Grace went on in her distraught voice. 'Thinking he'd been killed, when all the time . . . He could've had the guts to write and say we was finished.'

'Men have a queer way of going about things,' Rose said drily.

She led Grace back to the chair to sit down, and

knelt beside her, holding her and letting her cry, as Margherita had done for her only a few months ago. For days and weeks afterwards she comforted her sister through the shock of this betrayal and, perhaps Grace's most hurtful realization, that at least if he had been truly dead, she could still have carried on believing that he loved her.

During her first weeks at home, Rose had to try to adjust to all the details of living back in an England freshly recovering from war.

Closest to home were the changes which had taken place in the court. The only familiar faces left were the Pye family and Mabel Gooch's household. The two sisters from number four had both died during the war, one quickly succeeding the other, and the house was now occupied by an old couple. Moonstruck House still had occasional tenants, who never stayed long, probably more because of its atrocious state of repair than any other kind of blight on the place. And there was a new family at number three.

Apart from learning the names of the new neighbours, she found she had to carry an identity card, use a ration book and clothing coupons still and register with the grocer and the butcher. There was the damp, drizzly weather and the worn, grey people around her, many of whom – with some justification she soon realized – gibed at her for being 'well out of it' down there in Italy.

The elections that year also shocked many people by removing Winston Churchill as prime minister and replacing him with Clement Attlee.

'How could they do it to him?' Grace demanded. 'After all he's seen us through. They'll be throwing the king out next.'

Rose, who had looked round at her country with new eyes on her return, had heard all the voices clamouring for change and decided to join them. Things had to be moved on, to be improved after the war, otherwise what was the point of it all? She didn't tell Grace, but her vote had gone to Attlee, and she rather suspected Sid's had as well.

There was talk of all kinds of changes, of visions almost unheard of before the war. Of a 'Welfare State' – better support for the out of work, for big families – even for getting looked after when you were sick. Who would not vote for that?

During all this time when change seemed to be constantly in the air and Rose struggled to endure this regressive state, as it felt to her, of living back at home, she had one more adjustment to make – really the biggest of them all.

When she walked in from work one afternoon, Alfie was waiting for her.

'Look who's here!' Grace said as Rose pushed open the door. There was a note of warning in her voice, Rose realized. 'Don't waste this opportunity,' she was saying. 'Make the most of him. You don't know how lucky you are.'

'Alfie!' Rose cried, more startled than pleased. She had known he must come home soon if he had survived the war, and no one had heard that he hadn't. But she had kept pushing the thought from her mind.

There he was, in his slightly too big demob suit, thin and pale, his hair cropped so short there was not enough of it to stick up in its unruly spikes. He looked older, Rose realized. His jaw was stronger as if his whole face had broadened a little.

'How are you?' she asked, full of confusion. So strange him being there, looking much the same, yet with these small changes which were all that signified nearly six years' absence.

'I'm all right.' Bashful and nervous, his eyes lingered over her wonderingly. How her figure had filled out! His eyes moved hungrily down over her breasts, her curving sides. She was wearing a tight-fitting jumper of moss green, and a straight tweedy skirt cut with all the meagreness of war garments, which she had managed to alter so it fitted her.

'You look a treat,' he said.

Rose blushed. She wasn't ready for this, this directness, this talking as if the war had passed in only a few days and nothing had changed.

'Have a cuppa tea,' Grace said firmly, pouring hastily from the brown teapot. 'He wouldn't have one till you got here, Rose. Come on, sit down both of you.' She handed Sid a cup and then sat at the table with Rose and Alfie. Rose watched her smile at him – about the warmest smile she had seen on Grace's face since she'd arrived home.

'I'm sorry to hear about Sam,' Alfie began awkwardly. 'He were a good bloke.'

Rose and Grace both nodded. 'Thanks,' Rose said. 'Yes, he was.'

'Where was it? Out east somewhere?'

'Burma,' Grace told him.

Again they all nodded sadly, lost for words. They didn't talk about the losses of the war much; everyone bore them privately.

'Grace tells me you was in Italy?' Alfie said. 'What the hell were you doing there?'

'ATS. I was a driver,' Rose said, feeling suddenly prickly. His voice held a slight mockery, as if he didn't believe it. 'Was through most of the war.'

'You mean they let you loose on them trucks!' Alfie chuckled, looking at Grace as if expecting her to confirm the joke. 'God Almighty, what a thought!'

Rose gave him a hard, defiant look. 'So where've you been all the war then? Found a better hole to go to, did you?'

She saw her words had hit home. Alfie turned red and looked down at his tea cup.

'It weren't my fault,' he said. 'That's how it was, going into France. If you'd been there you'd have seen.'

Prisoner of war through the whole thing. It was a hard homecoming. Not much to brag about.

'Sorry,' Rose relented. 'It must have been grim for you.'

'Thought at times we'd be there for the rest of our lives,' he said. 'It was only hearing from people . . .' He turned to look at her with a hurt expression in his eyes. 'You could've written more.'

'I did!' Rose exclaimed guiltily. She knew that her communication with him, especially once she had reached Italy, had been the bare minimum. 'I'm sorry. We were very busy.'

It was hard for her even to look at him. Had his feelings stood still during the war? What else did you have to change them when you were locked up in a prisoner of war camp?

'It was such a long time,' she said wearily.

'Come out with me tonight,' Alfie said suddenly. He wanted to be with her away from the others. Kiss her. Get back on their old footing. After all, she was the girl who had promised to be his wife.

Walks, the flicks, evenings spent at her house or his, with Mrs Meredith fussing adoringly round them both. It was more peaceful at Alfie's. To make ends meet, Mrs Meredith had taken in a lodger, a widow in her fifties, but she kept herself to herself most of the time.

Rose found Alfie easy undemanding company. Gradually she remembered that he had made her laugh sometimes, that he was kind and generous. That he adored her, and being adored was warming in itself, even though the feeling was not mutual and she knew it. During the winter of 1945–6 they met almost daily. Alfie soon found work amidst all the rebuilding of the city. When both had finished for the day they met up, already washed and changed, and spent the evening together. Anything to get out of Catherine Street, with Sid morose, often half drunk, and Grace sad, quiet and dutiful.

'When we're married,' Alfie said one evening, 'you

won't have to work any more. Not having my wife working.'

Rose looked round at him startled. It was growing dark and they were walking away from Catherine Street after he'd come to pick her up.

'Oh – and what d'you reckon I'm going to do all day long then?' she said indignantly. He had not even asked her to marry him again yet.

'You'll be looking after the babbies, won't you?' he said, as if it was obvious.

He had voiced something that she had not realized yet in herself. Was this not the one thing left that she really wanted? Babies – children? Passion, locked deep in her as a part of the past, did not seem accessible now. Perhaps it was something you could only have for a short time, a dream time, not part of real life. She didn't see much passion in the tired, struggling people around her.

But babies. Something in her surfaced and said yes. Please. If she could have nothing else out of life now, she could have children. That was what Alfie was offering.

In April 1946, in St Joseph's Church, Birch Street, Rose became Mrs Alfred Meredith.

CHAPTER 31

MOSELEY, BIRMINGHAM, 1949

'Rose? Coo-eee. Rose!'

Rose's neighbour Joan walked down the side of the little prefab house, pulling her eighteen-month-old son Freddie by the hand. She found Rose pegging washing on the line. As she called out again she saw Rose start violently. She turned, the peg-bag in one hand and the other laid over her heart.

'Oh, Joan. I was miles away. You didn't half make me jump.'

'Well, who did you think it might be – Jack the Ripper?' Joan moved over to the line. 'Here, let's give you a hand with the rest of this lot.'

She was a sturdy woman in her early thirties with heavy arms and legs and long, thick brown hair. She soon had the rest of the washing pegged out. Then the two of them turned to watch Freddie and Hilda, who were both bent over something that had caught their attention at the other end of the garden. Hilda was growing up to look the image of her father, though her hair was more manageable than Alfie's and hung in wispy strands round her head.

'Mom!' Hilda shouted imperiously. 'Come here – look!'

'You'll have to watch her,' Joan said. 'She's turning into a right little madam.' It was said inoffensively and Rose knew it to be true.

'I know. Sometimes I don't know how to deal with

her. Mind you,' she laughed, 'that's what they all said about me!'

After a moment Joan said, 'Actually the reason I came over was, I was wondering if you could have Freddie for a bit of today. Dave's off sick like, and he can't stand his noise . . .'

'And you need a break,' Rose finished for her. 'Yes, course I can have him. If you bring a bit of something over for his dinner he can stay all day. Be good for Hilda – she's better when there's company.'

Joan's fleshy face broke into a broad smile. 'Are you sure? Thanks Rose. Oh, what a difference it makes to have good neighbours, eh? Now, if there's anything I can do for you – bits of washing or anything you just bring it right over.'

'Right,' Rose said. She loathed housework. 'You're on.'

As Joan left, full of gratitude, Rose watched her with an amused expression. She wasn't at all sure she believed the story about Dave being poorly, but it didn't matter. The fact was, Freddie was a good kid but Joan couldn't stand to have him round her. Not day in day out. Any excuse and she brought him over to Rose. And she wasn't the only one. 'Oh, I 'spect Rose'll have him' was a common refrain among her neighbours with small children.

One way or another, most days the house was full of them, sometimes with their mothers, but more often without. In fine weather there were often five or six, with Hilda playing Queen Bee at the centre of it all, bossy, perverse, but generally easier to handle when there were other kids about.

'I don't know how you manage it,' the other women would say gratefully as she ran her unofficial little nursery. 'You're a godsend!' And they repaid her with admiration, company and small offerings they could spare out of their rations. They took in her washing and ironing, and sometimes even offered to clean her house – all of which seemed less fraught than spending their time in the company of their offspring.

This was how Rose filled her days. Alfie wouldn't allow her to work, so she managed in her own way to do what she loved best, caring for small children.

Rose used everything she could get her hands on for those kids. Alfie didn't mind how she occupied them, so long as the mess was all cleared up by the time he came home. Often the mothers didn't come to collect their children until the afternoon, and they'd stop and have a cuppa, sometimes bringing their own tea. They sat round as their little ones told them in shrill, excited voices all they had done during the morning.

'We helped Rose in the kitchen!'

'She gave us a apple and toffees!'

'I sat on the potty!'

And Rose smiled delightedly at them all, at their enjoyment of coming to her house.

'When you going to have another then?' Joan asked when she came round later that afternoon. 'Hilda's two now, ain't she? Don't want to have too big a gap.'

'When it comes, I 'spose,' Rose called through from the kitchen. She was mopping Hilda's cotton dress where she'd spilled her drink down it. 'Can't have one any sooner than that, can I?'

'You do remember what you have to do, don't you?' another of the women teased. 'They don't just grow inside by magic after the first one, you know!'

'You try telling my old man that!' Rose quipped back, going back to join them in the living room.

It was partly a joke. But after the women had left, Rose's emotions were stirred up by this conversation, leaving her unsettled and sad. There was much less lovemaking between her and Alfie than there had been in their early days of marriage and it was nearly always at his demand. Although she wasn't sorry he left her alone more nowadays, she did wonder why it was taking her so long to conceive another child. Was there something wrong? She had taken the risk with Falcone but there had been no baby then either. Often she wished there had been. Perhaps she wasn't able to bear many children?

She thought she had put behind her all those painful feelings of longing and restlessness which had plagued her after the war. She had even managed to quell her frustration at being married to Alfie, burying her desire for a wider, more challenging life by putting all her energy into her most lasting and satisfying love – small children. If this was her life, then she must make the best of it. Look at George, locked away for what might be as much as five years. And Grace, who had been denied the opportunity to achieve even her modest aspirations. She had not been accepted for training by any of the local hospitals, and was still at home, still taking jobs in factories and keeping house for Sid. Wasn't she, Rose, lucky? She should strive to return Alfie's kindness and affection and build a life which was good for both of them and for Hilda.

She had made an enormous effort to create this new life, like a person who has had a couple of limbs amputated and must adjust to new ways of living.

'It's good to see you looking happier,' Alfie had said to her recently. 'All that looking back to the war – don't do anyone any good, you know.'

She knew he resented her war, even though she had told him only the barest details of her life in the ATS. His own had been so limited, so unheroic. She tried for her own peace of mind to block out her memories. It was another country, another time. Over.

She submitted dutifully to Alfie whenever he turned to her in bed. She had almost forgotten the feelings her body was capable of. Alfie was quickly aroused and very soon satisfied. Invariably he mounted her almost immediately after a kiss and a quick feel of her breasts and he would enter her, almost unable to wait until he was inside, and then it was over. Rose patiently held his slim, pale shoulders time after time as he murmured 'Oh, Rosie, Rosie' into her left ear, feeling nothing except his moist, softening member withdrawing from her. He expected nothing more, and seemed never to notice that she got as much excitement from peeling potatoes as from his lovemaking. He was content. He had a good, pretty wife who other men envied him for. She never complained, so she must be all right. He was not aware there could be anything more and Rose had shut out any expectation that there might be.

But if she could not even have more children . . . She began to shake, her body letting out the tension that her mind had been keeping so tightly under control. She sat in the little living room as Hilda sat watching her with wide, frightened eyes. Finally, the tears came and Hilda began to cry too.

Rose picked her up and cuddled her. 'It's all right love, don't you worry. Mommy's just feeling a bit poorly, that's all.' She felt steadied by the child's warm body.

Could there ever really be love between a man and a woman? Mr Lazenby, Alfie – both used her in their way. And what about Tony? That was unreasonable, she knew, but in her state such terrible thoughts came. Worst of all, the one she tried to keep furthest from her mind persisted. What about Falcone? Had his words, his confusion, the looks of tenderness and desire that she had from him all been his way of using her? Of getting what he wanted and then dropping her for a 'higher calling'? Had she been deluded even when she responded to a man with every fibre of herself? All these doubts stabbed into her mind.

Though she had tried to avoid thinking of Italy, and especially of Il Rifugio, she knew that what sustained her and kept her feeling worth something was the knowledge that she could truly love and be loved in return. If no one else ever showed her that, then Falcone had done so. Try as she might to forget Italy and him, the thoughts still came to her from time to time.

Sometimes she dreamed of him, seeing his dark, serious eyes close to hers. In some of the dreams he was telling her how much he loved her. She saw herself back in the Finzis' house with the moon slanting through the windows on to their naked bodies. Or in Il Rifugio, making love with him on the thin straw pallets where she had first seen him sleeping. In other dreams he kept telling her over and over again that he had to leave her. He was cold and distant, cruel even. She would repeat the feeling of desolation of returning to Il Rifugio to find him gone. Sometimes she would wake crying, finding Alfie stirring next to her. The depth of her disappointment that he was not Falcone made her weep even more – harsh, quiet tears that she could never share with him.

A few weeks earlier she had had a letter from Gwen. She and Bill had compromised between their two sets of parents and settled in a small village in Berkshire. Bill was working in a bank in the nearby town.

'We're not very far from where we all started out together!' Gwen had told her. She already had a son and a daughter, Edward and Elizabeth, and was expecting her third child.

'I must say, I'm awfully happy,' Gwen wrote. 'Bill is a good husband and father and provides wonderful protection against Mummy when necessary! I should so love you to see E and E and to meet Alfie and your little Hilda. Perhaps we shall all be able to meet up one day?'

Gwen had apparently found a settled, serene sort of happiness with someone she loved. It was possible. But Rose knew she did not love Alfie.

As she sat that afternoon, holding a now rather drowsy Hilda and looking blankly over the child's shoulder, she knew starkly that though she had settled for what she could get, for filling her life with children, it was not and never could be enough.

She had to believe in her love for Falcone and his for her, even knowing she would never see him again. Without that life seemed worth nothing.

CHAPTER 32

Rose was hanging decorations on a little Christmas tree when she heard the banging on the door. With her were Hilda and Freddie and another little girl, all squabbling eagerly over the few baubles and the home-made foil stars.

'Hey! Anyone in?' a voice shouted.

She went to the door. Outside stood two men, struggling to support Alfie between them, his arms pinned over their shoulders and his body sagging between.

'About time,' one of the men said. 'He's a dead weight.'

Rose looked at them all, dumbfounded. Alfie's head was lolling to the right and his eyes rolling strangely from side to side like those of an idiot.

'Move out the road,' the older of the two men grunted at her. 'Let's get him on the bed. Silly bugger's got himself properly tanked up. Been a right game getting him over here on the bus, I can tell you.'

They hoisted Alfie into the bedroom and half laid, half threw him on to the pink-candlewick-covered bed. His eyes rolled upwards and then he closed them.

'He looks terrible,' Rose said. The sight of him really disturbed her. She stood close to the door holding back the three curious children. 'What's got into him? He's not a big drinker.'

'Oh, he'll be right as rain by tomorrow. Must've been putting it away while no one was looking. He'll have one hell of a head on him in the morning!' The younger man laughed knowingly.

The other, more serious, said to Rose, 'You'd better tell him, though, one more do like this and he'll be out of a job. He's lucky they're not putting the boot behind him today like. He'll have to watch himself.'

Still startled, Rose watched them go as they called out cheerfully, 'Tara, Alfie. See you in the morning.'

'Save it till Christmas next time, mate!'

Rose sat the children down in the next room with a beaker of rosehip syrup and a biscuit each, and came back in to her husband. He was lying with his eyes closed, but when he felt her unfastening his boots and pulling them off, he opened them.

'Rose?' he murmured indistinctly. 'I feel terrible.'

'Well, what were you thinking of?' she asked him. She knelt down by the head of the bed. 'No wonder. You're not used to more than the odd pint.'

'No.' Alfie's voice sounded thick and strange; out of his control. 'I told them – I kept saying . . . I haven't had a drop. Nothing.'

Rose frowned. 'What d'you mean? Look, you don't have to make a big secret of it. Was it something the others gave you? Whisky?'

'No,' he slurred back. 'I told you . . . nothing. I don't know. I'm scared, Rose.'

Suddenly very alarmed, she bent close to him and smelt his breath. There was not a trace of alcohol on it. She stood up quickly. 'I'll get a doctor.'

By that evening Alfie was in Selly Oak Hospital. Rose left Hilda with Joan and went in to see him. She found him lying in a long ward with rows of beds along each side, his face almost as white as the stiff pillow case and his eyes closed. Rose stood for a moment looking down at him. His hair was sticking up on top of his head and still looked greyed from the dust at work. His neck was bent rather awkwardly to one side as if he had a crick in it, and the shape of his body underneath the thin covers looked slight suddenly, and vulnerable.

'Alfie?' she said softly. On the floor by the bed she put the little bag of his possessions she'd brought in: pyjamas, shaving brush and razor, and the day's paper, thinking he'd have been feeling better.

His eyes opened slowly, trying to focus. He also seemed to be trying to smile.

'How you feeling?'

'Bad,' he said. 'Never . . . had anything . . . like this . . . before.'

She reached under the covers suddenly, surprising them both by taking his hand, feeling compassionate and protective towards him as she would have done towards a child.

'They'll look after you,' she told him. 'Soon see you better.'

Alfie nodded slowly and his eyes closed again. 'Sleepy,' he managed to say.

Rose sat by him until he was deeply asleep and then went to speak to the matron, a tall, well-spoken woman with a sheaf of papers in her hand. She had a brisk, forbidding air which suggested she might be kind so long as you submitted to her totally.

'My husband, Alfred Meredith,' Rose said, rather timidly. 'Do you know what's wrong with him?'

'Mr Meredith,' the woman said, her grey eyes scanning the ward for inspiration. 'Ah yes, the *ataxia* – new admission. No. Too early to say I'm afraid. Could be something quite simple but you never know. Might be a few days before we're sure.' She made as if to walk off.

'But how long will he be here – please?' Rose called after her. The woman seemed more intimidating than any officers she had come across in the ATS.

'Oh, I couldn't possibly say,' Matron replied. She noted something down on one of the papers she was holding. 'Let's wait and see what they say in the morning, shall we?'

Rose walked desolately out of the echoing hospital building to catch the bus home. Seeing Alfie lying there had come as a terrible shock to her. He looked so broken and helpless. Though she did not love him with anything approaching passion, she knew that it mattered to her a great deal what happened to him. She relied on him, on him being there with her, on his bland optimism and steady kindness. She had simply grown used to him. And he was Hilda's father. She was really frightened.

Before she reached the bus stop she changed her mind. Hilda would be asleep by now at Joan's. It was already dark. Instead, she made her way to Catherine Street. She felt completely churned up inside and she needed to see them, to tell them what had happened. Grace may have hardened herself to many of the problems of others, but she could always summon up sympathy for anyone who was sick.

Rose knocked on the door of number five. Outwardly the house looked much better than it had in the old days. The back-to-back terraces in Catherine Street were among a number that had been 'soled and heeled' by the council, who could not keep up with the demand to build new houses and had decided to patch up some of the ones they already had. New roofs, windows and doors had made the whole place look smarter. The front door was painted a cheerful sky blue.

'What you doing here?' Grace asked when she opened the door.

Rose walked in amid the smell of meat cooking and the gaslight which seemed so much dimmer than the electric they had out in the prefabs. She noticed there were no signs of Christmas about the house.

'Where's Hilda?' Grace demanded anxiously.

As Rose sat down, Grace stood by the table, hands on hips. She was dressed in a drab brown skirt and fawn blouse, on top a flowery apron which Rose realized with a pang had been cut down from an old dress of Dora's. Grace's hair was fastened up in an old scarf, the end tucked in at the front, to keep her hair out of the way while she was working.

'Hilda's with Joan,' Rose said. 'I've been with Alfie. He's in Selly Oak. Been taken bad.'

Grace automatically reached out and poured Rose a cup of tea. 'In hospital? What's up with him?'

'They don't know.' Rose began to cry at last, the worry and shock of the afternoon finally released.

Grace leaned close to her sister's dark head and put an arm round her shoulder. Rose got a whiff of the sweaty smell from under her arms, sharp, but somehow comforting.

'They brought him home at dinnertime. Looked as though he'd had a skinful. He was all over the place – eyes rolling, could hardly get a word out of his mouth, the lot. And he hadn't touched a drop.'

Grace looked quizzically at her. 'You sure he's not just having you on? After all, what with Christmas coming up – you know what they're like.'

'No,' Rose sobbed. 'He hardly drinks ever. He'd never lead us on and make us think he was bad when he wasn't.' She looked into Grace's concerned eyes. 'When you were nursing, d'you remember seeing anyone like that – like Alfie is now?'

Grace shook her head. 'I've seen blokes in a proper state – shocked and that. But not like you said. Never heard of that.' She patted Rose's arm with sudden kindness and Rose could hear the wartime nurse coming out in her. 'Anyhow, the doctors do all they can, so there's no point in fretting all night about it. You should get back to Hilda before she thinks she's lost both of you.'

As she spoke, the door opened and Sid pulled himself into the room. His hair, so dark when he was a young man, was now a powdery grey.

'Dinner ready?' he asked Grace, and she got up to spoon out the meat and vegetables.

'Alfie's in Selly Oak Hospital,' Rose told him, and tried to explain what was wrong. She wished overwhelmingly that Dora was there for her to turn to.

'Oh ar,' Sid said. Then through a mouthful of swede he commented dispassionately, 'Blooming shame. I always thought he looked a weak little runt though.'

Rose stood up abruptly. 'Time I was going,' she said bitterly. She put her coat on. 'Tara Dad. I see you're much as usual.'

Sid raised one hand as a goodbye, but Grace followed Rose out into the yard.

'It's no good expecting anything from him,' she said, with more gentleness than Rose had heard from her for a long time. 'He lives in his own little world now and the rest of us might just as well not be here.' She touched Rose awkwardly on the shoulder. 'If you need anything, come to me, all right?'

Rose smiled at her. 'Still here, aren't you – after all this time. Running about after everyone.'

Grace shrugged rather evasively. 'Looks like that's what I'm good for, don't it? Now remember what I said. Just ask for help if you need it.'

Humbled, Rose kissed her quickly on her rough cheek. 'That's nice of you,' she said. 'Ta.'

Alfie spent Christmas 1949 in hospital. Hilda kept saying, 'Where's my Dad?' Rose brought her in to be with Alfie for a short time, walking into the warm ward from the icy air outside. When Hilda saw him she ran to him, dressed in her little red coat and black boots, her hair tied up in two pigtails.

'Hello little monkey,' Alfie said as Hilda hurled herself at him. He was propped up on several thick pillows. His voice sounded stronger now and his words were easier to understand.

'Not on the bed, please,' a nurse said as she walked past. 'I know it's Christmas, but we still have to keep the rules.'

'She's a real daddy's girl,' Rose told her apologetically. 'Been missing him like anything.' She lifted Hilda down on to her lap. The nurse walked off in her heavy black shoes, smiling.

'How are you?' Rose asked. 'You look a bit better today.'

'I feel better,' Alfie said. He was even wearing one of the coloured hats they'd all been given to jolly things along for Christmas, and the soft orange tissue paper kept slipping off his clumps of hair. 'It's wearing off a bit. My hands felt all queer, sort of numb. Scared me, I can tell you.'

His pale face suddenly lit up with an adoring smile. 'It's lovely to see you, Rosie. Give us a kiss, will you?'

She stood up and leaned forwards to kiss him. Affectionately she straightened the orange crown. 'I'll have to bring some Brylcreem in,' she joked.

But Alfie was staring at her with a seriousness which silenced her. 'I love you,' he said. 'You know that, don't you? I should tell you more often. Only when you're always about I forget . . . But, if anything was to happen . . .?'

'I know,' Rose said. She couldn't look at him straight, and felt her cheeks turning red. Hilda was pulling at her skirt, impatient at this conversation which took the attention away from her.

'You'll be home soon though, won't you?' Rose said brightly.

They didn't tell her then. It was a couple of days later. A condition affecting the nerves, the doctor with the grey hair and distant eyes said. Very hard to predict how it would progress. Some patients lived normal lives for years. Attacks and remissions, that was the pattern. Sometimes he'd be perfectly all right, sometimes not.

'Does he know?' Rose asked. Her eyes rested on the doctor's dark blue tie.

Looking out of the window beyond her, he said, 'He's known for a little while. He's had the chance to think about it. Said he'd rather I told his, er, family myself.'

'What about work?' Rose asked. 'Will he be able to carry on?'

'Your husband's a builder I see.' The doctor made a sharp, regretful intake of breath. 'Very difficult. Building's not a good job to be in with his condition. Any work off the ground, on scaffolding for instance, could cost him his life if he had another of these attacks. You must impress that upon him strongly, Mrs Meredith. He can't afford to be careless with himself.'

'Course I'm going back to work!' Alfie said. It was January, snowy, and thick fog covered the city, so dense that the traffic was having trouble passing along the streets. 'I feel fine. Don't s'pose they'll be doing a lot today anyway, but I've told them I'll show me face and see what's cooking. Don't you worry, Rosie,' he said, seeing her anxious expression. She was standing at the door with Hilda in her arms. 'I'll keep me feet on the ground. After all, someone's got to be the breadwinner round here!'

After he'd kissed them both they watched him, Hilda waving as he walked away, fast disappearing into the fog.

Two months later Alfie collapsed again. This time he was at home, and the attack seemed even more severe. Rose was terrified by the fear and distress on his ashen face. A pattern emerged. Hospital, a recovery period, a time when he felt weaker perhaps, but more or less normal, and then another attack. By the late summer of 1950 he was barely recovering between each one. His legs, from which he was gradually losing all sensation, finally became paralysed. He could do very little without help. Alfie had become a permanent invalid.

CHAPTER 33

CATHERINE STREET, BIRMINGHAM, JANUARY 1951

'This house is all pongy!'

Little Hilda, only a few months off her fourth birthday, sniffed distastefully as she eyed up the place that was to be her new home. She had grown into a pale, rather scrawny child, her brown hair scraped back into a high ponytail, the end of which did not even reach as far down as the back of her neck.

'Moonstruck House.' Mabel Gooch's gruff voice came from the edge of the room, where her barrel-shaped body was leaning up against the doorframe. Mabel, still the matriarch of Court 11, had aged from a woman with a strong, handsome face into one who looked almost masculine, with a hint of a moustache gathering on her top lip. 'Bet you never thought you'd end up here, eh, Rose?' There was a strong hint of satisfaction in her voice. But then she added, 'Still, it's good to know there's someone decent living here for a change. God knows, we've had some rum'uns in here, I can tell you.'

'It'll have to do us,' Rose replied flatly. 'I can't keep up the rent where we are.'

Like number five, Moonstruck House had been soled and heeled. All the windows were in, the doorframes had been replaced and the roof fixed. But on the inside it was a different matter. The smell of damp was unmistakable and there was mould growing all along the walls under the windows. In the downstairs room there was still some paper on the walls – a yellowish colour with clusters of dull pink flowers and a border of green cheese-plant leaves a few inches from the ceiling. A few sections of it near the floor had been ripped off upwards, and in other places the corners were curling back.

Upstairs, both rooms showed the barest traces of paper. Otherwise it was bare plaster, some of which had fallen or been gouged out in places where through the holes you could see the bare brick. In the second-floor room the floorboards opened up suddenly to the stairwell which plunged down in a corner. It was bleaker than number five had ever been.

'Never had anyone in long enough to take a pride in it. But you could soon cheer it up, give it a lick of distemper.'

Rose nodded absently. Mabel noticed how painfully thin she had become again. Even her pre-war clothes hung on her now and her eyes seemed more prominent in her face.

'He'll have to have a bed downstairs,' Rose was saying. She was grateful to Mabel for sticking around to talk things through. 'I can't get him up the stairs of a night. And anyway,' she added resignedly, 'it's hard to get him out of bed in the first place nowadays.'

'Like that is it?' Mabel shook her head sympathetically. She felt suddenly rather maternal towards Rose. 'Well, you'll have to make it as easy on you as you can. You working and night school and that. Don't worry' – she patted Rose's shoulder with her thick hand – 'we'll see you through. Your mother would've done the same for any of us.'

There were tears of gratitude in Rose's eyes as she turned to her old neighbour. 'Yes,' she said. 'I know she would.'

They did fix Alfie up with a bed downstairs, along the wall away from the front window. Rose put up some net to stop people gawping in. The Pyes lent her a hand one weekend in filling in the worst holes in the walls and giving the place a couple of coats of whitewash upstairs.

Rose scrubbed down all the floorboards with disinfectant and laid down what she had in the way of old peg rugs and little off-cuts of carpet they had acquired in Moseley.

Alfie half sat, half lay watching her one Sunday morning as she attempted energetically to carry on turning the place into somewhere they could call a home. It was cold and she had built a fire and was sweeping up the scullery.

'You should get out of bed,' she told him patiently. 'You know what the nurse said about you getting sore if you lie about all day.'

Alfie looked up at her languidly. 'It's so cold,' he protested, in the strange, slurred voice he spoke in now. 'And you've got too much to do already, Rosie.'

'I can do that later,' Rose said, growing impatient. 'Come on – let's get you up.'

Hilda appeared from upstairs as Rose was preparing a bowl of warm water to wash her husband. 'What can I do?' she whined.

'D'you want to come and help me give your dad a wash?' Hilda had grown very used to seeing her father's body since he had been ill. His place at the centre of all that was going on made his a very public illness.

'No,' Hilda said, sitting on the bottom step of the stairs and kicking at the wood with her heels. 'S'boring. And smelly.'

'Well go out and play then,' Rose said, trying the temperature of the water in the bowl.

'Don't want to.' Hilda's face twisted into the expression of stubborn sulkiness she often wore nowadays. 'You're just trying to get rid of me.'

'Yes,' Rose snapped. 'I am. Sitting around moaning at me. Now do as you're told and get out there with the others.'

'Me dad'd never be so horrible to me,' she said snidely as she pulled her old coat on.

Silently Rose began soaping Alfie's scrawny white arms. He had lost all the muscle tone that his building work had given him, and the translucent skin seemed to cover bone and little else. His arms had become stiff and awkward, and she had to lean on them to bend them. She washed under his arms, the light brown wiry hair turning white with soap. She'd tucked a towel under his shoulders so as not to wet the sheets. Gently she wiped his face, and then slid her hands flat under him to turn him so that she could wash his back. The nurses had showed her how – the lifting and bed baths. How to position a little container between his legs to catch the urine which dribbled from him beyond his control.

When she had turned him back over and was washing his chest she realized he was watching her, and that tears were rolling down his cheeks. She stopped what she was doing and stroked his hair which was rather greasy and needed cutting.

'What's the matter?' she asked softly.

'I'm sorry, Rose.' The sobs shook his body, his thin, gentle face growing pink and streaked with the tears. 'You shouldn't be having to do all this.'

'Ssshh,' she said, trying to soothe him, tears of sorrow and pity filling her own eyes. 'Don't say that. I've told you. I'm your wife, aren't I? Who else should be looking after you?'

'But living back here.' Alfie's voice came out horribly slurred from the disease and his distress. 'It was the last thing you wanted. I was going to do so much for you, Rosie, give you so much. I'm sorry . . .'

In the early days, when she had first begun caring for him, he had wept like this often, full of remorse, frustration and fear as to what was going to happen to the family. He had worried how they would live on sickness benefit alone. About how Rose would manage, and what would happen to Hilda. And in sheer horror at what was happening to his body. Worst of all had been the times when, at first, he had still wanted to make love to her.

'Rosie, come here,' he'd beg, wanting things to be all right, for at least that to be possible between them. She would lie in his arms as he took her breasts in his hands, touching her, kissing her desperately, trying to force some sensation into the limp lower half of his body. Sometimes he would say, as he had never done when he was well, 'Will you help me? Will you touch me?'

Pityingly she had taken him in her hands, trying to kindle him, caressing the soft, small part of him which could feel nothing, and trying, more for his sake than for her own, to arouse him. He would lie watching her with a fixed expression of concentration on his face, longing, willing himself, and it was that desperation she saw in him which made her cry, and his failure and shame which brought on his own tears, so that they would end up lying in distress in each other's arms, in a strange way closer than they had ever been before he was ill.

They no longer attempted lovemaking now. Rose cared for him and he, most of the time, just accepted that this was how it had to be. Seeing him in this broken state she grew to realize how grateful she was to him, and that she did indeed care for him, not as a lover – which she never had and never could – but as a kind, familiar friend, and the way she would care for a child or any sick, fragile creature.

As she dried his tears that cold morning, he appealed to her in a whisper, 'Give us a kiss, will you?'

She bent and kissed his lips, smelling the rather stale, sour smell of him despite the wash. When they had kissed she smiled kindly at him. 'I'll change your sheets again. Come on – let's get you into a chair.'

'I'm sorry,' he said again.

'It's not your fault,' she told him, touching his bony shoulder. 'Look – it's all right.'

In a way it was. Her feelings at that time were so mixed, so mercurial that at times she could barely make up her mind what she felt about anything.

Moving back into Catherine Street had symbolized for her the end of any aspirations of her own. The circle had closed. Now she was back just where she began and could hope for nothing better. But in another way it had been a relief to see the familiar old faces and know she could always rely on them for help. At that moment that was her greatest need.

At other times she was overcome by an extraordinary exhilaration, even through all the tiredness. It was like a resurgence in her of someone entirely forgotten. There was the thrill of risk, and the challenging sense that she was in charge. She could no longer be dependent and passive. She began to experience some of the zest for life she had felt in the army. Now at last she could do something.

'I'm going to have to earn more than the odd bob or two,' she had said to Grace. 'I'll have to learn how to do something. I'm only fit for the factory floor or a shop.'

So she had started the evening classes. She signed on for three evenings a week at Sparkhill Commercial School over on the Stratford Road. English, typing and shorthand, she decided, would stand her in the best stead for the future. Meantime, whatever job she got they would have to make the best of it until she was trained to do something better.

She applied for a job working in the offices of a firm in Burton Street, only a couple of streets away from home: Turner's Metal Smallware.

Since it was so near at hand she was able to run home in the lunch hour and give Alfie a few moments' company as well as hastily making Hilda something to eat. The rest of the day either Mabel or Gladys Pye saw to her and she played with the other kids in the court who were too young for school.

Her duties at Turner's ranged from seeing to the outgoing post, of which there was a great deal to be sealed and stamped on the cranky old franking machine, to helping actually to pack the goods: shining piles of hairgrips and hairpins and metal coathangers and straight pins, which were boxed up and sent out to shops all over the country.

Though the work was often tedious and she felt guilty leaving Alfie and Hilda, the fact was she had no choice in the matter if they were all to eat. As her mother had done before her, she was going to keep her family, though at the moment the money was never enough. Mrs Meredith helped them out a little when she could, but it was the kindness of the neighbours which really kept them going: Gladys popping in saying, 'Look – we've a couple of portions of stew left over. You have it, Rose. It'll go bad else'; or Mabel coming by with a loaf or a cake or a pat of margarine. Even the neighbours who she had not known all her life pitched in. Rose sometimes wept at their unquestioning generosity.

Often in the evening, when she had walked the couple of miles to Sparkhill after a hasty bite to eat, she would sit for two hours learning the intricacies of Pitman shorthand, her whole body throbbing with tiredness. Despite that she was one of the best in the class. She practised at every opportunity. Whenever she had to write something down she would think how to do it in shorthand.

'Some people have a natural bent for shorthand,' the tutor told her, smiling. 'And you're certainly one of them.'

Rose beamed with delight at learning something new and being praised for it.

One evening, when she had been going to Sparkhill for a few months, she walked down the front steps of the school with some of the other girls from the class. They were chatting, groaning over their typing speeds on the heavy Underwood machines. It was a warm evening, still light, and the air was soft and still, scented with fading laburnum and lilac. Occasionally a car passed by on the Stratford Road.

'I'm tired,' Rose sighed as they reached the pavement. 'I've a good mind to get on the bus and to hell with it.'

'Money down the drain,' her friends reminded her cheerfully. 'Bus or bread.'

Rose smiled. 'It's a good job you're here to keep me in line. Anyway, by the time I've been into town and out it'll take me just as long. And at least it's still light.'

They said their goodbyes and set out in different directions.

Rose turned, still smiling from the friendly company, to walk towards the side street where she would turn off towards home. She caught a whiff of roses from the gardens and breathed in the scent, so different from the usual smoky smells of the city.

Just before she turned off the Stratford Road, wondering whether Hilda had played Grace up about going to bed, she felt a hand settle firmly on her shoulder. Startled, she turned with a gasp, and behind her she found a handsome, and suddenly familiar face grinning at her.

It was Michael Gillespie.

CHAPTER 34

MARCH 1952

Again she woke from a vivid dream, those dreams which came only occasionally now. She realized her face was wet with tears. It had been so vivid.

They were in Il Rifugio, alone in the storeroom where she had first seen Falcone on the maize-straw mattresses. The others may have been around somewhere but the two of them were alone, and knew they would not be disturbed. She did not recall any particular words, or that they had spoken at all. What was most overpowering was the atmosphere of tenderness and passion as they loved one another. She remembered his body, slim and strong and dark, in every detail, as if they had only truly been together the night before. And the look on his face, his delight in her and care for her and her own sense of giving herself unreservedly and with joy.

For a moment she lay wiping her eyes, still completely taken up in the mood of the dream. Then other thoughts forced themselves into her mind, thoughts which filled her with excitement, but at the same time with strong pangs of guilt. Michael. She had agreed to meet Michael tonight. Though her conscience and common sense cried out not to do it, she knew that she would go.

She had seen Michael a number of times, at first only occasionally and seemingly by chance, after their first meeting. Seeing him there had truly delighted her.

'Michael!' she'd cried in wonder. 'You're alive. All this time you've been alive!'

He'd laughed at this, bending his strong body down to

give her a kiss on the cheek. 'Oh, I'm alive all right. Even survived the River Po and that's saying something, I can tell you. Sea of corpses it was when we crossed.' His expression lost its exuberance at the memory. 'But that's long in the past, and we both came through it, eh?'

'I was never in much danger down there,' Rose said. 'Hell of a lot quieter than it was here really.' She stood staring at him, amazed at the thought that the last time she had seen him had been outside the stables at Caserta. And it was so precious, that memory, that link with the war. Just those few minutes when they had stood together with Tony. Someone else who would remember him, remember the place.

'You living round here?' Michael asked.

'No. Been to school.' She outlined briefly what she was doing, told him about Alfie and Hilda.

Michael let out a whistle of sympathy. 'That's really rough. You poor kid. I thought you wasn't looking as bonny as when I saw you in Italy. But you always did have guts, I'll say that for you, Rose. Can't see my wife getting out earning a living.'

'You're married then?' They were still standing where he had caught up with her, Michael pressing one of his shiny black shoes up against the wall facing him as they talked. A tram made its way noisily along the road.

'Oh, yes. The wife and I live on down there a way. Edge of Hall Green.' He pointed down the Stratford Road. 'Mary her name is. Good Irish girl. I've a lad too – Joseph. He's two.'

Rose felt a pang at the name Joseph. For a second she calculated how old her own Joseph would have been now. Fourteen this year. A grown lad, perhaps just starting out on a job.

'I've got the bookies down the road,' Michael was saying proudly. 'My own little outfit. Gillespie over the door. Doing well. You know how it is with a growing family. We've another on the way – due in October.'

'I'm glad. It's really good to see you.'

'Listen – come for a drink with me,' Michael urged.

He went to put an arm round her shoulders and usher her along. 'Jesus, you're skinny! We can have a quick one in the Mermaid.'

'I can't,' Rose told him regretfully. 'Sorry Michael, I just can't. I've left my husband and kid all day.'

'OK,' Michael said easily, removing his muscular arm from her shoulders. 'Then let me walk you home.'

'Well . . .' Rose hesitated. 'That'd be nice. But what about your wife? Weren't you on your way home?'

Michael made a quick, dismissive gesture. 'Oh – she'll be off to bed any minute. She gets tired, what with the babbies and that. Anyroad, I'm out most nights to tell you the truth. She never kicks up a fuss.'

All the way back to Catherine Street they chatted and reminisced. Michael told her he had met Mary, his wife, three years ago.

'It was one of these Irish dos. Lots of booze and the music going and all the couples dancing and all the old'uns getting sick for the home country. She was fresh over here and she stood out. Really pretty face she had – well, she still has, except she's got a bit of fat on her after having Joseph, of course. But she's a good lass. Looks after me all right.'

'Bet that takes some doing,' Rose teased him. She realized, as ever with Michael, that she had began to flirt with him. 'Not sure I'd fancy the job myself!'

'Would you not?' Michael sounded mock wounded. 'I'd've said we'd have made a pretty fine team, you and me, Rosie.'

Rose realized he was not entirely joking, and she blushed in the dusk. Guiltily, she knew she had not felt so alive, so stimulated by anyone's sheer presence, in months and months. She steered the conversation on to less personal things.

When they said goodnight at the end of Catherine Street, Michael gave her another kiss on the cheek.

'Come for a drink another time,' he called, turning back towards Sparkhill.

Inside, to her surprise, she found Sid dozing in the

chair beside Alfie, who was also asleep. She crept in, and Sid roused himself as she closed the door.

''Bout time,' he said, looking up at her with the bleary eyes of an old man. 'Our Grace has gone home to bed.'

Rose looked at the clock. She had taken half an hour longer than usual to get home. Had she and Michael really spent so much time talking? It had seemed to pass in seconds.

She saw Sid out, giving herself a ticking off when she remembered how much help they were giving her.

She and Michael met for a brief drink some weeks later, but then it was months before she saw him again. There was no English class on the Thursday evening before Christmas, and they arranged to meet then. Rose knew she was deceiving Grace, who would spend the evening with Alfie. But sometimes she thought Grace would be lost now without her role in Rose's house. It had become part of her life. And Rose hungered for company, for interest and someone to have a good talk with.

As she sat opposite Michael in the busy Mermaid pub, she found all her doubts disappearing, and relaxed back into enjoying his company. They made an attractive pair, Michael in what looked like a new dark blue suit, his hair cut perfectly and greased back, and Rose with her long hair curling down prettily over her shoulders. She looked beautiful, especially when animated by her conversation with Michael.

They started talking about general things: Michael's business, the way money was so tight still, and of Michael's satisfaction that Winston Churchill had been re-elected to office in October.

'Now things'll get back to rights again,' he told her, with the almost superstitious regard in which some people still held Churchill. 'All that Labour lot messing about. What we need is a proper government – someone who knows what they're doing. Been like rats from a sinking ship, all these people looking to go abroad to work. What good's that to our country?' He pushed back his stool. 'Another?'

Rose watched him going to the bar. He still walked with the trace of a limp which had stayed with him from his injury in Italy. He was a fine-looking man with strong features and those direct blue eyes, always a hint of mischief in them.

He's a bit of a chancer, she thought. Bet he gives that poor wife of his the runaround. But she couldn't resist being with him this evening. He was a connection with the past, and being able to go out and meet him made her feel she could laugh and be her age again, for a short time at least, instead of driven, worried and overworked.

'I was just thinking,' he said, sitting down with their drinks, a pint for him and port and lemon for her. 'If you're out working all day, who looks after your husband?'

'Neighbours. I moved back to the Birch Street area again when Alfie was taken bad. They all help mind Hilda, my little girl, too. Me and Grace do the shopping between us – I mean, who's got the time to stand in a queue for hours on end? Anyroad, that's all that's left of the family now. My brother George is . . .' Blushing, she looked down at the table. 'He's in Winson Green.'

'Jesus! What for?'

'Burglary. He went bad on us during the war. I was away of course, so I hardly saw it coming. But Grace had him all through. She's done with with him. She don't even go and visit.'

'But you do?'

'When I can. Only every month or two, and he's due out soon anyroad. He's my brother. I always had a soft spot for him as a kid. I s'pose it was after the evacuation – he ran away, and he was never the same after he came back. It's as if—' She looked up at Michael, and he saw that tears had filled her brown eyes. Gently he leaned over and laid one of his large hands over hers, which were clasped tensely together on the table.

'It's as if he went off like a pint of milk. You can't get through to him any more. When I go over there' – she grimaced at the thought of the dark stone walls and towers of the prison – 'he sits there, all pinched in the face. All hard looking. I don't know who he is any more.' Slowly she pulled her hands away.

'I'm sure you're doing the right thing,' Michael told her. 'Though God knows, with all you've got on your plate no one'd think bad of you if you didn't go.' Then he asked gently, 'And your husband – Alfie, isn't it? How much can he do?'

'Nothing.' Rose sounded very matter of fact. 'It's got to him very hard and very fast. He doesn't move out of bed. Can't do anything for himself at all. Someone has to be about all the time.'

She took in Michael's appalled expression, realized that he was reaching for her hands again, but she kept them under the table. At that moment she felt that if he touched her she might just turn into his arms and cry out all the worry and tiredness and frustration of the past months. She longed for such comfort, to be able to lean on someone as solid and kind and reviving as Michael.

'Oh, Rosie,' he said. 'You poor, brave kid.'

She could think of nothing else to say to him, and was relieved when after a few moments he started talking. As she wiped her eyes she realized that her telling him about her own life and worries had released him and he was now able to disclose to her his own.

'When I met Mary, I thought I'd found the best woman ever,' he told her. 'She was pretty and sweet. She looked up to me and I loved her. I really thought the world of her, Rosie . . .' He hesitated, and as she looked across at him she saw confusion in his face.

'But . . .?' she prompted.

'I don't know if it's having the babbies that's done it. Joseph's a great kid, and now we've got little Geraldine and she's a bonny babby. But Mary, she's got time for nothing else. What with feeding Geraldine at night and both of them on all day. And she frowns all the time.

You may smile, Rosie, but before I'd hardly seen her crease her face in that way. She was the sweetest girl . . . But now she's got a line, as if someone's taken a pencil right down.' He pointed to the little bridge of flesh between his eyebrows. 'She never had that before.'

Rose leaned across the table and pointed at her own face, so that a man at the next door table watched with a puzzled expression. 'Look – I've got one too. They ought to call it the mother's mark!'

'But I don't get it . . .' Michael trailed off, frowning. 'You've got more worries than she has. She's not got a care in the world. All women have kiddies, but they don't go all mardy on you like Mary. She ain't got time for me, not in any department.'

He sat in gloomy silence for a moment, his deep blue eyes staring unfocusing across the bar. Around them people were laughing and two old men had started singing 'Roll out the Barrel'.

He brought himself up with a jerk. 'Sorry, Rosie. Didn't mean to bring you here and pour out all my troubles. You won't want to come again?'

She knew it was an invitation.

'But don't you think sometimes, looking back to when we was kids at Lazenby's, we were full of all we were going to do. What was it you went on about? Teaching kids, wasn't it? And I was going to run the world, have a big business . . .' He chuckled bitterly. 'And now look at us.'

'But you're doing all right?'

'All right. That's about the sum of it. But I wanted more, much more than that. Maybe that's where I went wrong.'

They talked a little while longer before Rose told him she really had to go in order to get home at the normal time. They walked back together, further into the darkened city, where the points of greatest light and noise were the pubs on corners and down side streets.

'Meet me again, won't you?' he asked as they parted, and she nodded. She knew that this meeting, and the way they had found they could confide in each other, had sealed their need to see each other.

Before she could stop him, he took her in his arms briefly and kissed her hungrily on the lips.

As she walked into Court 11 she tried to push from her mind what had just happened. It was a mistake, the result of an evening of resuming old friendship and sharing emotion. She wouldn't let it happen again.

Quietly she released the catch on the door and pushed it open. For a few seconds she stood startled in the doorway, watching unnoticed before Grace turned, conscious of the draught from the doorway.

Alfie was lying as usual, on one side in the bed. They had to turn him every couple of hours to relieve the pressure on his bedridden body, which opened up his skin into deep sores. Grace was sitting beside him, tenderly holding one of his hands in her own.

Unsettled, and feeling strangely guilty at the apparent intimacy of the scene, Rose moved in briskly, pretending not to have noticed. Alfie's eyes opened and his face lit up as far as it was able into his lopsided smile.

'Everything all right?' she asked. 'Hilda asleep?'

'She's well gone,' Grace told her.

Rose poured some tea for all of them.

'These sores, Rose.' Grace pointed at Alfie. 'They're not getting any better, are they?'

Rose sighed, sipping the warm tea. 'It's a losing battle. I don't know what else we can do.'

The two of them gently turned back Alfie's bedclothes, and he stirred slightly, his eyes closed again. A rank smell emanated from him, a mixture of sweat and urine and the discharge from the sores.

'We'll turn him,' Rose said. 'I'm glad you waited. It's a job on your own.'

They slid their arms under Alfie's inert body, pulling him gently across the bed, and rolled him over on to his other side.

Grace tutted. 'Sheet's wet again. We'll have to change it.'

Manoeuvring Alfie's body from side to side, they pulled out the bottom sheet and smoothed over another one. Washing and more washing. Rose carefully wrapped his reddened heels and elbows in soft cloths to help protect them against the bed's chafing.

They eased Alfie out of his pyjamas. His limbs kept stiffening into muscular spasms, so that for minutes at a time they could not straighten his arms enough to slide on a fresh pyjama jacket.

Before they replaced the trousers, Rose turned her attention to the worst sores at the bottom of his back. On the right side, the top part of his buttock was beginning to break up, the skin all red and cracked, and they were doing all they could to prevent it getting as bad as the other side. On the left a full-blown sore had developed into a discoloured, oozing hole large enough to hold a golf ball. It looked appalling, though Alfie said he was not aware of much pain from it.

Rose carefully pulled off the lint dressing and grimaced. From inside oozed a yellowish grey, foul-smelling liquid. 'We'll have to dress it again,' she said.

The nurse had recommended packing the wound with lint and a concoction of whipped egg whites, something which Rose had a decreasing amount of faith in as a remedy. When they had finished they tucked a bottle between his legs to try and keep the urine off the sheets, and covered him up again.

'D'you want your tea now, Alfie?' Grace asked him gently. Almost imperceptibly he nodded his head.

Rose met Michael on other occasions after that. What was the harm in meeting a friend, she reasoned. Except – and the thoughts hovered around and were pushed to the back of her mind – she couldn't bring herself to tell Grace.

Michael was like a lifeline. How could she give that up when the rest of life, the drab, everyday routine of illness and Turner's and rationing and struggle offered so little?

As she got out of bed that March morning, the dream of Falcone gradually sliding from her mind, she tried to quell her excitement at the thought of meeting Michael in the evening. After all, they were both married people with families meeting for a chinwag. So why should her feelings be so stirred?

CHAPTER 35

'I needn't go tonight,' she told Grace, her guilt making her wish that her sister would demand her presence. 'I'll stay if you think you'll need me.'

Alfie had a bad cold which had gone to his chest, and she had been helping Grace to prop him up so that he could cough and clear his lungs.

'No, you're all right. You go,' Grace said, seating herself on the wooden chair beside Alfie's head. 'I can always fetch Gladys in.'

Rose wondered if she was imagining that Grace really preferred it when she was out of the way. Or did she suspect that Rose was not going to a class at all?

'Well, all right,' she agreed. 'I'll get back as early as I can.'

'No need.' Grace pulled some knitting out of an old cloth bag. 'We'll get on fine – won't we, Alfie?'

As she walked into the cosy light of the Mermaid she saw Michael raise an arm to her. He was as usual dressed immaculately. She had never seen him wear anything the least bit worn or shabby. He had on a dark blue suit which emphasized the already powerful outline of his body.

'Sorry I'm late, Michael,' she gasped, sitting down at last with relief on the bench opposite him.

'Oh, no need to apologize.' He got up as she unbuttoned her coat. 'What'll you have?'

Clearly he'd managed to fit in a couple of drinks

already. When he came back to their table with the glasses and sat down, Rose immediately sensed a tension between them, something which made her self-conscious, and she found it hard to look him in the eyes.

She chatted to him nervously. They must keep things normal and conversational. Within bounds. She must not let him touch her hands across the table as he had done before. Otherwise she could not carry on persuading herself that she was justified in meeting him.

'Your family all right?' she asked. 'How's Mary? And the babby?'

'Mary's getting more sleep nowadays,' Michael told her. He was sitting with a generous tumbler of Scotch in front of him. 'They're all OK. They're doing fine.'

He sounded evasive, as if he didn't want to go into how things were between him and Mary. Rose had begun to realize that Michael only found it possible to confide in her if she first disclosed something about herself or showed emotion in front of him, and she was deliberately keeping that at bay.

Suddenly Michael said, 'I've been meaning to ask you something. About your . . . about Alfie.' Rose waited. 'Well, how is he?'

Rose was puzzled. 'Well, he's not too good. He never is of course. But he's got a chill at the moment.'

'I meant . . .' Michael looked down at the floor between his legs. 'Is he never going to get right again?'

'No. There's nothing anyone can do for him. No cure. Michael, you know that. I've told you endless times.'

He shook his head sadly. 'I thought – I was just making sure.'

'Anyroad,' Rose went on. 'The next thing is George is coming out, next week some time. God knows I've wished him out of there often enough, but now he's really coming I don't know what the hell we're going to do with him. I'm scared at the thought, Michael, to tell you the truth.'

'Where's he going to live?'

Rose shrugged again. 'I s'pose he'll have to come

home. I mean where else? Grace hasn't said a word about it and Dad might as well have forgotten who he is. We'll just have to see if he can hold down a job.'

'Can he do anything?'

'Thieving. He's good at that.'

Michael laughed, pulling out his cigarettes. Rose felt as if his blue eyes were piercing right through her. 'You only see your family as they are, don't you, Rosie? Not like me. Always wanting to put Mary on a pedestal like a plaster statue.'

'Well, how else?' Rose joined in his laughter and accepted a cigarette. 'Bit late to go making up fairy stories about them, isn't it?'

'Not for me. It's just the way I like to dream about people.' And again the sadness crept back in to his eyes. 'Trouble with statues on pedestals is that one way or another they keep getting knocked off.'

Then he asked, with the kind of intensity she had started to dread from him, 'What about you, Rosie?' He asked the question as if he wanted something from her: some pronouncement or decision. 'What are you going to do?'

'I'm going to look for a new job,' she told him. 'I should be able to get better money now, so I'll be looking around. I've got one place in mind, but really I'm being a bit cheeky. It's in town, with a solicitor. But I might as well have a try.'

Michael was draining his glass as she spoke. He put the glass down excitedly. 'Maybe I could find you something. I'm sure I could.'

Rose decided to treat this as a joke. 'Let me try out my wings first before you rush in to rescue me. But thanks for the offer. Now, let me get the next one in.'

But Michael stubbed out his cigarette with sudden resolve and picked up his coat. 'Come on, Rosie. It's not cold out. I'll take you to see my place. It's only a walk along the road.'

'Your house?' Rose asked, astonished.

'Jesus, no. I'll show you the business.' Seeing her hesitate, he urged her, 'Come on, what's the harm? I'd be proud for you to see it. You'll be home with time to spare.' He took her arm.

It was a cloudy night and mild, with a threat of drizzle. The shop was only a few streets away, and they walked in silence, well apart, as if they were afraid even of their hands touching by accident. It was an apprehensive, embarrassed silence. Rose knew why he was taking her there, and he knew that she knew. It all seemed inevitable after their meetings, but suddenly so very uneasy. Not at all a comfortable progression from confiding friendship to possible lovemaking, but driven, and somehow at odds.

He stopped outside a quite smart-looking shop front and, looking up, she saw 'GILLESPIE's' in bold dark letters above the window. He didn't go into the darkened betting shop. Instead he led her up a narrow staircase, between walls covered with brown, chipped paint and smelling of stale cigarette smoke and general dirtiness.

'Not too nice, that bit,' he apologized when they reached the top. 'Come on in here. This is my office.'

He produced another key, and she stood waiting behind him, looking at thc weave of his suit, depressed by the smelly seediness of the staircase and wondering what to expect from the room on the other side of the door.

'People have to knock to come in here,' he told her proudly.

Once he had pushed the door open and switched on the light she looked round in real surprise.

In contrast to the staircase, the room was freshly decorated in cream paint, and she found her feet suddenly cushioned by what looked like brand new carpet with a crimson background patterned with fashionable skater's trail curves in black and white. All the furniture was brand new as well: a sideboard, its wooden veneer still gleaming with the sheen of newness, and two easy chairs covered in a vivid green woven fabric. In the middle of the room stood an enormous desk behind which Michael evidently presided from a chair covered in bright red and black material.

'Blimey, Michael!' Rose said, laughing. 'This furniture's a bit bright, isn't it?'

Proudly he joined in her laughter. 'Right up to the minute that,' he told her. 'Makes a change from all that blooming depressing brown stuff, doesn't it? Makes me think of nothing but the war that does. Mary still likes it though. So I thought, well, if I have to put up with all that old fashioned look at home, then I'll have my own little place here where I can do just what I want!'

Although the room did not seem all that warm, Michael took off his coat and hung his jacket over the back of the red chair. Rose watched his broad, muscular frame with some curiosity as he went over to the sideboard and squatted down to open one of the low cupboards. He was really such a stranger to her.

'I'll get us another drink,' he said. 'Will you be having a nip of Scotch? Haven't got much else.'

'Oh – no ta,' Rose replied quickly. She already felt light-headed from the pace he had set drinking in the Mermaid. 'If I have any more I'll get bad.'

Unbuttoning her coat, she walked round Michael's very tidy desk. From one of the frames facing his chair Mary smiled sweetly back at her. Face like an angel, Rose thought. Poor cow. Her wavy hair looked as if it must be a middling brown, and the camera had caught her glancing up, as if it had taken some persuasion to make her look in that direction at all. Round her neck you could just see a small crucifix gleaming at the bottom of the picture.

She's lovely, Michael, Rose wanted to say. She's beautiful. But she couldn't bring herself to speak. To say such things would be to bring Mary into the room between them.

There was a second photograph, evidently more recent, of Mary holding the baby Geraldine, with Joseph leaning into the picture beside her. The little boy's expression was solemn. Geraldine had that startled kind of baby face, all eyes. Michael's eyes. Mary was smiling. Did being married to Michael make her happy, Rose wondered?

She realized Michael was watching her. She glanced up at him. His eyes looked slightly glassy: at once sad and lustful. She pitied him, but with a sense of panic. Everything about this was wrong.

'Come away from the window,' he said. She didn't resist when he took her by the hand and led her to a corner of the room. She wanted, needed him to hold her, to allow herself to feel excited by him. She wanted that dreamlike, swimming feeling which would allow her to make love with him, give herself up to the swell of it and forget everything else.

As soon as he moved against her and they began to kiss, she felt her body come alive with all the sensations she had not known for so long. His hands reached insistently inside her clothing to touch her skin, to close over her breasts, and her eyes closed as she gave way to the pleasure of it.

Michael released her slightly, his eyes half closed. 'God. It's been so long since she's let me.'

Something like icy water sluiced through her mind and she was out of the dream, eyes wide open and seeing herself and Michael with clinical clarity as if from a distance. She was in a room above a betting shop, with a man's body pressed to hers, his black hair close to her cheek. Black hair which could almost have been Falcone's but wasn't. A man who aroused her, filled her with sexual desire, but whom she did not love. She thought of the last time she was forced to the floor by a man in an office where photographs of his family looked on from the desk, and she knew that whatever it was she'd desired of these few minutes, she could only ever see them as cheap afterwards. Soiled and cheap.

Michael felt her stiffen and straighten up, withdrawing from him. She pulled on her blouse, buttoning it over her breasts.

Michael's eyes opened and he made a despairing sound. 'Oh God, Rosie,' he implored her. 'Don't pull out on me now. Please.'

She removed his arms from round her and moved away, rearranging herself. 'It's not that I don't want you. You know that. But I can't do it. I feel as if everyone's here watching us – Mary and Alfie and everyone. I'm sorry, Michael.'

He turned from her abruptly and went to pick up his glass, draining the last gulp from it. He lit a cigarette and sat down on one of the green chairs in silence. She knew he was not going to try to force her.

'I don't go with women, you know,' he said finally. 'That's not the way I was brought up. It's just – you're different Rosie, I can talk to you, and we go back a long way. There was always something there between us, wasn't there?'

'There was. And there is, in a way. But I can't do this. We'd be doing wrong to so many other people.'

There was an awkward silence before Michael spoke. 'What you said, about your husband, him being bad and that. I mean you and him, you don't . . .?'

'Not any more, no.'

'Then why?'

'He's still my husband. He's had enough bad luck without his wife going bad on him. And there's Mary. I looked at that picture and I thought I'd like her if I met her. That's daft I know, because what difference does it make? But I couldn't do it to her either. Or to myself.'

'But they'd never know. I don't want to hurt anyone either. It's between you and me, Rosie. Even if it's only the once, it's just for us.' His blue eyes suddenly looked very young in their appeal.

'I'm not going to come here any more, Michael.'

'Not come?' He made to stand up and she turned away from him. 'What? Not even for a drink now and then?'

'I can't. If I keep coming it'll always come to this, won't it? Because it's always there between us. Sooner or later I'd give in to you and I'd hate myself for it. And you wouldn't be happy either. Not in the end.'

Michael shook his head. 'You always were more grown up than me, Rosie. I can't help admiring you for it. Come here, will you? Just for a moment?'

She went to him and they held each other again briefly.

'Go and give Mary some of your time,' she told him as they released each other. 'And your kids. They're what matters. If you stick with them I bet things'll work out.

Michael kissed her. 'I hope you get that job of yours. I'll miss you.'

She told him she would walk back alone and he let her out of the office and the door on to the street.

She was late home again. Grace was sitting in her usual position by Alfie's bed. The fire had burned down to a glow in the grate, and beside Grace lay a long skein of knitting which she had abandoned out of sleepiness.

She said nothing when Rose came in through the door, but her whole manner spoke of reproach. She bundled her things into the cloth bag and placed it pointedly beside the door. Still in silence the two of them settled Alfie down for the night. Usually they talked and made tea while Alfie dozed, but tonight he lay watching them as they went about their tasks, their eyes not meeting each other's nor a word passing between them.

They re-dressed his sores, though this time the sheets had stayed dry and did not need to be changed. When he started coughing again they supported him between them by his skeletal shoulders and dosed him with linctus, waiting until he was calm again.

Eventually Rose asked Grace, 'D'you want a cuppa?'

'No ta.' Grace took her apron off. 'I'll be glad to get home to my bed. And not before time either.' Rose could hear the anger pressed into her voice.

'By the way. I'm stopping the classes. I'm ready to go for a better job now.'

Normally Grace would have looked pleased for her and asked questions about where and how much. 'That'll be a relief for everyone, won't it?'

Rose sighed. 'I can be home evenings.'

Grace continued to look huffy, busying herself with her bag. 'Well – we'll see about that, won't we?'

Then she was gone.

Rose boiled some water on the gas and made tea. She poured for herself and Alfie and helped him, spooning the sweet liquid into his mouth. Often when she came in he was sleepy and hardly seemed to notice she was there. But tonight he was wide awake, partly perhaps because of his troubled breathing. She knew he was watching her as she moved round, tidying away the cups and getting the room ready for the morning because it was always such a rush.

She went over to him. 'Would you like me to turn you again? Would it help you to breathe better?'

'No. I'm OK.' He carried on staring up at her. His gaze seemed to hold a knowing sort of wisdom which made her feel ashamed. In the end she could bear it no longer.

'What? What Alfie?'

In his stumbling, slurred way he brought out the words, 'Wanted . . . something . . . more than . . . half alive . . . did you?'

She knelt and laid her head down on the bed next to the thin curve of his body. 'I'm sorry,' she whispered. 'I'm so sorry.'

For a moment he managed to stroke her hair before his arm went into spasm again.

'You deserve . . . better,' he said. When she looked up at him she saw he was crying too.

'I'm going to be here now,' she told him. 'Evenings and all. I'm going to get a better job and work hard – for all of us. I'll make things better if I can.'

She took one of his stiff hands in her own. 'Grace makes you a better wife than I do, doesn't she?'

She looked into Alfie's wet face, and reached across to wipe away his tears.

'But you're . . . the wife . . . I want. Always. You know. I love . . . you.'

CHAPTER 36

George Lucas stood outside the entrance to Winson Green Prison for the first time in over four years and heard the heavy gate shudder behind him. He stood for a moment or two in the overcast March morning, turning his pinched face this way and that, trying to take in the fact that after all these months he could make choices about his own movements. He appeared weighed down by the responsibility of it.

He looked even thinner after his time inside, giving the impression that he had grown taller, like a plant that has bolted up in poor light, and his skin had a yellowish, waxy look. Under his arm he carried a small bundle of the few possessions he had with him when he went into prison, and these he carried wrapped in a strip of white towelling. With his old, threadbare jacket pulled close round him and a crushed-looking brown felt hat pulled over his cropped hair, he began to walk slowly away from the prison in the direction of Birch Street.

The same morning Rose made her way into the middle of Birmingham. She stopped at the entrance to some narrow offices squeezed in near the bottom end of Temple Street. Screwed to the wall beside the heavy wooden door was a brass plaque which read, 'LAURENCE ABEL AND MATTHEW WATERS: SOLICITORS'.

Rose checked there were no stray bits of fluff on the full navy blue skirt she was wearing, and adjusted the collar of her white blouse, relieved they wouldn't be able to see the mend in the right sleeve under her thick navy cardigan. On her head she wore a little felt hat with a narrow brim in a royal blue which looked striking against her jackdaw hair and, to finish off the outfit, some high-heeled black shoes. She wished the shoes had been navy as well, but the neighbours had rallied round to help her out and lend her clothes for her interview and she had had to take what she could get. She peered at her faint reflection in the window of the corridor leading to the office. Nothing seemed to be amiss, so she patted the hat gently and said in a whisper, 'Come on, Rose Meredith. Get yourself in there.'

She was precisely on time. When the door opened she found she was facing a tall blonde woman of about forty with an immaculately made-up face, who looked at her appraisingly and then held out her hand with what Rose could only feel was disdain.

'Good morning. Mrs Meredith?' The 'Mrs' was definitely unenthusiastic. 'I'm Miss Crosby.'

Miss Crosby had a small outer area to work in off which led the two offices of Mr Waters and Mr Abel. Each had a slim wooden sign on his door. Miss Crosby sat down behind her heavy black Olivetti with an affected caress of the back of her skirt. Every hair on her head sat in precisely the right place.

Brassy cow, Rose found herself thinking.

'You have a very satisfactory recommendation from Sparkhill Commercial School,' Miss Crosby said. 'Your shorthand and typing speeds are well within our requirements. Have you kept them up?' she asked suspiciously.

'I've only just left the school.'

The woman's stony blue eyes watched her coldly. 'You've been employed as an invoice typist in the pool of a small firm. Do you really imagine you're capable of taking a job as a personal assistant to a professional solicitor?' She spoke the words 'personal assistant' as if the position was second only to membership of the royal family.

'I think I can do the job,' Rose told her. 'I've got good speeds, I'm well organized and I'm a very good worker.'

'Perhaps I should make it clear what is required here. I have been secretary to Mr Waters, the senior partner, for several years. It is only in the past month that he has gone into partnership with Mr Abel, who has come to join us from Manchester. Mr Waters will be retiring in a couple of years – that's why Mr Abel is now named first in the practice.'

Rose had the definite impression that Miss Crosby's nose had been put out of joint by all these changes.

'Mr Abel needs his own personal assistant, since I am fully occupied with all Mr Water's affairs. If we were to take you on – and I have my doubts as to whether you'd be up to it, quite honestly, Mrs Meredith – you would be working under me. Is that clear?'

Rose nodded. 'Do I have to be seen by Mr Abel?'

'Oh, that won't be necessary,' Miss Crosby told her briskly. 'Mr Waters and Mr Abel leave all that sort of thing to me.'

Miss Crosby seemed on the point of pronouncing one way or another as to Rose's prospects with Abel and Waters when one of the inner doors opened and an energetic figure bounded out of the office. Rose saw a man with a round, cheerful face wearing a suit which looked good quality but was somehow comically ill-fitting on him, who bustled across the room, a newspaper tucked loosely under one arm.

'No, no, don't get up,' he said. 'I'm Laurence Abel. So, Miss Crosby, is this my new secretary or do you have a whole line of others waiting breathlessly outside?'

'I was just discussing with Mrs Meredith whether she is really suitably qualified for the position.'

Just then their interviewee, who had been looking anxiously up at Mr Abel, let out a loud gasp. Rose's hand rose automatically to her mouth to apologize for the sound.

'What's the matter, Mrs Meredith?' Laurence Abel joked. 'Is my presence too much for you?'

'I'm sorry. It's just – you'll think I'm very odd, but I noticed your newspaper.'

Laurence Abel frowned as if he had forgotten he was carrying the thing. He pulled it out and spread it out on the desk. It was a copy of *Corriera della Sera*.

'It's Italian,' Rose explained unnecessarily.

Miss Crosby was looking at her as if she thought Rose had lost her mind. But she had Laurence Abel's avid attention.

'I used to speak it.' Rose glanced anxiously at Miss Crosby. 'I was there for nearly two years. In the war.'

'Good Lord!' Mr Abel cried. Rose was almost sure his feet left the ground in his enthusiasm. 'How marvellous! You mean you really speak it? Can you remember it?'

Suddenly he launched into a list of questions, mostly in energetic Italian, but with the odd English word thrown in when he got stuck. Having heard Rose's replies he said, 'You're obviously a darn sight better at it than I am. Come on into my office for a minute.'

He led her into what seemed a surprisingly orderly room for so chaotic-looking a character: the walls lined with shelves of all his files and reference books with gold lettering on the spines.

'You know, I really should be working,' Mr Abel said, leaning back at his desk, his podgy stomach pushing out the front of his shirt. 'But I can't throw up an opportunity like this.'

Rose found herself telling him about the ATS and a little about Il Rifugio and her feeling that she belonged in the country.

'I know what you mean about the sense of belonging,' Mr Abel agreed eagerly. 'I had exactly the same feeling. I go back as often as I can. Couldn't do without it.'

'You go back?' Rose was amazed. She never imagined such a thing. Italy was part of the war, not accessible at any other time.

'About once a year. Managed a quick visit before moving down here. It's not quite the other side of the world you know.'

'It is when you've got no money.'

Laurence Abel looked at her in silence for a moment. 'If you came to work here, would you agree on a condition that when we're not actually dictating letters, we'll speak in Italian?'

Rose grinned at this bizarre request. 'That'd be lovely.'

She almost danced into number five that evening to tell Grace the news.

'I've got the job!' she cried before she was even properly through the door.

And then stopped abruptly. Grace was standing by the table wearing her apron and a grimmer, angrier expression than Rose could ever remember seeing on her face before. Sid was sitting on the other side of the room by the fire, but was for once intent on what was going on. And at the table sat George, his hat lying in front of him, a cigarette in his mouth, his defiant eyes staring down at the table.

'Oh my God,' Rose said. 'I'd forgotten it was today.'

'That's obvious,' George said bitterly. He pulled the cigarette out of his mouth, wincing as if it tasted bad and held it in one hand, tapping his fingers on the table.

'Well – what's going on?' Rose asked. The atmosphere was pure acid.

'He thinks,' Grace's voice grated out, 'that he's going to come swanning back in here to live as if nothing had happened – and have me waiting on him hand and foot again no doubt. And then' – she leaned down and shouted into George's face – 'I s'pose you'll just be off thieving and getting into more trouble and expecting the rest of us to carry the can for you! No. I'm not having it. I'm not having you back here. You can go where you like, go to hell for all I care, as long as you're not coming in and out of here.'

George sat in silence. He had walked most of the day, with no money for food as he made his way home, putting off going to the old house where he had grown up, skirting round it time and again, until by the afternoon he was so hungry and weary from the unaccustomed exercise that he had finally slunk into the court.

Sid had opened the door and when it dawned on him who had arrived, he said, 'You'd better come in, but I don't know what your sister'll say.' He'd let him have tea and bread and jam and a slice off a leathery bit of leftover beef.

Rose could tell that, for all his toughness, George was upset. She was horrified at what she was hearing from Grace. Grace hadn't been to see him once in prison and was turning him out now as if he was a stranger who meant nothing to her at all.

No one had spoken after Grace, but she leapt to her own defence as if they had, her hands clamped to her waist. 'Say what you like. You come in here and I go – simple as that. You can go rot for all I care.'

George looked over at Sid for some sign of authority, of contradiction, but saw only his father's watery eyes staring defeatedly back at him.

Sid shrugged tiredly. 'You'd better do as she says.' He couldn't have Grace walking out on him, after all.

'George.' Rose spoke more gently and he was struck even at that moment by the difference between his sisters: Rose's animated beauty despite her thinness, compared with Grace's haggard, bitter face.

Rose laid her hand on the back of his chair. 'What are you going to do, George? Find a job and get yourself straightened out or what? You can't go on the way you've been. You don't want to end up back in there, do you?' She looked with pity at the side of her brother's face with his shorn brown hair. He was a sad sight.

'I dunno,' he said. 'What can I do?'

'Never done a straight day's work in your life.' Grace's voice drilled on into him. 'Come as too much of a shock to you, wouldn't it?'

Rose frowned at her to shut her up. 'Look,' she went on. 'If you'll say you're going to try and find a job, I'll help you. There's a few going round here – and if you promise you're not going to go fooling about looking up all your old pals who're no good for you, I'll have you to live with us. Hilda can move down to sleep with me. You can pay me a bit of rent and I can always do with someone else about to help with Alfie and that. But just you watch yourself.' She wagged a warning finger in front of George's face. 'Any sign of trouble, of anything, and you're out. Right?'

George nodded in silence.

'You'd better get your lodger off home Rose,' Grace told her. 'I'm late with the tea already and what there is is only enough for two.'

George picked up his meagre bundle of possessions and slunk out with Rose across the yard to Moonstruck House. They were both well aware that other eyes were on them from the windows.

'Never thought you'd end up here, Rose,' George said as they went through the door. 'Thought you had ideas well above this place.'

'When did having ideas ever do anyone any good?' She felt completely deflated after her euphoric mood earlier. She turned to Alfie, ignoring George's horrified expression as he set eyes on him.

'You remember my brother George? He's coming to lodge with us for as long as he can keep his nose clean.' Then more kindly she said to George. 'I s'pose you're hungry. I'll get something on in a minute.'

Hilda, who was sitting near her father, gazed at George with interested eyes. She liked men: they picked her up and paid her attention and played games with her. 'Is he a real brother?'

'My brother. Your uncle.'

'This is your kid?' George asked astonished. Though Rose had told him what Hilda was getting up to on her visits, the child had never progressed further than babyhood in his mind.

'This is Hilda.'

Hilda was standing in her little flowery frock, lips pursed ready to give George a kiss. Rose watched her brother's confusion. Any such display of affection was something unusual enough in their family, and to George was a part of life long forgotten. Kissing a child was something he could barely imagine how to do. Slowly he bent down until he was level with Hilda, who popped a kiss on his cheek. As he stood up she rubbed her lips. 'You've got prickly cheeks, like Grandad,' she said. 'But I'm glad you're coming to live with us, Uncle George.'

CHAPTER 37

JULY 1952

'What're you doing here?'

The moment Rose opened the door of Moonstruck House she felt herself tense up, infuriated. George was supposed to be out at work, at yet another of the jobs she had found for him. Instead, he was just sitting there, smoking.

'I asked you a question.'

'Oh, don't go on. You get to sound like her over there.' He nodded in the direction of number five.

Rose was almost afraid to hear his reasons for being at home at this time. Had she wasted yet more time and energy helping him to find a job which he had either just walked out of or got the sack from for idleness and bad timekeeping?

In the end he said, 'Couldn't stand that bloody place. Got on me nerves. I thought bugger it and came home.'

'Got on your nerves!' Rose flared up at him. 'You're an idle little sod, that's what you are!'

She strode over to him furiously and snatched the cigarette from between his fingers. 'And you can put that bloody fag out and all. This is my house, and if you're living here you do as I say.'

'Leave me alone, can't you?' George snapped back.

Rose went to the window and flung it open, throwing the stub of cigarette, still burning, out on to the ground.

'Uncle George is going to buy me a bicycle,' Hilda chimed in from by the fireplace.

Rose swung round. 'And pigs might fly.'

After George had slammed out of the house, Rose went up to her bedroom. She felt despair wash through her, as strong as any she had experienced since her first days back at home after the war. The summer afternoon air drifted in through the window, and she could hear children shouting and laughing in the courts around them. The long, lonely evening stretched ahead of her.

Tears began to slide down her face. She lay face down on her bed and let them come on like a child. For so long she had been so busy, so driven by all the necessities in her life that there had been no time to think about anything. She found herself remembering her first meeting with Diana, and the dress with the pink sprigs of roses. How much hope she had had in those days!

Even lately she had persisted in believing that if she tried hard enough things would come right in the end. God knows, she had made enough effort with George. She had goaded him on day after day to look for work. And when she could manage to find the time, she walked the streets herself on his behalf, even in her own dinner breaks. Finding him a job was not especially easy, though there was plenty of work to be had. She saw vacancies for toolmakers, die-sinkers, stampers, rivet-makers and a whole host of other skills. But George had no skills.

The only jobs he was able to get were of the most menial; the unskilled, heavy work of stacking and loading and cleaning up after those doing the better-paid jobs. The money was never up to much and George had neither the application nor the staying power to stick to the work. Rose knew, and feared, that he could make easier and quicker money elsewhere.

'Why can't you give it a bit more time?' she'd implore him when feeling more patient. 'Can't you try a bit more than you do?'

Usually he'd just shrug off her questions, her encouragement. Once he turned to her and said, 'Give it a rest will you, Rosie? I'm no good for anything, so just don't keep on.' And she'd seen a wooden, beaten expression in his eyes.

But she had still believed, naïvely, that given a few more chances, a bit of help, he could go back to being someone more like the old, sparky George she had known as a child.

She heard the door downstairs open and voices. It was Grace. Since she had spent so much time looking after Alfie, she still kept up a slightly proprietorial air over his care and was always popping in to check things were being done properly.

'Where's your mother got to?' Rose heard her say to Hilda, before shouting up the stairs.

'Be down in a mo,' Rose called back, trying to make her voice sound normal and not weepy.

Grace stood leaning up against the sink in the little scullery that was still filled with gloom despite the bright sunlight and echoing summer sounds from outside. She had her hair wrapped up in a scarf as usual and wore her shabby brown skirt and flat, sloppy shoes. She looked as if she might be well on in years compared with Rose, who was still smartly dressed from work in her floral skirt and pink blouse, although she had taken off her heels to lie down.

'Coming round to my way of thinking, are you?'

Rose nodded miserably in reply.

'I warned you. You could've saved yourself the bother. You know who's sniffing round here again, don't you? Ronnie Grables.'

Silently Rose got on with peeling potatoes.

'Did you hear me?'

'He wouldn't. Not after all this.' Her secret fears about George seemed to be being confirmed one by one.

Grace let out a harsh, cynical laugh. 'None so blind as them as won't see,' she said. 'How do you know what he'd do? You don't know where he is now or what he's doing, do you?'

That evening she sat down with a new copy of *Corriera della Sera*. Alfie was asleep. Rose looked across at him. His face was moist with perspiration. It seemed so strange, him lying there and her in a tussle with this language she might never have any proper chance to speak again.

Why she carried on with it she wasn't even sure. After her initial enthusiasm at Mr Abel's offer, she had had to ask herself, who she was kidding?

At first she found the reading a terrible struggle. And she felt triumphant when she managed to make sense of short sentences, then longer ones, and gradually whole paragraphs. But tonight she was finding it hard to concentrate. She was very unsettled and anxious. It was partly because of George, of course. He had not come back for the evening meal and was still out somewhere. Doing what? Who with? Her mind followed him anxiously out into the streets.

And there had been an incident at work which had in a strange way brought her a little closer to her odd colleague Ella Crosby, and yet at the same time she felt depressed because of it.

It had dawned on Rose only gradually that Ella Crosby was in love with Mr Waters. At first she thought she was reading the signs wrong. Of course a secretary looked up at her boss with attentiveness when he came in to give her some work. But surely not always with the gaze of hungry pain that Miss Crosby directed at Mr Waters? Say something to me, it seemed to say. Just one extra thing which is not on the subject of work and which shows me you even notice me! But the longer she worked there, Rose found the situation at first unbelievable, then pitiful. She began to warm to Miss Crosby for that, if for no other reason.

That morning the two of them had been working hard at their typewriters with a stack of papers in front of them when Mr Waters' door opened. Miss Crosby and Rose both looked up.

Mr Waters was very tall, almost unhealthily thin looking, with such sallow, papery skin that when Rose first saw him she had thought immediately of the cemetery at

Naples. He was carrying a sheaf of papers in his left hand, and Rose saw Miss Crosby's cheeks turn a deeper red under all the powder as he laid them down rather impatiently in front of her.

'I'm sorry, Miss Crosby,' he said. As always he was polite, but there was a tetchy edge to his voice. 'I'm afraid we really can't send them out like this. They'll all have to be done from scratch. Rather a waste of time, of course. Still, I'll leave them with you. I know you'll do your best.' Without another word, he drifted back into his office again.

And to her horror, Rose saw Miss Crosby bring her hands convulsively up to her face, and she realized the woman was trying to hide approaching tears. She could feel her pain and embarrassment across the room. Rose wondered what to do. She decided to carry on typing for a while to give the woman time to recover.

Eventually, when she could see that Miss Crosby had regained some of her control, she stood up and said carefully, 'Never blooming satisfied, are they? D'you fancy a cup of tea?'

Miss Crosby nodded.

Rose was saddened by this. Did no one ever love the right person, she wondered? Were so many people really doomed to spend their lives longing and wishing and never happy?

She got up to check on Alfie and Hilda and brewed herself a last cup of tea for the night. She felt so tired that she was tempted to stop reading. But if she did stop, then what? On this night in particular she would start thinking and brooding. As she had been reading Italian she would find Falcone insistent in her mind and she did not want her emotions disturbed again.

She was settled in bed beside Hilda's warm body and already drifting off to sleep that night when she was aware of George coming back into the house, his loud, thoughtless tread on the stairs up to the attic. It had not long struck eleven o'clock. Rose closed her eyes and turned to lie with her back against Hilda. Where he had been and what he had been doing were not things she wanted to think about now either.

As the months went by things did not improve. George gave up any pretence that he was going to try and hold down any sort of job and yet Rose could not bring herself to throw him out. He came and went, back to his old pattern of disappearing for days at a time, paying her odds and sods of rent but nothing regular. She never knew where he was and she worried and Hilda sulked and was unsettled. But there was no trouble as such, no police round, nothing that she could actually hold up in front of him. Only the constant anxiety and suspicion which left her feeling worn down and angry.

Alfie's health was an increasing strain. Grace came and helped them often again now, apparently glad to be back in her role as nurse. Alfie went through chest infection after chest infection, his weakened body wracked by terrible coughing. Time and again she got for him the new wonder medicine – antibiotics, which fought off the infection for a time before it returned again, apparently stronger and more tenacious than before. She was mystified by his strength, how he managed to keep going after all these months. For what, she often wondered guiltily. What reason does he have to live any more?

As the autumn wore on and the days closed in, dark, and often foggy and wet, she was finding it hard to hide her strain and exhaustion at work. Her face looked pale and sunken and she was bone thin. Both Laurence Abel and Ella Crosby noticed.

'Is there something worrying you?' Miss Crosby asked one afternoon when Rose was yawning over her typewriter and struggling to keep her head clear. 'You don't seem quite yourself.' She blushed slightly, unaccustomed to trying to extract confidences from others.

It was a relief to tell her.

'It's my husband. He's very bad. I've been up a lot nights.'

'Oh, I'm sorry,' Miss Crosby said rather stiffly. She suddenly felt rather moved by the pale, lovely young woman in front of her. 'If there's anything I can do . . .'

'I don't think so.' Matter-of-factly, Rose added, 'We don't reckon he's got long left. There's not much anyone can do.'

'I didn't realize . . .' Miss Crosby looked genuinely sorry. 'I had no idea it was as bad as that.'

A kind of numbness overcame Rose, as if she could bear feeling no more. She was waiting for Alfie to die. Not because she willed it, but because she knew it must come. It was plain in his face. The nurse who came in tutted and said so in hushed tones as well. And now life was strung between these nights of waiting, watching his struggle with his weak, helpless body.

One December evening when she had finished work, she walked home from the bus stop in a wet dusk. The wheels of cars and buses hissed through the puddles, and she could hear the soft, rhythmic sound of windscreen wipers even over the engines. The red lights of the cars seemed to glow more warmly in the rain.

Inside the house she was slowly peeling off her wet coat when there was a tap on the door, and to her surprise she saw Sid standing there with his cap on, the raindrops shining on his dark, stubbly cheeks.

'Someone to see you,' he said. 'Over at our place. She's been waiting.'

He turned his back and went on his crutch back across the court. Frowning with irritation at him, Rose slid her coat back on again. He could at least have told her who it was.

'Stay with your dad a minute,' she said to Hilda.

She followed Sid across the wet bricks and stepped into number five. She saw someone stand up immediately and move towards her. The face had aged, of course, and looked tighter somehow, but was instantly recognizable.

'Rose – my dear!'

A moment later she was being drawn into the arms of Catherine Harper-Watt.

CHAPTER 38

Rose could hardly take in Catherine's sudden appearance. Here she was, thinner but still beautiful, her thick hair arranged in an elegant chignon and wearing an obviously expensive suit tailored in slate blue and black checks and all nipped in nicely at the waist. She sat on the old wooden chair by the table in Grace's poor kitchen looking quite at ease as she might anywhere, so accustomed was she to mixing with anyone and everyone. Sid and Grace had taken their meal over to eat with Alfie.

Rose began to chop off florets of cauliflower for cauliflower cheese, waiting for the pan of water to boil.

'I know this'll sound rude,' she said. 'I'm ever so pleased to see you. But why are you here tonight suddenly?'

'No, it's a good question.' Catherine remembered that even as a child Rose had always gone straight to the heart of things, no messing about. 'The practical truth is that I'm here in Birmingham because I was sent down to a meeting in the Town Hall. More of my organizing and interfering with other people's lives.' She smiled.

'I have to admit this isn't by any means the first time I've been back, and I've thought of calling in on you. I came this evening to see if anyone could tell me your address, and to my astonishment I find the person I'm talking to is your father! But I'm sorry not to have warned you, Rose dear. I had fully intended to write you a better letter after you wrote to us so kindly during the war. And to have come and looked you up much sooner. But I just

– even now it's . . .' She laid the palms of her hands flat on the table in front of her. 'I just couldn't do it.'

Rose put down her colander, realizing with consternation that Catherine's voice was breaking up with tearfulness. She reached out to provide the family comforter. 'Let me get you a cup of tea while we're waiting.'

'I knew I must at some point,' Catherine told her, accepting the cup of strong tea. 'When we moved to Manchester and got settled in, Diana made a lot of friends, of course. She was always that kind of girl – you remember how open and friendly she was. But you know, despite all the differences between you two, I don't think there was ever anyone she cared for as much as she did for you. Perhaps we make very few real friendships in our lifetime. When I think of Diana's childhood now, that's the first thing that comes to my mind – you and her.'

There was a moment of silence. The two women looked at each other across the poorly lit kitchen and Catherine saw that Rose's brown eyes were full of tears.

'It's ten years since she died, and it's taken me all this time. Only . . . I know I've got William and Judith, and they're a great support to me and both doing so well. But losing Diana, losing any child is just . . .'

'I know,' Rose said gently.

'You poor girl, what a time of it you've had. Here am I, carrying on. Of course you know how it feels.'

'You know I met Diana. At New Street Station?'

'She told us. She was so delighted. You see she thought she'd done something terribly wrong when she didn't hear from you. After she got your letter I remember her saying to me, "If only Rose had told us. Why d'you think she felt she couldn't? I wanted to be her friend whatever." It's all right' – Catherine stood up and took Rose by the shoulders, seeing her really beginning to cry on hearing this – 'she understood. You poor child. You were young and afraid, and so . . .'

'Ignorant,' Rose finished for her, sniffing.

'Well, yes, you were in a way. But so very bright and

lively with it.' She embraced Rose briefly, and then the two of them carried the food to the table.

'I haven't talked about Diana,' Rose said as they ate. 'Not for years. There's been no one I could tell. No one round here would want to know anyway.'

'I should have done this years ago!' Catherine said later as she laid down her knife and fork. 'What a chump I've been, thinking it would all be terrible and gloomy. You won't be able to keep me away now, Rose. But for tonight' – she looked at her slender wristwatch – 'before I have to go I want to hear a lot more about you.'

Their shared memories allowed Rose to open up and relax in a way she had not done for years. The Harper-Watts' talent for helping others to confide and Catherine's motherly concern for her made her feel she could say anything.

She told her about Dora's death, about her war and Sam and Grace and Grace's fiancé; about the factory at Castle Bromwich and about the ATS. And to her own relief, pleasure in fact, she told her about Italy and Il Rifugio and the drops, and quite straightforwardly she told her about Falcone. She explained too how things had been since the war, with Alfie and Hilda and her work, and Alfie's illness.

'So at least I've got myself a more decent job,' she finished, 'which means we're doing a bit better now. But Alfie's very bad. No one thinks he's got long, to be honest with you. To tell you the truth, Mrs Harper-Watt—'

'Call me Catherine, please.'

'Well, Catherine then. The one place I always hoped I'd get away from was Catherine Street. I had all these ideas. And here I am. Square one.'

Catherine smiled sadly. 'You had so many dreams, both of you, when you were children.' She watched Rose's face carefully as she asked the next question. 'And this man, this priest. He was something very special to you?'

Rose paused. 'He wasn't a priest then. But yes. Like no one else, ever.'

'Oh Rose!' Rose saw the sympathy in her eyes.

Catherine suddenly started and looked at her watch again. 'Heavens, I shall have to go.' She got up and put on a soft grey wool coat, belting it round the waist. 'The time has gone so quickly,' she said. 'Now listen, my dear. Thank you for feeding me at such short notice. And please thank your family for putting up with this disruption. It was most kind of them all.'

As they stood at the door, she said, 'I'm so glad I came.'

Rose nodded with pleasure, not sure what to say, and Catherine kissed her quickly on the cheek. Smiling, and suddenly elated, Rose watched her smart figure disappear quickly out of the court.

Two days later when she arrived back from work she found a long white envelope waiting, addressed in black ink in Catherine's beautiful italic script. Under their Manchester address on the thick, white paper she read,

> My dear Rose,
>
> I hope you will not take this amiss. I am not at all sure whether I conveyed to you when we parted on Tuesday just how much our meeting meant to me. You and Diana were so special – but then I think I *have* said all that.
>
> I should be most grateful if you will accept the enclosed. It is not meant to be seen as charity or anything you need take offence at. You'll know I have always had means of my own, and I should love you to think of yourself as something of a daughter who need not feel ashamed of accepting a gift from me. I should like to think that as soon as circumstances allow, you, who were such a dreamer as a child and whose dreams have been so consistently pushed aside by events, might be able to put this little offering towards fulfilling those dreams in some way, whatever that may be. I would gladly give you

more if you were not too proud to ask. I can't do anything for Diana, but I have at least found you.

I told Ronald about my visit to you and he was overjoyed (a very Ronald word!) and sends much love to you, as do William and Judith.

I do hope to see you again before long, if you don't mind.

With much gratitude and affection from us both,
Catherine H-W.

Folded in the sheet Rose found ten £10 notes. The moment she had read through the letter and had re-read it in wonder, she pushed both it and the money hurriedly back inside the envelope. Pulling out one of the loose bricks from round the fireplace she arranged the envelope neatly behind and replaced the brick. No one else need see that money just now.

But she thought about it endlessly as she got on with the evening's chores. Dreams? What dreams did she have left that were not buried almost deep enough to have been forgotten? She had no clear idea what she might do with such a sum of money. Except for one thing.

'I'll do something special for Grace,' she thought. Grace, whose life had been so lacking in excitement, who had always stood by her and helped out when she was needed, even if she did have a good moan about it. She'd think of some way, however small, to pay Grace back. She deserved it.

'He ought to be in hospital,' the nurse kept saying, tutting over Alfie. 'He's in a terrible state! Look at those sores, and hark at his chest!'

'We've done the best we can,' Rose told her exhaustedly. 'And he doesn't want to go.' Even Alfie himself had tried to impress this on the nurse in his more lucid moments.

The new doctor who had started coming supported Alfie's wishes, rather to Rose's surprise. 'You know that your husband has not much time left?' she told her gently.

'So everyone keeps saying. To be honest with you we've all wondered how he's kept going this long with what he's been through.'

As Sid had put it only yesterday, 'You'd never have thought that weak little runt'd have held out like this, would you?'

The past weeks had, of course, prepared Rose. Several times she had walked warily over to Alfie, her own breath stilled in her throat, thinking he'd stopped breathing altogether. But each time there had been a pause and then his loud, laboured breathing had started up again. They could talk very little now. Mostly his eyes were closed, so he did not take in what she or Hilda were doing. But paradoxically her life revolved round him more and more: on his washing and feeding routines, or simply being there as much as possible, even though the nurses were spending more time there during the day, and one neighbour or another was constantly with him.

For the first time she had seriously begun to think how she would feel after he died, and again to her surprise, the thoughts which came filled her with apprehension verging on panic. For what was her life now without Alfie to care for?

Hilda had begun to say to her at night, 'Will Dad still be here in the morning?' The mother of one of her classmates had recently killed herself and it was always on Hilda's mind. And people kept saying Alfie hadn't long.

'I hope so,' Rose would tell her, with decreasing certainty. 'Don't get all worked up about it. Just go and give your dad a kiss, love.'

The night he died, Grace was there as usual. They took it in turns, each sleeping half the night in Rose's bed, and sitting for the remainder downstairs with Alfie. It was agonizing and exhausting. Each of his breaths seemed to demand from him such effort. And his poor, contorted body looked so corrupted by the illness.

Occasionally Rose allowed herself to think of him as he was when she had first met him before the war, and she would weep at the sight of him now. He had become such a strange thing in the room, his unconsciousness a mysterious barrier against them all. Was it simply sleep, or had he already begun to leave her behind?

Grace ran up the stairs and pulled on Rose's shoulder, rousing her from a light, confused sleep.

'What? WHAT?' She sat up at once.

'It's just – he's changed. I can't tell you. You'd best come and see.'

The two sisters skimmed down the cold stairs again in their nighties.

Alfie's breathing had grown even louder and more irregular. Watching him from the bottom of the stairs, Rose felt he might rise bodily off the bed in his attempt to capture his next vital lungful. His chest rose and fell, rose and fell, the rasping breaths hauled in and out. Then they stopped.

Hypnotized by the rhythm, for a moment both women carried on staring at him. The silence continued. They looked at each other, unable to move.

Then Rose rushed over to the bed. She took Alfie's emaciated wrist and felt for a pulse. For a few seconds the tips of her fingers felt for the delicate blood vessel. Nothing.

'He's gone,' she said solemnly.

It was Grace who fell to her knees by the bed wailing 'Oh Alfie!' and laid her head down on the covers beside him.

The burial took place in the cemetery where they had laid Dora. Unlike the overcast day in 1940 when Rose had stood beside Grace and Sid at that graveside, the day was a crisp, bright one in February, with the old rusty leaves of autumn crackling underfoot. The beauty and calm of the cemetery with its mature trees and sloping green areas dotted with the silent stones moved Rose. Alfie's death and all the suffering of his life weighed heavily on her. She had lost a friend, and the focus of years of care and energy. The future lay blank in front of her. But what felt worst was the knowledge of how little of herself she had really given to him. Everyone kept telling her how marvellous she'd been, what a staunch wife. And it was true that she had served him and cared for him in his physical need. But no more.

After the ceremony, Rose held Hilda's cold little hand in hers, with Grace supporting her on the other side, as they followed the slow progress of Sid and Mrs Meredith along the curving path. George had not made an appearance. Grace's face was as drawn with misery as Hilda's and Rose's own.

'A couple of days more,' she said softly to Rose, 'and he'd have died exactly a year after the old king.' She seemed to find this comforting.

Rose nodded, squeezing her arm. A little further on she said, 'Grace, if he'd asked you – back in the early days – would you have married him?'

Grace kept her eyes down, looking at the dry twigs and pine needles along the path. 'You know I would. And not just then either. Any time. Right up to the end.'

Then she looked round at Rose with a most wistful smile on her thin face. 'But it was only you he had eyes for. Ever. You know that, Rose.'

And then she stroked her sister's arm as Rose finally began to break into sobs beside her.

CHAPTER 39

AUGUST 1953

For months after Alfie's death Rose felt tired to the very core. It seemed a huge task just to get to work in the morning. Through the end of the winter and the lightening days of spring she dragged herself around feeling only half alive, as if Alfie had taken a part of her with him, her own youth seeping away gradually through his illness.

She missed him more than she had ever imagined possible. One thing had been certain, ever since she moved to Moonstruck House: that Alfie would always be there. Whenever she came down in the morning or in from a class or work, there he was, almost as she had left him. Wakeful and watching her, providing as much conversation as he could manage, or dozing, semi-conscious – but there. Now, just as certainly, the room was empty of him.

But like a gift, from somewhere within her, her vitality and zest were returning. She had other things to think about. George for a start. And, with a certainty which increased with each summer day, she knew what she was going to do with her money from Catherine Harper-Watt. One of the things that she had thought most unattainable, that Laurence Abel had talked of yet still sounded like a fantasy, was now within her grasp. Italy. She would go back, and she probably even had enough money to take Hilda.

'It's a barmy thing to do,' she thought to herself, almost giggling with excitement. It was a baking hot Saturday. On the sunny side of Court 11, near the brewhouse, Rose was standing bent over an enamel bucket, swilling through some of Hilda's clothes. A few children were listlessly playing marbles in the shade. 'I could do up the house, move out even. I could buy us all new clothes or furniture, or just put it away for a rainy day. But I'm damned if I'm going to!'

Italy was her dream now, and Catherine had prescribed the money for a dream. She could go and visit Margherita and Francesco. She still received cards from them at Easter and whenever they had had another child, always with entreaties to visit. It was clear to her that this was what she must do. Just as her idea of what she could do for Grace had come to her with equal force a couple of months earlier.

As June approached, coronation fever had struck the court, the city, the entire country and, of course, Grace, who showed the kind of excitement that only a royal occasion ever brought out in her.

'A queen!' she cried. 'Oh, isn't it going to be lovely to have a queen for a change! Elizabeth the Second. Doris at work says it's going to change everything. Things'll never be the same again. Oooh, what I'd give to live down London!'

For weeks beforehand the talk and activity all centred round bunting and flags and plans for street parties and big celebrations with brass bands and fireworks.

'What if you could go?' Rose said to Grace one day in May. 'You know, go down and really see it, in London?'

'I'd give my right arm,' Grace replied. 'But we'll hear it all. And we might get a sight of one of them televisions somewhere. And all the pictures'll be in the papers.'

'No,' Rose told her. 'You're to go. Down to London, on the train. It'll be my treat.' She blushed at sounding like Lady Bountiful with her sister. 'Look – you've done nothing but help me over the past few years. I'd like to pay you back a bit. One way I can think of anyway.'

Grace's face had gone pink with excitement. 'But – you can't afford that, can you? It'd mean the price of the train and . . . and new stockings, and . . .'

Rose grinned. 'That's all right. Listen. No one else need know about this, but when Mrs Harper-Watt came she gave me a bit of money. It doesn't matter how much, but take my word for it, it's enough for you to have a new frock and your rail ticket. And I'll stand you taking Doris as well if you like.'

Grace was flabbergasted. 'But why don't *you* come? If you've got enough money for the two of us?'

'I'm not that keen really, you know that. Go on – go with Doris and get into the spirit of it. You'll have much more fun with her.'

So Grace went, feverishly excited and wearing a new peach-coloured frock. She and Doris sat out all night in the Mall with a flask of tea and their sandwiches with all the other thousands of people breathless to catch a glimpse of the new monarch. And she came back brimming full of it all: the procession and the flags and trombones and all the aeroplanes flying over, and how the woman next to them had shared her ham sandwiches with them because they'd run out, and how everyone cheered and cheered when she came out of Westminster Abbey and stood there for hours with their little flags despite all the showers.

So it went on for days and weeks after. Rose was never in any doubt as to whether she'd made the right choice.

Things with George, though, were getting worse and worse, and Grace's excursion brought things to a head.

'So who paid for that, then?' he demanded.

'I did, if you must know.'

'Where d'you get the money from?' he asked in his usual sneering tone.

'Some of us do a job of work if you remember.'

She watched her brother with loathing that day as he sat smoking, as usual. Fag after fag, flicking the ash towards the fireplace and missing half the time. All the sympathy she had mustered for him had evaporated over the past few months. God knows she had tried. But he had given her no respite, and not an ounce of help or sympathy. He sickened her. He couldn't even be bothered to come to her husband's funeral. Things she had hoped never to say tumbled out of her mouth.

'I used to think it might be worth helping you out,' she spat at him as he sat staring indifferently at the floor. 'But you're a useless sod if ever there was one. Other people have problems and get on with their lives, but not you. Poor old George. You sit on your arse and wait for everyone to run round you. And then you turn round and go back to thieving and wasting your stupid, useless life away.'

George's head whipped round savagely. 'Who says I'm thieving?'

'Well, aren't you? You're up to something. Out all hours and mixing in with God alone knows who. Anyone out at the time of night you come in is up to no good. And you're not stony broke are you? So where's it all coming from if you're not nicking it?'

'Leave me alone, you silly cow!' George yelled at her. 'Stupid nagging bitch. You're all the bloody same!'

Rose watched her brother's face, its expression of pure malice. His grey eyes were the coldest she had seen for a long time. Shuddering, she thought of Mr Lazenby.

'I tried with you,' she said more quietly. 'I'm the only person who's even tried.'

'Only so everyone could tell you how bloody marvellous you are. You thought I'd come in here and be your dogsbody, looking after that cripple of a husband of yours, and your stupid kid. But now people can start doing the running for me for a change.'

'What d'you mean?'

George sat down again, nipping his cigarette nervously between his lips. 'Never you mind – sis,' he said contemptuously. 'You just go on being a good little girl and working for your nice law man. I s'pose he's giving you one, is he?'

'Get out. Take your things and get out of my house.'

George turned to her with mock casualness. 'Going to make me?'

Thinking back over this now as she wrung out the

clothes, Rose could feel the rage rising in her again. Things had settled down for the moment it was true, but sooner or later she was going to have to face up to it. She pegged out the clothes and flung the water down the drain. She had to do something about George. She simply could not stand the sight of him.

In September everything changed at work. She reached town rather late that morning, trying to hurry in her tall slim heels through the usual sounds of thumping and drilling and all the dust and mess that signified the resurrection of the city. She hoped Ella Crosby would not notice she was late.

Climbing the stairs up to the Abel and Waters offices, she became aware of more crashing about and shouting from inside. What the hell's going on? she thought, hurrying even more. It sounded as though the offices were being ransacked.

She cautiously pushed the door open and was greeted by an incredible sight. Near his closed office door, as if trying to take refuge from it all, stood Mr Abel.

'No – please!' he cried as if that was the last straw. 'Not the typewriter, please! They're so expensive! Ah Rose – Mrs Meredith. Thank goodness you're here!'

Across the room was strewn what looked like the entire contents of Miss Crosby's desk. There were shorthand pads open and spread over the floor, files and typed letters and crumpled sheets of carbon paper, wodges of new stationery with sheaves of envelopes fanning out across the carpet, and against the wastepaper basket the blotter stood tipped up at an angle. A typewriter ribbon lay unravelled in black coils across the layers of paper.

Ella Crosby still seemed to be searching for things to throw, a snarl of fury trapped for the time being in her throat.

'What's happened?' Rose asked. 'What on earth's going on?'

'It's . . .' Mr Abel tried to explain.

'The stupid, selfish, miserable old—' Ella Crosby finished the sentence with a screech of fury. She thumped her fist down on the desk and the sight was so melodramatic that Rose wondered for a second whether she was putting it all on.

'What the heck have you done?' she demanded of Mr Abel.

'Not me!' Laurence Abel squeaked. 'God in heaven, not me! It's Mr Waters.'

'He's only gone and died, hasn't he?' Ella shouted. 'He's gone and damn well died on us!'

'It was a heart attack,' Laurence Abel explained. Last night. Someone found him this morning lying on the floor downstairs.'

Rose walked cautiously over to Ella Crosby, who had sunk down on her chair and was sitting sobbing at the desk.

'Miss Crosby,' she said gently. Somehow she did not dare touch the woman. 'You've had a shock. Why don't you go home and have a bit of a rest? Take the day off?'

Ella Crosby looked round at her slowly, rather stunned. 'But I've made such a terrible mess. I'm so sorry. I should clear it all up at least before I go.'

'No. You're all right, I'll do it,' Rose told her. 'Go on. We'll see you in the morning.'

Slowly Miss Crosby picked herself up, wiping her face with a handkerchief, and went out of the door.

Ella Crosby applied for another job. Laurence Abel was left with the sole running of the practice, and Rose stayed on with him. It took several weeks before things began to settle down.

'I'll be able to pay you a bit more now,' he told her. 'You'll be doing more work for a start.'

'Well, I'm not going to complain about that,' she told him.

'But,' he went on, 'come hell or high water I'm going to take the time off that I'd planned. Complete folly of course in the circumstances, but I can get someone to stand in for me and do at least the basics for a fortnight.'

Rose smiled at him without the sense of wistfulness that she had always felt before whenever he mentioned his trips to Italy. It was her secret. She was going to go as well! It didn't matter how soon, but she was going.

She realized that Laurence Abel was looking at her with unusual intentness.

'I'd have thought you must be in need of a holiday too,' he said. She noticed that his cheeks were turning pinker as he spoke. 'You could – er – come with me. I mean, don't get me wrong, Rose. I know how much it'd mean to you to go. I'd be happy to pay for you.' He laughed nervously.

Rose was so startled she could for a moment think of nothing to say. What was it he was actually asking her? He had been extremely kind and understanding to her during the last weeks of Alfie's life. But now she was back to being a single woman, was he trying to push things further? She wanted to believe the best of him, but she found her old mistrust flaring up again.

She sat staring down at her typewriter, her cheeks burning. She could feel his own discomfort even though she was not looking at him.

'I'm sorry. Don't take that the wrong way, will you? I wasn't expecting . . . anything of you. I'd just enjoy the company.'

She wanted to believe him. She looked up shyly at him. 'Thanks. But I couldn't just go, anyway. I've my daughter to think of.'

When Laurence Abel returned from his trip in November, it sharpened even more her own longing to go.

'Hilda,' she couldn't resist saying one night as she pulled the bedclothes up round the little girl, 'how would you fancy coming away on a little trip with me?'

'To Weston?' Hilda asked eagerly, half sitting up.

'No, not Weston. But we might see the sea.'

'Ooh yes!' Hilda said, and wriggled with excitement. Then she wrinkled up her nose. 'Would Uncle George have to come with us?'

Her uncle had been losing his glamour as the months passed and all his promises failed to come true. Since Alfie died, she had clung increasingly to Rose, the one really reliable person she had left, and they had grown much closer.

'No, not Uncle George,' Rose said. 'We don't want him along with us, do we? It'd just be you and me.' With a sudden rush of affection she leaned over and kissed Hilda's warm cheek. 'Now you go to sleep and dream all about it, eh?'

As she made herself a cup of tea she resolved that before she and Hilda went anywhere, she had to get George out. She sat down, kicking off her shoes and stirring sugar into her tea.

She hadn't seen him for two days. Perhaps she could threaten him with the police? Call his bluff? She had absolutely no proof that he was doing anything, but she knew him too well and he had to be up to something. She couldn't just throw him out. She had tried that. She began to think of something that would work. Money. She could bribe him. She put her cup and saucer down. Give him some cash for a clean pair of heels? Perhaps she could spare some of Catherine's money. That would mean she would have to delay her plans a little, but it would be worth it. She could save the rest up gradually.

She went over to the fireplace and jiggled the loosened brick out of the wall to recount the money.

Her fingernails scratched against the brickwork. For a moment she scrabbled around, not believing it. Where was the envelope? Growing frantic, she slid her hand all round the inside of the cavity. Nothing.

A horrible suspicion filled her mind. Heart thumping hard, she ran up to the attic, to George's room, where she had not ventured for weeks.

The stench of stale cigarette smoke hit her immediately. With trembling hands she held the candle high and looked around. The bed was unmade and the old cupboard door was hanging open. Beside the bed lay the only remains of George to be seen in the room: a white saucer brimming over with cigarette stubs.

A week later a letter arrived from Catherine Harper-Watt. They kept up a regular correspondence, but this letter was different and short. Rose read it through several times, the full implications of it taking time to sink in. Finally she laid it down, shaking with anger and embarrassment.

My dear Rose,

Just a quick note to let you know that all is well and I am most happy to have been able to help. The fact that you felt able to send your brother here when he needed assistance is most gratifying to me, and he seemed such an interesting and purposeful young man.

I was able to let him have £50 to help him on his way, and we left him at Piccadilly heading north to his new life feeling we had truly done someone a service. Perhaps this removes a burden from you, and of course of that I am also glad.

We are all well. Judith has announced that she is at last to be married to her teacher friend Robert. How old that makes me feel!

I shall write again, but I just wanted to set your mind at rest.

Loving greetings,
Catherine Harper-Watt.

The winter months passed very slowly. Rose felt as frozen inside as the weather outside. Even work seemed less enjoyable. To her surprise she missed Ella Crosby, and it was lonely sitting in the outer office on her own.

She could not bring herself to write and tell Catherine the truth. For a start it might sound as if she was asking for more money. She had not even told Grace what had happened. Now she did not have Catherine's money as a back up, she felt compelled to save as much as she could of her wages, scrimping along as a matter of habit.

Laurence Abel was keener than ever to speak Italian whenever possible, and although she went along with it, it only rubbed in the fact that she never seemed to get anywhere in her life.

What she needed to do now, she told herself, was to forget all this foolish hankering for something that was past, and build the best future she could for herself and her daughter. Hilda, after all, was the future.

The bus drew up with its brakes shrieking. Climbing inside Rose realized she had the chance of a seat and squeezed across to sit next to the window. It was a surprisingly warm spring day and the bus felt hot inside. She was on her way home from work, tired and stuffy in the head.

On her lap with her bag was her last newspaper from Laurence Abel, a December copy of *Corriera della Sera*. She knew she was feeling too inert to make any sense out of it at that time in the afternoon, but she opened it up, taking care not to wave it in the face of the man next to her.

The words seemed to shout at her, from a small news item in the middle of the second page. She blinked hard and tried to make sense of it.

'Vatican makes example of rebel priests', was the headline above the words that had drawn her eyes: Paulo Augustino Falcone. Father Paulo Falcone.

Many of the words in the article were unfamiliar to her as she seldom bothered to read stories connected with the Church.

She tore home, the paper not even properly folded in her hands. Once she was sitting down at the table with her dictionary she began to make more sense of it.

Three priests were referred to in the story. All of them

had preached or taught on issues of faith or morals in a manner which had come to the displeasured attention of the Sacred Congregation for the Doctrine of the Faith. Rose had no idea what that was so she skipped over it. The story said that the Vatican had decided to clamp down on these three to provide a moral example to the rest of the Catholic community. Consequently, all three had to some degree been silenced by suspension from their duties as priests.

Rose skimmed over the details about the other two.

> The most severely reprimanded of the three and also the youngest is Father Paulo Augustino Falcone, ordained three years ago in the Dominican house of San Domenico Maggiore in Naples. His radical views on issues such as poverty and contraception, and his calling to question the obligatory state of celibacy for all priests have resulted in his being banned from teaching, preaching, or celebration of the Mass.

Rose sat staring across the room, only realizing after a moment that Hilda was prodding her arm.

'I'm hungry, Mom. What's for tea?'

In a dreamlike state Rose got up and started spreading margarine on bread, the past still crashing in around her. Just reading his name like that rekindled such strong feelings.

'I said I wanted jam!' Hilda protested, swinging her legs crossly against the chair when the food arrived.

Rose stared, confused, at the slices of bread. Instead of jam she had put margarine on them twice.

He was still there: he was real. And now, after all his agonizing, all those years of training, his commitment to the priesthood was leading him into what, she recognized, devoid as she was of any real understanding of the Catholic faith, must be a good deal of pain and confusion.

'Mom! Listen to me! Can I have some jam? Is there any cake?'

Now she knew with a kind of frightening clarity that whatever it took, whatever the outcome of it, she had to go there. Finish things if necessary. She had to see Falcone again.

Standing by the table with the saucer of strawberry jam in her hand she said to Hilda, 'You know I said – ages back – that we'd be going on a journey? Well, I've been saving, and I'm going to go on saving our money until we've got enough to go – together. What d'you think of that?'

'Smashing,' Hilda said. 'Now please give me some of that jam!'

CHAPTER 40

SEPTEMBER 1954

'You really going tomorrow then?' Grace's voice held a definite tone of disapproval.

Rose was folding clothes into a decrepit old suitcase of Alfie's that had stood for years in her bedroom. 'Looks like it, doesn't it?'

'Beats me why you want to go off over there,' Grace said, shifting her weight to lean up against the doorframe. 'You could've gone anywhere for a break – a week by the sea at Rhyl for a quarter the price. I'd have thought you'd have had enough of over there in the war. They say it's ever so dirty and smelly.'

Rose smiled. 'Do they?'

'And you could've left Hilda with me and our dad. No need to go dragging her along as well.'

'I want her to come,' Rose said. 'She's seven, old enough to see it and remember. And Margherita's got kids. They can all play together.'

'You sure you've got enough money? Is that Mrs Harper-Watt paying for you to go?'

'No,' Rose said briskly, pushing a pair of shoes down into the side of the suitcase. 'She sent me some money for my birthday so I put that in the pot.' She turned to look squarely at Grace. 'The money she gave me after she came that time—'

'How much was it?' It was something Grace had always been dying to know.

'A hundred quid.'

Grace's eyes widened in astonishment. 'Blimey. She must be rolling in it!'

'When I'd taken some out for you and some other bits and bobs, there was still about eighty left. George had it off me.'

'You gave him eighty pound?' Grace screeched at her, standing absolutely upright now.

'Course I didn't. He pinched it, when he went off. And he stopped by in Manchester and conned some more out of her on the way to wherever he's gone.'

Grace stared at her, speechless for almost half a minute. 'Did you tell her?' she managed to say at last.

'No. Couldn't really, could I? It'd have sounded as if I was on the scrounge or something. What we're going away on is what I've saved, bar the ten pound she sent me.'

'He should be strung up.'

'Probably has been by now, for all we know.' Rose shut the case and struggled with the rusty fastenings. 'There – all set. Oooh.' She gave a little jump. 'I can't believe it, Grace. I'm really going – for ten whole days!'

'Nor can I,' Grace said drily, though she was smiling. 'Must be mad.'

With rhythmic, comforting sounds, the Naples train eased its way out through the suburbs of Rome. It was not very crowded and they had seats facing each other. Hilda, exhausted already from the excitement of a very long day – travelling on an aeroplane! – was dozing, her head lolling against the window. Rose felt she could not have slept even if she had been heavily drugged. She watched Hilda, her cheeks soft and lovely in the gentle light of the approaching sunset. Her perverse, self-willed but lovable daughter, here with her in Italy. Bringing these two parts of her life together seemed quite extraordinary.

She turned her attention to the regal Roman buildings outside the window. Even in the suburbs many of the tenements had a grandeur about them, with their flaking paint in yellow or terracotta or pink, and the contrasting greens and blues of the wooden shutters. Rose took in a deep, satisfied breath. This country! Whatever happened while she was here, at this moment she felt deeply content just to see it, to take in all the half-forgotten things that she loved about it. Fig trees and peeling trunks of eucalyptus softening the sides of buildings, the washing strung across narrow side streets glimpsed as the train hurried past; the baskets and buckets hanging outside windows ready to be let down to receive a delivery of bread or groceries. All the different smells that were so peculiarly Italian, the trace of drains and cigarette smoke mixed with the evening air – and she was sure she could smell the *prosciutto* between chunks of white bread that the elderly woman was tucking into on the seat across the passage.

As the light began to fade they passed through miles of fields, with small towns and villages strung along the railway line. Part of the land was fallow now that the summer was closing, and some fields held late crops of hay or spindly maize, with mules and carts still out collecting the dry cobs. On the left ran the line of the mountains, sometimes close enough to see the dark green cover of trees, sometimes smoky grey outlines in the distance, the foothills of the long spine of Italy.

When it was completely dark outside and the lights were on inside the train, Rose pulled Margherita's latest letter out of her bag. It seemed incredible that in a few hours she and Hilda would be sleeping in Francesco and Margherita's flat, and waking with the sun to meet their children.

'*Carissima Rosa*,' Margherita's bold writing looped across the cheap piece of paper.

> We are so happy that you are coming and bringing your daughter with you. How excited we all are about seeing you – it seems now only like a dream!
>
> I hope you will forgive our little place – it is small and cramped with all of us in it, but we can always find the space for such a welcome guest.

Your train will arrive in Naples at about 22.00, and Francesco will be there to meet you, we promise you faithfully. I hope you will recognize each other! Please stand in the area near the ticket office and he will come to find you.

We wait in eager anticipation of your visit – and until then, love and blessings from us all.
Margherita.

The train began passing between buildings again, some of them higher than any Rose remembered from the war. Like Birmingham, she thought. The war has given us all a new face. As they rattled past tenements and factories still dotted with lights, and junctions with roads where cars, lorries and carts waited facelessly behind the gates, she began to smell the sulphury city smell.

He's out there somewhere, she thought. His city. The train was slowing now from its hectic pace so that the buildings slid past instead of being whisked immediately from view. They were replaced by light and the concrete of railway platforms as they drew to a halt in the great yawning central railway station in Naples.

'Hilda!' She leaned across and shook her gently. 'Come on, love. We're here.'

Francesco spotted her the moment she and Hilda walked out from the railway platform. Before she had even had time to look for him he was beside her.

'Rosa!'

'Francesco! Oh, Hilda, this is Francesco.'

And their arms were round each other, laughing and exclaiming and oblivious to anyone else in the huge, echoing station.

'*Come sta?* Are you well?'

'*Bene – benissimo!*'

'I think you've got a bit fatter, you know.' Rose prodded him playfully. 'It must be married life!' She found herself speaking slowly, feeling her way into the language again.

'But not much, truly. With six children you don't get

fat! And you – you look lovely as ever. A little different perhaps . . .?'

'Older – but then who isn't!'

Francesco bent down and Rose watched as he smiled warmly at Hilda who glanced doubtfully at her mother before smiling back.

'Welcome, *piccola.*' He pinched one of her cheeks affectionately. Unsure, Hilda drew her face away. 'We have a lot of friends at home for you to play with.'

Rose explained this to Hilda in English.

'She'll come round,' she told Francesco. 'By tomorrow night she'll be bossing them all about even if she doesn't speak the same language. Oh – I can't wait to see them all!'

Still laughing and joking, with Francesco carrying her suitcase, they walked out to a side street near the station.

'My brother Carlo lent me his car,' he said, unlocking a shiny red Fiat. 'He works as a salesman,' he said with slight mockery. 'Impoverished school teachers like me don't have cars. In any case, if we did we'd never all fit in it.'

Rose watched him curiously as he settled Hilda on the back seat and stowed her case away. It was true he was not as painfully thin as he had been during the war, but despite her teasing he was still a slim man. And he really did look older, much older. She remembered his pointed, aristocratic face as she had known it before: that aquiline nose and the striking blue eyes. But there was something different now. He looked – she kept glancing at him as he drove them home, struggling for the right word – he looked more *ordinary*. That was it. And did she look so to him? Had she ever seemed extraordinary? Perhaps it had been the war, its romantic element of adversity and drama that had lent them all a touch of romance. Was this how everything would look now she was back? Ordinary? And if so, would that make it any less of a pleasure to be here, now they were all back to everyday life?

'Why did you move to Pozzuoli?' she asked, as Francesco steered the car rather joltingly out west away from Naples to the small town along the coast.

'My job is in Pozzuoli, the school. I try to cram some history into their unwilling heads. And my brother lives there, so we can borrow his car!' he joked. 'No – but it is smaller, and quite cheap. It's OK.'

'And you're happy there?'

'Happy enough,' Francesco said with a shrug. 'Yes, why not happy? It's not a question I often find time to ask myself.'

It was not a long drive and soon they pulled up in a side street outside a pale, four-storey building. It looked pinkish in the streetlight.

'We're on the first floor so it's not too much of a climb,' he told her.

Rose could hear dogs barking and a buzzing sound, something electric. Cats shrank in and out of the shadows.

'Margherita is on tenterhooks to see you. And with any luck all the children should be asleep by now.'

The three of them climbed a dark, rather musty-smelling stone staircase. As they got near the top they heard a door open. Margherita must have been listening for them.

'Francesco?' Rose heard her soft, so familiar voice.

'Yes. We made it,' he called to her.

And there she was, outlined in the dim light from the flat. Rose almost stopped climbing the stairs in astonishment. Was that really Margherita? The figure of the woman standing at the entrance to the flat was plump and thick limbed, her long hair draped down over her shoulders.

Before she had had time to take in fully the changed appearance of her friend she was at the top and they were embracing and kissing, both with tears of joy on their cheeks.

'At last you are here!' Margherita cried. 'I have been so longing to see you! Come in. Come and have some coffee and we will get you settled in. And you, little Hilda – I have some milk for you, *cara*'.

Francesco disappeared to take the car back to Carlo. Margherita disappeared for a moment and came back cradling a baby who had a shock of thick black hair.

'She is wakeful tonight,' she told Rose. 'This is my little one – Magdalena. She is nearly six months.'

Rose smiled wonderingly at the baby and called Hilda over to admire her too.

'She's lovely, Margherita. Quite beautiful. You have so many children already.'

Margherita smiled with the gentle wistfulness that Rose remembered. She had not really changed so much once they got talking.

'I have been blessed with so many little lives,' she said. Then with a despairing look she passed her free hand down over her waist and right hip. 'But that is why I am so fat. You would have walked past me on the street, eh, wouldn't you? With each one I seem to gain kilos and they never go again. We Italian women are fated this way. Whereas you – you look just the same!'

'Well, I've only had one, haven't I?' Rose laughed.

Margherita led them into a little kitchen with a tiled floor and pale blue walls.

'I am so happy to scc you.' Margherita sat suckling the child. 'I really missed you when you left. And you left us so sadly.' She smiled quickly and then switched the conversation.

'Your little girl is lovely. Hilda, you are beautiful! She is the same age as my Marco, so they will be able to play. But of course the older ones will have school tomorrow – and Francesco too! We shall have a nice lot of time together. Come now.' She stood up, fastening her blouse. 'You can have a look at my babies.'

Suddenly extremely weary, Rose followed her along a little passage to the bedrooms. The children had all been moved in together to leave a room for her and Hilda.

As Margherita pushed open a door the light fell on some of the children, some in beds and two on the floor. Rose learned the names of the quiet, sleeping faces.

'Come. We can talk tomorrow.' Margherita leaned

over and kissed both of them again. 'Thank you for coming – you have made me so happy.

For two days they did hardly anything but talk. Margherita did not mention Falcone and at first Rose was content to enjoy simply being there. She soon felt at home in the chaotic, ramshackle flat with its crumbling paint and old furniture, shelves and surfaces spilling over with books and papers and children's clothes and drawings and toys. And she helped Margherita with her chores as they got to know one another again.

While the three older children were at school, Hilda settled into playing with the others. Caterina, who was three, looked up to her as if she was some kind of pale English goddess, and they soon found ways of communicating. And little Giovanni followed them about and they fussed over him and chivvied him to join in their games.

Rose learned that Margherita and Francesco were, as he had put it, 'happy enough'. But they were constantly worried about money, like so many of the families around them. Though Margherita clearly had a Neapolitan adoration for all her children, Rose noticed a suppressed kind of restlessness about her.

'How many children d'you think you'll have?' Rose asked her the second evening. They had spent the day shopping for food and walking in the town and were preparing spaghetti for the evening meal.

'As many as God gives me.'

'You're not serious!'

Margherita looked round at her, and Rose saw a look of desperation in her eyes.

'What else can I do? There's no way of stopping it. The Church tells us that if we limit our relations to the time in the month when it is safe . . .' She sighed. 'For some women that works. For me, it doesn't make any difference. I couldn't easily say this to anyone else, but I wonder sometimes why I studied. Why do they allow us women to have an education if our fate remains the same

– to bear child after child and bring them up in poverty because there are too many of them?'

The tears welled up and ran down her cheeks. Rose put her arms round her.

They had barely even mentioned Il Rifugio during those two days. Rose was growing anxious and frustrated. She was eager to reminisce – one of the things she had most looked forward to about coming. In the evenings, once the mayhem of the children had died down for the night, they sat in the stuffy little flat drinking cheap wine and eating bread and late summer fruit, and talking, but they avoided the subject she most longed to discuss. If she asked a question they moved quickly on to something else. Most resolutely they did not talk about Falcone. Up to now she had not been able to bring herself to mention his name either. But to be here so near him, yet as closed off from him as she had been in Birmingham, was agonizing. She found herself constantly watching for his face among the crowded streets, even though they were not in Naples.

By the third morning she was beginning to feel that if she or someone did not mention Falcone soon she would explode. She walked with Margherita down to the little port to go to the fish markets, the stalls strung out along the front next to the sea. Hilda was fascinated by the fish. They strolled along with the vivid blue of the Mediterranean on one side, dotted with sunlight and coloured boats. And on the other, wooden tubs painted pale blue inside seethed with live eels or shellfish like piles of coloured pebbles, or small silver and orange fish flitting about in the shallow water. On the stalls behind lay heaps of prawns, and larger fish, already dead and glassy-eyed on banks of ice. Their smell was pungent on the air, and mixed with that of the sea and the drains.

'Oh look, Mom!' Hilda cried, running to bend over a row of tubs where lobsters tangled their claws together, crammed in in a brick-coloured mass. From a nearby one a number of large octopuses stared out balefully, some of their tentacles slipping experimentally out over the side and curling as they touched the ground. Caterina was chatting excitedly and Giovanni gingerly dipped his fingers in the water.

As they were occupied for the moment, Rose took Margherita's arm. Speaking loudly to be heard over the long, doleful cries of the fish hawkers, she said, 'I've heard what's happened.'

Margherita frowned. 'What?'

'To Falcone.'

Margherita's expression showed first astonishment and then apprehension. 'How did you know?'

'I read it in a newspaper. Why won't you talk about him?'

'We hoped you would think of him as a priest still. That nothing had changed. We wanted to avoid causing you pain – if that's what you would feel after ten years, of course. How could we know what you would feel? You might even have forgotten.'

Rose shook her head impatiently. 'You've seen him recently?'

'Yes, a month or so ago. We didn't tell him you were coming, by the way. He's in a lot of trouble. He began to question what the Church teaches and of course that disturbs a lot of people. He's obviously very unhappy. He loves his faith deeply, but he's so disillusioned, with the priesthood especially. And the hierarchy have come down hard on him. You'd think it might be enough to crush a person.'

Rose hesitated. 'Did he ever mention me – when you saw him after the war?'

'Of course. In the beginning.' She paused. 'I know I never thought he was cut out to be a priest, but that's for God to decide. He's had so much to bear, and whether now you should be part of this . . .'

Rose gripped Margherita's arm again with a determination that clearly communicated itself.

'I have to see him.'

CHAPTER 41

The church of San Domenico Maggiore was a forbidding building of stained, sandy-coloured stone.

Rose stood in the piazza looking at it. That Falcone had worked and studied here for so long was hard for her to imagine – a place which seemed to suggest such rigidity and conviction. She could not reconcile that with the man she had known; so tender and so confused.

Now the prospect of simply walking round the building to the seminary and knocking on the door seemed quite impossible. After all, what if he opened the door? She had been partly prepared for approaching the place by Margherita, who seemed to have decided that if Rose was going to do something of such doubtful wisdom she might as well give her as much help as she could. She had insisted that Rose leave Hilda with her for the day.

'Go to them and ask for Father Falcone,' she told Rose. 'Tell them that you want him to hear your confession. They may try to get you to accept someone else, but you can say you have something particular to ask him. If he's busy you can always go back later, can't you?'

I'll go and have a look at the church first, she said to herself. Get a feel of it.

She walked slowly over to the entrance. She was wearing a pleated skirt in a soft yellow poplin, cream court shoes, and a close-fitting navy blouse. The skirt swished luxuriously round her legs as she walked. She had felt very smart and feminine when she put them on, but now she was unsure of herself. Should she have worn something darker and more staid to come to a place like this?

The inside of the building was almost as austere as its exterior, the floor flagged in black and white marble on which her thin heels seemed to make far too much noise, and a ceiling which was plain except for frescos above the aisle, and even they were in restrained colours. There was very little else in the way of decoration.

She had evidently arrived just at the end of the Mass. As she entered people were beginning to stream out of the building. A few stayed in their places at prayer or moved to the front to light candles. Others stood round in small clusters talking. She watched those who were leaving bow to the altar and cross themselves and she made an attempt to do the same, overcome with a sudden distaste.

Bowing and scraping, she thought.

As she looked up towards the high altar, two figures caught her attention. Long white robes, with black cloaks over them which wafted out behind as they walked, seeming to glide across the floor. For a few dizzying seconds his face was superimposed on each of them. Then she focussed properly. One had white hair and was short and stocky. The other was tall and slim with black hair, but everything else about him was wrong; the nose too long, the eyes, brows, complexion all unknown to her. She stood watching. So this was his life, here, doing this.

Soon she was almost alone in the church, still standing there in the aisle. The younger priest had disappeared. She knew that if she did not act now she might never find the courage again.

She walked up towards the altar. The elderly priest was standing to one side in one of the choir stalls, leafing through a book. His thick, white eyebrows were pulled into a frown.

She wasn't even sure how to address him and when she spoke her voice sounded too loud.

'*Signore? Mi scusi!*'

The priest looked up with an irritated air. 'Yes. What is it?'

'I – I'm looking for Father Falcone.'

He stared at her for a moment, then with startling force he slammed the book closed so that dust flew up from the wooden choir stall. He stepped out and began to walk briskly away.

'Father Falcone is not here.' He spoke over his shoulder with unmistakable dislike.

Rose followed him for a few steps. 'Where is he – please?'

The priest stopped and turned round abruptly, obviously shocked. His first answer should have been enough. She was not supposed to question further.

'Father Falcone is away on retreat – again. Not, as one would expect of a priest in a position as serious as his, in a religious house of prayer, but' – he flicked his right wrist several times, dismissively – 'in some place of his own choosing. Where that may be I have no idea.'

He turned and was gone.

The impact of the old man's bitterness left her reeling and close to tears. Only as she was walking back along the black and white flagstones did she know just how consuming was her need to see Falcone. But she was no closer to finding him.

She sat down on one of the seats at the back of the church. His church, which felt so desolate now she knew he was not here. She stared up at the high altar, shrouded and mysterious at the far end of the church.

'Please. Please help me find him,' she found herself whispering. Perhaps his God would come to her aid?

She thought of him kneeling in here day after day. He was in deeper trouble than she could have imagined. He had felt the need – or been sent – to get away and think about things, and not for the first time by the sound of it. And he had even chosen to go somewhere they would not think of looking.

And then it came to her, making her catch her breath.

Of course! If Falcone needed time to think, her instinct told her, she knew the first place he would go. Not even questioning now the need that drove her on to find him, she ran out of the echoing church and across the piazza.

Less than an hour later she was on the train to Sorrento.

She might have revelled in being in Sorrento had things been different, but as it was she hardly took in the town at all. By the time she had walked up the road to the Finzis' house, having several times had to ask the way, it was one o'clock, and though no longer the height of summer it was hot enough to tire her. Her feet were sore from walking in her flimsy, high-heeled shoes.

The bubble of excitement and eagerness which had driven her on in the early part of the day had almost evaporated through weariness and thirst. She felt very nervous. All the things she had planned to say on meeting him again, the scenes she had so often visualized had vanished, and instead she could only think of flat, lifeless things. The day had gone wrong. And she was only guessing that he was here.

When she caught sight of the Finzis' house she slowed down, her heart hammering in her chest. The house had recently been painted in pale green, and the shutters in a darker shade, so that the whole place had a newer, fresher air about it.

What on earth was she doing here? If he really was here, what could she say to him? But to turn back now would be unthinkable.

Without waiting to summon up courage she knocked on the door. There was a pause before it opened and she was facing a middle-aged, heavily built man who stared at her in silence. He was chewing hard on something and clearly in the middle of a meal.

'Yes?' he said eventually.

'I'm sorry to disturb you.' Her heart was sinking. It

was all a mistake. The Finzis weren't here any more. 'I am looking for Paulo Falcone – Father Falcone.'

The man nodded. 'Yes,' he said abruptly, showing no surprise. 'Come in.' And she was stepping back into the Finzis' house.

The inside had also been painted, and as she walked through the coolness of the rooms it felt strange, less homely than she remembered. He led her immediately to the kitchen which was little changed from when she had stayed there.

Before she had time to collect her thoughts the man was saying, 'Paulo – someone to see you.'

Not their meeting as she had pictured it at all. She stood in the doorway looking into his face as their eyes met, trying to take in that it was really him. He was sitting at the table, fork in hand, dressed not in the white robes she had seen earlier, but in a shirt and trousers, both black and worn. He looked much the same as she remembered: serious, a little more careworn perhaps. Those large, long-lashed eyes stared back at her, puzzled. Whatever emotions may have been present in him, whether surprise or dismay, did not give themselves away in his face. He put down his fork and pushed the chair back.

'Rosa?' He stood in front of her, apparently unsure what to do. Then convention took over and he held out his hand. Somewhere in her mind she registered how warm it felt. She tried to smile at him, but her lips barely seemed to obey.

'Er – we were eating,' Falcone said, quickly. 'Will you join us and have some food?' He pulled out a chair for her.

'Thank you. That would be very nice.' She imagined him with the worshippers at San Domenico Maggiore, measured and courteous.

He gave her some of the tough bread and a dish of spaghetti with meat and tomatoes.

At the table Rose was shocked to recognize Clara

Finzi. She had aged greatly, her once plump cheeks sunken, her eyes watery and holding an absent expression.

'Clara.' Falcone spoke to her loudly. 'This is Rosa – from England. She stayed here once, during the war. When Angelo was still alive. Do you remember?'

He looked at her then. Rose found herself blushing. He remembered. Of course he remembered. And what else could he have said to the old woman, who just nodded, mumbling something indistinct. Clearly Clara did not recognize her.

'I'm sorry,' Falcone said with the same formal politeness. He gestured to the man who had opened the door to her. 'This is Lorenzo Finzi, the eldest son of the family. He has been living here with his mother since Signore Finzi's death.'

'I'm sorry,' she said. 'About Signore Finzi.'

Both men nodded, acknowledging the comment.

'Where are you staying?' Falcone asked her.

'With Francesco and Margherita in Pozzuoli.'

Falcone smiled for the first time. 'And all their lovely family?'

'My daughter is with them.'

He looked attentively at her. 'You're married.' It was not quite a question.

'I'm a widow.'

'Rosa . . .' He stopped. 'How did you know I was here?'

'They told me you were on a retreat somewhere, and I thought . . .'

'They? Margherita and Francesco?'

'No. A priest. At your church. He didn't seem very happy at me asking.'

'You went to San Domenico?'

She nodded, unable to work out his reaction to this. Was he angry? Had she made things even worse for him? He was shaking his head gently from side to side, whether in amazement or displeasure she could not decide. She felt terribly embarrassed and clumsy, and longed to leave.

Even her clothes felt wrong. She was overdressed, a stranger even to herself.

She looked away from Falcone's face, down at his hands, dark against the red and white checks of the tablecloth. They looked so familiar that the sight of them brought a lump to her throat. Those gentle, loving hands. Incredible that the hands of this stranger beside her had once known her so intimately. She was a fool for coming, for reviving the memories. She would go immediately. She could not even finish the food on her plate. If she and Falcone could have anything to say to one another it was quite impossible here.

'I really have to go now.' Getting up nervously she said to Clara and Lorenzo Finzi, 'Thank you both for your hospitality. I'm very grateful.'

Falcone took her to the door. She felt the lump in her throat again as he walked behind her. She could not have imagined a meeting as dreadful as this. She had visualised conversations where he reinforced to her his priestly vocation, and stood up for his decision to leave her so abruptly: perhaps rejected her all over again and with even more force. Anything seemed preferable to this unreadable formality.

'I'm sorry for disturbing you.' She was having difficulty controlling her voice. 'I should not have come here.'

She turned and began to walk away down the road so he would not see her tears.

'Wait!'

Almost angry now, she turned to him.

'I . . . You must understand how surprised I am to see you,' he said lamely, walking to stand closer to her in the dusty road. She stood dumbly in front of him, hardening her feelings. She could not speak.

'I had no idea you were coming, and . . .' He stumbled over the words. 'You look so different.'

He turned aside from her, looking up at the trees on the opposite side of the road. He was breathing in fast, shallow breaths.

'Look . . . I'm sorry. I can't . . . Every time I speak it

condemns me.' He gestured despairingly with his hands. 'Seeing you again . . . Could you – would you come back?'

'When?'

'Tomorrow – afternoon? I'll be walking.' He pointed up towards the mountain. 'I often do at that time of day. Lorenzo will not bother us.' He seemed to recover himself a little. 'I'm sorry you have come so far and I am unable to – that I can't be more . . . welcoming today.'

In a dignified voice Rose said, 'I'll come tomorrow, if that's what you want?'

He nodded. 'Please, Rosa.'

She turned and walked back down towards the town.

It was a warm, languorous afternoon bathed in rich autumn sunlight which touched the fading leaves with gold. Walking to the house, she saw red blooms still on the geraniums, tiny children watching her from doorways and cats curled sleeping in the sun. She was dressed differently this time, her feet comfortable in flat shoes, feeling the warmth on her arms. She felt strangely calm, as if anything that happened was now up to him. She was here, come what may.

There were no signs of life at the house and she walked past. As she began to climb the first deep step to the Stations of the Cross, the sense of recognition hit her oddly – those stones, so unchanged. At every other twist of the steep path were the stations she remembered; the crudely painted little pictures each protected by its alcove of brick, which also held their tributes of candles and flowers. She looked fondly at them, though their actual meaning was mostly lost on her.

Perhaps she had come too early? They had not agreed on any particular time. She sat down on one of the steps and looked back. The town was just becoming visible through the trees, though they had grown and thickened. She thought back to the last time she had sat up here on one of these steps. She had been thinking of Sam, still soaking in the shock of his death.

She breathed in the smells of the herbs and trees around her. There was a light scuttling sound. A salamander dashed off into the dry grass alongside the path in alarm. Startled, Rose turned her head.

Falcone was standing watching her. He had come down from the chapel where he had spent some of the early part of the afternoon, thinking perhaps to meet her. As he turned the bend in the path he had come upon the sight of that familiar little figure sitting below him. He stopped, narrowing his eyes to make it out more clearly, as if perhaps it might be another dream. She had come to him many times before, dressed in the old black blouse and skirt, her hair taken up in a coil behind her head. It was an image that had haunted him against all the power of his will for the past nine years.

As she turned, she heard his voice saying softly, as if unsure, 'Rosa?'

She stood up and slowly climbed up to join him. When she reached the step on which he was standing she looked up at him solemnly. It was impossible for either of them not to remember their last time together in this place.

Falcone looked back at her, then as if in some way defeated by the sight of her, he directed his gaze away at the ground. But in that brief moment of contact the emotions she had seen in his eyes were all she needed.

Together they turned and began to climb.

'So,' she asked softly, 'why are you here up on this mountain instead of getting on with being a priest?'

'Well.' He sighed heavily. 'I'm in a mess.'

To his amazement, Rose suddenly grinned. 'Are you always in a mess, or is it just whenever I turn up?'

Falcone burst out laughing. The sound startled her. He stopped and leaned up against the rocky wall next to the steps.

'I had almost forgotten,' he said. 'How could I forget – how you . . .? All the time I'm surrounded by earnest, righteous people telling me I'm mistaken, that I must stop speaking my mind because it will threaten the whole fabric of the Church. And then you come along and blow right through the whole thing! But in answer to your question: since I'm no longer allowed to do any of the things that are normally the framework of my priesthood, they can't think what to do with me. They keep sending me off to "reconsider my position" on various questions. To examine my conscience and so on and so forth. So here I am, trying to do just that.'

'And are you getting anywhere?'

'Oh . . .' Falcone tilted his head back for a moment, wearily, as they walked on. 'No further perhaps than I should have got if I'd taken more notice of you when we used to argue back then.'

He turned to face her. 'I don't want to go over and over it again. It's – oh, it drags you down. Rosa, I'm so sorry about yesterday. Your coming here at this time was so extraordinary that I didn't know how to react. Why did you come?'

'I had to see you.'

They'd reached the little chapel and sat down together on the top step at the entrance, soaked in warm afternoon light.

She felt bold because there was no time not to be, but also because the priest figure had gone, and they could talk as immediately, as honestly as ever.

'I saw what had happened to you in the paper,' she said. 'There's a man I work for at home who gives me Italian newspapers. When I saw your name again, real like that suddenly, I knew I had to come. I don't know if you realize how cruel it was, the way you went and never spoke to me again. Your letter. It left me all ragged at the ends. I could never settle, not really. It never ended for me you see . . .' She trailed off, her cheeks burning and suddenly wet with tears. 'I always loved you.'

Falcone was sitting with his face in his hands. She longed to touch him, but hesitated, before gently laying a hand on his shoulder and stroking him.

After a moment, trying to control his voice, he said, 'Oh, Rosa, Rosa. Would you believe me if I tell you that not a day has passed without me thinking of you? Of how I treated you? When I saw Margherita after you'd gone back to England, she let me know very clearly just what I'd done. She was so angry with me. She would never show that she despised someone but she must have despised me then. It was another guilt to add to all the others. But at the time I couldn't – really couldn't think what else to do. I wouldn't have been any good to you, not then. Margherita even told me she didn't think I had a vocation to the priesthood. It's dangerous to say such things of course. I've had to find that out for myself.'

'Without Margherita I think I would have fallen apart.'

'But you married – your English husband? I knew that. When I heard, it made things easier for me in a way. To think that you were really taken from me. That you loved someone else.'

'No,' Rose said bleakly. 'That was my mistake. And I say that more for his sake than mine. I could never give him what he really deserved from me. I had learned what love was before that and I could never forget it. However much I tried not to think of you, you took something from me that I was never able to give again, to him or anyone.'

He turned to look at her and she saw his eyes were full of pain. 'Rosa – come here.'

And they were in each others arms, he rocking her gently as she laid her wet face against his chest, his own tears falling on her hair.

'I'm so, so sorry,' he said. 'All this time you have felt so much . . . And sitting here now I feel so close to you, as if I saw you only last week.'

'I feel it too,' she said through her tears. 'Paulo – what will happen to you?'

'I think I stopped being a priest in the way they define it a long time ago. When my conscience could no longer stomach some of the teachings, but I was expected to act as if I believed absolutely that they were God's laws. It's a sickening position to be in. Only I hadn't yet found the courage to let go of it. But now . . .'

She turned her face up to his and they looked into each other's eyes before they kissed, at first soft, quick touches of their lips, each still full of wonder at the other's presence.

Their hands began to rediscover each other's bodies. Rose wanted to touch every part of him: the soft curve of skin at the back of his neck, his shoulders, his warm flesh under the rough shirt, and she felt his hands moving hungrily over her hair, down her back and round to her breasts which ached for his touch.

In moments they were taken over by their desire for each other. He lifted her on to his lap and she sat astride him, her skirt riding up round her waist. She could feel his hardness pressing beneath her and his face was taut with the urgency of it.

She took his face between her palms, steadying him. 'I don't want you to regret this.'

'Never. This is not what I regret.'

When he came up into her their cheeks were wet with tears again before either of them had climaxed. Rose held Falcone tightly as he came, his body shuddering, hands gripping her back as if in pain. As she reached the height of her own pleasure she cried out, 'I can't bear it' and heard him making reassuring sounds as if to a child.

They clung to each other for a long time as their breathing slowed, her cheek pressed against his, and he still deep inside her.

Afterwards they sat very close, talking until shadows slipped over them and cooled them as the night drew in and mosquitoes whined round their heads. There was so much to share, to tell of their lives.

When it had grown almost completely dark, Rose got up, stiffly and reluctantly. 'If I don't go now I shan't even catch the last train back.'

It was not easy to move away from this place where

the communication had grown up between them again, from roots which had never been destroyed.

'Can you come again?' Falcone asked with sudden awkwardness. 'Bring your daughter so that I can see her?'

'I'll bring her tomorrow. But then you must come and see Francesco and Margherita. They'll think I've deserted them. Are you allowed to?'

Falcone shrugged. 'I suppose so. If not, then it will be just one more transgression to add to all the others.'

They stood at the top, reluctant to take the first step, as if fearful that going back down to the rest of the world might destroy what had happened there that evening.

'Look – I'll have to go.' She could see his eyes watching her, the faint remainder of evening light shining in their dark surface.

'Don't leave me again,' she said.

Falcone moved towards her. 'My love.'

And then they held each other, very gently this time, like old, fragile friends, standing together between the dark shapes of the trees in the scented night air of the mountain.

Margherita and Francesco were both waiting up for her, though it was very late by the time she let herself into the flat. She had long missed the last bus to Pozzuoli and had had to take a taxi.

They were very relieved to see her, and the glow on her face was unmistakable to both of them as she walked in, startled to find them both up. Margherita was watching Rose's face intently and Francesco handed her a glass of wine.

'Well?' he demanded. 'Come on – what happened?'

'Rosa?' Margherita said more cautiously. 'Holy Mother – what have you both got yourselves into this time?'

Rose put her glass down. 'One moment. I just need to go to my room. I'd like you to do something for me.'

She stayed long enough to kiss Hilda and return to them carrying a flat package.

'Francesco, have you still got your record player?'

She smiled when he nodded in reply. 'Play this for me then.'

And she drew out his old gift to her: the long unplayed recording of 'J'attendrai'.

CHAPTER 42

ITALY, JUNE 1957

The voice she could hear shouting somewhere in the house was unmistakable, and though it was impossible to make out a word of what was being said, she smiled to herself in amusement.

It must have been quite a house once, she thought, examining it before going right up close. Certainly more promising than she'd expected when she was travelling out here on the train. All those drab little towns north of Naples! Cellina itself was one such town: small, poor and more or less featureless, except for one redeeming sight, a little church she had caught a glimpse of, with a vivid turquoise dome. Otherwise the place seemed to consist only of that one square, the Piazza Garibaldi, streets of ill-kempt houses and a few dismal shops.

But this house, out towards the more peaceful western edge of the town, reassured her. The doctor's house. It stood detached, and behind it was an orchard, planted with a mixture of citrus and apricot trees. The place was in need of some repair, of course, but these things took time – and money.

What pleased her most about the front of the house was the tiled plaque obviously newly attached to the wall beside the front door. In dark green letters on a cream background it read, 'ORFANOTROFIO DIANA – ORPHANAGE DIANA'.

She banged on the heavy brass door knocker, and as she did so caught sight of a man, stooping under the weight of a heavy box of vegetables, hurrying round the side of the house with an annoyed expression on his face. He flung the box into his little three-wheeler truck, and started up its rough, coughing engine to rev off down the road.

As she watched, the door opened.

He looked different from how she had imagined, more gentle and approachable, and certainly more casual, in his cotton trousers and open-necked shirt. Not at all her image of an Italian doctor. Despite Rose's descriptions she had visualized someone in a suit and perhaps rather aloof. Instead – what warmth in those eyes! Although slightly startled, they already held a welcome.

'Dr Falcone? I'm Catherine Harper-Watt.'

His face creased into a delightful smile. In awkward English he said, 'Of course. We wait for you.' He beckoned in that Italian manner, almost as if shooing her away. 'Please come.'

As she stepped into the house she heard the voice again: 'Paulo – *chi e?* . . . Oh Catherine it *is* you. At last!'

Rose ran forward and the two women flung their arms round each other.

'Oh, I'm so glad you've come to see us!'

'I heard you even before I arrived,' Catherine told her teasingly. 'You seem to be familiar enough with the language to hold your own!'

Rose chuckled, translating what Catherine had said to Falcone.

He also laughed, shrugging in mock despair. 'You should tell her that now you've learned to swear in Italian as well there's no stopping you!'

Rose repeated what he said. 'It's just that bloke who comes round delivering the veg. He always tries to palm off all the old frowsty stuff on me. I'm sure it's because he thinks I'm a foreigner and I won't notice. So I gave him what for this time. Anyway, come on through and let's get you settled. I'm dying to hear all the news.'

Falcone took Catherine's bags to her room, and the three of them went through to a huge, white-tiled kitchen at the back of the house. The room was slightly clinical with its grey lino on the floor, and a huge white sink and steel range. But there was a pot simmering on the top of it which was homely, and on the windowsill above the sink stood several flowering plants.

Four children, all between the ages of two and four, were sitting at a large wooden table in the centre, tucking into thick chunks of bread. Watching them was a plump-faced young woman who was sitting with her rounded arms resting on the table. The children fell silent at the sight of Catherine, their brown eyes watching her every move as their little cheeks bulged like hamsters' with the bread.

'So these are part of the family,' Catherine said. 'I shall have to learn all their names.'

'This is Anna Lucia,' Rose said, indicating the young woman, who nodded and smiled back amiably. 'She works here now every day except Sunday. We couldn't do without her.'

Rose placed a bottle and some glasses on the table.

'There are nine children here so far – and Hilda, of course. The older ones are at school and we do the best we can with the rest. There's about room for a couple more.'

Falcone put a hand on Rose's shoulder. 'Shall we take them out for a run about when they've finished? Then you can talk.'

Catherine watched smiling as the little ones all climbed down from the table and followed Falcone and Anna Lucia out of the door.

'You seem to have got yourselves organized quite speedily,' Catherine said, accepting a glass of wine and some of the bread.

Rose looked at her gratefully. 'We couldn't have done it without your help.'

'And the help of some worthy WI women in the Manchester area,' Catherine reminded her. 'They've been quite fired up by the idea of this place. You have a little money from the town now?'

'Yes. That's something. You've come at a good time.' Rose sat down. 'We've just heard that Paulo's registered to practise again, so now he can go back to what he's meant to be doing. It's a bit of a relief too, because the money his father left is all but gone. There've been so many extras to get the place going.'

'And for your wedding.'

Rose laughed. 'That didn't set us back much. It must've been one of the quietest weddings ever to happen in Italy! Which was fine by me and it was all we could afford. And another reason was that even after the dispensation came through so we could get married it took him quite a while to get used to the idea that he wasn't a priest.

'I didn't care what we did so long as I could just get back over here with him. You'd think with all the time since the war that another couple of years wouldn't make much odds, but I've never known two years go so slowly!'

'You were very patient,' Catherine told her. She leaned forward to take off her soft fawn cardigan. 'How beautifully warm it is here! And you're looking positively marvellous, my dear!'

Rose was dressed in a frock in her favourite navy, a colour which always flattered her dark looks, and her hair was taken up in a swinging ponytail. Catherine was noticing for the first time just how beautiful Rose could look. Her face had always been attractive, arresting even, but now, the one ingredient which had been lacking before – the bloom of happiness – had transformed her.

'You must work hard with all these children, but I must say you don't look at all worn down by it.'

'Well, we've got Anna Lucia. And Paulo's been around a lot – though that'll change when he's back to being a doctor. I s'pose it is tough, but I love doing it, that's all. Doing what you like isn't too difficult is it?'

When Catherine had settled into the tiny spare bedroom, Rose showed her round. It was a spacious house, with five bedrooms and plenty of room to accommodate the growing 'family' downstairs.

'The surgery will be here,' Rose said, opening up a

room beside the front door. 'It was where Paulo's father worked, so he can soon get it all set up again.'

The room must have been much as the older Dr Falcone had left it, with shelves of books and an old wooden desk with a crucifix hanging behind it. Against the opposite wall stood a high, flat examination bed.

After their little tour she led Catherine out of the back door of the house. They sat out on a terrace where so much grass had grown up between the stones that they were almost completely hidden. Rose found some old wooden chairs on which there was still some peeling brown paint.

The scents of honeysuckle and other flowers that Catherine could not identify filled the air, and pink bougainvillea burst its colour all over the wall along one side of the garden. On the dry grass under the trees Falcone was entertaining the children by teaching them to turn somersaults, while Anna Lucia stood by giggling.

'He's very good with them.' Catherine watched Rose carefully as she looked over at her husband, happy to see the love so plain in her eyes. She had come to feel as protective towards Rose as if she were her own daughter and she was anxious to see her happy.

'He's so much freer now – laughs more than I've ever known. Hilda loves him, she really does. He's the first proper dad she's ever had. Of course her real father was special to her, but he could never play with her. And she's teaching him English! I think she's picking up Italian quicker though.' She turned to Catherine. 'Tell me how things are at home. Any news?'

'Well, most of it's reasonably good. I stopped by in Birmingham on the way. Grace sends all her love of course, and . . .' She paused. 'I asked her if she'd like to come out and see you both.'

'You mean . . .?'

Catherine held up a hand, embarrassed. 'I'd love to help. Don't say any more.'

'Oh, thank you!' Rose actually clapped her hands together with delight.

'Paulo!' She shouted across to him. 'Catherine is going to send Grace over to see us!'

He smiled and waved back, and was promptly toppled to the ground by the two four-year-olds who shrieked with laughter. Rose and Catherine laughed too.

'I can't get over how fast Birmingham is changing,' Catherine said. 'All those tall buildings going up. Real skyscrapers. Of course you'll have seen a lot of it, but the centre of the city seems to be altering almost beyond recognition. They're going to redo the Bull Ring completely you know.'

'I know.' Rose sighed. 'Sometimes I wonder if I'll know any of it if I go back. In a way I'm glad not to see it happening.'

'But the big news is that they're going to demolish Catherine Street and all the others round it.'

'What? Grace never told me.'

'She's only just heard. Apparently they've got the choice of moving out somewhere on the edge of the city or having one of the new flats close by. Grace says she's determined to stay near the same spot. She thinks the suburbs will be all kippers and curtains and your father would embarrass her by still insisting on cutting up his squares of newspaper for the lavatory. She made me laugh over it in fact. And he seems prepared to do whatever she wants. To tell you the truth, he barely said a word the whole time I was there.'

'That's Dad for you,' Rose said. 'Poor old Grace, though. He always had a soft spot for her and she's never really had a break from him. I don't s'pose he'd have lived for long with me even if I had stayed around to let him. We'd have fought like blooming alley cats.'

'Grace seemed remarkably cheerful, I thought.'

'I don't half miss her,' Rose said thoughtfully. 'Fancy the old place going, though. I knew they were going to get round to it some time, but it really will be the end of an era. Can't picture Grace in a new flat. But then I 'spect she can't picture me over here either.'

'There is one piece of bad news,' Catherine said hesitantly. 'Your brother George has been arrested. In Glasgow.'

'Glasgow?'

'That's where he went, evidently, on your money and mine. Oh yes, Grace wasn't going to let me go without putting me straight about that. For goodness sake, Rose, you should have told me. I wouldn't have been angry. Anyway, for some reason he gave the police the Birmingham address. Perhaps he hasn't got a fixed abode up there.'

'What's he done this time then?'

Catherine shifted her gaze to the ground. 'I'm not certain.'

Rose looked at her closely. 'You *do* know, don't you?'

Catherine gave a painful sigh. 'Well, all right, yes. He's been acting as a pimp. Lining his pockets quite successfully I gather.'

Rose's mouth fell open. 'A pimp? My God. All that time he was with me! To think – what did I have in my house?'

She sat silent, shocked, until Catherine thought of something else.

'A more cheerful piece of news. Grace said she'd heard from Alcester. One of the twins? Apparently she's recently had her first baby. A little boy called Jimmy.'

Rose smiled, shaking her head in wonder. 'Dear little Susan. Fancy.'

They spent an uproarious few hours when the older children arrived back from school. Hilda, a tanned and healthy ten-year-old, was thrilled to find someone else in the house who spoke English, and chatted away non-stop to Catherine.

Once they were all fed and in their beds and Anna Lucia had gone home, Rose cooked a meal for the three of them. They ate in what was still the dining room of the house, with its dark, formal furniture. Rose put candles on the table. A bowl of nectarines and green grapes glistened in the light at the centre of it.

They ate tagliatelle and fried fish, with a salad of huge, succulent tomatoes by the side of it, and drank the rather harsh local red wine.

Catherine watched Rose and Falcone together. She found she liked him immensely. Though most conversation had to take place through Rose, she noticed that he listened attentively when she talked, as if eager to make out her words. Every so often he would join in a joke with them, exploding into wholehearted laughter which transformed his rather serious face. Sometimes when he laughed he would reach over and touch Rose's hand for a second, and Catherine saw her smile back at him, the shadows from the candles moving tenderly over her face.

She asked Falcone, 'How are people reacting to you now that you're back here? They must know you've been a priest?'

'There's been some disapproval, from a few. Those who did not know my family mainly. But the welcome we have had I owe entirely to my father.' He laughed softly. 'It's the reverse of what it says in the Bible – that a prophet is never welcome in his home town.'

'Also you're a doctor and you and your wife are caring for children who would otherwise be destitute?'

'I'm sure that also helps,' he agreed.

'And you have made an old woman from England very happy with your Orfanotrofio Diana,' she told them, slightly self-mocking.

'Old, my foot,' Rose interrupted.

Looking at the two of them and what they were creating here, Catherine knew she had before her a strong couple. She was longing to tell Ronald about them already. It was all so right. So improbable at first sight, but so entirely right.

'I must toast your future,' she said, raising her glass of

the inky red wine. 'Here's to the Orfanotrofio Diana – and to you both, with all my heart.'

They raised their glasses.

It was a time of night that Rose always loved, and on this night it was particularly special. When her husband was asleep, his hands resting softly against the curve of her back, she slipped off the huge, lumpy bed and went to sit for a while by the window. She opened the shutters a crack so that she could just see the half-moon casting its light on the trees behind the house.

She was excited and stirred up by all the news from England, and at the same time had a sense of enormous joy in her life. She was becoming certain that she would have another piece of news to tell first Paulo and then Catherine this week: that soon she would be adding another child to the household, a real brother or sister for Hilda after all this time.

She sat for some time with no clear thoughts in her head, just fragments of the day passing through. Then she went quietly out of the room and through the upper floor of the house, looking in on all the children who lived here in their care. Every bed was full tonight with Catherine sleeping at the end of the corridor.

Finally she climbed back into bed beside Falcone's warm body. Impossible as she knew it to be, she fancied as she lay down that she could feel the child moving inside her.